THE SKIPPER
"Swede" Stromburg didn't give a damn for rules and regs, all he cared about was getting his men through this war alive.

THE COPILOT
Easygoing and smartmouthed, Pat O'Riley possessed the luck of the Irish and the smooth good looks of a movie star.

THE NAVIGATOR
Bill Lancaster was the intellectual, a brilliant engineer who had a passion for cars and a way with women.

THE BOMBARDIER
Former jitterbug champ of East Chicago, Lennie Balzac was a cocky SOB with unerring instinct for the target and a taste for bootleg booze.

THE TAIL GUNNER
Nick Galvani was an Italian from New Jersey, a newlywed, and a compulsive worrier.

THE NOSETURRET GUNNER
An amateur violinist, a bookish loner, Lou Foulette confronted danger with a martini-dry sense of humor.

These were the men of
BOMBER CREW 369

BOMBER
CREW
369
The Reluctant Heroes

William C. Anderson

BANTAM BOOKS
TORONTO • NEW YORK • LONDON • SYDNEY • AUCKLAND

BOMBER CREW 369: THE RELUCTANT HEROES
A Bantam Book / October 1986

ISBN 0-553-26223-8

Published simultaneously in the United States and Canada

Bantam Books are published by Bantam Books, Inc. Its trademark,
consisting of the words "Bantam Books" and the portrayal of a
rooster, is Registered in U.S. Patent and Trademark Office and in
other countries. Marca Registrada. Bantam Books, Inc., 666 Fifth
Avenue, New York, New York 10103.

PRINTED IN THE UNITED STATES OF AMERICA

KR   0 9 8 7 6 5 4 3 2 1

To Candyce and Peter
with love

Foreword

In 1944 the European skies became the battleground for the most deadly aerial assault in the annals of military history. The U.S. Army Air Corps had the mission of breaking the back of the Axis powers by the sustained deployment of heavy bombardment.

Assigned to the Army Air Corps was the Fifteenth Air Force, one of the major commands in Europe employed to carry out this mission.

Assigned to the Fifteenth Air Force was one of the heavy-bombardment groups called the 451st Bomb Group (H).

Assigned to the 451st Bomb Group (H) was a closely knit fighting team of heavy bombers and aircrews known as the 725th Squadron.

Assigned to the 725th Squadron and manning one of the B-24 Liberator bombers was a group of ten men known as Bomber Crew 369.

This is the story of Bomber Crew 369.

In actuality, there was, indeed, a Bomber Crew 369. It operated out of southern Italy from 1944 to 1945. By virtue of letters, reminiscences of the crew, declassification of secret military documents, and thorough historical research, the true story of Bomber Crew 369 has been chronicled.

Meticulous attention has been paid to the actual dates and missions of the 725th. In the interests of capsulating time and simplifying the roles of actual personnel involved, certain license has been taken in fictionalizing some of the characters and dramatizing some of the events.

For the purist who desires to separate fact from fiction, it is quite simple. The incredible things happened. Some of the credible things did not.

This book is dedicated to the officers and men of the Fifteenth Air Force.

The plain man is the basic clod
From which we grow the demigod;
And in the average man is curled
The hero stuff that rules the world.

—SAM WALTER FOSS

Chapter One

Hq. 19th Replacement Battalion
APO 49
6 November 1944

Mr. Elwood Snodgrass
Internal Revenue Service
District Office
Boise, Idaho

Dear Mr. Snodgrass:

Reference your letter dated 20 October forwarded to me and just received. It's always nice to get letters from home.

It is with deep regret I learn that an audit of my 1942 income tax has turned up some questions. I would be very happy to bring my records and meet with you in your office at my earliest convenience. Unfortunately, I am now in Naples, Italy, with my bomber crew, at the convenience of President Roosevelt. My crew is being processed at this replacement depot for transfer to a flying base in southern Italy.

In a situation like this, I'm not sure whether President Roosevelt or the Internal Revenue Service enjoys the higher priority, but perhaps a determination can be made. In case it should come to a vote, you would certainly get mine, as Boise, Idaho, is a lot more attractive than Naples, Italy. Especially since the eruption of Mount

Vesuvius. They're still knee-deep in ashes around here.

Or perhaps we can resolve this problem by mail. If you would care to outline the discrepancies, I'll be happy to try to explain them. Suggest you correspond by V-Mail, it's much faster. My address will be:

Lt. Rolfe Stromburg
725 Bomb. Sq., 451 Bomb Grp.
APO 520, c/o PM, New York

Sincerely yours,
Rolfe Stromburg
2nd Lt., AC

Stromburg signed the V-Mail form, folded it, addressed it, and stuck a six-cent airmail stamp on it.

Then he swung out of the tent and headed for the mailroom.

"Geezus!" said O'Riley. "We damned sure better get there soon. My back teeth are floatin'."

Stromburg pulled back the sleeve of his shortcoat to expose the radium dial of his watch. "It's been ten hours. Should be there by now. Rain's slowing us up."

"I'll give 'em another five minutes," said O'Riley, grunting. "Then they're gonna have to stop this gut-churner. Or I'm gonna flood the ass end of this truck."

It had been six hours since their last relief stop. The ten men in the back of the truck rode silently, hunched over on the hard, let-down benches hinged to the side of the truckbed that brought numbness to legs, transmitted every chuckhole shock directly to the spine. Nightfall had brought the blackness of a tomb, and as though hypnotized, Stromburg watched the glowing tip of O'Riley's cigarette as it responded to the lurching of the vehicle, making free-form designs in the dark.

The six-by splashed into one final butt-banging pothole that brought groans from its riders, surfaced, and came to a halt. The ignition was turned off. Even deprived of electrical stimulus, the hot engine continued to cook its own combustion for several revolutions before it finally wheezed and backfired to a stop.

The sound of heavy rain pelting the tarp filled the silence left by the growling engine. "Either we're here," muttered Balzac, "or we've just busted an axle."

"Let's stay put," ordered Stromburg, "until we find out."

Muffled noises came from the cab, and several minutes later the back canvas flap was lifted. A ponchoed figure framed in the opening swept the interior with a flashlight beam. "*Hombres*," said a voice that had been deep-fried in tortilla oil. "*Bienvenida*. Welcome to sunny Italy. And Castellucia, home of the famous Four Fifty-first Bomb Group. I am your reception committee. Corporal Gonzales. Just call me Redeye. Anybody from San Antonio?"

There were no takers. "I'm from Ohio," said O'Riley, "and I'm drowning in my own kidneys. Can we cut the welcoming ceremonies short?"

"*Sí, señor*," said Redeye, throwing the canvas flap up over the top of the truck. "That trip from the repple-depple is a bitch-kitty. You *hombres* are crew Three Sixty-nine?"

"Affirmative," said Stromburg.

"Then if I can have a copy of your orders, I will sign you in on the morning report. We'll take care of the rest of the paperwork *mañana*. Who is the *gran patrón*?"

"Come again?" asked O'Riley.

"Who is the commander of the airplane?"

"I am," said Stromburg, reaching into his inside pocket for a copy of the crew's orders. "Second Lieutenant Stromburg." He extracted a mimeographed sheet and handed it to the corporal.

"*Gracias, señor*. Just climb out and follow me to your *casa*. Bring your bags."

Stretching the stiffness from their backs, the ten men fumbled to claim their luggage, abetted by the darting gleam of Redeye's flashlight. As the corporal lowered the tailgate, the ten men crawled out of the truck. There was a chorus of protestation as they found themselves sinking ankle deep in the cold mud. Grumbling and holding their bags up waist high, the men fell in behind their escort.

"Hope you *hombres* don't mind a little rain," Redeye threw back over his shoulder. "Good for the olives."

"You sure we didn't overshoot," grumbled O'Riley, "and land in Mexico? I'm gonna throttle that cheery wetback."

"Wait," said Lancaster, "until he gets us to someplace dry. Then I'll hold him while you throttle him."

The rain started coming down in earnest. Drenched to the core, the crew followed the bobbing flashlight in single file, cursing loudly as the cold mud seeped into their shoes. They came to a row of tents, barely distinguishable in the murk, and passed along them until Redeye's flashlight picked up the tent number he was looking for. He pushed open the framed door and entered, followed by the shivering men. "Here we are, *hombres*. Your little home away from home." His searching beam focused on a candle stuck to the top of an orange crate. He fumbled inside his poncho for a match. "In no time you goin' to be comfy as fleas on a hound dog."

"Redeye," said O'Riley, "don't think we're not grateful for the cheery welcoming ceremony. But if you don't point me in the direction of the nearest latrine, we're all going to be sorry."

"Latrine's down the trail," said the corporal. "About a hundred yards. You have to do *número uno*, or *número dos*?"

"For God's sake, man, I gotta take a leak!"

"Then just step out the door, Lootenant. All this rain it ain't gonna hurt the olive trees."

"God forbid," groaned O'Riley, making a hasty exit, "I should hurt the olive trees."

"There we are, *amigos*," said Redeye, torching the candle wick with a match. A pale luminescence flickered through the tent, exposing the top half of a fifty-gallon drum that squatted in the center. A chimney extended from its top to disappear through the canvas roof. Redeye approached the makeshift stove. "These stoves are kinda tricky. But once you get the hang of it, they don't blow up too often."

He opened the small door cut in front, picked up a can

of fluid nearby, and sloshed its contents into the stove. The smell of kerosene permeated the tent. "Fire's all laid. Only one small *problema*. We're burning olive wood. It's green and don't start too good. But this here kerryseen starts it right up." He lit another match, threw it into the stove, and slammed the door. There was a muffled explosion. "Soon be hotter'n a jalapeño fart in here."

The men gathered around the cold stove, hands outstretched. Stromburg looked around the Spartan interior of the tent. There was a camp cot in each corner, with three folded blankets on each cot. Near the stove was a squatty table fashioned from an orange crate. That comprised the furnishings. "You people," said Stromburg, "really know how to fight a war in comfort."

"*Sí*," said Redeye. "But weren't always this nice. Till we fixed it up. I got here weren't nothing but an olive grove. We hacked out a runway strip and put up these tents. These here are the officers' quarters. Soon as you *hombres* get dried out, I'll take the enlisted men to their tents."

"Are the enlisted quarters as nice as this?" asked Balzac.

"Little nicer. Got wood floors. Enlisted men sometimes a little handier with their hands." Redeye looked at Stromburg. "Meanin' no offense, Lootenant."

"No offense, Corporal. I'll go with you to get the men settled. Then we'd like something to eat. Haven't had a bite since breakfast."

"Big *problema* there, Lootenant. Mess hall is closed. Open *mañana*. Six o'clock sharp."

Stromburg reached for the corporal's shoulder and spun him around. "We seem to have a misunderstanding. I said we haven't eaten. I want my men fed."

"Oh, *yo comprendo, señor*." The corporal wiped his nose with his sleeve. "But I can do nothing. Even if the mess cook was here, he never would open after hours. Especially on a night like this. And especially since he went to an Italian wedding up in the village tonight. Ain't nobody going to bring him down."

"You seem pretty cocksure."

"I am pretty sure, Lootenant. Mainly on account of the wedding he went to is his."

Stromburg's eyes hardened. "My men have been straddling a bucking plank in an Army truck all day. We've had no lunch, we're wet to the core, and hungry as hell. If I can't get some chow for my crew, you and I are marching in to see the squadron commander."

"Lootenant, that is going to be one long march."

"Yeah?"

"*Sí*. On account of the CO went to the wedding. Best man."

Stromburg swore. "What the bleeding hell kind of war are you guys running here?"

The corporal smiled, revealing a picket fence of teeth. "Just stick around till the weather clears up. It will get better." He crossed his heart. "*Es la verdad.*"

Stromburg's shoulders sagged. "Okay, Corporal. No purpose in giving you a hard time."

"That is the way I look at it, Lootenant."

"Let's get the enlisted men settled."

"Roger dodger." The corporal replaced his hood and turned on his flashlight. As he started toward the door, the beam picked up a footlocker that had been partially obscured by the tent door. "*¿Qué es ésto?*" he asked.

"What's the matter?" asked Stromburg, hard on his heels.

"That footlocker. It should not be here."

"What's in it?"

"Personal effects. Of Señor Muldoon's crew."

"What are they doing here?" asked Stromburg.

"Ain't supposed to be here," said Redeye. "Should be on their way to the *familias*."

"Would you drag that by again?"

The corporal turned and faced Stromburg. "This was the tent of Muldoon's crew. Until two nights ago. Then they bought the farm. Over Ploesti. *Muy muerte*." Redeye shook his head. "It is not good leaving personal effects around like this. Is bad for the morale. I will pick them up *mañana*."

"You do that," said Stromburg.

Redeye held open the tent door as Stromburg and the enlisted men filed through. Just before ducking out himself, he addressed the three remaining officers huddled around the stove. "Hope you *señors* enjoy our little wars."

He was answered by the mute gaze of six eyeballs. "Ah, I almost forgot. Happy Thanksgiving, *amigos*."

Major Diddle was a small, nervous man with a slight tic and a laugh like the neighing of a horse. "Welcome to the Seven Twenty-fifth," he said. "The best goddamn squadron in the best goddamn group in the best goddamn wing in the Fifteenth Air Force."

Diddle paused, as if expecting applause. None came from the men of Crew 369 lounged in the chairs of the squadron briefing room. Diddle neighed and continued. "Since you gentlemen just arrived from the States, you've probably been reading about the new mission of the Army Air Corps. In official words, the Combined Chiefs of Staff have made the decision to use air power for the destruction and dislocation of the German military, industrial, and economic system and the undermining of the morale of the German people to the point where their capacity for armed resistance is fatally weakened."

Again Diddle paused, as if expecting some reaction to this pronouncement. Balzac, the bombardier, responded with the clicking of his nail clippers.

"What this means," continued Diddle, "is that we are engaged in strategic bombardment. The airplane has been given a definite assignment of its own, rather than being used in merely a support role. We're going to prove to the world—once and for all—the mighty potential of air power!" Diddle banged the podium with his fist.

Stromburg's stomach growled, and O'Riley crossed his legs in deference to full kidneys.

"By bombing around the clock! The RAF at night, and the mighty Fifteenth and Eighth air forces during the day. We're going to bring the stinking Krauts to their knees!"

Stromburg looked around at his vacant-stared crew. Feeling something should reward this proclamation, Balzac spoke. "Hooray!" he said.

Diddle neighed his appreciation, and warming to the subject, continued. "Finding our bombing losses unacceptable in striking high-flak and fighter-density targets such as Ploesti, Vienna, and Berlin to knock out ball-bearing factories and refineries that can be quickly repaired, you gentlemen will be pleased to know we've adopted a wiser course of strategy. The mission of the Fifteenth Air Force is now the job of destroying all communications. We're going to ignore the heavily defended industrial centers for the time being. Instead, we're going to knock out every marshaling yard, bridge, canal, and highway in the war zone. Let the Krauts produce their heads off. But if they can't move their oil, their gasoline, their ball bearings, their aircraft engines, their tank replacements—what good's it going to do them?"

"No good," said Balzac, taking the cue when he saw no one else was going to respond.

"Right you are, Lieutenant. We're making the enemy disperse their flak guns to cover all their key communications targets. They don't know when, how, or where we're going to strike next. And the campaign is already beginning to pay off. German fighters are running out of gasoline. So are the Panzer divisions. So we'll continue to use this strategy. And that, gentlemen, is an overlay of our mission. Any questions?"

There were no questions.

"I see I've done a competent job of explaining our mission. Now I'll turn you over to our operations officer, Captain Sheridan. He'll start you on your indoctrination and orientation program. Once again, gentlemen, welcome aboard. And congratulations on being assigned to the Seven Twenty-fifth, the best goddamn squadron in the best goddamn group in the best goddamn wing in the whole Fifteenth Air Force." Major Diddle stepped off the dais and strode in quick steps to the door.

"We're sure lucky," whispered Galvani, the tail gunner. "We might have been sent to some other squadron."

"AttensHUT!" barked Captain Sheridan. The men of Crew 369 lumbered to their feet as the major exited the briefing room. "At ease!" commanded Sheridan. The men flopped back into their seats.

The operations officer was a tall, boney beanpole from Corpus Christi, Texas. He wore his cap down over one eye, and his pants were tucked into a pair of high cowboy boots. He had a hooked nose that looked as though it could be employed to open beer bottles, and a pair of piercing blue eyes stared out of a face molded from an old saddlebag. "Welcome to wop country, men. Anyone here from Texas?"

No one admitted to being from Texas.

"Accordin' to the weather guessers, this cold front's gonna pass this afternoon. Means the squadron will be able to get on with the war, and give the bad guys another tug where the hair's short. Unfortunately, you gents won't be able to go on the mission tomorrow. Gotta get a little trainin' and indoctrination under yer belt first. Here's the skinny.

"Stromburg, you and your crew will take a local hop tomorrow with me. I'll give y'all a guided tour of the local territory. Check you out on combat procedures. Then we'll buzz over to the gunnery range and see if yer gunners can hit anythin'. Then we'll shoot some landin's if our PSP airstrip ain't sunk in all the mud. So much for tomorrow. Durin' the next couple days, each of yer men will take a mission with an experienced crew, flyin' in yer assigned slot. By next week, all goes well, you'll be able to take yer first mission as yer own crew."

"Joy to the world," muttered O'Riley.

"Got any problems, bring 'em to me. My tent door's always open. Got damn high morale in this outfit and intend to keep it that way. Any questions?"

"One," spoke up Stromburg. "We have a footlocker containing the personal effects of the former occupants of our tent. Any chance of delivering it someplace? I'd like to get it out of the tent."

"Personal effects? Whose personal effects?"

"Muldoon's crew."

"Muldoon?" Sheridan scratched his head. "Sure. Crew Two Thirty-four. Muldoon bought it on a low-level raid over Ploesti. Hit a smokestack. Damned fine pilot. Had a great future. What about his effects?"

"They're in a footlocker serving as a coffee table in our

tent. I thought it would be nice if they were forwarded to the next of kin."

"You mean they weren't?"

"Apparently not."

"Christ on a crutch! I'll see they're picked up immediately. Helluva note. As I say, we got a damn good morale in this outfit. And we intend to keep it that way. Any other questions?"

"Sir," ventured Foulette, the nose turret gunner. "In the enlisted men's mess. About the cockroaches in the cornflakes—"

"Okay, gents," said Sheridan. "I guess that about wraps it up. Just remember. I got an open-door policy. Come to me anytime with yer problems. See y'all in the mornin'. Start engines at oh eight hundred. Dismissed."

Stromburg and O'Riley had finished the preflight and were squatting under the wing waiting for the operations officer. O'Riley munched on a toothpick and stared pensively up at the nose of the B-24 Liberator. "That," he said, "has got to be the world's ugliest airplane. No wonder they call it the crate the B-Seventeen came in."

Stromburg followed his gaze. "It ain't very pretty. But don't knock it. Flies higher, faster, and carries a bigger bombload than the Flying Fortress."

"It's got no lines. An airplane should be streamlined. That boxcar was designed by the Pennsylvania Railroad. Looks like it should be in a roundhouse. Not on a runway. Look at that turret stuck on the nose like a carbuncle."

"Never forget the first time I took the damned thing off. The way it gobbled up runway I thought I was trying to get the *Super Chief* off the ground."

O'Riley sighed. "When I think I used to fly P-Thirty-eights . . ."

"Don't come bleeding to me with your troubles. Anybody stupid enough to try and fly under clotheslines deserves to be washed out of fighters. Especially when the clothesline belongs to the base commander."

O'Riley looked pained. "Punished, yes. But banned to B-Twenty-fours? As a *copilot*? That is cruel and inhumane treatment."

"You'll survive."

"Frankly, I very much doubt it."

Stromburg looked over at his copilot. Again he was smitten with a touch of envy. No question about it, O'Riley cut a handsome figure in his leather flying jacket, his officer's cap pushed back on his head at a jaunty angle, his pink twill pants thrust into the top of his cowboy boots. He had the innate Irish look of rugged good humor; a chiseled nose that commanded a broad mouth and square jaw; sparkling brown eyes that always seemed to be asking questions.

It had been almost four months since O'Riley ambled into Stromburg's BOQ at Chatham Air Base in Savannah, flopped down on the bunk, and introduced himself as the copilot of Crew 369. It was at this humid southern base where Stromburg and O'Riley really got to know one another while homesteading a couple of barstools at the Chatham Officers' Club, waiting for the rest of their new crew to come straggling in to the staging area.

With the arrival of the bombardier and navigator to round out the officer complement of the crew, they had moved their operations from the base club to the bar of the Savannah Hotel, where the hunting was much better. Here Stromburg first came to realize what an asset O'Riley would become to the crew. The lanky, broad-shouldered Irishman had but to saunter into the cocktail lounge and one could hear the breath being sucked into the heaving chests of every female present; and when he threw a leg over a barstool and ordered a beer in his rich, baritone voice, the clapper in every southern belle in the room gonged with delight.

Being eclipsed in the shadow of this handsome Irishman should have been discouraging to the other officers in the crew. But in truth the men were grateful, for although O'Riley had his pick of fawning damsels, he created such a wake in his passing that the roiling waters washed up more fine nuggets than there otherwise would have been to choose from. As a result, even the truncated bombardier, Balzac, had his choice of the man-hungry secretaries, schoolteachers, and defense workers who flocked to the Savannah Hotel like ants to a picnic.

Because of his easygoing, generous nature, O'Riley was also a hit with the enlisted crew members. He was always good for a loan, or a drink from the bottomless bottle of Jim Beam he kept sequestered in his footlocker. Although Stromburg had envied the likable Irishman and his natural attraction for the men, he was also grateful, for the two months of transition and crew training at Chatham had gone without a hitch. They had bombed ranges with flour bombs, strafed targets with the .50-caliber machine guns, shot touch-and-go landings, practiced formation flying, flew day and night cross-countries, simulated every type of in-flight emergency. Thanks in large part to O'Riley's laid-back contributions, ten men picked at random from all walks of life had been honed into a deadly, effective fighting machine over the alluvial swamplands of Georgia.

O'Riley tongued his toothpick to the other side of his mouth and looked curiously at Stromburg. "Swede, don't tell me you *enjoy* flying this aluminum confusion."

Stromburg thought a minute. "I honestly don't know. Fighters are where the glamor is. The romance. The wild-blue-yonder crap. But when we went through our psychological batteries of tests as cadets, the shrinks ordained me for bombers. Probably because I'm too slow and stupid to fly fighters. But I don't give a rat's ass. I'm flying. And I've always wanted to fly. And frankly, I like a big airplane. I don't want to have to fly in something you have to squeeze into like a corset. I like to get up and walk around. Have a cup of coffee and go back and gab with the tail gunner. Take a pee standing up. I guess I just like the creature comforts."

"To each his own."

"Amen."

"Mornin', gents." Sheridan clumped up in his cowboy boots, a parachute slung over his shoulder. "Got this little beauty preflighted?"

"Ready to go, Captain," said Stromburg.

"Then let's mount the wind and make like a big bird."

For several hours they flew around the undulating terrain that comprised the spur of Italy's boot. Sheridan, standing between the two pilots, pointed out the towns of

Foggia and Barietta and Bari; the villages of Cerignola and
Canosa di Puglia and Andria. He pointed out emergency
landing strips and extreme-emergency landing strips. All
the while he kept up a steady chatter in his Texas drawl,
grilling the crew members on emergency procedures: fire
in flight, ruptured hydraulic lines, electrical system failure,
frozen relief tubes—every conceivable mishap. "If anythin'
can go wrong, as the old saying goes, it'll go wrong in an
airplane. Especially this one. And when trouble comes, like
grapes, it comes in bunches. Stromburg, you handle this
flyin' machine middlin' well. How much time you got?"

"Four hundred and seventy-five hours and thirty-two
minutes. Roughly."

"'Bout par for the course for you lads comin' in from
the repple-depple these days. Where did you take your B-
Twenty-four trainin'?"

"Chatham Field. Savannah, Georgia."

"Christ on a crutch! Know it well. The old Savannah
Hotel still standin'?"

"Still swinging," said Stromburg.

"Great place. Never forget the night I ferried a B-Two-
dozen into Chatham. Went into town, saddled up a stool in
the bar of the old Savannah Hotel, and settled down for
some serious drinkin'. In walked a herd of schoolteachers,
out on the town. Among them was the most gorjus, two-
titted heifer you ever saw in your life. Took some doin' to
corral her, but I managed. Got her up to my room and she
turned out to be a wildcat. Nympho." Sheridan sighed.
"Christ on a crutch, it was somethin'! First time I ever wore
spurs to bed."

"That's a heartwarming story," said O'Riley.

"Fond memories that," said Sheridan. He blinked the
glassy look from his eyes. "But let's get on with the war.
Head for the base, Stromburg. We'll make a couple tactical
peeloffs. Shoot some landin's."

"Roger." Stromburg swung the big bomber around.

"Now, when ya come in from a mission," explained
Sheridan, "ya gotta bunch of birds low on gas, all headin' for
the nest at the same time. So you gotta land in a helluva
hurry. Here's the way we've worked it out. The squadron
circles around the field while the flights peel off one at a

time. In elements of three. Now, the critical part of this billy-do is the number-three man. As you come over the runway, this dude's gotta really rack it over and get it around, cause if he don't, he's gonna have the birds behind him spread out all over Italy. Okay. You're the number-three man. Flyin' right toward the runway. Now, just as you reach it, rack it over, do a three-sixty, and squat her down."

Stromburg, concentrating on his traffic-pattern altitude, airspeed, and drift, watched the end of the runway approach eight hundred feet below him. When directly overhead, he wheeled the big bird around in a thirty-degree bank, called for gear and flaps down, started his descent, and searched for the end of the runway. He spotted it, leveled out for the downwind, banked again, and leveled out for a long final approach.

"Make this a touch-and-go landing," ordered Sheridan over his shoulder.

"Roger." Stromburg flared out just right, catching the runway with barely a jar. He dropped the nosewheel onto the runway and poured the coal to the bomber for another takeoff. Again airborne, Stromburg turned to the operations officer, a smug look on his face. "How was that, Captain? A typical Stromburg grease job."

"*How was that?*" thundered Sheridan. "A piss-poor tactical approach. Like you had all day. You land like that and yer gonna end up with twenty bombers on top of you. Let me in the left seat. I'll show you how it's done."

Smarting, Stromburg crawled out of his seat and changed places with the lanky Texan. They circled around and headed for the runway. "Okay, copilot," said Sheridan, "when I give this thumbs-down signal, you drop everythin'—gear, flaps, and yer drawers, if necessary."

"Yes, sir," said O'Riley.

Over the end of the runway at traffic altitude, the Texan floorboarded the left rudder, rolled the control column left to the end of its travel, and jerked his thumb down. The heavy machine whipped up into a near-vertical bank as Sheridan pulled the throttles back to their stops. The blare of the gear-up warning horn filled the cabin as the G-forces of the tight turn added lead to the extremities of the crew.

"Goddamn!" muttered Stromburg, trying to keep erect standing between the pilots. "You're exceeding structural limitations of this airplane!"

"You'll know we've done that," said Sheridan, grunting, "when the wings peel off."

The unsafe-landing-gear warning light blinked red, and as the stomach-churning bank was continued, the wind whistled eerily above the sound of the gear-up warning horn as unprogrammed aerodynamics were challenged. Stromburg watched the ground approach at sickening speed. "The left wing!" he shouted. "You're gonna plow up—"

An instant before the runway approached, the left wing snapped up, the ship flared, and the wheels touched the runway the second the green landing light came on. Nonchalantly, Sheridan lowered the nose, then added full power for another takeoff.

In the air, Sheridan cleaned up the takeoff checklist and turned to O'Riley. "That's how we do it down Texas way."

"Geezus!" said the copilot, staring at him in open-mouthed admiration. "You fly this thing like a P-Thirty-eight."

"You also," said Stromburg, overcoming a dry mouth, "landed before you got a signal your landing gear was down and locked."

"That's the trick," said Sheridan. "Takes about eight seconds for the gear to get down and locked after the lever is actuated. If yer copilot's on the ball, comes out just about right. And even if you had to land with the gear partially extended, you've saved a couple minutes. Which jest might be the time needed to prevent some cowhands from plowin' up the north forty with dry gas tanks. I know this ain't what they taught you in the Training Command. But this is combat. And yer soon gonna find there's a whale of a difference. Okay. I'll switch places with O'Riley and be yer copilot. You crawl back into the left seat and we'll practice this till you get the hang of it."

For two hours Stromburg went though his paces until his flying suit was wringing wet. It came hard at first.

Stromburg, by nature conservative and with an inborn respect for the published limitations of any piece of precision equipment, treated a flying machine with awe and reverence. But under the malevolent glares and chafings of the operations officer, he eventually overcame his own resistance and began racking the bomber over and pivoting it on its wingtip to Sheridan's satisfaction.

"There may be hope for you yet, boy," drawled the instructor as Stromburg executed a three-G pitchout that even drained some of the blood from the Texan's face. "Jest one point of caution: Only do tactical maneuvers like this when yer comin' home from a mission with an empty airplane. With yer bombs gone, most of yer ammo expended, and gas tanks nearly dry, yer light as a feather. You can rack this old bird around pretty good. But don't try it with a bombload. Yer jest liable to make the old gal swayback."

"I'll remember that," said Stromburg, wiping the sweat from his eyes.

"Pilot from waist," came a squawk over the intercom.

"Go ahead, Hannigan," answered Stromburg.

"Skipper, I think you're getting the hang of it. On that last approach the tail gunner threw up twice."

Stromburg grinned at his instructor. "Think maybe we'd better knock off landings for a while?"

"Roger," said Sheridan. "You 'bout got the old gal broke to the reins. Let me in the left seat. We'll mosey over to the gunnery range. Put the freeloadin' passengers in the back end to work."

The deep blue of the Adriatic sparkled in the afternoon sun as Sheridan herded the airplane along the coastline. The water looked very inviting to Stromburg, still dripping with sweat from the physical and mental exertion of mastering the huge flying machine in untried maneuvers. The instructor descended, skimming low over the white-washed houses of the resorts and fishing villages that lined the beach. Stromburg sucked in his breath. "Damn! I never realized parts of Italy were so beautiful."

"Yep," said Sheridan. "Hunks of it are almost as fancy as Corpus Christi. Only one thing wrong with Italy."

"What's that?"

"It's fulla Eyetalians."

Stromburg grinned. "You got something against Italians?"

Sheridan snorted. "Christ on a crutch, I guess! Hate the garlic Fashists. They spent the first half of this war tryin' to clobber our ass. When the Allies started winnin', they changed sides."

"I'd say that wasn't too stupid."

"They got no goddamn spine. They'll follow whoever throws 'em the biggest breadstick."

"They've had their political problems."

"I hope to spit in yer mess kit. They're more mixed up than a hog's breakfast. Don't ever turn yer back on 'em."

"I'd appreciate it if you didn't talk that way in front of my tail gunner. Galvani is Italian. First generation. Before we left the States we had dinner at his folks' house. Finest, warmest people I've ever met."

"That's different. They're *American* Eyetalians."

"There's a difference?"

"Hell, yes. The American Eyeties had to take an oath of allegiance to the Stars and Stripes. At least they got something to believe in." Stromburg mulled this and was about to respond when Sheridan changed the subject. "Up yonder is the gunnery range." Sheridan pointed to a remote, unpopulated stretch of beach. In the water just off the beach were series of floating oil drums painted with red and white stripes to make them stand out from the clear blue water. They were anchored in a zigzag formation.

"The gunnery range here is posted off limits to the Eyetalian fishermen," continued Sheridan. "'Though I don't know why. A few fifty-caliber slugs up their ass would serve the bastards right. And there's something the Army Air Corps definitely does not want us to do, and that's hairass the wop fishing boats."

"How would one go about harassing the fishing boats?" asked Stromburg.

"I'll show you." Sheridan's eyes became slits as he searched the horizon. Suddenly his face brightened as he spotted a speck of white in the distance. "There's one of the varmints." He shoved the throttles, took a firm grip on the

controls, and pushed the yoke forward. The ship descended
until it was a dozen feet from the water. At three hundred
miles an hour the bomber thundered toward the white rag
bobbing in the blue water that was rapidly turning into the
billowed sail of a fishing boat.

"*Yaaahoooo!*" roared Sheridan, as if a man possessed.
Within minutes they were upon the boat, and just as
Stromburg was sure the mainmast was going to crash
through the cockpit, Sheridan nudged back on the controls
just enough to clear the mast by inches. Then he whipped
into a turning climb so he could witness the havoc created
by the miniature hurricane of the bomber propwash.

As they pyloned around the boat, Stromburg strained
over from his copilot's seat to see the hapless fishing boat. It
was all but capsized. The whipstream had snapped the
mainmast, and its sail was settling over the boat like a huge
shroud. Two men were struggling in the water.

"Ride 'em, cowboy!" yelled Sheridan. There was a
malevolent look on his face as he watched the men
struggling to get back onto their boat. "Always remember,
Stromburg. That is something you never want to do.
Hairass the Eyetalian fishin' boats. The good colonel will
really fry your ass if he finds out."

Struck dumb, Stromburg could only stare at the
homely face of the Texan.

"Ole Armbruster caught Hail Columbia the other day.
Made the mistake of buzzin' a fishin' boat with a radio in it.
When he landed, the wing commander was waitin' for him.
Armbruster denied everythin' and woulda probably gotten
away with it. But when he opened the bomb-bay doors,
about a yard of mast fell out. They sure nailed ole
Armbruster."

"Captain!" sputtered Stromburg. "What the hell did
you do that for?"

Sheridan flashed his parted teeth at his student. "Jest a
demonstration, pardner. Wanta be sure yer up on our rules
and regulations."

"Demonstration, hell! You could have *told* me. That
was a crappy thing to do!"

Sheridan's grin faded. "A crappy thing to do. That's

what I said when I got the telegram about my little brother. He's now fertilizin' the sod at a place called Salerno. He was with the Fifth Army when Mark Clark invaded Italy. Picked up a chunk of lead in the head, delivered by an Eyetalian sharpshooter. Don't tell me about crappy things, friend."

Stromburg stared at the Texan, his jaw slack.

"Don't waste time broodin' about the ass-lickin' olive chompers. We got our hands full with the Germans. The Krauts ain't gonna win any personality contest, either, but by God, they're men!"

Taken aback by this flash of emotion from the easygoing Texan, Stromburg searched for words. "I'm sorry about your brother, Captain—"

Sheridan turned to Stromburg and gave him a lopsided grin. "Forget it. I don't generally lip off like that. It's jest that those goddamn wops make my hackles rise. How about you gettin' in the left seat and flyin' yer own dam airplane. We'll sashay over to the gunnery range. See if yer gunners can hit anythin'. And maybe if we're lucky, some spaghetti-snapper's boat will get lost and wander into the firin' range."

For the next hour Stromburg made passes over the firing range at different altitudes while his gunners strafed the bobbing targets in the water. The Liberator is a huge porcupine, bristling with armament. Fifty-caliber machine guns poke out of the nose turret, the top turret, tail turret, waist positions on each side, and a ball turret that can be extended from the belly of the plane. When a gun is fired from any position, a distant hammering shakes the airplane. When all guns fire simultaneously, the bomber vibrates like a jackhammer.

The upper turret bothered the pilots the most. Situated right above the flight deck, the ear-banging cacophony of its twin .50s sent teeth fillings to vibrating and flight instruments to dancing. Stromburg was rapidly developing a splitting headache.

"Christ on a crutch!" said Sheridan. "Did you ever hear such a hellacious racket? This ole bucket shakes like a pup tryin' to pass peach pits. O'Riley, crawl back into yer copilot's seat. I'm goin' back to the rear. See if these gunners of yers can hit the broad side of a barn."

"Right, Captain," said O'Riley, changing places with the instructor. Sheridan disappeared into the bomb bay.

As they made their strafing passes, Stromburg looked back over his shoulder to watch the tracer-marked trajectory of the bullets as they splashed into the water, marching up to the bobbing barrels and covering them with a hail of lead, smoking and frothing the target. He grinned with satisfaction as his gunners peppered the floating targets right on the money.

Presently Sheridan returned to the flight deck. "Tell the cowhands to quit firin'," he said into Stromburg's ear.

"Pilot to all stations," obeyed Stromburg. "Cease firing."

As the din quieted, Sheridan reached across Stromburg and picked up his mike. "Sheridan to all stations. Okay, you ranchhands. Yer hittin' yer targets purty good, but yer trigger-happy. Yer firin' too quick. Yer sprayin' bullets around like a drunken Indian. Establish yer lead and yer rate of closure, then start firin'. Make yer shots count. Conserve yer ammo. Ain't nobody makin' ammo deliveries over Vienna when yer out of bullets and the fighters hit you on the way home. Let's try it again. This time get yer target lined up afore you pull the trigger." Sheridan handed the mike back to Stromburg and checked his watch. "Let's make a couple more passes, then we'd better head for the barn. Get this beast stabled before today's mission returns."

"Roger." Stromburg circled around for another pass. "Pilot to all stations," he intercommed. "Couple more passes and we'll hang it up. You heard the captain. Let's see nothing but bull's-eyes."

The pilots winced as the chattering of the guns reverberated through the flight deck. As they neared the end of the strafing pass, Stromburg started to pull back on the controls to make a climbing turn for another run. Unaccountably, the control column suddenly started bucking in his hands. It was all he could do to hold it. "What the hell?" He shot a worried look at Sheridan. "The damn rudders are chattering—"

"Christ on a crutch!" Sheridan yanked the microphone from O'Riley, yelled into it. "All stations! Cease firin'!"

As the firing ceased, the controls quit jerking. Gingerly Stromburg tested them. They seemed to comply as he reached for altitude. "Controls respondin'?" asked Sheridan, breathing down Stromburg's neck.

"Seem to be okay. Rudder's a bit sluggish."

"Yer damned lucky." Sheridan addressed the mike. "Sheridan to all stations. Okay, which one of you sad sacksa shit decided to shoot holes in the rudder?"

There was no answer.

"I repeat: Which one of you commodeheads decided to ventilate the control surfaces?"

Finally a numbing silence was broken by a faltering voice. "I'm afraid I did, sir."

"Who the hell are you?"

"Balzac, sir. Second lieutenant. Serial number one nine four—"

"I don't give a rat's ass about yer serial number. How much damage have you done to the tail surfaces?"

There was a pause, then, "Doesn't look too serious, sir. Seem to be a few holes in the stabilizer. Quite a few in the rudder."

"Great shootin'. We'll put you in for a marksman medal. What the hell were you doin', Balzac?"

"Gun jammed, sir. I was trying to clear it when a live round cooked off and started to fire. Didn't realize it was pointing at the—"

"Christ on a crutch! As bombardier, Balzac, yer also the armament officer. Yer supposed to know your weapons. Let me explain somethin' from a pilot's point of view. That thing stickin' up out there behind you that looks like a barn door—ain't. It's called a stabilizer. On it is attached a thing called a rudder. The rudder comes in handy when the pilot wants to do little things like turnin' the airplane. It's one thing for the Krauts to shoot it fulla holes. That's what they get paid for. To keep Krauts from shooting it fulla holes is what you get paid for. You ain't gettin' paid for puttin' holes in yer own airplane. Got that straight?"

"Yes, sir. You got a tactful way of putting things, sir."

Sheridan handed the mike back to O'Riley. "Herd this bucketa holes back to the corral. I'd rather go out on a combat mission than a trainin' mission with your crew. Helluva lot safer."

"Damned embarrassing, Captain," said Stromburg. "I'll have a talk with my bombardier when we get back."

"You do that. Just make damn sure the idiot knows whose side he's on."

"Yes, sir. It won't happen again."

"For yer sake, I hope not. You may not live to tell about it."

As soon as the airplane was parked in its revetment, Sheridan swung down through the bomb bay. "Mission's about due to return. I want to be in the control tower when they land. After debriefing, Stromburg, I want to see you."

"Yes, sir." The lanky Texan disappeared through the hatch and started sprinting across the field.

Completely drained, Stromburg slumped down into his seat. "Well, Pat," he said, "we're really starting off this war with a bang."

"You might say that," said O'Riley.

"What do you think of our Texas friend?"

"He's a pistachio nut. But I'll give him his due. He sure knows how to fly an airplane."

Stromburg nodded. "I have a great crew. Sheridan thinks I fly like an old grandmother, and on our first checkride our own bombardier shoots our airplane full of holes."

"Wouldn't it be terrible," said O'Riley, "if they wouldn't let us join their little war? Just made us pack up and go home?"

"Somehow I don't think that's going to happen."

"Don't sweat it, Swede. If they don't like us here, we'll go start our own war someplace. Like Switzerland. I understand those Swiss women—"

"We have something to be thankful for." Stromburg turned to his copilot, smiling in spite of himself.

"What's that?"

"If somebody *had* to shoot holes in our airplane, I'm

glad it was Balzac. Can you imagine what would happen if it had been our tail gunner? With an Italian name like Nick Galvani? I think Sheridan would have gone back and thrown him out of the airplane."

O'Riley grinned. "You got that right."

"Hey, Lieutenant!" Stromburg turned around to confront a ground maintenance man who was peering at him from the bomb bay. "I thought this was going to be a training mission, Lieutenant."

"It was, Sergeant," said Stromburg.

"You got a tail end full of holes."

"Yes, Sergeant. I know we got a tail end full of holes."

"I didn't know German fighters were ranging this far south."

"I didn't, either."

"They damned near clipped the control cables. You're lucky, Lieutenant."

"Yes, Sergeant," said Stromburg, crawling out of his seat. "This crew is shot in the ass with luck."

Chapter Two

Dearest Mom and all the relatives:

Hi, all you swell guys. How's everything in Seattle? Today was a red-letter day. I received a bushel of mail, the first since we left the States. Even gave O'Riley, my copilot, a couple of letters from Sis, as his creditors in Cleveland have given up writing him, and he didn't get any mail at all.

Well, we're comfortably settled in our tarpaulin foxhole at our permanent squadron. Any similarity between combat and the recent movies is strictly coincidental. But any comparison between our 725th Squadron and the movies of World War One hits the nail right on the head. Sis, as an old movie buff, you remember *Hell's Angels* and *Wings* and *Sergeant York*. They could have been filmed right here in our squadron. Except for the sophisticated bombers we're flying, instead of Spads and Nieuports, the scene hasn't changed a bit since the First World War. The guys even sing "Lili Marlene" at the club.

We're squatting near the little village of Castellucia di Sauri, which I don't think you'll find in the family atlas. But it's near Cerignola, on the heel of the Italian boot. Our airstrip is carved out of a rancho that's been liberated from a wealthy Italian admiral. The Army whitewashed the buildings and outhouses (you should see an Italian john); made the stable into a briefing room; olive drying rooms into squadron operations and S-2; servant quarters into supply offices; and the group commander moved into the main house. The officers and enlisted men live in tents clustered around the airstrip.

Haven't had much time to get bored. All my crew members have taken their check-out missions with experienced crews, and tomorrow we make our first mission together. Everyone except my copilot, O'Riley, who will be replaced by a combat-experienced copilot. From then on, if all goes well, I'll fly all the missions with my original crew.

Mom, I think it's nice you're getting letters from the families of my crew members. I don't blame them. With the skipper they've got, since misery loves company, it's nice to seek solace from one another. In response to your request for a thumbnail sketch of each one, so you'll be better able to correspond with their families, I'll give you one in each letter. Starting with my copilot.

Pat O'Riley, as you can see in the crew picture we sent you from Savannah, is a tall, easy-going, handsome bachelor of Irish extraction, who hails from Cleveland, Ohio. Oddly enough, his dad is over here in England, a maintenance sergeant with the RAF. Pat hopes to take leave later on and visit his dad in London.

Pat's a natural-born pilot, in many ways a much better pilot than I am. But he seems content, for the moment at least, flying as copilot. He gets all the stick time he wants, without having to shoulder the responsibilities of an aircraft commander. In time I hope to get him checked out with his own crew. At any rate, we get along great, and his infectious grin and easygoing approach to things are welcome counterpoints to my sometimes uptight attitude. The whole crew thinks he's tops. Needless to say, his Irish blood makes him full of the old blarney, and he has quite a way with the women.

Well, that's it for now. I'm glad you're enjoying your work at the Boeing plant. With you and Sis both building B-17's, the war can't last much longer.

My love to all the family, and a great big smacker for you.

Swede

P.S.: I see in *Stars and Stripes* that the Superforts have bombed Tokyo. Since the Allies have launched a major offensive in the Rhineland, I'll be home before you know it. So please don't worry.

Stromburg addressed the V-Mail form, then tried to summon the ambition to take the letter to the mailroom. He had brought his cot outside the tent to take advantage of the unusually warm day, and the bright sunlight felt good soaking into his olive-drab uniform. Maybe a short nap would be in order before making the trek to the mailroom. He had just stretched out when his attention was commanded by a grunting noise near the tent. He shaded his eyes with his hand.

Balzac was puffing into view, straining with the weight of a large load he was pulling on a rope behind him. Curious, Stromburg rose on his elbows for a better view. The sunlight danced brilliantly off the large aluminum, torpedo-shaped object his bombardier had in tow. "What the hell," asked Stromburg, "is that?"

Balzac pulled up to Stromburg's cot and stopped to get his breath. "What does it look like? It's a P-Thirty-eight wingtip tank, of course."

"Of course. Where did you get it?"

"Oddly enough, off a P-Thirty-eight."

"Do tell. What do you suppose the P-Thirty-eight pilot is going to say when he discovers one of his long-range fuel tanks is missing perhaps?"

"Don't think he'll be too upset. Mainly on account of

he crash-landed on our strip last week, and they bulldozed the plane off the runway so our bomber mission could land. It isn't in very good shape. Neither is the pilot. They neglected to take him out of the plane before they bulldozed it off the runway."

"Interesting." Stromburg looked curiously at his bombardier as the little Pole wiped the sweat from his face with his handkerchief. "May I ask what you're going to do with a salvaged P-Thirty-eight wingtip tank?"

"You may. I am building a furnace. For our tent."

Stromburg was only mildly surprised. "I should have known."

"I should think so. I've had enough of a stove that gobbles wood faster'n you can haul it, belches smoke, then craps ashes all over the floor."

"So, naturally, you're going to build a furnace."

"Naturally. With the help of my serf here."

O'Riley came ambling up to the tent, a coil of aluminum tubing slung over his shoulder. Stromburg looked up at his copilot. It did not surprise him that the six-foot-three Irishman would be carrying the lightweight tubing while Balzac struggled with a load as big as he was. The lofty, laid-back copilot was the exact antithesis of the diminutive, ballsy bombardier. With the attraction of complete opposites, it was only natural that the Mutt and Jeff team had become as close as the shell on a coconut.

O'Riley sat down on the end of Stromburg's cot and pulled out a Lucky Strike. "Leonardo Da Vinci here," he said, glancing at Balzac, "is building a furnace for our tent."

Stromburg nodded. "So I hear. May I ask just how you intend to approach this undertaking?"

"Simplicity itself," said Balzac. "See that wooden cradle there next to the tent?" Stromburg craned to observe a sturdy wooden platform that had been erected between the tents. "That cradle has been designed so this wingtip tank will rest securely on top. High enough above our stove to permit gravity flow. We fill the tank with oil, from which it will flow through this attached aluminum tubing to terminate in a box of sand at the bottom of the stove. We will regulate the flow of oil, thus the heat, with this simple little shutoff valve. *Voilà!* A clean, smokeless, trouble-free oil furnace."

Stromburg considered this. "Might work. Only one problem: Where are you going to get the oil?"

"Least of our worries. Every time the maintenance men change oil in the airplane engines, they end up with barrels of dirty oil. We can have all we want. And for a paltry pittance, I have arranged to keep our tank filled."

"How paltry a pittance?"

"Two packs of cigarettes a week."

Stromburg's brows puckered. "Odd that should be the payment. Especially since I'm the only officer on the crew who doesn't smoke up his cigarette rations."

"That is odd," said Balzac. "But as our lovable aircraft commander who's vitally concerned with the morale and welfare of his men, we know that no sacrifice would be too great. Right, O'Riley?"

"Right," said O'Riley. "And we we want you to have a feeling of involvement in our project. The warm feeling of having made a contribution."

"How," said Stromburg, "can I ever thank you?"

"There will be time for that later. Would you care to give a hand?"

"I'll give a hand. And, it appears, most of my cigarette ration."

Stromburg blinked at the flashlight beam, batting his eyes to try to erase the probing light that was exploding in his sleeping brain.

"*Buenas días, hombres,*" came the tortilla twang of the orderly, Gonzales. "Drop your cocks and grab your socks. Ees time to go stun the Hun."

"Now that you've permanently destroyed my night vision," grumbled O'Riley, "will you douse that damn klieg light? Geezus, Redeye!"

"*¡Caramba, señors!* We do not seem to be in a very good mood this beautiful mornin'," said Redeye, going out the door. "Truck to the chow hall leaves in twenty minutes."

O'Riley sat up in his cot, rubbing his eyes. "So help me, before this war is over I'm going to neuter that cheerful sonuvabitch."

"You sound like Irving Berlin," said Lancaster. "He had a thing about buglers."

"I'm going to do more than amputate his reveille," grumbled O'Riley. "I'm gonna circumcise his tamale."

Stromburg groped for the matches under his cot and lit the candle on top of the orange crate. As the match flared he checked his watch. "Four ayem. What an ungodly time to go to war."

"For the first time in my life," said Lancaster, shivering as he pulled on his thick woolen socks, "I think I hate the damn Germans."

Further conversation was muted as the men fumbled around in the semidarkness, pulling on their flying suits, then their bulky, electrically wired outer garments. Finally came the thick, fur-lined boots and the nylon-inserted electrically heated flying gloves. Thus rigged out like some twentieth-century clan of awkward gladiators, they picked up their flight bags and waddled out of the tent toward the waiting truck.

"Why is it?" said O'Riley with a grunt, throwing his flight bag up on the truckbed, "that I never think to take a pee until I'm all zipped up in this frapping straitjacket?"

"Just tie a knot in it, O'Riley," said Balzac. "If you can find it."

"If you can find it? You're a riot, Balzac. A real riot." In the act of climbing into the truck, O'Riley suddenly stopped. "Why, you dirty bastards!"

"What's the matter?" asked Stromburg, looking at his copilot.

"What's the matter? Hell, I don't fly this morning! Ewing is your copilot on this mission."

"That's right."

"Then why the hell did you get me out of the fartsack?"

"Nobody got you out of the sack. We just naturally figured you got up to see us off. To launch your old buddies off into the thick of the fray on their first mission."

"Screw my old buddies. I'm going back to bed." He pulled his flight bag off the truck. "And I hope to hell your relief tubes freeze up."

"That is not," said Balzac, "a very nice thing to say."

O'Riley gave his crew the finger, then turned on his heel and started back toward the tent.

"Sometimes," said Balzac, grinning, "it's hard to figure our copilot out."

"You might say that," said Lancaster, grabbing hold as the truck lurched off into the predawn darkness. "But as Plutarch put it, 'All men whilst they are awake are in one common world; but each of them, when he is asleep, is in a world of his own.'"

Balzac looked sleepily at the navigator. "That's how Plutarch put it?"

"That's how Plutarch put it."

"Well, bully for old Plutarch."

The mess hall for the 725th Squadron was on the far side of the olive plantation, housed in a converted outbuilding that had formerly served as part of the stables. This fact was not particularly a problem to the head cook, a surly ex-stevedore named Schultz, who had been drafted from the Brooklyn docks and whose only culinary experience had been a speed course in the Army's mess school, where he earned his degree in Food Deappetizing.

Tons of Lysol and whitewash had failed to compromise the stench of equine residue from the former occupants, and the breakfast staple of Army chow known as chipped beef on toast, or better described as SOS ("shit on a shingle"), was even less popular at the 725th, even though Schultz stoutly denied the accusations that his recipe included the real thing.

The kitchen was in the center of the long building, flanked on one end by the officers' mess and on the other by the enlisted men's. The one kitchen catered both mess halls, serving the same food to both.

Heeding the advice of the experienced crews seated at the long tables, Stromburg and his officers eschewed the chipped beef in favor of scrambled dehydrated eggs and inch-thick slabs of toast lathered with a Cosmoline falsely advertised as butter, all made partially palatable only when larded with large amounts of orange marmalade. The

coffee, however, was another matter. There was no denying
its virtues, particularly if measured by its strength. It was
announced properly brewed by Schultz only when it could
clamp a stirring spoon and hold it upright in a vise grip of
rigor mortis.

The food may not have been appetizing, but it was hot
and filling. Abetted by the coffee that gave a hearty caffeine
lift to sagging spirits, the warm mess hall provided a mood
elevator that raised the chilly predawn grunts and grumbles
into a semblance of conversation that may not have been
sparkling but was at least civil and at times animated as the
crews pondered the upcoming mission.

"You Three Sixty-nine?"

Stromburg put down his coffee mug and turned to face
the owner of the hand that rested on his shoulder. "My
crew is Three Sixty-nine. Yes."

"I'm Ewing. Your copilot for today's mission."

Stromburg found himself looking into a pair of pale
blue, watering eyes. So this was Ewing, the experienced
pilot who had been assigned to fly today's mission with him.
Whereas all his other crew members had taken a mission in
their assigned slots with experienced crews, the aircraft
commander did not do this on his first combat flight.
Instead, an experienced pilot was assigned to occupy the
right seat, replacing the regular copilot, so that the AC
could not only be checked out in combat flying but could
also be advised on the techniques of crew management in
combat situations with his own crew.

The more experience gathered by flying as an inte-
grated team, the faster the crew was declared combat-
ready. For this reason the replaced O'Riley was back in his
warm sack making loud z's while Stromburg was drinking
coffee that tasted like carbolic acid and shaking hands with a
small pilot with watery eyes. A man, thought Stromburg,
could grow to hate his copilot.

Stromburg reached up and shook the proffered hand.
"I'm Swede Strom—"

He was stopped with a flashed palm. "I don't want to
know your name." Stromburg stared at the man in puzzle-
ment as he withdrew his hand. "How do you like our

cuisine here in the fighting Seven Twenty-fifth? Ain't it the shits?"

"Ranks right up there with the coffee."

"Schultz's own recipe. It's about half chicory, half horse dung, and half hydraulic fluid. But it does wake up the inner man."

Stromburg started to introduce his bombardier and navigator when again Ewing's hand shot up. "No introductions. Nothing personal, fellas. I just don't want to know your names."

Stromburg looked closely at the lined, pouchy-eyed face of the short, skinny copilot. "If that's the way you want it, Ewing."

"That's the way I want it. No offense." Ewing sat down beside Stromburg and poured himself a cup of coffee from the chipped enamel coffee pot. "Ever had breakfast with the Hollywood Air Force?"

"The Hollywood Air Force?"

"The Eighth Air Force in England. Do you know the flight crews over there get fresh eggs and steak for breakfast?"

"No," said Stromburg. "I didn't know."

"If they served those glamor boys a meal like this, the cook would end up using it as a suppository."

"Do I detect a note of bitterness toward our B-17 comrades?"

"Bitterness? Ha!" Ewing took another big swig of coffee. "Why should we be bitter? Just because they go up in their dandy little flying machines, earn their flight pay, then duck into town to spend it on horny British women who speak English, why should I be bitter? After all, we're in sunny Italy, ass deep in mud, and we get our pick of all the sheep that graze in the south pasture. What makes you think I'm bitter?"

Stromburg finished his coffee, looking curiously at the unrecognizable dregs in the bottom of the cup. "You're overlooking one thing, Ewing."

"What's that?"

"Look at all the beautiful olive trees around you. Bushels of olives just yours for the taking."

"You're right. I'm being a bastard. What would happen to all the martini drinkers if it weren't for sunny Italy? I must start looking at the bright side."

"Good lad." Stromburg noticed that Ewing's hand trembled slightly as he lit a cigarette.

"So, Three Sixty-nine, you're about to take your first mission. How do you feel about joining our little war?"

"How do I feel?" Stromburg thought a moment. "Apprehensive, I guess. And a little scared."

"Good. Healthy signs."

"How many missions do you have in?"

"Too goddamn many."

"How many is that?"

"Any number over zero is too goddamn many. But if you have to be specific, this will be my twenty-ninth."

"Good for you. Only seven more to go."

"Don't count on it. We used to have to complete only twenty-five missions, then we could go home. The day I completed my twenty-fifth, they upped it to thirty-five."

"The hell! I can see why you might be a little bitter."

"A little bitter?" He snorted as he butted his cigarette in his coffee cup. "Not me. I have no reason to be bitter. After all, I'm still alive. I'm the sole survivor of my original crew."

Stromburg studied the lined face of the copilot, who had aged far more than his years. "My God, Ewing—"

"Let's knock off this maudlin horseshit. Bad psychology to tell war stories to a green crew before the first mission. Scratch all the above. And let's just hope Vienna isn't our primary target today. If it is, you're apt to find your copilot seat empty during the bomb run."

"Vienna? That's a bad target?"

"Never mind. Sorry I brought it up."

"All right. If you don't want to talk about it." Stromburg checked his watch. "I guess we'd better get going. The last truck is leaving."

"Yeah." Ewing rose and led the way toward the door. "Wouldn't do to be late. Sure as hell wouldn't want them to start the war without us."

Seated with his crew officers and Ewing, Stromburg looked around at the briefing room of the 451st Bomb Group. A large building that formerly served as a drying room for olives, it now contained a small raised stage at one end of the room, commanded by a podium in its center. The wall behind the stage was covered with maps and charts with plastic overlays, and in the center was a drawn curtain. On the stage several staff officers were milling around, fussing with the wall charts. The rest of the room was taken up with folding chairs that now contained the flanks of the officers of crews belonging to the 724th, 725th, 726th, and 727th squadrons that comprised the bomb group.

Presently a major at the podium hit a ramrod stance and yelled, "Attention!" Entering from the back of the room, a bird colonel strode toward the stage as the men in the assemblage lurched to their feet and hit a brace. When the colonel reached the stage he took a stance by the podium and addressed the group.

"Be seated, gentlemen." With a clanking of metal chairs, the officers resumed their seats.

"That's Colonel Sterling," whispered Ewing to Stromburg. "Group commander."

Stromburg nodded, appraising the tall, slender figure of the colonel. He was a striking man, dressed in military pinks and blouse with sharp military creases that could shave a boar. He was tanned, looked ruggedly fit, and his regular features were surmounted by a shock of curly black hair. "Looks out of place here," Stromburg whispered to Ewing. "He should be back in the States leading a bond drive."

"He just got back," muttered Ewing.

The colonel addressed the major at the podium. "Start the briefing, Major." Then he crossed over to the side of the stage, where he observed with folded arms.

There was dead silence in the briefing room as the group operations officer began his briefing. "Today, men, the target is the Blechhammer South Oil Refinery."

There was a murmur in the assemblage as the crews greeted this information. A hissing exhalation came from Ewing; then he muttered, "At least it's not Vienna."

As the major nodded to a lieutenant standing by the closed curtain, the officer pulled the drawstrings that exposed the large map of Germany that had been overlaid with acetate sheets. The course to the target had been inscribed with heavy lines on the overlay. The major advanced on the map with his pointer.

"The Four Fifty-first will pick up the IP here, turn to a heading of five eight degrees for the angle of attack. Bombing altitude will be twenty-six thousand feet. The target elevation is six hundred and six feet. The weather is forecast to be CAVU, bombing will be done visually, all ships will drop off the lead bombardier. Bombload will be five-hundred-pound GP's, intervalometer set at forty feet.

"This will be a maximum effort. Groups will be at bombing altitude and go into right echelon five minutes before IP. There will be two PFF aircraft leading able flight for navigation only. Ball turrets will be lowered when cruising altitude is reached. Two cartons of chaff will be dispensed following normal SOP.

"Call signs will be as follows: Four Fifty-first, 'Surething One'; Four Sixty-first, 'Surething Two'; Four Eighty-fourth, 'Surething Three.' Escort will be twenty P-Thirty-eights, twenty P-Fifty-ones—call sign, 'Fruittart.' Recall call sign will be 'Sweatshirt.' Radio discipline will be strictly enforced. Any deviation from standing operational procedures will be noted in the mission flimsies being handed out to the pilots. Navigators will pick up their maps and mission kits following the briefing. Rendezvous procedures are outlined in the flimsies."

As the major droned on, Stromburg looked questioningly at Ewing. "My God, that's a lot to remember."

"Don't sweat it," said Ewing. "Most of this poop will be in the flimsy. All you have to do is memorize it."

"Whatever the hell a flimsy is."

"We will start engines at zero seven one five," continued the major. "Taxi at zero seven two five, take off at zero seven three five. Depart base in formation at zero eight three eight at six thousand feet. And now for the Intelligence briefing. Lieutenant Davidson?"

A young officer dressed in olive greens approached from the sidelines, took the pointer from the major, and crossed over to one of the wall maps that was bedecked with large orange circles.

"Good Lord," whispered Stromburg. "The Intelligence officer can't be over eighteen! He's got pimples."

"Wrong," said Ewing. "He's pushing the hell out of twenty. A late bloomer. But he's a sharp little bastard."

"Our Intelligence reports indicate," said Davidson, cupping the end of the pointer with his hands and leaning on it, "that the Blechhammer Oil Refinery is back in business. Although it was well clobbered on our last mission, the Germans have been working around the clock to get it back into production. It has the highest repair priority, as Hitler desperately needs gasoline and lubricants for the Wehrmacht, which thanks to our heavy-bombardment operations is getting critically low."

"I thought we were only going to bomb communications targets," whispered Stromburg.

"You will find," said Ewing, "that our strategy changes from time to time. Keeps the Krauts on their toes. Only consistent thing you can really count on is our inconsistency."

Davidson had turned to tap the flak map with his pointer. "The route to the target will skirt the heavy flak concentrations here, here, and here. However, the Germans aren't all that keen about having their refinery blown up and have brought in their biggest guns, ranging from seventy-five to one hundred fifty-five millimeter. Consequently, flak over the target will be from moderate to intense."

"Davidson has a great knack for understatement," muttered Ewing. "Flak'll be so thick we'll have to fly on instruments."

"Be alert over the Austrian Alps," continued Davidson. "As you know, the Germans have mounted heavy antiaircraft guns on train flatcars, and since they're being continually shuttled around, they're not noted on the flak charts. So you can encounter moderate flak at any time in the vicinity of railroad lines and marshaling yards. Enemy fighter action is forecast to be minimal, due to the shortage of fuel for the Luftwaffe. Some resistance may be encountered near the target, just before turning on to the bomb run."

Davidson turned from the map to consult an Intelligence folder in his hand. "On the world front, the Russians have encircled the Czech hub of Kassa. On a grimmer note, the German counteroffensive has opened in the North. Von Rundstedt has breached Allied lines with fifteen Nazi divisions and is smashing toward Liège. Our American troops have been surrounded at Bastogne. And so, gentlemen, this war is far from over." He closed the briefing folder and looked out at the assemblage. "When you gentlemen pick up your rescue kits for this mission, you'll find there have been a couple of changes. First, the fifty dollars in greenbacks formerly included to assist you in escape and evasion in case you're shot down will no longer be part of your escape kit. Instead, a piece of paper and a stubby pencil like this have been included. If you fall into Partisan hands, you may write an IOU for any amount necessary to guarantee your escape, and it will be honored by our government.

"And secondly"—Davidson held up a tiny object between his thumb and forefinger—"this tiny compass has been included in your escape kits. It's quite accurate and small enough to be shoved up your rectum, where it'll be difficult to find in case of capture."

"Only pilots will be able to read that," murmured Balzac.

"Why is that?" asked Lancaster.

"Because they're the only ones on the crew with their head up their ass."

Balzac received a sharp elbow in the ribs from Ewing. "Knock it off, bombardier."

"And we have a new SOP for our Vienna missions," continued the Intelligence officer. "If you happen to be shot down over Vienna, take streetcar number nineteen to the end of the line. There you'll be met by members of our underground."

"Good God!" said Lancaster. "This guy's crazy. Can you

imagine walking through Vienna with your parachute over your arm, asking Germans for directions to catch streetcar number nineteen?"

"You will find," whispered Ewing, "that our Intelligence is more of an art than a science."

"I will conclude the Intelligence briefing with this one thought," said Davidson. "Remember, there are only six more shopping days until Christmas."

This attempt at levity was met with snarls, grunts, and dire mutterings as the briefing was turned over to the weather officer. The fact that the target was forecast to be clear met with more disgruntled rumblings. When the meteorologist concluded his briefing, the ground commander came to the podium.

"All right, men, if there are any questions they'll be answered following the briefing. I don't need to tell you how important it is to annihilate this target. Let's do it right, so we won't have to go back. The faster we dry up Hitler's gasoline supply, the fewer fighters we're going to have to face on future missions. You have seen the Stat reports. You know how effective our bombing missions have been in crippling the German war effort. The sooner Hitler says 'Uncle,' the sooner we can all go home. So let's give it our best bloody shot!"

"Sounds like a football coach," said Stromburg.

"He's a regular Knute Rockne," said Ewing. "Pep talk number twenty-three. Now here comes the lowering of the boom."

"Now a word for you pilots," continued the commander. "Some of you are getting sloppy. The bomb photos of our last mission showed that some of our bombs were way to hell and gone out of our target area. The Krauts don't need us to plow their potatoes for them. When we have a visual sighting of the target and all the ships bomb off the lead bombardier, there's no damn excuse for not having a tight bomb cluster on the target.

"I don't want to hear any more of this crap about frozen bomb-bay doors and malfunctioning intervalometers. If this happens, you damn sure better be able to prove it when you're back on the ground. Okay. I'll be in the lead ship on today's mission. And when I say tuck it in on the bomb run, I goddamn well mean tuck it in! I don't want to see any daylight between wingtips. And I want to see the nose gunner on Dog Flight sniffin' the ass end of Able Flight. You guys know how to fly formation. Today you're damn well going to prove it."

"Witness," hissed Ewing, "the lowering of the boom."

"I witness," said Stromburg.

"Stand by for a time hack," said the colonel, checking his watch. "In ten seconds it will be zero six two seven. Nine, eight, seven . . ." The officers set their watches for the countdown. ". . . three, two, one—hack! Zero six two seven." Sterling folded his hands behind his back and looked around the room. "Now, men, let's show the folks back home how the best damn group in the whole Army Air Force does its stuff! Go get 'em!"

Balzac jumped to his feet, the fever of excitement showing in his face. "Let's go get 'em!"

The men were ordered to attention as Sterling walked off the stage. When the CO had left the room and the men had been dismissed, Ewing relaxed from his brace and turned to Balzac. "Are you the guy that yelled, 'Let's go get 'em'?"

"Yes, sir," said Balzac. "The colonel gave a hell of a pep talk."

"Did you notice you were the only one in the whole briefing room who did anything but grunt?"

"I don't know," said Balzac, beginning to redden. "I just thought the colonel should know we're all behind him. That we're going to do our damndest to liquidate the nasty Nazis."

"Well," said Ewing, staring at the little bombardier, "rah, rah for you."

Balzac pulled himself up to his full five feet and three inches. "Say, what the hell's the matter with this outfit? It's got no damn spirit!"

"We'll talk about spirit after your first mission. You'll find out it's a little difficult to generate a hell of a lot of enthusiasm for spending the day flying around and getting shot at by very large cannons. Now, you and your navigator go pick up your mission kits." Ewing turned to Stromburg. "You come with me, and we'll pick up the mission flimsies. I'll try to answer your questions."

As Ewing herded Stromburg to the rear of the briefing room to pick up the secret operations orders, Balzac looked after him for a moment before turning to Lancaster. "That Ewing worries me," he said. "I think his spirit is broken."

"We'll discuss it further," said Lancaster, "when we have twenty-nine missions under *our* belt."

Balzac shook his head. "Got to have esprit de corps. That's why we're going to lick the Nazis. We got it and they ain't."

"That's nice to know, Balzac. But let's keep our little secret from the Nazis. Okay?"

Chapter Three

19 December 1944
Somewhere in Italy

Dear Bob:

How goes it, older brother? I hope this short note finds you and Echo Dell and all the kids in great shape. And that your new plastics business is flourishing.

Well, today's the day. In about an hour I saddle up Old Paint and dash off to parry with the enemy on my first mission. Ever since I read Stephen Crane's *Red Badge of Courage* I've wondered how I would stand up under the stress of combat. Now I'm about to find out.

An interesting sidebar: I figured up the other day that the average age of Crew 369 is 20½ years old. I'm the old grandfather with my twenty-three years. One of my waist gunners is nineteen years old. If our average age is taken into account, my crew couldn't buy a drink at a bar. They're still wet behind the ears. Yet, we're about to crank up and operate the most sophisticated engine of destruction ever devised by the warped mind of man. Talk about growing up in a hurry!

But to get to the point of this missive. I know nothing will happen to me. I'm a lot more worried about getting blown up by our tent stove than by the Germans. But if I should slip on a banana peel or something, I know I have your assurance that little Ann will be taken care of. We both know that my short-lived marriage was a disaster. I think we were both just too damn young. There's nothing but a vacuum where a man's love for his wife should be. Whether Thelma and I can patch it up after the war, I seriously doubt. But I do know that little Ann means everything in the world to me. So if anything should happen, I know you and Sis will see that she'll be well taken care of. I have made her the beneficiary of my GI insurance, and that will help a little.

Enough of this. It's time to go. Will write more later. Give my love to Mom, Sis, and your swell family. And I don't want to hear of you saving up your meat stamps for when I come home. You use them, ya hear? Those kids of yours need red meat. In fact, those nephews of mine should have *raw* meat.

Speaking of meat, I think I'm getting horny. Been a long time since I've pitched a little woo.
Swede

P.S.: I won't tell you where I'm writing this, but Chick Sale would be right at home. And a Sears, Roebuck catalog would sure be a vast improvement over this sandpaper peddled as GI toilet paper.

In the cockpit of the B-24 Liberator number thirty-two, better known as *Bombbastic Barbera*, Lieutenant Ewing was reading the last items on the Before Starting Engines checklist as Stromburg performed the duties. "Mixtures rich," muttered Ewing.

"Mixtures rich," repeated Stromburg, pushing the mixture levers forward.

"Props high RPM."

"Props high RPM." Stromburg shoved the propeller controls to their limits.

"Before Starting Engines checklist complete," said Ewing, putting down the plastic card.

"Roger. Standing by to start engines."

"Now we wait for the tower flare. Should be in about two minutes. You know the signals?"

"Affirmative. Green flares mean we go, yellow flares mean stand by, red flares mean stand down and go back to the sack."

"Correct. Now, the most important part of the pre-takeoff checklist is not listed. But be sure you make a mental note." Ewing turned to Daringer, who was leaning over their shoulders. "Engineer, are the flight lunches aboard?"

"Yes, sir," said Daringer.

"And coffee?"

"Two jugs."

"Very well. Waging war is ridiculous. Waging war on a growling stomach is insufferable. Always make damn sure your lunches are aboard. Miserable as they are."

"I'll make a note," said Stromburg.

Ewing pulled up the sleeve of his flight jacket to check his watch. "Okay, look over there at the tower. Five seconds . . . four . . . three . . . two . . . one . . . hack!" Precisely on the word "hack," two green balls of pyrotechnics shot out of the control tower, climbing high in the sky to stand out in the early-morning light.

Stromburg thrust out three fingers, rotated them to signal the ground-crew fireguard, then energized the switches that started the huge propeller of number three engine to rotate. It coughed several times as Stromburg toggled raw gasoline into its cylinders, then with a roar the Pratt & Whitney power plant kicked into life as Stromburg reined in its 1,830 horses. Engines number four, two, and one followed suit in that order.

As the engines warmed, the two pilots ticked off the Before Taxi checklist and checked the magnetos. Then Stromburg fanned out his thumbs to the ground crew. The wheel chocks were removed. At precisely 0725, the lead ship of Able Flight started rolling out of its revetment and onto the taxi strip that led to the runway.

"Since we're flying the number six slot in Baker Flight," said Ewing, "we'll fall in line behind number fifteen over there in that revetment. See it?"

"Roger," said Stromburg. "Number fifteen." The two men watched silently as one by one the planes lurched out of their revetments to fall into their places in line on the taxi strip.

"What an ungodly beast," said Ewing as aircraft number fifteen taxied by them. "Look at them. Like a herd of old pachyderms heading for an elephant graveyard."

Stromburg nudged the throttles forward and fell into place behind number fifteen. "All that aluminum!" he said, glancing up ahead. "A belching, backfiring aluminum river."

"Yep," said Ewing. "A helluva way to treat good pots and pans."

The pilots ran through the Before Takeoff checklist as they taxied; then at exactly 0735 the lead ship rolled onto the active runway and with a blasting roar started its takeoff roll. At precisely thirty-second intervals the ships ahead of Stromburg followed, bumping down the rough pierced-steel planking to wallow into the air like some overweight dodo bird, fighting propwash and the gross weights that sorely pressed the airplane's aerodynamics.

When his turn came, Stromburg taxied onto the runway, lined up, locked the brakes, and listened to Ewing count down the seconds. Five seconds before his departure time, Stromburg started advancing the throttles until they were almost to their stops by the time the copilot said, "Firewall it!" Stromburg released the brakes and with a lurch started down the runway as he bent the throttles to their stops and cranked the manifold pressure of the engines up to war emergency power.

"God!" he muttered, bouncing in his seat as the wheels transmitted the uneven steel planks of the strip to send shock waves reverberating throughout the aircraft. "This bird sure likes to devour runway!"

"The B-Two-dozen has a great affinity for Mother Earth. Especially when carrying a maximum load like this."

"I'll buy that!" Stromburg began to sweat as he saw the end of the runway approaching faster than his airspeed indicator was climbing. He watched grimly as the muddy slough of the overrun fast advanced, and then as the steel

planking started to give way to mud, he horsed back on the
control column, literally hauling the airplane into the air.
The staggering bomber divorced the rough runway to
encounter the rougher turbulence of prop-churned air.
With all his might Stromburg wrestled with the controls,
allowing the aircraft to sink down into the valley as the
mushing airplane hovered at stall speed. "Gear up!" he
ordered.

"Gear coming up," replied the copilot, complying.
With the reduced drag of the retracted gear and the milking
up of the flaps, the airplane slowly began to assume more
the characteristics of flight than of fatality. Stromburg
banked around to search for his flight leader.

"My God!" he said, wiping the sweat from his eyes.

"You made many max-load takeoffs?" asked Ewing.

"One. That one."

"Mind a couple of suggestions?"

"Hell, no. Not if they'll prevent making very large
divots in Mussolini's golf course down there."

"Okay. First, be sure you're up to max power, with the
superchargers cranked in, *before* you release the brakes.
With a load like we're carrying, you need all the head start
you can get."

"I'll buy that. I started rolling a little too soon."

"Second, we were slow getting the cowl flaps closed.
They create a hell of a lot of drag until they're closed. In
this weather there's not much chance of the engines over-
heating."

"So noted. Cowl flaps closed sooner."

"Third, and you won't find this in the manual, but most
of the pilots have the bombardier stand by to jettison the
bombs on takeoff. If you lose an engine during the critical
takeoff speed with a max load, ain't no way you're going to
get this crate back onto the runway in one piece. So if an
engine conks out, first thing to do is give the bombardier
the signal for bombs away. Then you got a chance."

Stromburg looked over at the copilot. "You mean spray
the landscape around here with bombs?"

Ewing shrugged. "Take your choice. You want to cover
the local terrain with a few unarmed bombs, or do you want

to pave it with aluminum? Not to mention ten delicate torsos? Personally, I opt for the former. And if you look below us, you'll see there are people who agree with me. Those furrows were not made by Italian tractors."

Stromburg looked down at the scars in the fertile dark ground that fanned out from the end of the runway. "See what you mean."

"One final suggestion: My first pilot used to insist that all the crew members shake their grates before takeoff. He claimed it might make the difference between getting airborne or not, in a tight squeeze."

Stromburg grinned. "I doubt it. But why not? A takeoff like this one will scare the crap out of them, anyway."

"You're beginning to get the picture, Three Sixty-nine. You'll soon see why we have the Italian laundries working around the clock."

It took a full hour of circling the base before the group was assembled in formation. Stromburg located Baker Flight and slipped into his number six slot to complete the Baker Flight formation, which then took its place to the right of the six ships that comprised Able Flight. Charlie Flight flew to the left of Able Flight, with Dog Flight just behind and below Able Flight. At exactly 0858 the formed group departed the base at 6,000 feet to rendezvous with the 461st and the 484th bomb groups. Then an armada of bombers thundered across the spur of the Italian boot and out over the quiescent blue waters of the Adriatic Sea.

"Let me spell you off for a while," said Ewing, looking over at the perspiring pilot who was jockeying throttles and controls to keep the lumbering bomber tucked into formation. "Hate to see you working so hard."

"You got it," said Stromburg, gratefully relinquishing controls to the copilot. "Let's see how an old experienced pro handles this wallowing whale."

"You will notice," said Ewing, settling in his seat and gathering the throttles in his gloved hand, "that at no time during these delicate maneuvers do the fingers leave either hand."

"I notice." Stromburg was immediately taken by the

smooth manner in which Ewing kept the big bomber at precisely the right position off the lead ship. Once in place exactly where he wanted to be, he barely touched the throttles or controls.

"The secret of flying formation," said Ewing, "is to anticipate rather than overcontrol. You'll notice some pilots continually fight the airplane, and come down after an eight-hour mission ready for the rubber room. Take it low and slow, think ahead, anticipate your corrections, and then make them very slight. And use your trim tabs. That's what they're for."

Stromburg was visibly impressed. "You do nice work, Lieutenant."

"Nothing to it. You just have to be smarter than the airplane."

"I'll remember that."

"In the meantime, you might have your gunners arm and test-fire their weapons while we're over water. We'll be crossing Yugoslavia soon, and Tito takes a dim view of our spraying lead around his homestead."

"Roger." Stromburg thumbed the intercom button and gave the order to the crew.

"And tell them to watch where they're shooting," added Ewing. "Our squadron buddies would appreciate it if we didn't shoot any of them down."

Stromburg nodded and relayed the information over the intercom. Then the aircraft began to vibrate sporadically as in turn the waist guns, ball turret, nose turret, and top turret .50-calibers were readied for combat. As the final readiness report was forwarded to the cockpit, Stromburg turned to the copilot. "We're hot to trot."

"Good show. Now I suggest you put on your oxygen mask. We're starting our climb to cross the Alps. When you're hooked up, you can take the controls and I'll get into my gear."

"Roger."

"It'll start getting colder than a marble cutter's ass. You might plug in your heated suit while you're at it."

"Wilco." It took nearly ten minutes for Stromburg to affix his oxygen mask to his leather helmet, adjust it, and set the oxygen regulator on Command. Next came plugging in the microphone that was built into his oxygen mask, and the goggles with the electrically heated wires that dissipated the perspiration steam. Then he inserted the plugs of his electrically heated suit and gloves into their sockets and adjusted the rheostat. Now looking like a Hollywood costumer's bad interpretation of a man from Mars, he took over the controls so that his copilot could likewise attire himself.

"What I like about this job," said Stromburg, testing his oxygen mask mike, "is the snazzy uniform."

"Right," said Ewing, donning his equipment. "Sexy as hell, ain't it?"

At twenty-two thousand feet the formation passed over the snow-garlanded peaks of the Carnic Alps, then turned on a heading that would take them across Austria. So far the flight had been smooth, and except for a malfunctioning turbo supercharger on the number three engine, had been gremlin-free. This mechanical problem required a bit more work by the pilots in keeping a tight slot in the formation, but since it affected the engine's performance only at high altitude—where the supercharger rammed more of the rarefied air into the engine's carburetor—it would not affect the engine's performance at lower altitudes and was not given undue concern by the pilots.

As the formation wheeled around on its turning point, Ewing thumbed his intercom button and addressed Stromburg. "We're over territory now where the folks ain't too friendly. This is a good time to don flak suits and helmets and man battle stations. Advise your crew to be on the alert for enemy fighters."

Stromburg nodded and verified that all stations had received the message. With the engineer's help, Ewing draped the heavy lead flak suit over his body and put on the steel, uncomfortable flak helmet. Then as he took the controls, Stromburg was similarly decked out in the protective garb. "Damn!" he muttered into the mike. "This thing weighs a ton."

"Believe me," said Ewing, "when the flak starts coming up, you won't even notice it."

"Pilot from tail gunner," came an interruption over the intercom.

"Go ahead, Galvani," replied Stromburg.

"We got visitors. Six o'clock high. A large formation."

"Can you identify them?"

"Not for sure. But they're coming closer."

Ewing got on the intercom. "Hold your fire until positive identification. Repeat: All stations hold your fire until positive identification." Ewing turned to Stromburg. "That should be our boys. We're supposed to pick up our fighter escort here."

"Pilot from tail. Looks like they're going to buzz the formation." Then, with obvious relief, "They're Mustangs! God, ain't they beautiful!"

The pilots strained to see the fighters come in over the formation. "You'll notice," said Ewing, "that the fighter jocks don't come in too close. Just close enough to be identified. They've had too many of our green gunners take potshots at their tail feathers."

"I notice they're staying out of our gunners' range," said Stromburg, watching as the fighters climbed back to altitude to take a position above and to the rear of the bomber formation.

"Hate fighter pilots," said Ewing. "Every damn one of them thinks he invented the airplane. But I have to admit it's comforting to know they're back there riding shotgun."

"I believe it," said Stromburg.

"Copilot to ball gunner."

"Come in, sir," responded the squeaky-high voice of Waverly.

"That ball turret is on a swivel for a reason. Use it, and keep your eyeballs peeled. We don't expect too much action from enemy fighters, but there're usually a few diehards who come up from below and hit us in the belly. Stay on your toes."

"You're talkin' to a ballet dancer, Lieutenant."

"Good. That goes for you waist gunners, too."

As the waist gunners acknowledged, Ewing put his

hands on the controls. "Let me take her for a while. We'll be coming up on the IP before too long, and you're going to be busier than a one-legged man in an ass-kickin' contest. So relax a spell."

"Okay, Ewing. You got it." Stromburg lifted his hands from the controls and slumped down in his seat. As he did so, he looked curiously at his gloves. Perspiration from his palms was being turned to steam by the electrically heated gloves and was wafting in little spirals to the roof of the cockpit. "Would you look at that," he murmured to Ewing.

Ewing nodded. "Interesting phenomenon, isn't it? Wait till we get over the target. It'll be like a steam bath in here. You can tell your heart and your head to have courage, but there's no dictating to your palms. Dead giveaway."

"I guess. God, would I love a cup of coffee."

"Shame the guy who dreamed up wars couldn't dream up a way to drink coffee through an oxygen mask. Do you know the B-Twenty-nine Superforts are pressurized? The crews don't have to look like Martians. They fly at thirty thousand feet in their shirt sleeves."

"I don't want to hear about it."

Twenty minutes later, Ewing turned to Stromburg. "This is our last turn before the initial point, where we start the bomb run. If you want to take over, I'll help you get ready for the IP."

"I got it," said Stromburg, taking the controls.

"Bombardier from copilot."

"Come in," said Balzac, his voice bubbling with excitement.

"Are the bombs armed?"

"Affirmative. Arming pins removed. Intervalometer is set. Standing by to toggle bombs."

"Roger. You will release bombs only on command of the pilot."

"Understand. But I will track the target on my own bombsight. Just in case the lead bombardier screws up."

"Okay. Just don't get carried away. Now I want a report from all stations that you have flak suits and helmets on." One by one the stations responded compliance, then, "Waist gunners, are you ready to dispense chaff?"

"Roger, sir," said Hannigan, the right waist gunner.

"Okay. We'll tell you when we turn on the IP. Then start throwing it out to beat hell."

"You can count on that."

"Still no sign of enemy fighters back there?" The response from all stations was negative. Ewing reflected on this, then cocked his head at Stromburg. "I don't like it. It smells fishy."

"What smells fishy?" asked Stromburg.

"We were picked up by enemy radar the minute we crossed the Alps. By now every Kraut in Germany knows there's a large bomber formation heading for the Fatherland. But not one damn enemy fighter has come up to challenge us."

"From a neophyte's point of view, I'd say that's a reason for rejoicing, not despairing."

Ewing shook his head. "I don't like it."

"Maybe the Intelligence officer was right. Maybe we are drying up their gasoline supplies. Keeping the Luftwaffe on the ground."

"I don't trust Intelligence officers worth a damn. But if he is right, it'll be the first mission we haven't had some fighter contact." He checked his watch. "Anyway, we're about ten minutes from the IP."

"Pilot from tail gunner."

"Go ahead, Galvani."

"Skipper, we've got a straggler B-Twenty-four coming up from the rear. Looks like he wants to join our formation."

Ewing snapped upright in his seat. "Did you say a straggler?"

"Yes, sir. Must have dropped out from one of the other flights and is joining our formation."

"The hell. Can you see his markings?"

There was a pause before the tail gunner responded. "Yes, sir. There's the old orange ball on the tail. It's a plane from our group, Lieutenant."

"That a fact." Ewing shot a look at Stromburg as he thumbed the intercom button again. "Engineer, fire a red-yellow flare. Immediately."

"Yes, sir." Daringer moved to the flare rack, pulled out the color-coded flare, and rammed it into the flare gun. He then stuck the muzzle of the gun through the small flare-gun porthole and fired. The colored fireballs burst out of the top of the plane in a low arc, whipped by the windstream.

"Okay, tail gunner," said Ewing, "keep an eye on that straggler. He'll respond with a flare. I want to know the colors."

"Roger," said Galvani. "I got him in my glasses."

Stromburg's eyes were riveted on the lead ship as he kept the bomber tucked in tight. Steam was coming from the gloves that clenched the controls. "What's this all about, Ewing?" he asked.

"You'll soon find out," came the curt reply.

"Copilot from tail gunner. The straggler just fired his flares. Red-yellow. Repeat. Red-yellow."

"Red-yellow!" repeated Ewing. "You sure of that?"

"Positive, sir."

"Oh, shit! Okay, tail gunner. Let's see if you can hit anything. Start firing at him!"

There was a pause, then the sound of a microphone being slapped with a gloved hand. "Sir, I seem to be having trouble with my mike. I thought you said—"

"That's what I said, tail gunner. *Shoot the sonuvabitch down!*"

There was another pause, then, "But, sir! You mean fire at one of our own planes—"

"Goddamn it, man! This ain't no debate, it's an order. *Shoot the bastard!*"

"Yes, *sir!*"

Ewing flicked the radio switch from intercom to command and pushed the transmitter button. "Fruittart. You reading Surething One? Over."

The voice of the P-51 flight leader responded immediately. "This is Fruittart. Reading you five square, Surething One. Over."

"Roger, Fruittart. We got an uninvited guest knockin' at the back door of Baker Flight. How about takin' care of him?"

"Wilco, Surething One. Have him in sight. We'll yank the welcome mat. Fruittart out."

As the vibrations of the tailguns were felt in the cockpit, Stromburg stole a quick glance at the copilot. "Would you mind telling me what the hell's going on?"

Ewing met his eyes for a brief second. "You read the flimsy. What's the identification response when you're challenged?"

Stromburg started fumbling in his flight suit for the mission information. "It's right here—"

Ewing reached over and slapped his hand. "That info ain't going to do you a damn bit of good on that sheet of paper. That poop's got to be right here." Ewing tapped his temple. "Memorize that goddamn mission flimsy. You're going to learn that combat flying is split-second timing. When the shit hits the fan, you don't have time to run to the library!"

Stromburg felt his gorge rising at this uncalled-for chastisement. "Now, just a minute, Ewing—"

"Just a minute, hell! If you ever found time to read it, you'd know that the identification response to today's mission challenge is green-yellow. Not red-yellow!"

Stromburg tried to digest this. "So maybe the guy made a mistake. Maybe the poor devil's got engine trouble and is trying to join our flight for protection. No reason to shoot at the poor bastard—"

"I checked the four flights of the Four Fifty-first. The airplanes are all tucked into position. No holes. No stragglers. Beginning to get the picture?"

Stromburg shook his head. "No. Where in hell did the straggler come from?"

Ewing noted the fire sparking in Stromburg's eyes, even through his goggles. "Okay. I'm coming down a little hard. A guy on his first mission can't be expected to know everything. I'll explain. The Germans have patched together some of our bombers that have crash-landed in Germany and Austria. They've made them flyable, complete with proper squadron markings and identifications. Then, on a mission like this, they send one up, hoping we'll think it's a straggler and let it join our formation—which, I'm sorry to say, we have allowed in the past."

Stromburg shrugged. "I still don't understand. Why in hell would the Germans want to send up a plane to join our formation?"

"Simple. When they're flying on our wingtip, they know our exact altitude. To the foot. They know the winds aloft. When we turn on our IP and open our bomb-bay doors, they know our exact heading, position, and target. They radio this information to the German ack-ack gunners. All the sharpshooters have to do is crank this information into their tracking computers and we're sitting ducks. As soon as the straggler knows we're on the bomb run, he peels off. He doesn't want to get shot at any worse than we do."

"Well, I'll be damned!"

"Don't ever sell the Krauts short, my friend. Anybody who calls the Germans *Dummkops* ain't got his head screwed on straight. Anyway, that's why we came up with the coded flare identification challenge. At least we can find out if a straggler is one of us." As Stromburg absorbed this, Ewing addressed Galvani. "Copilot to tail gunner. How's it looking back there?"

"Damn, Lieutenant!" came back Galvani's hyperventilated voice. "You should have seen those Mustangs zero in! That poor *paesan* looked like a chicken in a wolf pack. She spiraled down in one big fireball of flame, then exploded." He sucked in his breath. "Hell of a way to treat a good airplane. Especially one of ours."

"Yeah. Hell of a way."

Stromburg's mind spun as he tried to come to grips with this strange art form known as military combat. Concentrating on the lead ship, he throttled back slightly to stay in formation as it slowly banked over to the left.

"Copilot to all stations, look alive," Ewing said. "We're turning on the bomb run. Bombardier, stand by to open bomb-bay doors. You waist gunners prepare to dispense chaff." As Ewing barked orders, Stromburg was startled to see a bright metallic blizzard emanate from the waist of the lead ship. He nudged Ewing, bringing it to his attention. "Copilot to waist," said Ewing, acknowledging. "Start throwing out chaff."

"Yes, sir," came a response from the rear.

Stromburg watched entranced as the narrow strips of aluminum foil, resembling Christmas tree tinsel, streamed from the lead plane. Cut at precise lengths, the aluminum chaff, or "window," was designed to confuse the enemy's radar, the electronic echoes fogging the German radarscopes to make target tracking more difficult. "Don't know how effective this stuff is in jamming enemy radar," muttered Ewing, "but it gives the boys in back something to do to take their minds off the flak. Speaking of which . . ."

Stromburg looked curiously at the first flak burst. A gray, mushroom-shaped specter of smoke appeared mysteriously in the distant sky. And then it was followed by another and another as the smoky symbols began to dot the sky at exactly their flight level. "So that's flak," murmured Stromburg. "Doesn't look very dangerous."

"If you can see it," replied Ewing, peering nervously at the shell bursts, "it seldom is. Damn! Should have shot that friggin' straggler down sooner. The Kraut gunners got out altitude nailed. This is going to be a shootin' gallery."

Concentrating on keeping his exact position off the lead ship, Stromburg noticed out of the corner of his eye that the smoky mushrooms were becoming more frequent. "Flak bursts seem to be getting blacker," he managed through a dry throat.

"We're gettin' into the range of the big guns ringing the target. Bigger the shell, the blacker the flak."

"That's nice to know," said Stromburg, wishing he could wipe away the sweat that was crawling into his eyes. Then he saw the bomb-bay doors on the lead ship suddenly roll up to expose the bombs nestled in their racks. "Pilot to bombardier. Bomb-bay doors open."

"Bomb-bay doors coming open," repeated Balzac. The whistling of wind filled the cockpit as Stromburg reached for the trim tabs to compensate for the new aerodynamics of the plane. He was just adding throttle when his fingers suddenly froze on the quadrant. He had glanced over to see if the ship opposite him in number five position had likewise opened its bomb-bay doors. At precisely this second a flash of flame gushed from the number five ship,

and then the aircraft, unbelievably, began to break in two,
as if some invisible giant had taken it by the nose and tail
and cracked it over its knee. Mesmerized in horror,
Stromburg watched as the insides began spilling out—the
ammo belts hanging momentarily in midair as if to garland
the bodies of the gunners frozen in an eerie tableau for a
brief second in space before beginning a slow, plunging
descent.

Ewing had also witnessed it, and turned to see the look
of mute terror in Stromburg's eyes. Ewing unclipped his
oxygen mask, reached over, and punched Stromburg hard.
"Goddamn it, man! Fly your airplane! You're falling back!"

Stromburg shook his head as if to try to clear it of the
image that refused to register in his brain. Then, more by
instinct than reasoning, he shoved the throttles forward.

"Copilot to navigator," said Ewing, his voice brusque,
businesslike. "Number fifteen just took a direct hit. Going
down. Mark this position. Waist gunner, watch for chutes.
Bombardier, stand by to toggle bombs."

The other crew members acknowledged; then Hannigan reported from the waist. "No chutes, skipper. The
plane broke in two. Front half is on fire."

"Roger," said Ewing.

Back in formation position, Stromburg glanced with
glazed eyes at his copilot. "Dinsmore was flying number
fifteen. I met him this morning in the latrine. He shared
some of his stateside toilet pap—"

"I don't want to hear!" snapped Ewing. "Get ready for
bombs away. And the second we drop the eggs, be on the
ball. The lead-ship pilot will go into wild evasive action.
He'd be beholden if you didn't run into him."

Stromburg nodded numbly. The sky was actually
beginning to darken from the flak bursts. An occasional
"whomp!" could be heard as well as felt, rocking the big
bomber, causing Stromberg to fight the controls. On the
formation thundered, not wavering from the altitude and
predetermined angle of attack that would give the bombardiers hunched over their Norden bombsights the necessary
time and stability of platform that would allow an unerring
bomb pattern to erupt on the oil refineries coming up
below.

"Waist gunner to pilot," said Hannigan. "Number six ship in Charley Flight is on fire. Going down, but I see chutes."

"Count 'em," said Ewing.

"Number three ship in Dog Flight just rolled over on its back," said Galvani. "Rear stabilizer's gone."

"Copilot to crew. Make a note of all casualties. Now stay off intercom until bombs away."

Stromburg hung on gamely, sticking to the lead ship like glue in spite of the antiaircraft bursts and the sudden deviations made by the lead ship in response to the bombardier's last-minute corrections as he lined up on the target. Then he saw the first two five-hundred-pounders separate from their racks in the lead ship's bomb bay, and like baby porpoises unwilling to leave their mother's breast, fly along under the aircraft for brief seconds until gravity overcame velocity, to send them with noses pointing down as they hurtled toward the earth below.

"Bombs away!" said Stromburg, not noticing until the words came out that he had yelled it.

"Bombs away!" echoed the voice of Balzac, likewise screaming in high-pitched excitement. With a flourish the bombardier triggered the intervalometer that would, with split-second precision, respond to its preselected interval of timing that would release the bombs in a pattern calculated to do the maximum damage. "Now it's our turn!" yelled Balzac. "Take that, you Kraut bastards!"

Grimly Stromburg held on, fighting vainly not to overcontrol as he kept the lead ship in sight through the black smoke, compensating for the rough air and the fluctuating weight and balance of the plane as the heavy bombs spewed out. It seemed to take forever for the bombs to stop coming from the bay of the lead ship. "Looks like a big goose taking a crap," said Ewing, observing the bombs. "Doesn't it?"

"A damn well-fed goose," agreed Stromburg.

"Okay. That's the last one. Get ready for the rally off the target. Copilot to bombardier. Let us know when the last bomb goes."

"There she goes!" yelled Balzac. "All bombs away!"

"Then," said Ewing, "rack this mother over and let's get the hell out of here."

Stromburg found himself jerking the throttles back to their limits to keep from overrunning the lead ship, which had suddenly tilted up on its left wing in a near-vertical bank, to dive down in a screaming turn that would abandon the dangerous altitude the Germans were claiming with such unerring accuracy. "Hold on to your hernia belts!" roared Stromburg as the plane racked over, straining to stay in formation.

In a matter of seconds the flak was exploding harmlessly above them as the ships gathered in a loose zigzagging formation in a wide sweep that would turn them toward home. As they swung around in the turn that took them abeam of the target area, they could see the huge geyser of black smoke boiling up into the sky that marked the former location of the Blechhammer South Oil Refinery.

"Man!" yelled Balzac, barely able to contain himself. "Did we clobber that sonuvabitch! Man, oh, man!"

"Looks like a good strike," said Ewing. "All right, all crew positions check and report battle damage. Starting with the tail gunner."

"Got a few holes in the left stabilizer," said Galvani. "Don't look too serious."

"Got some daylight showin' back here, skipper," said the cool voice of Hannigan. "Where there shouldn't ought to be any daylight. And some bad news. The peckerheads put a hole in our coffee jug."

"Those dirty birds," said Lancaster. "That's hitting below the belt."

"A crappy thing to do," said Ewing. "Okay. The worst is behind us. But we aren't home yet. So stay on your toes and watch for fighters."

Some six hours later, Stromburg and Ewing were slumped into chairs in the squadron dispensary, waiting while the enlisted men lined up for their shot of mission whiskey. Stromburg, utterly drained, rubbed his eyelids with the tips of his fingers, then looked over at Ewing, who was drumming the arms of his chair with his palms. "Can't say I care much for your little war."

Ewing turned red-rimmed eyes on Stromburg. "Why the hell do you say that? Uncle Sam's about to buy you a free drink."

"Yeah." Stromburg idly watched the white-frocked medic pouring two-ounce shots of Seagram's Seven Crown into rows of paper cups, which were picked up by the airmen as they passed by in line. "I have to admit the fringe benefits make it all worthwhile."

"Glad you think so. I'm signing you off as combat-qualified."

"Oh?"

"You'll do all right, Three Sixty-nine."

"I'm not all that sure I want the job. Didn't they say at debriefing that six ships out of our squadron didn't come back?"

Ewing nodded. "About par for the course. Look at the bright side. Eighteen crews came back. And yours 's one of them."

"Let's see. We lost six out of twenty-four. That's about twenty-five percent losses."

"Not quite. One ship went to Switzerland, another made it to Yugoslavia. Another crew bailed out over the Alps. There'll be a few more crew members straggling in."

"That's still a hell of a high percentage rate."

"The Air Corps considers a ten percent casualty rate acceptable on a large mission."

"The Air Corps may consider it acceptable, but I sure as hell don't. At ten percent attrition, statistically a guy will get shot down once every ten missions. We have to put in thirty-five. So if we're lucky, we'll get shot down only three and a half times before we can go home. I'm not all that crazy about the odds."

"Trick is to stay in the ninety percent bracket that comes back. Do that thirty-five times and you're home free."

"How many times have you been shot down?"

"Twice. I never learned the trick."

Stromburg studied the face of the small, nervous pilot. "You were a big help today, Ewing. You taught me a lot. You were cool and calm under fire."

A sad grin warped Ewing's lips. "Cool and calm? You got a funny description of scared shitless."

With the airmen taken care of, the medic brought over two paper cups of whiskey and handed one to each of the men. Ewing brought his to his lips and downed it in one gulp. Stromburg did likewise. He wiped his lips and blinked the water from his eyes.

"One thing I want to know," said Ewing, lighting a cigarette. "There were times during the mission when I swear I heard violin music. Especially when we were descending and had the engines throttled back. Am I hearing things, or did you hear it, too?"

"You heard it. That's Foulette, our nose gunner. He likes to bring his fiddle when he flies."

"Now, hold it." Ewing took a deep drag from his cigarette. "You mean your nose gunner plays the damn violin on a mission?"

"Yeah. He says it's a good place to practice. There's not much to do up there in the nose-gun turret when there's no enemy planes to shoot at. Is there?"

"Probably not. So your nose gunner practices the violin."

"Yeah. Only problem is, he's not very good."

"He's terrible."

"That's why the enlisted men like him to practice in the nose turret. You can hardly hear him. Balzac complains occasionally, the bombardier's station being so close to the nose turret. But if it makes Foulette happy, I'm all for it."

"Just be damn sure he keeps his eyes peeled. He's liable to get a German tracer up his Stradivarius."

"He stays alert. He's a good man."

"You ask me, most of your crew members got a large rip in their marble bag. Especially that bombardier of yours—"

Stromberg turned watering eyes on the copilot. "Ewing, why are you flying copilot? You could be a first pilot anytime you wanted."

"First pilot? You kidding? No dice."

"Why not? It would be a hell of a lot easier job than wet-nursing green crews."

"No. Aircraft commanders have a lot of responsibilities. And a crew. A crew they get to know. And like. People with names."

"You got something against names?"

"Yes. Names get linked with faces. Faces that you have breakfast with. Faces that don't show up for dinner. I don't want to identify any more faces during this bloody war. I told you I'm the only one left of my original crew. Their names and faces will always haunt me. I don't want to be haunted by any more people. I just want to finish my missions and go home."

"So that's why you wouldn't be introduced to the officers of my crew at breakfast this morning."

"You got it." Ewing rose slowly to his feet and headed for the door. "Nothing personal." He paused at the door and turned to look Stromburg in the eyes. "I'll see you around, Three Sixty-Nine." He turned and departed.

Stromburg rose and went to the door. He leaned against the jamb, watching the stooped, retreating figure as it shuffled down the dirt road—a hundred-year-old man barely through puberty. He tried to think about the sad little copilot. About the mission. About the colossal stupidity of this insane war. But he felt nothing. Only the liquid fire burning in his gut gave any clue that he was alive at all.

He clenched the paper cup in his fist, flung it at a wastebasket, and headed for his tent.

Chapter Four

Dear Sis and everybody:

Everyone should have a sister like you, Sis. I got your package last week. You really know how to shop for a guy who has everything. Naturally, the peanut butter can that shoots out three snakes when you open it was the biggest hit. It will keep people from rummaging around in my footlocker. I gave the pencil with the rubber lead to my navigator, who's still trying to figure it out.

The pooper cushion is really appreciated. Unfortunately it's been confiscated, as one of the lads put it in a chair in the squadron commander's office, and it wasn't noticed until General Twining happened to drop by on an inspection trip. It was noticed when the good general sat down. I think our squadron CO is going to enjoy his new assignment in Adak, Alaska, as the sewage disposal officer.

One other slight problem was the teaspoon that melts when you stick it into a hot cup of coffee. We tried it on old Schultz, our chef at the mess hall, and when he stirred a cup of his coffee and half the spoon melted, he looked up beaming and said, "Now, that's what I call a cup of coffee!" We've been having a little trouble with Schultz's java on missions lately, as it keeps eating through the Thermos jugs.

Anyway, as you can see, the package was certainly appreciated. Many thanks, Sweetie.

Another thumbnail sketch for Mom, this time our navigator. Bill Lancaster is a rather handsome, quiet chap—a sort of intellect who quotes from the classics a lot. He hails from Dearborn, Michigan, and he wants to finish college after the war so he can get a degree in engineering. Wants to design cars for the Ford Motor Company. He's a very likable guy once you penetrate his somewhat somber facade, and one cracking good navigator. He has one nagging setback: He gets airsick. On every flight he throws up about fifteen minutes after takeoff. Then he's all right. This, of course, doesn't exactly endear him to his crew. Especially our bombardier, as he likes to use Balzac's flak helmet. There are times when this causes something of a rift in bombardier-navigator relations.

Things are going great here. We've had two missions now, and they've both been milk runs. And the stove only blew up once last week. So tell Mom there's absolutely nothing to worry about. We'll all be home before you know it. General Patton is on the warpath and is hitting the southern flank of the Bulge. And we're dropping food and medical supplies to our troops trapped in besieged Bastogne. Things are looking up.

I can't get over you being the inspector on ball turrets in the B-17's. I have a mental picture of you trying to fold up your six-foot frame into that tiny ball turret. Our ball-turret gunner is only five foot six, and he has trouble. But if anyone can do it, you can.

Give my love to everyone at home, and save a bunch of hugs and kisses for you and Mom.

Swede

P.S.: Am enclosing a money order with this letter to buy some Christmas presents for Ann. It's a little late, but so was payday. She'll be with

Thelma's parents in Oregon this Christmas. At least I hope so. They're good people.

Stromburg returned from the mailroom to find a flurry of activity behind his tent. Balzac and an enlisted man were digging for all their worth as O'Riley stood nearby, leaning on a shovel and kibitzing. Balzac was nearly up to his waist in a hole that measured some five feet square.

"Would you mind telling me," asked Stromburg, "what the hell you're doing to our homestead?"

Balzac stopped shoveling for a moment, wiped dirt from his eyes, and looked up at Stromburg. "Swede, I want you to meet an old buddy of mine. Sergeant Warner."

The sergeant stopped his labors long enough to pop a half-assed salute. "Glad to know you, Lieutenant."

Stromburg acknowledged the salute and the introduction. "Warner here," continued Balzac, "is from the armament shop. He loads our bombs, ammunition, all that kind of stuff."

"That so?" asked Stromburg, appraising the short, muscular enlisted man who was smiling up at him with a grin that joined both ears. "What are you building, an air-raid shelter?"

"What we are doing," said Balzac, "is adding some class to this dump."

"You're building a swimming pool."

"No. But you're close. Remember the last two times we had to traipse clear down to the showers half a mile away, only to find there was no hot water?"

"I remember."

"And how we had to take turns scrubbing each other's goose pimples?"

"I said I remember."

"Okay. That will soon be just a memory. For we, with the help of good old Sergeant Warner, are going to have the only tent in the squadron with hot and cold running water. And, are you ready for this—our own hot shower."

Stromburg pursed his lips. "That a fact?"

"Warner here is not only the best armaments man in the squadron, but in civilian life he's a plumber. With his help we've designed this masterpiece, and we will no longer have to sit downwind from everyone at the mess hall."

"Just how do you intend to achieve this miracle?"

"Simplicity itself," said Balzac. "Tell our lovable old aircraft commander, Warner."

"Shouldn't be too difficult, sir," said Warner, warming to the spotlight. "What we're doin' now is diggin' the drain. For the runoff. We'll dig this down about six feet, fill it with gravel, then put a duckboard over it. Should take care of the waste. Then we'll use some tubing from salvaged airplanes, and coil pipes through your stove and into a hot-water tank. Presto. A hot shower."

Stromburg chewed this. "Sounds good. Only one question: Where's the water going to come from?"

Balzac grinned. "We've already solved that. For a small remuneration, the water truck driver that fills the tanks at the mess hall and the community shower will also fill our tank."

"I see. And that small remuneration wouldn't by any chance be cigarettes? From my ration?"

Balzac moved over to Warner and clapped him on the shoulder. "See, Warner, didn't I tell you about our lovable first pilot? Perceptive, shrewd, bright. No wonder he's the best pilot in the squadron. And on top of all that, he's generous to a fault."

"Yep, you told me," said Warner.

Stromburg looked down at the two men grinning up at him from the hole. He pointed his index finger at Balzac and then crooked it in a beckoning motion. "Come with me a moment, bombardier."

"Where are we going?"

"We're going to have a little chat." Stromburg strode away as Balzac scrambled out of the hole. When Stromburg was out of Warner's earshot, he waited for Balzac to catch up. "Two things," he said. "One, how often is that contraption going to blow up?"

"No problem, Swede," said Balzac, looking up at him as he brushed the dirt from his trousers. "Shouldn't blow up any oftener than the stove."

"That is not the world's greatest recommendation. Your running around with bandaged hands all the time is raising hell with the morale of the new troops checking in. They think your injuries are from combat, not from trying to cook popcorn on an experimental stove."

"Picky, picky."

"And second, how have you managed to subscript the labors of Sergeant Warner? Or should I ask? You know, you've already committed just about all of my cigarette ration."

Balzac spread his hands. "Skipper, would I do a thing like that to you?"

"Yes."

Balzac looked down at his toes. "You sure know how to wound a fella."

"You'll recover. Now level with me. Armaments men have a hell of a lot to do besides building hot showers for officers. What have you promised Warner?"

Balzac suddenly became preoccupied with the toe of his left flying boot, which was drawing designs in the dirt. "Warner and I just happen to hit it off. We became friends when I was building the oil furnace for our stove. He's the best scrounger in the whole damn—"

"What, Balzac, are you promising Warner?"

Balzac looked up into Stromburg's face. "What the hell is there about pilots that make them so damn suspicious all the time?"

"Pilots are only suspicious when they have flak-happy bombardiers. Now just what are you promising Warner, and how much is it going to cost me?"

"Well . . . if you must know. I just told him that if he'd like to help with the shower, we'd get him laid. That's all. A damn small price to pay for—"

"You told him *what*?"

"Now, Swede, don't get all adrenaline. You know the ground crews don't get a chance to go into town very often—"

"You told Warner we'd get him *laid*, for God's sake? What are we going to do, trap him a sheep?"

"Now, look. It's very simple. We're taking the laundry

run into Foggia tomorrow, right? He knows a dandy little whorehouse in town. We'll all chip in two bits, and *violà!* Warner will get his ashes hauled, we get ourselves a hot shower for our tent. What could be simpler? Just a brief stop at Madam Grabballi's."

"Madam Grabballi's?" Stromburg tried to ignore the beaming grin that was flashing at him. "Balzac, have you forgotten the Army VD lectures? There's more clap and syphilis floating around here than you can shake a pecker at. We officers are supposed to see that the enlisted men keep their damn flies zipped. Not take up collections to send them to a two-buck whorehouse."

"I thought of that, too. Two bucks is a little steep. But Warner says they throw in a bottle of wine."

Stromburg's eyeballs rolled to the heavens. "Why the hell couldn't I have been a fighter pilot? All alone in an airplane. No crew. No bombardier—"

Balzac slapped him on the shoulder. "I knew we could count on you. I knew you wouldn't let your buddies down. Your valiant crew that flies into battle, shoulder to shoulder with their beloved leader."

"Balzac, you are so full of—"

"Ah-ah! Just remember. No more cold showers. No more goosebumps."

An efficiency expert might have found fault with the operation. But no one at the 725th Squadron saw a thing wrong with using a four-engine bomber as a laundry truck, filling it with dirty laundry for the weekly trip to the requisitioned quartermaster laundry in Foggia. The flight that took twenty minutes by air would take a day in a truck, and it gave the flight crews a brief respite from the isolation of the remote Italian boondocks in which they were stationed.

Although the services of Stromburg's gunners were not needed—there had never been an instance of enemy fighters ranging deep into southern Italy to shoot down a laundry van—nevertheless, Stromburg found his full crew complement showing up at the flight line for takeoff. This unusual eagerness to fly was abetted in no small measure by the underground communications network spreading the joyous news that Sergeant Warner was going, and he knew the best whorehouse in Foggia.

Landing at the bustling Foggia airport, the laundry special was met by a large GI truck, and the cargo was transferred in record time. It took some persuasion to convince the driver of the truck that his vehicle could be entrusted to the flight crew and his services were not required; this was somehow achieved during a huddle participated in only by the enlisted men, in which certain goods changed hands, and Stromburg had no desire to delve into the matter.

Then with Stromburg at the wheel, Sergeant Warner squeezed into the front seat between him and Lancaster, and the rest of the crew piled atop the dirty laundry in the rear. The truck was soon off the airdrome and winding its way through the crooked, cobblestoned streets of the large, dirty, Italian city called Foggia.

A short time later, heeding instructions from the sergeant, Stromburg wheeled the big truck off into a side street flanked with decrepit buildings whose peeling white-wash had long ago surrendered to the unkempt rigors of war and weather. "That's it, Lieutenant," said Warner, pointing to a small door wedged between steel-shuttered shops. "That's Madam Grabballi's." The truck pulled up in front of the door, and before it could stop, the armaments man leaped from the cab yelling back, "You guys wait here a minute! Be back in a flash!"

The men watched as Warner knocked loudly on the door, at the same time pulling on a cord that was obviously attached to a bell somewhere in the inner remoteness of the building. Presently the door cracked open, Warner talked for a moment to a figure barely visible in the doorway, then he ducked inside. The door closed.

Stromburg nervously drummed the steering wheel with his fingers as Lancaster lit a cigarette. The navigator caged his lighter, then squinted at Stromburg through the smoke. "Swede, you seem a mite nervous."

"Nervous? Me?" Stromburg stopped drumming his fingers and looked over at the navigator. "Now, why in hell should I be nervous? We've commandeered a truckful of dirty laundry, which I've just parked in front of an off-limits whorehouse so the men I'm responsible for to keep mentally and physically fit can all get laid and get a dose of the clap. Now, why should I be nervous?"

Lancaster grinned. "It's a jolly war, isn't it?"

"A lot of laughs. A little different from Boise, Idaho." Stromburg looked around at the dingy, rubble-strewn street. "A little different."

"Boise, Idaho." Lancaster blew a smoke ring at the windshield. "How did you happen to pick Boise, Idaho?"

Stromburg shrugged and leaned back in his seat. "Good question. I guess it sort of picked me. There was a job there. And it's a great little town. Clean, green, uncrowded. Capital of Idaho and still under thirty thousand people. Lots of good hunting and fishing. And Idaho's a beautiful state."

"So I've heard. And that's why our young Horace Greeley went West to set the literary world on fire."

Stromburg grunted. "A job on a weekly newspaper ain't exactly setting the literary world on fire. We printed the county legal notices, obituaries, monthly meetings of the garden club. I spent a hell of a lot of time selling advertising, and even more time trying to collect for the ads I sold. I even melted lead, set type, and helped run the press. But once in a while I'd get to write. Even had a little column of my own. And then, just before Uncle Sam beckoned, I got to be a stringer for the Associated Press. Made ten cents a column inch. So, naturally, I bought me a Packard."

"Naturally." Lancaster squinted at his pilot. "So that's what you want to do after the war? Write?"

"No. I don't think I want to. It's the world's poorest-paying profession. But I'm afraid I have to."

"You *have* to?"

"No person should ever set out to be a writer. At least that's what the pros tell me. Writing isn't a vocation. Nor an avocation. Writing is a compulsion. Some people just *have* to write. I'm afraid I'm one of them."

"Interesting."

"Not really. Problem is, I'll probably turn into a lousy

writer. To paraphrase Hemingway, I'm happy only when I'm writing. It's a hell of a disease to be born with."

"Well." Lancaster flipped his cigarette butt out the window. "At least when this thing's over, and if you live through it, you'll have something to write about."

"I'm not too sure." Stromburg raised his hands and looked around "Who in hell would believe this?"

Lancaster squinted his eyes. "I think it was Ben Franklin who said, 'The next thing most like living one's life over again seems to be a recollection of that life, and to make that recollection as durable as possible by putting it down in writing.' I suggest you keep a notebook. Give Ben a run for his money."

"That'll be the day. Besides, I'm not too sure anyone would want to relive these days."

"They just might. Anyway, get yourself a notebook. Keep a diary. I'll help you with your spelling."

"I've already started one. And if I get stuck, I'll call on you."

There was a noise at the door. Suddenly it swung open and Warner popped out, all but engulfed by a weird assortment of bubbling, laughing women. Wearing short skirts and blouses, some unbuttoned to the navel; their faces a mask of bright red lipstick, pancake makeup, and eye shadow; the motley collection of assorted baggage ranged the age spectrum from nubile youth to last-chance senility.

Warner led his concubines to the rear of the truck, a diminutive Pied Piper, his flute a bottle of red wine, which he swung by the neck. "Welcome to Paradise," he said as the men boiled out of the back of the truck.

"Good God!" exclaimed Lancaster, recoiling from a blast of garlic delivered by a mouth that suddenly invaded his ear. He jerked back to bring into focus the face of a woman of matronly age who was regarding him not unkindly.

"You wanna make ficky ficky?" asked the woman, grinning with a mouth that contained more gum than teeth. Lancaster was startled to find his hand suddenly captured and thrust deep into the woman's blouse. His fingers encountered a sagging pouch of dried, nippled leather. "I show you good time. Very good ficky ficky."

"Thanks, no," said Lancaster, retrieving his hand and rolling up his window. "Some other time." This gesture was met with a gummy grimace and a volley of Italian words from the face pressed to the window.

"What's the matter?" asked Stromburg, chuckling. "You don't want to make ficky ficky?"

"Christ!" said Lancaster, lighting up another cigarette. "If this is the best whorehouse in town, I'd hate to see the worst."

There was a loud, shouting, shuffling of positions on the sidewalk as the two forces met, underscored by the loud voice of Warner as he attempted introductions. "Men, these women don't speak much English. But this is Isabella, that's Maria, that's Sophia, and over there's Tiny Tits Albertti and Big Boobs Bargolli. . . ."

As the women displayed their wares and the men shopped, O'Riley and Balzac disengaged from the throng and moved over to the cab of the truck. With some effort they dislodged the matron who was still haranguing Lancaster, and Lancaster rolled down the window.

"Somebody," said O'Riley, watching the scene, "must have left the door open to the zoo."

"Interesting collection," said Balzac, tapping the truck with his swagger stick as he watched the pairing up. "Oh-oh!" He flipped his swagger stick under his arm and nudged O'Riley. "Do you see what I see?"

"If you're referring to those two chicks over by the door," said O'Riley, "I see."

"Be right back." Balzac tracked a great-circle route around the crowd and approached the two women who stood in the doorway, smoking and coolly appraising the activities. They appeared to be a cut above the frenetic menagerie grouped on the sidewalk; their skirts were split up the sides to expose shaved legs evidently more accustomed to embracing the thighs of eager soldiers than the backs of donkeys, and their tight-knit sweaters displayed uplifted contents that had not as yet entirely succumbed to the forces of gravity.

The three officers watched as their bombardier became involved in an animated conversation with the two women. After a moment, he turned on his heel and marched back to the truck, his gait even livelier than usual, his swagger stick slapping a lively tattoo on his shanks. "Swede," he said, "I think it would be in the best interests of the service if I were to stay here and see that our boys keep out of trouble. I'm sure a man of your stature can handle the laundry detail without me."

"Okay, lover," said Stromburg. "We'll try."

"And," said O'Riley, grinding his cigarette under his heel as he returned the wink of the taller of the two women standing by the door, "I think it would be wise if I stuck around to see that our bombardier stays out of trouble."

"Okay, you two," said Stromburg, "I'll be back in a couple hours. And for God's sake, watch out for the MP's. They're swarming all over this town."

"Wilco," said Balzac. "See you anon."

As the two men headed for the women in the doorway, Stromburg turned to Lancaster. "Bill, do you want to stay here and see that our copilot stays out of trouble?"

"No, thanks. After seeing the best whorehouse in town, I'll stick with the dirty laundry." Stromburg kicked the truck into gear and started backing out as the sidewalk throng headed for the doorway, shouting and laughing. "Just remember the old saying, 'It's better to wash your dirty linen in public than to remove your shorts in a private two-buck whorehouse.'"

"Who coined that little gem?"

Lancaster shook another cigarette out of its pack. "William E. Lancaster. A fine figure of a man."

Even with the help of the Army's concise Italian-American language handbook, it took Stromburg and Lancaster nearly an hour to ferret out the quartermaster laundry in the twisted, dogleg streets of the city. But once located, with the considerable help of an MP directing traffic on the main thoroughfare, the exchange of clean laundry for soiled was quickly made, and the two officers found they had time on their hands before they were to pick up their errant crew.

At the suggestion of the quartermaster laundry officer, the two men rode off in search of the Foggia USO Center, where it was rumored one could get a good cup of coffee and a doughnut that did not taste like sawdust. This sanctorum was finally located near the train station, where they parked the truck on a nearby side street. "Do you think it's safe to leave the truck here?" asked Stromburg, getting out of the cab.

"I don't know," said Lancaster. "I've never parked a laundry truck in Foggia, Italy, before."

"Hard to lock up a rig with a canvas top—"

"Hey, GI Joe!" Stromburg looked down at the source of the interruption that was tugging at his sleeve. A small, tattered youth looked up at him through dark eyes the size of saucers. "You want to meet my seester?"

"Good Lord," said Lancaster. "Get a load of that pint-sized pimp. He can't be ten years old."

Stromburg kneeled down to eye level with the sales-man. "No, son. I don't think we have time to meet your sister. Although I'm sure she's a very nice girl."

The youth cupped his hands and stuck them out in front of his chest. "She got big boom booms. She look like Betty Garble. She a virgin."

"I'm sure she is. Some other time." Stromburg rose, looking uncomfortably at the pleading eyes that were appraising him sadly.

"Hey, GI Joe. Only two pack cigarettes. She got very big boom booms."

Stromburg shook his head. "Sorry."

The lad held up one finger. "One pack cigarettes?"

"No. But I'll tell you what. How would you like a Hershey bar? With nuts?"

The eyes became puzzled. *"Come?"*

Stromburg reached into his flight jacket to produce a candy bar. He held it in front of the lad, who began to salivate visibly. "You watch truck." Stromburg motioned as he talked. "Don't let anyone near. *Capish?"*

The little head started nodding. *"Capish.* No one come near truck."

"When we come back, this candy bar is yours."

In a flash the youth clambered up over the tailgate to squat on the pile of bundled laundry. He folded his arms over his chest. "I watch. No one come near."

"Atta boy." Stromburg pointed to his watch. "Be back in thirty minutes." The two men headed for the canteen.

"Now, about the credentials of your security guard," said Lancaster as they crossed the street. "That's like hiring a cat to guard the mice. You want to make a bet that just the laundry disappears, or the whole truck?"

"No bet. I just felt sorry for the little bugger. Did you notice those eyes?"

"Like a couple of Stutz Bearcat head lamps."

"Mussolini must be proud of himself. He and Hitler sure know how to improve a country."

"And we have to come halfway around the world to make it safe for democracy and hip-pocket pimps." Sniffing the aroma of brewing coffee, they opened the door of the canteen. "As Bill put it, 'War at best is barbarism.'"

"Good line," said Stromburg, ushering Lancaster through the door. "Didn't know Shakespeare wrote that."

"He didn't. A general by the name of Bill Sherman."

"That a fact? Didn't know generals could write."

"He printed with a Crayola."

The two men went through the cafeteria line, picked up their coffee and doughnuts, and found a table in a far corner of the crowded room packed with servicemen of all branches. Taking a sip of the hot coffee, Stromburg smacked his lips appreciatively. "Damn, it's good to taste coffee that doesn't make your eyes water."

"It is at that," agreed Lancaster.

"Is this a private war, fellas?" The two men looked up to see a plumpish young lady in a Red Cross uniform standing at their table. "Or can anyone join?"

The officers rose and Lancaster pulled out a chair. "Please join us."

The woman smiled and sat down. "I'm Frances Adams. Your friendly doughnut dispenser."

"And we're a couple of your friendly hired killers," said Lancaster. He introduced Stromburg and himself, as they

appraised the young woman. She had pale brown eyes that
smiled out from under thick brows that met above the nose.
Strands of black hair had escaped the tight bun on the back
of her head to frame her face in parentheses. "It's a real
treat to converse with an attractive young lady who speaks
English and smells unlike garlic."

"Go on with your flattery," she said, smiling as she
glanced at the wings on their uniforms. "I'll bet you're a
fighter pilot," she said to Stromburg.

"No, worse luck. We're with a bomber outfit based
near Cerignola."

"That must be the Four Fifty-first. We don't see too
many of you fellows here."

"Only once a week," said Lancaster. "On washday."

Her brows formed an inverted V. "On washday?"

"Yes. Once a week we fly in the weekly wash."

"You *fly* in the weekly wash?"

Lancaster nodded. "A whole bomberload. You see,
when aircrews have to fly with pilots like Stromburg here,
there's a whole lot of linen that gets dirtied. Mostly shorts.
Creates such a logistics problem that we have to fly our
laundry back and forth."

"What an awful thing to say," she said, smiling
sympathetically at Stromburg. "I don't believe it."

"Believe it," said Stromburg. "I have more dirty shorts
than anybody. Even I hate to fly with me."

"Well, just let me know when you make your next
laundry run. I'd like to throw in a few things."

"We'll let you know."

"Where are you fellas from?"

"Lancaster here is from Dearborn," said Stromburg.
"I'm from Boise, Idaho."

Her brows lifted. "Boise. You don't say. I went through
training with a girl from Boise. It's a small world."

"Really? What was her name?"

"Wilson. Kathleen Wilson. A very pretty—"

"Not Kathy Wilson!" Stromburg spilled his coffee.

"Kathy Wilson. A very pretty redhead. Do you know
her?"

"You bet I know her. And she's not a pretty redhead,
she's a gorgeous redhead."

"Yes, you could call her gorgeous. Of all the room-mates to get stuck with, I had to get Kathy. Can you imagine my chances for a date with her around? And what's worse, she's as nice on the inside as she is pretty on the outside."

"I used to go to high school with her. We had a big crush all through my senior year."

"Wait a minute!" Her brows gathered. "You said your name was Stromburg. Do they call you Swede?"

"Yes. Among other things."

"Kathy used to talk about a guy named Swede. Did you play basketball?"

"I played at it."

"Well what do you know!" She pushed herself back from the table to appraise him. "So you're Kathy's Swede! Well, I'll be damned."

"As you say, it's a small world."

"She always dated a lot. With some real nice guys. But do you know, your name always kept cropping up. Especially after she'd had a glass of wine or two."

"I'll bet."

"It's true. You know, I think she's still carrying a torch for you."

"Oh, come on! She kissed me off a couple of years ago. When I went to work on a newspaper. Said I was hopelessly irresponsible."

She shook her head. "I just don't believe that."

Stromburg held up his right hand. "It's true. And she was right. I was completely irresponsible. I bought a Packard when I was making fifteen dollars a week. Went into debt. One of the reasons she sent me packing."

"She said you never wrote her when she went off to college."

"Of course I didn't. What do you say to a girl who says she never wants to see you again?"

"Honestly! You men! And your insufferable pride."

"Now, wait a minute. How about you women? And your uncompromising female logic?"

"I think," said Lancaster, picking up his coffee cup

and rising, "this would be a good time to put a head on my coffee. How about you folks?"

Frances shook her head, and Stromburg pushed his coffee cup toward the navigator. "Thanks, Bill."

Lancaster departed with the empty cups. Stromburg toyed silently with his spoon as Frances studied him through lowered lids. "Well," she said, "I guess you got the last laugh. Running off and marrying another girl."

"Yep. I got the last laugh, all right. Nothing like being married to a rodeo queen."

"A rodeo queen?"

"Thelma was the rodeo queen of the Idaho State Fair."

"Do tell." She made a tent of her fingers and tucked it under her chin. "How is married life?"

Stromburg broke a portion off his doughnut and idly munched it. "Good doughnuts."

"Thank you. You didn't answer my question."

"You can barely taste the sawdust. The ones we get on the flight line taste like—"

"Did you know that Kathy is stationed here in Italy?"

Stromburg quit chewing. "No, I didn't."

Lancaster arrived with brimming coffee cups. "I trust," he said, "that in my absence you've worked out the incompatibility of insufferable pride and uncompromising logic."

"All worked out," said Frances. "And I'm glad you're back. We may need an adviser."

"Or a referee," added Stromburg.

"I'm here to serve," said Lancaster, handing Stromburg his cup.

Stromburg checked his watch. "It's time we headed for the barn. By the time we pick up the crew and get the ship loaded—"

Frances looked around. "Isn't your crew here with you?"

Lancaster cleared his throat. "We left them off at the Christian Science Reading Room. The boys have turned religious since they started flying with our venerable skipper."

"Yes," said Stromburg. "They've seen the light. They

have coffee and doughnuts at the reading room, and a refined, quiet atmosphere for playing chess and writing letters home."

"Very commendable," said Frances.

"Yes," said Lancaster. "We have a very commendable crew."

"Well," said Stromburg, "let's gear up." He took a large swig of his coffee and turned to Frances. "It's been very nice talking to you. Thanks for sharing your time."

"My pleasure. And I know you're not interested, but just for the record, Kathy Wilson is stationed in Florence. At the Army's Twenty-Fourth General Hospital. Just in case you happen to be in the neighborhood."

"Thanks. So noted for the record. But I won't be in the neighborhood."

"Of course not. I just thought I'd mention it."

Stromburg rose. "Let's hit it, navigator."

"Swede, we have time to finish our coffee."

"You stay here and finish. I'll get the truck and bring it around."

"Okay, sorehead. Give me five minutes."

"You got it. So long, Frances."

"Good-bye, Swede. I hope to see you again."

"Me, too." Stromburg picked up his hat and headed for the door.

Frances followed the tall figure with her eyes, then turned to stare at her hands clenched on the table. "Me and my big mouth. I've upset him."

"Not to worry, little lady. Swede's a pilot. All pilots are weird, irrational, jumpy, and downright odious."

Her eyes traveled to the wings on his chest. "And navigators?"

"Navigators are an entirely different breed. Cool, compassionate, understanding, and just downright lovable. To a man."

She grinned. "And humble."

"To a fault."

She idly picked at the doughnut crumbs on Stromburg's plate. "What is Swede's wife like?"

"I don't really know. I've never met her. According to

her pictures, she's a very pretty gal. Sort of the horsey type. Swede seldom mentions her."

"I have the feeling things aren't going too well between them."

"I think that's a fair assumption. As I say, Swede's pretty tight-lipped about her. He did say something one night, though, when we were both in our cups at a party. Something to the effect that he didn't mind having a cowgirl who loved cows, but he did draw the line at her loving cowboys. I have the impression he caught his cowgirl horsing around. If you'll pardon the expression."

"How sad."

"Yeah. Swede's a good troop. He doesn't deserve that. Come to think of it, no one deserves that."

She shook her head. "It almost makes you want to cry. When I think of that beautiful Kathy Wilson—"

He reached over and patted her hand. "Then let's just not think of it. Let's change the subject. We could talk about us, for instance. I'm single. Are you?"

She dabbed at a dampness in her eyes. "Of course."

"Great. Then what say we launch into a torrid, knee-knocking, bone-crushing, heart-thumping, clothes-ripping romance. Just the two of us."

"Just the two of us?" She looked at him and smiled. "Just the two of us."

"As long as I don't smell like garlic. Right?"

"As long as you don't smell like garlic."

"You're right about navigators being a different breed. You left out the fact they're also crazy. Crazy as a loon."

"Just another facet that adds to our seductive charm."

"All right. We'll give it a test. I happen to know where there's a nice, cozy, black-market restaurant. Where you can get fresh eggs fixed any way you want."

"Fresh eggs? Right out of the chicken?"

"Right out of the chicken. Next time you come, maybe we can arrange a rendezvous at Mama D'Amico's."

"If that's a promise, I'll personally soil every sheet in Cerignola to expedite the mission."

"That's a promise."

The sound of a truck horn reverberated through the

canteen. Lancaster bolted his coffee and jumped to his feet. "That's Swede. And if I don't go, he's not above driving that damn truck in here."

"Then best you go."

"You'll be hearing from me, Frances."

"I hope so, Bill." As he turned to go, she grabbed his sleeve. "You sure you know where to pick up your crew?"

"Yes. We have a rough idea."

"If you just follow the main drag and turn right at the end, you'll run right into it."

"You sure of that?"

"I'm sure. It's the only whorehouse in this part of town."

Madam Grabballi's was not exactly the run-of-the-mill house of ill repute. Between wars, it was a leathergoods factory overlorded by a plump, pince-nezed widow whose spouse had long ago been beckoned to the great slaughterhouse in the sky. During wars, however, there was an acute shortage of raw materials, as animal hides were not unwrapped from live carcasses that were shipped to far-flung corners of the globe to feed the troops. It became an economic necessity, therefore, for Madam Grabballi to replace scarce rawhide with abundant manhide in the form of visiting soldiers.

By the simple expedient of converting drying, tanning, and cutting rooms into cozy cubicles, spraying them with Evening in Paris perfume, and reorienting the job description of her employees, Madam Grabballi's House of Leather quickly became Madam Grabballi's House of Happiness. Nor did the morale of the employees suffer from this transition, as nearly all of the women preferred massaging the skin of live men to tanning the hides of dead cattle. And in truth, the workers at Madam Grabballi's were not exactly looking forward to the end of the war.

With the help of the madam, who spoke no English but who was very articulate in the universal language of love, Stromburg and Lancaster finally tracked down all the errant members of Crew 369 and with no little difficulty engineered the separation from their inamoratas. Balzac was last to be found, eventually located in a top-floor loft where, bereft of all raiment save dog tags and swagger stick, he was giving jitterbug lessons to a trio of bare-breasted nymphets with the aid of a wheezy, windup Victrola.

It took the combined strength of both Stromburg and Lancaster to heave the last of the boisterous revelers into the truck atop the laundry and slam shut the tailgate. A fast inventory produced two bobbing-breasted stowaways who were returned to the madam, and the Army truck finally bounced off down the street to leave the Pasture of Rapture in a cloud of dust.

It was one last stop before reaching the airport that brought even more wailing and cries of anguish from the crew than the forced evacuation from Madam Grabballi's. Pulling up in front of the train station, Stromburg brought the GI truck to a halt, dismounted, and unlocked the tailgate with a shooing motion. "Okay, all you lovers. Out!"

"Where are we?" asked Sergeant Warner, trying to bring Stromburg into focus.

"We are at the train station. The train station has a public rest room. Inside the public rest room is a pro station—a facility that all you cocksmen are now going to take advantage of."

This pronouncement was met by a chorus of protestation as the men dismounted. "A pro station?" managed Balzac fuzzily, falling off the truck and all but impaling himself on his swagger stick.

"A pro station," repeated Stromburg, picking up the bombardier. "P-r-o. Short for prophylaxis. As you may recall, a prophylaxis is the best defense against venereal disease."

"What the hell you talkin' about, *bwana*? I didn't do a damn thing but dance!"

"The rest of the crew sure as hell weren't dancing. This great idea was your brainstorm. Now we gave you your picnic. It's over. So go in there and shake your blanket."

"Absolutely not," said Balzac, pulling himself up to full height to stare at Stromburg's Adam's apple. "Pros are undignified. And messy as hell. Let us not forget, Lieutenant Stromburg, that you are talking to an ossifer. And a gentleman. By act of Congress."

"I'll remember that. In the meantime, get your little butt in there, and take your men. Everybody in the squadron uses the same latrines, and nobody wants to get the clap second-hand. Now *move it!*"

"Is that an order?"

"That's an order."

"Why, you sonuvabitch."

"Sonuvabitch, *sir*."

"Very well. Sonuvabitch, *sir!*" Balzac saluted with his swagger stick, did an about-face, and pulled himself up to a semblance of attention. "All right, you men. Fall in! Form a column of twos."

There was considerable confusion as the men milled around, giggling and scratching, trying to gather into a loose formation.

Stromburg turned to O'Riley, whose long frame was leaning against the tailgate. "How about you, Pat?"

"I'll sit this one out." O'Riley ground his cigarette under his heel. "I emerge from this fishfry with the family jewels untainted."

Lancaster grinned. "What happened?"

O'Riley shook his head. "Not a damn thing. I must be getting old. But there's something about bad teeth and hairy armpits. Taking a pro would be more fun than diddling the ghoul I ended up with."

Stromburg chuckled. "Know what you mean."

"You should have come with us," said Lancaster. "Maybe we're all getting old. Hell of a note when a doughnut hole looks good."

"All right, men. Atten*shit!*" Balzac had finally gotten the men into two straggly columns, which on command jerked themselves into a wobbling formation. "Right . . . face!" Again confusion reigned as wine-soaked brains tried to sort out their starboard side; then finally the formation was all heading in the same direction. Balzac pointed his swagger stick in the direction of the railroad station. "All right, men. To the pro station!"

"To the pro station!" chorused the men.

"Forward . . . harch! Hup . . . toop . . . threep . . . four . . . how about a little song, men?"

The formation reeled uncertainly toward the train-station entrance, cadenced by the loud voice of the little Pole strutting alongside, his swagger stick tucked under his arm. As the men broke into an enthusiastic, if cacophonous version of "Off we go into the wild, blue yonder," the three officers at the truck watched mutely.

Lancaster finally broke the spell. "John Gay put it nicely: 'So comes a reckoning when the banquet's o'er,— The dreadful reckoning, and men smile no more.'"

"I'd say," said O'Riley, "the men will be smiling for a long time."

Stromburg grunted as he watched his crew disappear into the pro station. "I'm discovering there's a lot about this man's Army that my recruiting sergeant never told me."

Chapter Five

Dearest Mom and family:

Peace on Earth, good will toward men.

Just returned from a little Christmas Eve service over at the mess hall, conducted by Chaplain O'Flaherty. You'd like him, Mom. He's a typical red-faced, wonderful Irishman—not exactly a stranger to a wee drop of the poteen, as he calls his homemade Irish whiskey. With the help of Lennie, my bombardier, the chaplain makes his own nectar of the bogs in a still concocted from the innards of a crashed German Messerschmitt. The stuff they distill would gag a maggot off a gut wagon, or in the words of the father when he tasted his latest batch, "A sudden jolt of this has been known to stop a victim's watch, snap his gallusses, and crack his glass eye right across." I think he stole that quote from Irvin S. Cobb, but it's sure descriptive.

In the spirit of Christmas this good man of the cloth shared his latest brewing with the members of his flock, and needless to say, there was a goodly turnout for the Christmas Eve services. Lennie was on hand to help with the festivities, but I think he overdid it sipping Christ's blood, as he ended up falling off the stage while conducting the visiting Foggia boys' choir.

Come to think of it, I don't believe I told you very much about Lennie, our illustrious bombardier. He can charitably be described as a character—a cocky little Polack who is small but wound tight, with the curious, kinetic energy of a young puppy. He measures barely five foot two from pedal to pate, and it took a lot of determination and no little political pull on the part of him and his family to get a waiver for his induction into the service.

He was the jitterbug champion of East Chicago, has a hair-trigger temper, possesses more brass than a depot spittoon, wears his officer's cap with the grommet removed and slung back on his head like a snood, and with his swagger stick under his arm it's been rumored that Balzac is the model for comic-strip *Terry and the Pirates'* Hot-shot Charley. Or maybe it's the other way around. In any event, I spend a lot of my time trying to explain him, and bailing him out of hot water with the brass.

But I wouldn't trade him. He was the sharpest bombardier in his graduating class, and as the crew's armaments officer he works very closely with our enlisted men. Since he's so completely irreverent and outspoken, naturally the enlisted men think he's the greatest thing since Ernie Pyle.

I must admit he's got me buffaloed. For on those occasions when I've had to chew him out, he grins up at me with that pixie smile that spreads from ear to ear and makes dimples you could lose marbles in, and I generally end up laughing. Heck of a way to strike the austere tone of discipline and respect into one's crew members. Anyway, I hope you meet him someday, Mom. I'll try not to throttle him until the war ends.

And I think the war will end soon, honey, and we can all come home and get on with our lives. At least if it takes spirit to win a war, we should

button it up soon. When German General Von
Rundstedt encircled some American troops during his drive toward Liège, he demanded their
surrender. The American colonel in charge responded, "Nuts!" Last we heard, the surrounded
Americans are still fighting. It's this kind of spirit
that will eventually spell victory for the Allied
cause.

The thing I hate most about this dumbhead
war is that it splits family up. This is especially
bad during holidays, doubly bad during the
Christmas season. Especially when one has a
close-knit family like ours.

I miss your traditional fried-oyster feed on
Christmas Eve, Mom, and the crazy festivities of
Bob and Echo Dell and their happy clan as they
prepare for Christmas. Kids are what the Yuletide
season is all about, and your grandkids are about
as great as they come. And my whacky sis and her
great hubby, Joe. And the smells of Christmas—
the mistletoe, the raw-oyster dive-bombing, the
huge tree, the smells of Christmas cookies and
oyster dressing and baking turkey . . .

I'd better knock this off. I seem to be working
up a first-class case of homesickness. We'll just
look ahead to next year when we'll all be home
and we can have Ann with us. God, how I miss
that little toad!

Well, it's sacktime. Have an early-morning
call for a milk run in the morning. Just hope we
don't lock antlers with Santa's reindeers on the
way to the target.

All my love, and a very Merry Christmas to
each and every one. An especially big boodle to
you, Mom.

                                    XXXXXXX
                                    Swede

P.S.: Darned near forgot to tell you about little
Luigi. I think I mentioned our weekly laundry
run to Foggia. Well, my crew took it last week,

and when we landed at Foggia we loaded the dirty laundry aboard a truck to take it into town and exchange it for clean laundry. Bill Lancaster and I dumped the crew members off at the USO to play Ping-Pong, then he and I dropped by the Red Cross snack bar for a doughnut and a cup of java. Before going inside I used a candy bar to bribe a little Italian boy to watch the truck.

As it turns out, this ingratiating little bandit not only watched the truck, but he somehow ended up smuggling aboard our plane, and now he's watching our tent. This is a responsibility we really don't need, as now we have to feed and shelter the little moppet until we can locate his family and ship him back. He claims he doesn't have any folks, but we've got the International Red Cross trying to locate someone who will claim him.

The little tyke can't be much over ten years old and is very small for his age. He's wiry tough and has survived his environment by adopting the characteristics of the coyote to satisfy the demands of a stomach that seems to be bottomless. Cunning and bright, his insecurities cloaked in a mantle of feisty toughness, little Luigi has become sort of a mascot. We've given him a little cot in the corner, and between what we can scrounge from the mess hall and eke out of our ration allowance, we're keeping him fed. In return, he makes our beds, keeps the tent clean, shines our shoes (ever seen a pair of polished tennis shoes?), and performs small jobs, like stealing everything that's not nailed down.

War does, indeed, make strange bedfellows.

P.S. ½: We finally got to see *Going My Way* at the mess hall the other night, I didn't know Bing Crosby had it in him. You are right, Sis, the Old Groaner deserves an Oscar.

Finally signing off,
Swede

"Bombs away!" shouted Balzac.

Stromburg tucked into number five position as close as he could to the lead ship in the second element. The bombardier's intervalometer ticked off, carefully spacing the release of the twelve five-hundred-pound bombs from their racks in the bomb bay. Adjusting the trim tabs to compensate for the shifting airplane weight, Stromburg unriveted his eyes from the lead plane long enough for a quick sweep of the horizon. Oddly enough, there was very little flak at their altitude; only a few bursts far above at nine o'clock, which may have been directed at the escorting P-51's. There were no enemy fighters to be seen.

Stromburg took a deep breath and prepared for the rally off the target as soon as the last of the lead ship's bombs fell free. Maybe this was actually going to be a milk run. Maybe they had caught the marshaling yards at Wels, Austria, asleep at the switch. Or maybe the Germans had figured the Americans would not be so un-Christian as to drop bombs on Christ's birthday.

This mission had turned out to be a sort of Christmas present for the crew, as the primary target was scheduled to be the synthetic-oil plant in Brux, Czechoslovakia, an installation well defended by nearly four hundred flak guns, and one of the roughest targets in Europe. But deteriorating weather had dictated that the alternate target of the Wels Marshaling Yards replace the primary, a decision that was not contested by any of the crew members.

"That's the last one, *bwana*," said Balzac, hunched over his bombsight. "Let's get the hell outta here!"

Stromburg was ready when the lead ship suddenly banked sharply to the left, its bomb-bay doors sliding down their runners to close the gaping void in the belly of the plane. He nudged his throttles forward to compensate for his wide-turn swing to stay in position off the lead ship, sticking to it closely as it made a sweeping dive off the bomb run. As the whole formation of twenty-four bombers wheeled around to pick up its heading for home, Balzac suddenly let out a loud yip from his position in the greenhouse. "Gawd damn! We clobbered it! We dropped 'em right down the smokestack of that locomotive. Look at the secondaries!"

Stromburg craned around to see the target behind his left wing. Smoke was billowing up, almost to their altitude, stark black against the snow. "Looks like we lucked out. Hit an ammo train."

"Holy donkey hockey! You talk about precision bombing! Look at those craters marching right up to the railroad tracks. It's going to be a helluva long time before the Chattanooga Choo-Choo toots through those marshaling yards. Damnit, Balzac, what a bombardier you are!"

"Do you think," asked Stromburg, relaxing a bit as the formation leveled off, "that the lead bombardier might be given a little of the credit? After all, you did drop your bombs off him."

"That's Sam Eppstein flying lead. The kid's got promise."

"Isn't he the squadron's lead bombardier?"

"Affirmative. I had the drift killed and the course corrected nicely in case his bombs got hung up."

"Glad to hear it. Now would you mind interrupting your back-slapping long enough to close the bomb-bay doors?"

"Roger, *bwana*. Bomb-bay doors coming closed. But I do not appreciate your acerbic tone. Let us never forget the fact that the only reason we have pilots on bombers is to steer a movable platform from which bombs may be dropped. As directed by the bombardier. Let us not forget our respective roles, pilot Stromburg. You are but a lackey in the overall mission. An airborne chauffeur, if you will."

"Land a Goshen," said O'Riley, shooting a pained look at his pilot. "Would you listen to that, now. My aged old grandmother was right. She used to dangle me on her knee and tell me that the three most useless things in the world are the runway behind you, the altitude above you, and a wise-ass bomb tosser."

"True," said Stromburg. "I wonder if there's any regulation against dropping the bombardier along with the bombs."

"Let's try it next time," said O'Riley. "I'm sure no court-martial would ever convict us."

"Just keep it up, comedians," said Balzac, "and I'll demonstrate the trapdoor Lancaster and I installed under the pilot compartment."

Stromburg received a negative battle damage report from his crew, along with the cheering news that not a single plane had suffered battle damage. As the formation slowed down to long-range cruising speed for the trip back home, Stromburg established his ship precisely in his slot behind the element lead bomber, warned his crew to stay alert for enemy fighters, and turned the controls over to O'Riley.

"I got it, coach," said the copilot, removing the flak helmet from its customary position over his crotch and placing it on his head.

"I wish to hell you'd wear your brain bucket on your head while we're over the target, sport. A lot of good you're going to do me if you pick up a headful of lead."

"The flak helmet is designed to protect one of man's most vital spots. A lot of good I'm going to do myself, not to mention hundreds of women who will go into mourning black, if my family jewels get shot off. If it's all the same to you, I'll establish my own priorities."

Stromburg sighed. "I'm not sure this war's big enough for both of us." He slumped down in his seat, flexing his fingers, letting the tension drain from him. He looked around at the clear sky, the only condensation being the vapor trails that issued from the bombers in long shafts of white. It was a beautiful, serene counterpoint to the violent eruptions that had rent the sky moments before in the peaceful, slumbering Austrian town.

Stromburg fiddled with the radio controls and finally picked up the Armed Forces Network station out of Foggia. It was broadcasting a Christmas program of choir music from the Mormon Tabernacle. He relayed the information to the crew so they could pick up the program on the COMMAND position of their individual radio selectors, and settled back in his seat to enjoy the music.

His thoughts light-years away, he idly watched a

housefly making its way across the frosted windshield that
was so cold the fly seemed to be tiptoeing. Stromburg
reached out, slid the finger of his glove under the fly. He
drew it closer to his face, watched as the fly seemed to
nestle down in the crook of his finger, obviously reveling in
the warmth of the heated glove.

Glancing across the cockpit as he kept the bomber in
close formation off the lead ship, O'Riley took in the scene.
"Your fly got cold tootsies, coach?"

Stromburg nodded. "You ever wonder about flies that
get trapped in airplanes? Suppose this fly knows it's making
good a ground speed of two hundred and forty miles an
hour just sitting on my finger? Without so much as a flap of
its wings?"

"Doubt it. I don't think Italian flies are all that bright."

"Don't be too sure. It was Italian flies that flew into the
paint on the ceiling of the Sistine Chapel. Eyetie flies that
buzzed around Leonardo de Vinci's cadavers. Some of these
Italian flies have a very rich heritage."

O'Riley shrugged. "All I know about flies is what my
aged old grandmother used to tell me. 'Patrick,' she'd say,
dangling me on her knee, 'flies breed disease. So keep
yours zipped.'"

"Your aged ole grandmother must have been quite a
woman."

"Aye, that she was."

"And you'd be well advised to heed her advice."

"Ain't too tough to do around here." O'Riley flew
silently for a moment, automatically making the small
adjustments that kept the big plane in formation. "I noticed
the railroad tracks we just blew up went right through the
center of town."

"Yeah," said Stromburg.

"Tough on people who were shortsighted enough to
build their homes and churches next to the tracks. How
would you like to have a Christmas present of fifty tons of
high explosives dumped in your lap?"

Stromburg didn't answer.

"It's a funny world. A few minutes ago we blew God
only knows how many people to kingdom come. Now we sit
here trying to keep a housefly from having cold feet."

Stromburg looked narrowly at his copilot. "You know those marshaling yards are a vital link in the German communications system. Who knows how many days we may have shortened the war by destroying it."

"Or how many lives we have just shortened in the process."

"Damn it, Pat, knock it off!"

O'Riley shrugged. "Okay, coach. Don't get all worked up. I know we're just doing our job. Maybe I'm feeling sorry for myself for having to work on Christmas Day."

"Pilots from navigator," broke in Lancaster's voice.

"Come in, nav," said Stromburg.

"You gents see that little town off in the distance at about three o'clock?"

Stromburg looked past the right wingtip to see a patch of brown in the white blanket below them. "Roger."

"That's the village of Hallein, Austria. I don't suppose either of you ignorami know the significance of that little village?"

"Hallein?" said O'Riley. "Doesn't ring a bell."

"I'll pass," said Stromburg.

"I figured you two would, knowing pilots as I do. That little town is famous for being the home of Franz Gruber."

Stromburg and O'Riley gave each other blank looks. "Well, what do you know," said O'Riley.

"Franz Gruber wrote the song you're listening to on the radio," continued Lancaster.

Stromburg turned the volume up on the command set, listened for a moment. "Franz Gruber wrote 'Silent Night'?"

"Of course," said O'Riley. "*That* Franz Gruber."

"It was Christmas Eve in 1818," expounded Lancaster. "Gruber, a schoolteacher, and a young priest named Joseph Mohr were getting ready for Christmas Eve services when they found a family of mice had taken over the church organ. It refused to properly blow and bellow. So Mohr knocked out some words, and Gruber improvised a tune strumming on his guitar. Thus, 'Silent Night' was born. Right over there in that little town. About a century and a quarter to the starboard."

"That a fact," said O'Riley, shading his eyes to peer into the distance.

"All part of the Lancaster Tour Guide service," said Lancaster. "Makes one think, doesn't it? If some marshaling yards ran through it, we might have had the privilege of blowing up the town that gave us the holiest of all Christmas songs. On Christmas Day."

"Really puts one into the Christmas spirit," said Stromburg, unhooking his oxygen mask long enough to inhale a sip of cold coffee.

"Yeah," said Lancaster, burying himself in his maps. "Ho, ho, ho."

"Pilot from tail gunner."

Stromburg wasn't enjoying this conversation, and he was glad for the intrusion from Galvani. "Come in, Nick."

"Sir"—the voice sounded pained—"I got myself a problem."

"Oh? What kind of problem?"

"It's kinda embarrassin'. But my pecker is frozen to my gun barrel."

Stromburg blinked. "You seem to be coming in garbled, Galvani. Say again."

There was a pause; then, "I said it's my tallywhacker. Damn thing's frozen to the left barrel of my tailgun. Ouch! Damn, that smarts!"

Stromburg shot a look over at his copilot. "Maybe it would help if you started at the beginning, Galvani."

"Yes, sir. I had to take a leak. Was using the relief tube when we hit that bumpy air back there. My dingus flopped out and slapped against the gun barrel. You know how cold this damn gun is at our altitude. Now my jabberwocky is stuck to it and I can't get it off."

Stromburg watched O'Riley's face bloom into a large grin. "Sorry to hear that, Nick. You can't peel it off?"

"If I peel it off, it'll leave the skin there. That ain't no way to treat an old buddy."

"Well," chimed in O'Riley, unable to keep a chuckle out of his voice, "you keep telling us how well endowed you are. Couple inches shouldn't be missed—"

"This ain't funny, Lieutenant."

"No," said Stromburg, compassionately, "from where you're sitting, I don't suppose it's very funny." He reached over and punched his copilot, who was about to explode with suppressed mirth. "I'll take over, O'Riley, before you fly into the lead ship."

"You got it," murmured O'Riley, relinquishing the controls and reaching for his handkerchief.

"Well, as I see it," said Stromburg, preoccupied with getting the ship tucked back into formation, "only one solution to your problem."

"What's that?" asked Galvani, fear showing in his voice.

"You have to get that gun barrel warm."

"Yeah, skipper. That makes sense."

"And only one way I know of to do that."

There was a moment of silence on the intercom, then a small explosion. "No! You don't mean—"

"I do mean. Unless you can come up with a better solution. You have to fire your guns."

"Holy owl shit!"

"Just squeeze off a few rounds. Enough to warm your gun barrels. Then your little problem will resolve itself."

"You mean my big problem."

"Okay, your big problem."

"But the recoil on these fifty-calibers—"

"Who knows?" said O'Riley. "You might discover a cheap thrill."

"I want a discharge," said Galvani with a moan, "but this ain't what I had in mind."

"Just bite the bullet," said Stromburg, "before frostbite sets in. That happens, the little bugger's liable to fall off."

"Frostbite!" cried Galvani, trying to come to grips with this new menace. "Oh, God!"

"Go ahead and fire at will. Try not to hit any of the ships in our formation."

"Oh, God A'mighty!" came a final lament through gritted teeth. There was a long silence; then suddenly the chatter of the tailgun vibrated in the cockpit.

Stromburg gave his copilot a wincing look as O'Riley wiped at his eyes with his handkerchief. Finally the tail gunner reported. "Holy shit!"

"How was it?" queried Stromburg. "You all right, Nick?"

"Sufferin' Jesus!"

"Damn it, man! You all right?"

"Yeah, skipper, I think so. My tallywhacker's a little worse for wear. But it's back in my pants."

"Well, hooray!"

"Talk about a blast! Tore off a hunk of skin but didn't even notice it. I think I just fell in love with my tail gun."

"Better get some sulfa and a bandage on your wound. I'll send Balzac back to give you a hand."

"Thanks, skipper, but no thanks. No officer is layin' a hand on my privates. I'll bandage it myself."

"Then you're okay?"

"I'm okay. Just tell the guys to lay off the horny stories for a couple of days."

"Okay. No erotic stories. Since you got wounded on a combat mission, I'm going to put you in for the Purple Heart."

"No favors, skipper. What'll I tell my kids when they ask to see where I got wounded? Let's just forget the whole thing."

"Don't blame you, Nick," said O'Riley. "Anybody can get a Purple Heart. But just think—you'll be the first in your block to have a purple hard-on."

"That ain't funny, Lieutenant."

Lieutenant Balzac had made arrangements with the maintenance personnel to be notified whenever an airplane was placed in Class 26—damaged to the point where it could not be practicably repaired. Several times a week the bombardier was apprised of such an event, generally the result of a crash landing due to malfunctioning battle-damaged equipment. There is no more fertile field anywhere for a collector of gizmos, whatnots, geegaws, and framstrams than in the innards of a wrecked airplane. Like a coroner who loves his work, Balzac was never happier than when plundering aluminum carcasses in search of tubes, switches, valves, and all manner of assorted hardware to feed his ongoing efforts to modernize the tent. With his heater and shower operational—between explosions—he was now designing a swamp cooler that would air-condition the tent in the summertime.

He had just been alerted to the crash of a British Lancaster that had used the base as an emergency landing field. This had proved to be a problem when the brakeless bomber overshot the runway and ended up in a farmer's sheep-shearing pen. Armed with his hacksaw and wire cutters, Balzac was heading for the area when he heard his name being called. He stopped, looking around for the source of the hailing, and saw that he was abeam of the Officers' Club. He stepped over to the dark doorway and entered, blinking his eyes to accustom them to the gloomy interior.

The Officers' Club was not exactly plush. An amateurish artist's rendering of a naked maiden with wine spouting from both breasts into champagne glasses was the sole decor that covered the wall behind the rough-hewn bar and six tall barstools that comprised the 725th's Officers' Club. A whitewashed horse stall, the pungent odor of used hay still lingered to give an aromatic touch. On the bar were three large bottles, all containing grain alcohol. To one of the bottles a bit of iodine had been added to give the flavor of Scotch, to another a bit of vanilla had been added to give the color of Bourbon, and the third was untampered alcohol for those who preferred either gin or vodka. Beside the three bottles was a large can of grapefruit juice, the only mix available.

As his retinas grappled with the dim light, Balzac brought into focus the slender figure of Lieutenant Sam Eppstein, the squadron's lead bombardier. Eppstein was never seen without his hat, even in the mess hall, as he was sensitive about the creeping, premature bald spot that was rapidly taking over his skull. He had deep-set, sad eyes separated by a large aquiline nose that was reddened by a bad cold. He sniffed, wiped his nose, and motioned for Balzac to sit down. "Balzac, join me in a small beaker."

Balzac looked around in indecision. "Can't do it now, Sam. Have a mission of urgency."

Eppstein patted the barstool next to him. "It can wait. Must I remind you you're in the company of the squadron's lead bombardier? We bubble-chasers must stick together."

Balzac edged his buttocks onto the barstool. "Okay, Sam. For a minute." He looked closely at the weeping eyes of the bombardier. "You look like hell. What are we celebrating?"

"Coupla things. Foremost, the fact that I have walking pneumonia. The flight surgeon just grounded my ass."

Balzac got a glass, poured a couple of fingers of alcohol into it, then slopped in some grapefruit juice. He reached over and touched Eppstein's glass with his. "I'll drink to that."

Eppstein drained his glass and reached for the bottle. "But that's not all I'm drowning in this liver-bleaching concoction. Want to know what else?"

"By all means." Balzac recoiled as the depth charge exploded in his midriff.

"I have come to a very important conclusion. Wanna know what it is?"

"By all means."

"Then I'll tell you." He honked into his handkerchief, and turned rheumy eyes on Balzac. "I know goddamn well our outfit is being sabotaged." He put his fingers to his lips. "But don't tell a soul."

"Sabotaged?" Balzac blinked. "What the hell are you talking about?"

"I'm talking about our planes. That have been blowing up right after takeoff. Where there's not an enemy plane or an ack-ack gun for hundreds of miles."

"Go on! You been belting too many potato squeezings—"

"I may be potted, Balzac, but I'm deadly serious. I'm an old-timer in this squadron. I'm one of the lucky ones who has survived a helluva lot of missions. Thanks mainly to my pilot, the old bastard we all love to hate—Captain Sheridan. Best goddamn pilot that ever sunk his spurs into an airplane."

"What has that to do with sabotage?"

"I've seen at least three ships blow up after takeoff. *Three ships!* For no goddamn rhyme or reason. Just kablooie! That's all she wrote!" He ticked off his fingers. "Three ships! And you know what else?"

"What else?"

"I'm not the only one who suspects sabotage. There've been some funny-lookin' characters around the squadron lately. Guys in trench coats with turned-up collars."

"Now I know you've had one too many."

"I know what you're thinking. You just mark my word. And on your preflight before you take off, go over every inch of your airplane. Like your life depends on it." He stirred his fresh drink with his finger. "Because it does."

Balzac shook his head. "You been reading too many spy novels."

"Just take it from your old squadron lead bombardier. It's true."

"Okay, thanks for the warning. We'll be on the lookout. But I'm not sure what the hell we'll be looking for."

"Bombs. Small bombs. That can be smuggled aboard. Probably in the nose section."

"But who the hell would do a thing like that?"

Eppstein shrugged his thin shoulders. "Who knows? Could be anyone. Could even be one of our own guys."

"Oh, come on!"

"Okay, okay!" Eppstein wagged his palm at him. "Don't believe me. But you're gonna be damned sorry if you don't. All I ask is that you go over your aircraft with a fine-tooth comb. Will you grant me that much?"

"Yes."

"Good." Eppstein took a small envelope from his pocket, produced two white pills. He put them in his mouth, chased them with a large gulp from his glass.

"Sam, it's none of my business, but shouldn't you go easy on that stuff?"

"Just following the doc's orders. He said to take two APC's and hit the sack. I'm gonna do that shortly."

"Good idea." Balzac started to leave. "I'll look in on you later."

Eppstein reached over and grabbed his arm. "Don't go yet, Balzac. I haven't told you the other reason I'm having this bout with brother Bacchus."

"Okay." Balzac took another swig of his drink. "If you want to talk, I'll listen."

Eppstein thrust his face inches from Balzac's. "Have you observed, old man, how people hate my guts?"

"Oh, come on, Sam. That's not true."

"It is true. Haven't you noticed how no one will sit near me at the mess hall? I go into the latrine and it clears out in minutes. I'm about as popular as pinking shears at a circumcision."

"Hold it. It's just because you're paranoid, Sam. You just aren't happy unless you think you're being persecuted."

Eppstein shook his head, took another drink. "No. People hate my guts. And I don't blame them. Goes with the territory."

"What goes with the territory?"

"If you're a good bombardier, people will hate your guts. Mark my word."

"I fail to see how anyone is going to hate your guts just because you're a good bombardier."

Eppstein stared at his confidant. "Don't you see? A good bombardier is not going to drop his bombs until he's sure of clobbering his target. I mean, there's no sense in cranking up a lot of expensive airplanes loaded with expensive bombs, burning a lot of expensive gasoline, getting strafed by enemy fighters, and shot at with large-caliber guns—unless there's a damn good chance we're gonna do some damage to the enemy. Right?"

"Absolutely."

"So in order to do that damage, it's up to you and me, and the other bombardiers in this squadron, to nail our target right on the button every time. Agreed?"

"Agreed."

"Then to properly hit that target, we have to have a good bomb run. Sometimes the bomb run gets screwed up. We may have a bombsight problem. Or an intervalometer problem. Or airplane problems, or the jet stream hits you and blows you off course. Or clouds can black you out on a visual run. Or bombing by radar we—"

"I get the picture, Sam. A lot of things can go wrong on the bomb run."

"So what do we do? We abort the run, and turn the whole formation around to come in for another try. Sometimes two or three times, until we get the bomb run down cold and have the maximum chance of clobbering the target."

"Of course that's what we do. I fail to see—"

"If I wasn't a damn good bombardier, I wouldn't be so crotchety about hitting the target. I'd just drop the bombs on the first run, not worry about where they landed, and get the hell out of the target area. But since I am a good bombardier, take pride in my job, and insist on doing it right, people hate me."

"Sam, you ain't making a hell of a lot of sense."

Eppstein took another long pull, draining his glass. He honked into his handkerchief, and turned to Balzac as he wiped his nose. "Don't you see? In order to do the job right, I may have to make several runs over the target area, which is full of flak bursts. By milling around up there, positioning for another run, they have plenty of time to nail our exact position and altitude. We're sitting ducks. Our squadron alone had lost dozens of planes on the second and third bomb runs. Is it any wonder people hate my guts?"

"Look." Balzac put his hand on Eppstein's shoulder. "You are off your rocker, buddy. Nobody hates a guy who's doing a damned good job."

"Oh, yeah?" Eppstein stared into his drink. "Tell that to the buddies of the guys who don't come home. Tell that to the next of kin. Tell them how great it is to have some eager beaver lead them through hell two or three times more than they're supposed to go."

"But it doesn't happen every time. The other day you creamed our target on the first run. And I mean— creamed!"

"That was a good run. Let's talk about Vienna last month. Had to go over the target twice. Lost four ships on the second run. Is it any wonder people despise me? I'm worse than the village hangman! I don't know how much longer I can carry all this guilt."

"Oh, come on, Sam. You're imagining things—"

"Oh, am I? Am I imagining the snake I found in my flying boot? Am I imagining the unsigned hate mail? Come on, Balzac. I'm about as popular around here as a whore at a church social."

Balzac shook his head. "It just doesn't make sense, Sam. No sense at all."

"I'm telling you this because you may someday be the squadron's lead bombardier. I want you to be prepared. Start growing a real thick, armadillo hide. You'll need it. There. I got that off my chest. Thanks for listening."

"Anytime." Balzac slapped the forlorn bombardier on the back as he slid off the barstool. "Cheer up, Eppstein. You do have people who appreciate what you're doing. Now, come on. I'll walk to your tent with you."

"No. You go on ahead, I'll stay here a spell." He reached for the bottle of alcohol and half filled his glass. He poured in a dollop of juice and gave Balzac a wan smile. "Gotta follow the doc's orders. He said to drink lots of liquids."

Chapter Six

26 December 1944
Sunny Italy

Dear Bob:

Well, brother, how goes it? Here it is the day after Christmas. I hope the Yuletide was a great one for you and the family.

Our mission Christmas Day turned out to be a real milk run. Our primary target was socked in, so we ended up hitting marshaling yards in a sleepy little Austrian town. All the ack-ack gunners must have been belting their eggnog, because the flak was so sparse we didn't lose a single ship. We didn't know it at the time, but the mission turned out to be the high point of the day.

When we landed, we found out the post-mission whiskey had been consumed by the medics in an orgiastic free-for-all, and there was none for the flight crews. This did not augur well with the crews, as attested to by several corpsmen who were last seen hanging from the squadron flagpole in their own straitjackets.

Then we were greeted at the mess hall with the saddening revelation that the Christmas turkeys had all been eaten by the ground crews. This came to light when we tried to carve a leg off the turkey-shaped hunk of Spam the cook had tried to disguise with giblet gravy.

Needless to say, from this point the holiday

appeared to be going downhill fast. Noting our
crew members emerging from the mess hall with
their morale down around their arch supporters,
O'Riley and I decided to do something about it.

So we invited the whole crew to our officers'
tent for a Christmas party. Naturally, they all
accepted. All we needed now was some grog,
food, decorations, and presents.

O'Riley swiped the Intelligence officer's jeep,
and he and little Luigi, our houseboy, made a
foraging expedition to an Italian village atop a
nearby hill. What Luigi couldn't steal O'Riley
paid for, and they came back with a case of good
vino, two dozen fresh eggs, and a ham Luigi
liberated from a smokehouse a split second before
an encounter with an Italian pitchfork.

Balzac made a raid on our so-called Officers'
Club and showed up with a gallon of grain alcohol
to which he eye-droppered enough iodine to
make a gaggable ersatz Scotch.

The enlisted men came lugging in a Christmas tree made from olive branches, gaily festooned with jeep reflectors, dog tags, and strips of
radar chaff. Toilet paper served yeoman's duty as
gift wrapping for the cigarette packs, beer bottles,
and candy bars I had left over from my rations,
and when spread under the tree they made the
whole scene quite festive.

Balzac has made friends with Sam Eppstein,
the squadron's lead bombardier, and Eppstein
joined us, contributing a large jar of gefilte fish for
the occasion, even though he was not real sure his
rabbi would endorse his celebration of Christ's
birthday with such a bunch of heathens.

Such reservations were soon dissolved in the
punch the enlisted men made out of the grain
alcohol, the one lemon they added doing little to
disguise the taste of residual fluid that came from
mixing the concoction in a hydraulic tank
scrounged from a bulldozed English Lancaster.

Mellowing into the Christmas spirit, Balzac decided we should sing Christmas carols and proceeded to conduct our choral group with his swagger stick. No one could remember the words to the carols, but we did remember the melodies, and I'm sure the Man Upstairs didn't object too much at hearing "Little Star of Bethlehem" lyricized by the words of "Roll Me Over in the Clover and Do It Again."

Or maybe he did. Which might rationalize why the Christmas tree caught fire in the middle of the festivities. More likely it was one of the Zippo lighters serving as Christmas tree lights that fell over on the olive branches and started the conflagration. At any rate, Daringer should not have tried to quell the flames by throwing his drink at it, for this had the proverbial effect of trying to put out a fire with gasoline. All of which explains why the tent caught on fire.

To make a long story short, roofless but undaunted, the enlisted crew members were not about to have the momentum of the party spent by such a minor item as a tent burning—especially since it was the officers' tent—and at their behest the festivities were adjourned to the officers' latrine. Once again protected from the elements, here the party was to flourish and flower into full bloom in the congenial if somewhat scatological surroundings.

The party might still be going full blast were it not for a couple of minor contretemps that finally summoned the constabulary. First, Balzac somehow managed to fall through one of the holes in the six-holer, which led to a heated debate as to whether it wouldn't be easier to train a new bombardier than to try to get this one cleaned up. After much discussion, however, he was finally—and regrettably—extricated.

The other misfortune occurred when the

executive officer, making a nocturnal visit in deference to nagging kidneys, arrived just in time to get his little toe blown off by an errant slug from a .45. Things are still hazy as to how this happened, but it has resulted in a speedy new squadron policy prohibiting the carrying of side-arms to the latrine. Truly a blow to our marksmen who like to sharpen their eye by taking potshots at passing jackrabbits while heeding Nature's nudge.

All told, you might say it was an interesting if somewhat unorthodox Christmas. I'll be able to tell you more about it after my upcoming command performance with the squadron commander, who I'm not sure has been properly imbued with the Christmas spirit.

So drop me a line and tell me how your Christmas spirit was. Give my love to everyone, Bob, and have a fantastic New Year.

> Your brother,
> Swede

P.S.: Best you not show this letter to Mom, knowing what a worrywart she is. I've enclosed a note you can give to her.

Dearest Mom:
Just a short note to tell you what a serene and peaceful Christmas we enjoyed rocking here in the cradle of Christianity. I know you are worried about my being homesick, being so far away from home on this most joyous of holidays. But the Army really takes care of its soldiers. The pictures you saw in the *Seattle Times* of the turkeys that were being sent to the troops overseas did, indeed, arrive. So everyone had a nice, old-fashioned Christmas dinner. These Army mess sergeants really know how to cook.

And thanks to the USO troupe that arrived, we didn't have a chance to get homesick, what with singing Christmas carols and all. So don't

worry your pretty head about me. Next Christmas
we'll all be together.
Hope your Christmas was a very merry one.
All my love,
Swede

The squadron's Italian barber looked as if he would be
more at home threading gondolas through the Venice canals
than guiding clippers through the hirsute mops of American airmen. Laughing brown Latin eyes surveyed the
world from under a hedgerow of black brows, and an
expansive handlebar moustache swooped over an ever-
grinning mouth that displayed a row of white, even
porcelain. From this cavity issued a booming, stentorian
basso profundo that would have sent the scenery to flapping
in Milan's La Scala. For this reason, Lancaster had prompt-
ly dubbed him Figaro, the barber of Seville, and the name
had stuck. Although Figaro could not converse in English,
he had no trouble communicating with his customers
through the magnificent sweepings and gesticulations of the
Italian to the opera born.

Stromburg and Lancaster now entered Figaro's domain, a whitewashed horse stall containing the single
antique barber chair, and tossed their caps at the sad-
dlepegs that adorned the wall. Recognizing Lancaster,
Figaro immediately leaped from the barber chair in which
he had been dozing, launched into an aria from *Aïda*, and
with a grand gesture ushered Lancaster to the chair.

Stromburg settled his flanks on one of the milking
stools that lined the walls and watched as Lancaster put his
arm around the barber and joined him in the finale of the
aria, the two voices making terrible harmony. Then the
men bowed to each other, Lancaster sat down in the chair,
and the barber whisked the cloth over him.

Stromburg applauded. "You two would make a great
down payment on a barber-shop quartet."

"Ain't it the truth," agreed Lancaster. "Figaro has one
hell of a voice. I think he could make it in opera."

"How goes it, Figaro?" Stromburg asked, picking up a
dog-eared copy of *Stars and Stripes*.

"Come?" asked the barber, cupping his ear in the direction of Stromburg.

"He wanted to know"—Lancaster switched to Italian—*"Come sta?"*

Grinning and nodding his head in understanding, Figaro clustered his fingertips, kissed them, and threw the kisses at the ceiling. *"Bello, bello!"*

"He said," translated Lancaster, "things are going beautifully."

"Glad to hear it," said Stromburg, smiling at the Italian. He addressed Lancaster. "Great to have a linguist in the crew."

"Just one of the many services rendered by your friendly navigator." Lancaster fixed his pilot with a questioning look. "Incidentally, how are things going with you? How was your session with the squadron CO? You need a blood transfusion?"

"Wasn't all that bad," said Stromburg, spreading out the paper. "Major Diddle lunched on my butt for a spell, but his heart wasn't in it. He said he's considering our crew for flight lead when we get more missions under our belt. Hard to lead an element of six ships into mortal combat when our crew's all confined to quarters."

"No kidding! Flight lead?"

Stromburg nodded. "If we stay out of trouble. Major Diddle said if our crew could raise as much hell with the Krauts as we have with the rest of the squadron, we'd all be going home by New Year's Eve."

"I think the good major is prone to exaggeration. Just because the exec officer lost a toe at our last party—"

"It's Balzac who seems to rub him the wrong way. Yesterday Diddle discovered he didn't have any electricity in his tent. He traced the wire leading from his tent to the squadron generator, found it had been tapped by a wire leading to our tent. He was less than euphoric to find the tapped wire terminated inside Balzac's radio."

Lancaster chuckled. "You mean our boy actually tapped the squadron CO's electricity to run his radio?"

"That's our boy."

"You have to hand it to him. The kid's fearless."

"That's one word for him. I can think of several more. The guy's going to be the death of me."

"He's good for you. Keeps you on your toes. You know you can't help but like him."

"Beside the point. I tried to get rid of him for a couple of weeks. Submitted his name as a candidate for the Army Exchange Program. I could use two weeks of peace and quiet."

"What's the Army Exchange Program?"

"It's some kind of deal laid on by the brass to indoctrinate officers in other branches of the service. For example, we send an officer to the front lines to see at first hand how the infantry operates. They send one of their officers to fly a couple of missions with us to see how the Air Corps functions. Supposed to make for better efficiency and teamwork between branches."

Lancaster peered up from his bent-over position while his neck was being trimmed. "Sounds like a good idea. Wonder how the brass happened to think of it?"

"Probably dreamed up by some sergeant. Anyway, we have an Army ground-pounder joining our crew next week. Our crew's supposed to furnish an officer to go to the Fifth Army. I submitted Balzac's name, but it bounced."

"Who bounced it?"

"Major Diddle. He said the Krauts were demoralizing the grunts enough on the front lines without sending them Balzac. So I submitted O'Riley's name. Diddle agreed with that."

"Why O'Riley? I'd have volunteered. Wouldn't mind at all seeing how the other half lives."

"Pat's got a dad floating around somewhere as a sergeant in the British Army, remember? He volunteered to go just on the off-chance he might run into him somewhere. There's a British contingent not far from the Army corps where Pat will be going."

"That's right. O'Riley should go. Be great if he could meet up with his old man."

"Chances are slim. Anyway, he'll be shipping off tomorrow. We'll have a substitute copilot for a couple of weeks. And an additional passenger to powder and diaper."

"Well, it might be interesting." Lancaster closed his eyes in ecstasy as the barber vigorously massaged his neck. "Bring on your gravel-scratcher."

"You Stromburg?"

Stromburg turned from his shaving mirror to look up curiously at the huge cloud that had drifted into his tent. The cloud was wearing Army fatigues and the insignia of a second lieutenant. "I'm Stromburg."

"Kebrowski." Stromburg found his right hand suddenly swallowed by a huge vise with fingers. Wincing, his eyes scaled the granite jaw thrust out at eye level, and climbed up the dour face that was appraising him sullenly. "Fifth Army."

"Ah," said Stromburg, retrieving his hand and trying to flex back the circulation, "our exchange officer. Welcome aboard, Lieutenant." He instantly recognized the famous West Point fullback from the spread in *Life* magazine. No wonder Alex Kebrowski had struck terror into the hearts of the nation's top college teams. His huge head was mounted without benefit of neck on shoulders borrowed from a Clydesdale brewery horse. A face that Nature had not been overly kind to to start with had not been enhanced by a permanent scowl etched by a succession of football coaches.

"So you're a flyboy."

Stromburg found himself impaled on a steely look that indicated Kebrowski was either naturally taciturn or had received one too many cleats in the crotch. He tried a smile. "That's right. I'm a small cog in the machinery of a bomber crew."

"Seen you flying overhead. Way up there above the mud and crap of the front lines. That's why I volunteered for this mission. I want to see what you airydales do to earn more dough than us infantry troops."

Stromburg cleared his throat. "I suppose you're referring to our flight pay."

"It's a crock of mule dung. And the way you zoomies get promoted! Sheeeit! You got full colonels in your Air Corps who are still playin' with their peter." He spread his huge hands. "Look at this. You guys livin' in tents! The life of Riley!"

"Not exactly the Waldorf-Astoria." Stromburg felt his gorge rising at this unwarranted attack from a stranger—famous fullback or no. "As to the claims of you gravel-agitators that aircrews are overpaid and oversexed, let me lay a couple of facts on you. During combat training, five aircrew members are lost for every ground-gripper. In combat so far, three aircrew members are lost for every infantryman on a per-capita basis. So, my friend, we may enjoy the life of Riley, as you so poetically put it, but statistically we don't enjoy it very damn long. If you think this flyboy is backing up to the pay table, you're out of your skull."

The huge man blinked down at Stromburg, then grunted. "We'll see about that."

"Right. I guess that's the purpose of this exchange program. To get a better understanding of each other's mission."

"In the meantime, where's the chow line?"

Stromburg pointed out the tent door. "The mess hall's over there. Across the runway."

"*Mess hall!* You guys got a *mess hall?*"

"That's right. Such as it is."

"A *mess hall!* Sufferin' sheep shit!" The big hulk stooped over to get through the tent door. "Next time I'm joinin' the friggin' Air Corps. You throttle-jazzers really know how to live! You got it made in the shade."

Stromburg idly wiped the soap off his face with his towel as he watched the big man stride out across the field. "So that's our exchange officer," he said to the image in his mirror. "Second Lieutenant Alex Kebrowski, All-American. This is going to be a lot of yuks."

The target: Trento Marshaling Yards in northern Italy. Angle of attack: 235 degrees. Bombing altitude: 22,000 feet. Target elevation: 642 feet. Ordnance: six 500-pound GP bombs.

Trento, Italy, was a bit north of Verona, and since much of the mission was to be flown over the Adriatic Sea, it was regarded as something of a milk run.

Stromburg climbed into the cockpit. As he buckled

himself in, he inhaled the smells of the big bomber. It was an indefinable odor—an amalgam of hot aluminum, perspiration, and the acrid tinge of cordite from the .50-caliber guns. He looked across at his copilot. "Something about the smell of a bombing machine. A smell you can taste."

Lieutenant Ewing, his original combat check-out pilot, had been assigned temporarily to replace O'Riley, who was somewhere on the front lines with the Fifth Army. "It's a smell that will haunt me forever," said Ewing, buckling himself in.

"And taste." He looked over at the copilot. "So, Ewing, you're counting down to number thirty-five. Then back to the land of the big PX."

Ewing nodded. "Four to go. And I'd appreciate it if you bring this tub back in one piece."

"Believe me, I'll do my best."

Balzac, followed by Lieutenant Kebrowski, made his appearance on the flight deck. Balzac was giving a running commentary on the functions of the ship and explaining the emergency procedures to the football player. It had taken a special requisition to gather up flying gear large enough to cover the athlete's huge frame, and at best it was still two sizes too small, making him resemble a huge outer-space monster that had been cursed with a very poor tailor.

Because of their common Polish heritage, Stromburg had asked Balzac to take the All-American under his wing and outfit and brief him on the survival gear and the emergency procedures. The two Poles had hit it off immediately, presenting an incongruous and somewhat ludicrous David and Goliath.

"You know our illustrious aircraft commander, of course," said Balzac, poking his head into the cockpit. "Our very own Captain Nemo. Like his prototype, he's completely mad and eccentric, but we've learned to love him. Especially since he makes out our officers' effectiveness reports."

"Sorry you missed the briefing, Kebrowski," said Stromburg, ignoring his bombardier. "It sort of gave a clue as to where we're going, and what we're going to do when we get there."

"Interfered with breakfast," said Kebrowski. "Know how long it's been since I had pancakes? *Pancakes!* With maple syrup! You hotshots sure got it rough!"

"And this is our venerable copilot," continued Balzac. "I'd introduce you, but he doesn't like to know people's names."

Kebrowski squeezed his eyes at the copilot, "You got something against names?"

"Nope," said Ewing, looking up from the checklist. "Only when they're associated with people." He looked at the big Pole curiously. "Your face looks familiar. Have we met before?"

"Not likely."

"Odd. Your face looks very familiar."

"It might connect if you knew his name," said Stromburg. "Our illustrious passenger here is not your run-of-the-mill ground-pounder. He's—"

Ewing stopped him with a raised hand. "I don't want to know. No names. No names."

Kebrowski stared at the little copilot, examining him as if he might have been impaled on a pin. "Do you guys have to have a loose trolley wheel to get into the Air Corps, or do you just get this way from flying without oxygen?"

Ewing returned to his checklist. "Don't fly any more missions than you have to, Lieutenant. I've seen a couple of exchange officers shipped home in wooden kimonos. Ain't no way to travel."

Kebrowski grunted. "Don't worry about me. I can take anything you flyboys can hand out." His eyes fell on an object swinging from the roof of the cockpit. It was a blue hand-knitted affair, resembling a one-fingered glove. It was closed at one end, open on the other, with two small cups laced on with white ribbon. "What the hell's that?" he asked.

Stromburg checked the object of Kebrowski's attention. "That's a peter heater."

Kebrowski stared blankly. "How's that?"

"It's a peter heater."

"You mean . . . you put that thing on your peter?"

"If you want to keep it warm, yes."

"Hell, that thing wouldn't even fit a flyboy."

"You're right. It's too small. That's why it's hanging there. It's become sort of a talisman. A good-luck charm."

Kebrowski fingered it curiously. "Who the hell needs a peter heater?"

"Our tail gunner had a little problem. The crew chipped in and had this knitted by one of the Red Cross gals, who made it from a design we drew. Big mistake. She made it way too small. Especially for an Italian."

Kebrowski's brows puckered. "What the hell you talking about?"

Two green balls of fire arced high over the control tower. "It's a go," said Stromburg, thrusting out three fingers to the ground crew. "I'll explain later, Kebrowski. Right now we got a war to fight. Ewing, let's crank up number three." The copilot toggled the number three engine into life.

As the lead ship taxied by his revetment, Stromburg gave his old mentor a thumbs-up salute. Captain Sheridan, the lanky Texan who had checked him out on his first orientation ride, was leading the squadron. As Sheridan trundled by, Balzac held up a porcelain object for the formation leader to see. Sheridan did a double take, then laughed as he taxied by.

"What the hell's that you're holdin' up?" queried Kebrowski, staring at the object in Balzac's arms.

"What the hell's it look like?" said Balzac. "It's a kitchen sink."

"Chalk this up as a stupid question, but do you guys always carry a kitchen sink?"

Balzac grunted with his load as he carried it back to the bomb bay. "Nope. This is a one-time deal. I liberated it from an old farmhouse up in the village." Balzac set the sink down and returned to address his aircraft commander. "Incidentally, Swede, you owe farmer Lugano two packs of cigarettes."

"Oh, do I?"

"Yep. For the sink. Took some doin', but I got him down to two packs."

"I'm glad to hear that. Warms my heart to know you're so frugal with my cigarette ration."

Kebrowski batted his eyes for a moment as he watched the little bombardier scurry around; then he said, "I was told that airydales are a little light in the loafers. But you clowns been munchin' loco weed."

"That because you don't understand about the kitchen sink?" asked Balzac.

"That's only part of it."

"Look," said Balzac, pausing in his duties long enough to stare up into the big man's face, "after this shootin' match is over, my kids are going to ask me what I did in the war. And I'm going to tell them that I was a bombardier on a big bomber, and we not only dropped everything but the kitchen sink on the lousy Nazis, but we also dropped the kitchen sink! Now, you stupid Polack, what could be simpler than that?"

Kebrowski wagged his head for a beat, then rehinged his lower jaw. "So when you drop the bombs, you're gonna throw out the kitchen sink."

"Small correction. While I drop the bombs, *you're* gonna throw out the kitchen sink. What the hell you think we brought you along for?"

As Ewing took in this exchange, he looked across the cockpit at Stromburg. "Your exchange officer ain't too bright. Your bombardier makes perfect sense to me."

"Yeah," said Stromburg, nudging the throttles forward and taxiing into number four position for takeoff. "He's a football player. Fullbacks get kicked in the head a lot."

Lined up in position as they waited to take the runway, Stromburg monitored the engine temperatures as his hack watch ticked down to takeoff time. Then Captain Sheridan taxied the lead ship onto the runway, lined up, brought his engines up to full power, and at precisely 0745 released his brakes, and the heavy bomber started bobbing down the runway. At thirty-second intervals the numbers two and three planes taxied onto the pierced steel planking and took off; then it was Stromburg's turn to follow suit.

Stromburg was becoming more proficient with experience, and this time he brought his engines up to full emergency power and trailed the cowl flaps before releasing the brakes. Fighting the turbulence from the preceding ships that churned over the runway in the still morning air, Stromburg lifted the bomber's nose, and the awkward machine lifted off well short of the runway's end. He banked over to join up with the other planes that were beginning to form into formation as they orbited overhead.

The needle of the altimeter was just approaching five thousand feet when he started to slip his plane into the number four slot, directly behind and slightly under the formation leader. And then suddenly the lead ship turned into a giant fireball. As Stromburg watched in horror, an explosion ripped through Captain Sheridan's cockpit. For a split second Stromburg's faculties were frozen in mute disbelief, and only a knee-jerk reaction caused him to horse back on the controls in time to keep the flying debris from striking his own plane. For a brief instant frozen in time, Stromburg could see into the topless cockpit as it slid underneath him. Captain Sheridan and his copilot were slumped over the controls like rag dolls; a large, red, brain-flecked hole gaped through the back of the leather helmet that housed what used to be the Texan's head. Stromburg gasped for breath as a fist of nausea slammed him in the pit of the stomach.

"What the goddamn hell!" roared Ewing. "Gunners, search for ack-ack guns. We're over *friendly territory*, for Christ's sake! See if you can spot any guns down there in the hills." Ewing looked over at Stromburg. "You all right?"

Stromburg nodded, swallowing hard to discourage the breakfast that threatened to surface. He dropped back to avoid the confusion in the formation that was reforming. The number two ship took over the lead, the number three ship slipped into the number two slot, and Stromburg closed in to the left of the lead ship in the number three position. As if nothing had happened, the new formation continued its orbiting as Sheridan's plane erupted into a billowing sheet of flame to mark its funeral pyre in the green, alluvial hills.

The gunners reported no chutes.

"That crazy sonuvabitchin' Texan!" said Stromburg

with a moan. "He gave me my orientation ride. Hottest damn pilot that ever strapped an airplane to his butt. Did you know he completed all his missions and volunteered for another tour—"

"I don't want to hear about it!" snapped Ewing. "The bastard bought the farm. He and his crew. They're gone. Now fly your fucking airplane!"

Stromburg blinked his eyes, trying to bring into focus the lead ship, which was a blurry outline. He wiped his nose with the back of his glove. "Pilot to crew. Anyone spot any guns down there?"

There was a negative response from the waist gunners.

"Damned if I understand it," said Stromburg, shaking his head. "No one sees any enemy guns. Yet the lead ship just up and explodes. The explosion must have happened inside the airplane. But how?"

"Maybe a fuel leak. Maybe a defective bomb. As you damn well know, anything can happen in this plumber's nightmare." Ewing's eyes narrowed. "And maybe that crazy damn bombardier's right. Maybe we really do have sabotage in the outfit."

"Sabotage? Balzac mentioned something about it. I thought it was just his paranoia. You don't think—"

"Hell, in this theater of operations—in this screwed-up war—I wouldn't be surprised at anything. Least of all sabotage."

"You're not serious, Ewing! How the hell could anyone—"

"Don't ever sell the Krauts short. We just saw an airplane blow up. Without an enemy gun anywhere. The Germans have always been good at sabotage. Hell, we could have a saboteur in the next tent."

"Sufferin' sheep shit!" Stromburg's view of the lead ship was suddenly blocked by the huge head of the football player. "What the hell's goin' on up here?"

Stromburg threw a backhand at the chest of Kebrowski. "What's going on," said Stromburg, "is that we're going to mount that lead ship if you don't get your big head out of my line of vision."

Balzac grabbed the arm of the big Pole and pulled him

out of Stromburg's line of sight. "Our venerable pilot would appreciate an unblocked view of the lead ship when he's trying to fly formation on it."

Kebrowski turned scowling eyes on the bombardier. "Tell me what went on back there."

"You're getting a taste of war in the sky, my friend," said Balzac. "We're just boring holes in the blue over friendly territory, minding our own business, and trying to get in formation. So far we've lost only one airplane. Wait'll you see what it's like over *enemy* territory."

Kebrowski was about to answer when his attention was commanded by activity at the navigator's station. He gazed in slack-jawed amazement as the slightly green Lancaster vomited into the kitchen sink that nestled in his lap. "Balzac!" yelled Kebrowski, unable to take his eyes from Lancaster. "Your navigator's sick. He's tossing his cookies."

"That's right," said Balzac.

"What are you going to do about it?"

"Not a helluva lot. He throws up pretty well all by himself."

"The poor bastard—"

"Lancaster's had a lot of practice. Does it on every mission."

"You mean—"

"Great idea bringing that kitchen sink. He usually throws up in my flak helmet."

Lancaster wiped a blue mouth with his handkerchief, and turned watery eyes on Kebrowski. "'The dog is turned to his own vomit again.' That's a quote from the New Testament. Peter's version, I believe." He turned back to his charts.

Kebrowski blinked, then slowly sagged his large carcass down in the far corner of the flight deck, where he just sat and stared, muttering to himself. "I left a nice, muddy, rat-infested foxhole for this. These weenies have all escaped from a rubber room. They've broken the string on their yo-yo. . . ."

"You can't do that, sir," said the white-frocked medic in the dispensary as Stromburg picked up two full bottles of

Seagram's Seven Crown and tucked them under his arm. "Regulations state—"

"Screw the regulations," said Stromburg. "This is to make up for Christmas Day, when you blood-suckers drank up all the mission whiskey. One bottle for the officers, one for the enlisted men."

"But sir—"

"Any problems," said Stromburg, nodding at Kebrowski standing at his side, "take them up with my secretary here."

The medic looked up at the mountain hovering above him and gulped. "I think we can work something out, sir."

"I thought we could." Stromburg scooped up a nest of paper cups, and the two men went out the door.

Outside the dispensary, Galvani was waiting. Stromburg handed one of the bottles to the tail gunner. "For you and the boys."

"Skipper, you did it! A whole jug for the enlisted troops?"

"A small emolument for services rendered to your country."

"Thanks, Lieutenant." The tail gunner clamped Stromburg on the shoulder and took off on a beeline for the enlisted men's area.

Kebrowski's eyes followed the retreating figure until it disappeared into the cluster of tents. "That tail gunner of yours sure walks funny. Like he's got saddle sores."

"He's got a sore joystick," said Stromburg, turning toward the officers' tents.

"He's got a what?"

"A sore pecker. Got a big bandage on it. Why he walks funny."

Kebrowski fell in step with Stromburg. "A bandage on his tool? What the hell for?"

"Got tangled up in his tail guns. Stripped the skin off it."

"Sufferin' sheep shit! How the bloody hell could a guy strip the skin off his pecker?" Kebrowski looked over at Stromburg, then raised his hand. "Forget it. I don't want to know."

Stromburg shrugged. "Suit yourself."

"Wait a minute. That thing hanging in your cockpit. That jock sock—"

"Peter heater."

"Whatever. He the guy you had it made for?"

"Affirmative."

"And it didn't fit."

"That's right. We had another made by Madam Grab-balli. Unlike the Red Cross gal, she didn't need a sketch. She made it from memory. It's so big it looks like a wind sock. Even you could get into it."

"I doubt it. So you hung the little jock sock in your cockpit."

"Peter heater. That's right. Every time we start the takeoff roll, we give it a little tug for good luck."

"Weird." Kebrowski wagged his big head. "You guys are weird."

"No argument. But don't forget one thing."

"What's that?"

"Our peter heater brought you home safe and sound."

Stromburg poured the whiskey into the paper cups and handed them out to the officers gathered in his tent. "Let's drink to our passenger here, gentlemen," he said, raising his cup. "To Kebrowski's first mission."

There was a round of hear, hears, to which Kebrowski emptied his cup and wiped his mouth with the back of his hand. "And to his last."

Balzac looked in surprise at the fullback. "What do you mean? One mission isn't enough to learn the ropes of flying combat in heavier-than-air machines—"

"One mission with you chowderheads is more than enough. Flyin' with eight-balls who carry their sandwiches around in their armpits. Sufferin' sheep shit!"

"So that's it," said Balzac. "My good man, have you ever eaten a frozen cheese sandwich? At twenty-six thousand feet it gets forty below zero. *Everything* freezes. so we stick our sandwiches inside our heated suits in our armpit for an hour or so before eating. Thaws 'em out. In fact, considerin' that Italian cheese, it enhances the flavor a bit."

Kebrowski shook his head. "If you space cadets are typical of the whole frappin' Air Corps, I'm damn glad to be in the infantry. Jesus, are those slit trenches going to look good!"

"But Kebrowski," said Lancaster, "this mission was a milk run. We didn't lose over ten planes in the whole group. Just because we had a small problem with number two engine—it's very seldom that an engine actually falls off the airplane like that—and the little incident with the honey bucket. Fortunately, we keep the john in the rear of the airplane, so when it got that direct hit and exploded, it covered only the enlisted men—"

"And, my good man," broke in Balzac, "you are not forgetting the pancakes with maple syrup? The hot showers? The houseboy who keeps your shoes shined? We got it made in the shade, I believe was your quote."

"Screw it," said Kebrowski. "I'm heading back to my outfit in the morning. No way are you weenies going to get me up in that airborne outhouse again. No way."

"That's the way I feel about it," said a slender figure who suddenly materialized in the doorway. "If man were meant to fly, he'd have been born with barf bags."

All eyes turned to the newcomer as Balzac greeted the squadron's lead bombardier. "If it isn't First Lieutenant Samuel Eppstein in the flesh. Sit down and have a wee beaker." Balzac looked closer at the figure weaving in the doorway. "On second thought, you look as though you might already have had a beaker or two."

Eppstein staggered over to the table, waving a near-empty bottle of wine. "I come bearing gifts." He produced a jar from his pocket and plunked it on the table. "I brought you some more gefilte fish." He looked dourly at the jar. "Christ, I hate gefilte fish. Why in hell were Jews burdened with this god-awful insult to the taste buds? Haven't Jews suffered enough? We're a tribe of masochists. Why in hell can't my folks send me smoked oysters? Or peanut brittle? I got a goddamn footlocker full of gefilte fish!" He crashed onto Balzac's cot, and except for Balzac's timely intervention would have done a somersault backward.

"Don't spill your wine," said Balzac, helping the bombardier to a sitting position. "Especially on my bed."

Eppstein took a deep draught from the wine bottle, wiped his lips with his sleeve, and looked vacuously at Balzac. "I should be dead. Right now I should be burning out there in that funeral pyre with the rest of my crew."

"Sorry, Sam." Stromburg reached over and gripped Eppstein's shoulder. "Sorry as hell about your crew."

"That skinny dumb Texan," said Eppstein with a moan, turning rheumy eyes on Stromburg. "That goddamn Sheridan was the best frigging pilot in the whole goddamn world. That sonuvabitch could land that airplane on a nest of robin's eggs and never crack a shell." He clutched Stromburg's arm. "What the hell *happened*, Swede?"

"Damned if I know, Sam. We may never know. All we saw was an explosion, looked like in the nose of the plane. We were just forming up our formation when Sheridan's ship blew. There was no collision, no sign of enemy guns. The damn thing just exploded."

Eppstein shook his head. "The same thing happened just before you guys arrived. We were just getting into formation over the field here when Heller's ship blew. Wiped out the whole crew on their next-to-last mission. Their plane almost crashed in the motor pool." He took another swig. "Something weird's going on. Planes just don't up and explode for no reason. Not even B-Twenty-fours."

"Certainly not when piloted by guys like Sheridan. He was a born pilot. Checked me out in tactical flying."

"Tex Sheridan. That goddamn Texan. Ran around in those cowboy boots acting so goddamn *macho*. Inside he was a cream puff. Know what his first name is . . . was?"

"No."

"Clarence. Ain't that a yahoo? A Texan named Clarence." Eppstein wiped his eyes and stared at Stromburg. "Do you know what it's like to have your whole goddamn crew wiped out? Three missions from going home?"

"I know," said Stromburg, trying to soothe.

Eppstein pulled away from him. "Like hell you know. Nobody knows. Not until you've gone through it. Leibowitz, O'Toole, Faraday . . . I should have been with those guys. *I should have gone down with my crew!*"

"That's insanity," said Balzac. "You have a bad cold. The doc put you on DNIF. You know you can't fly when you got a headful of snot. It all ends up in your ears. Now count your blessings."

Eppstein turned his head back and forth. "No, no, no. I'm the squadron lead bombardier. I'm supposed to help lead the goddamn squadron into the valley of death. I'm supposed to fly with my crew. Not sit around nursing a frigging head cold." He pulled out a handkerchief and blew his nose. Then he took another swig from the bottle and looked over at Balzac. "Did you know, fellow bombardier, that when we bombed the marshaling yards in Rome, we had all Catholic bombardiers in the lead ships?"

"I didn't know that, Sam," said Balzac. "I suppose that was a special precaution to assure the Vatican didn't get hit."

"Absolutely right. And you know what?" He fought eyelids that were beginning to curtain. "When we bomb Jerusalem, I'm gonna be in the lead ship."

"Good for you."

"Wouldn't do for anybody to blow up the Wailing Wall."

"Nobody's going to bomb Jerusalem, let alone the Wailing Wall. But I know one bombardier who's more than a little bombed. Let's get you into your sack."

"And miss the party?"

"It's not a very good party."

"Okay." Eppstein tilted up the bottle, finishing it. He smacked his lips and turned to Balzac. "I may need a little help, old buddy. Things are gettin' fuzzy."

"I'll take you home." Balzac put Eppstein's arm around his shoulder, then helped him up. As he did so, the dam broke. Large tears started coursing down the lined face of the bombardier.

"Oh, shit! I'm gonna miss that friggin' crew of mine."

"We're all going to miss them."

"It's sabotage, I tell you. We gotta find the bastards who are doing this!"

Balzac steadied the bombardier on his feet. "If it's sabotage, we'll unmask the culprits." The two shuffled through the door, Eppstein wiping his eyes.

"A Texan named Clarence," muttered Eppstein as they faded from earshot. "Ain't that a yahoo?"

"That's a yahoo."

A heavy silence settled over the tent following the departure of the bombardiers. It was finally broken by Kebrowski, who poured himself another shot of whiskey, downed it, then muttered to no one in particular, "You guys fight one shitty war."

Chapter Seven

10 January 1945
Southern Italy

Mr. Elwood Snodgrass
Internal Revenue Service
Boise, Idaho

Dear Mr. Snodgrass:

Just received your reply. This V-Mail really zips along.

I am truly sorry, Mr. Snodgrass, if you felt my letter facetious. But it definitely was not "snotty," as you put it. I know you're doing a very important job. But let me explain something. This morning a bomber on a strike mission blew up on takeoff. The third one this month. It rained aluminum around here for thirty minutes. I won't tell you what a body looks like that has bounced for a mile. Suffice it to say, it can ruin your lunch.

This might help explain why, on my current list of priorities, I'm not getting as exercised as I probably should about the deductions you questioned on my 1942 income-tax return. However, I realize you have your job to do, so I will try to explain the deductions in the limited space provided on a V-Mail form.

You question the set of barbells I contributed to the Salvation Army and deducted $75.00, the full price I paid for them. It is your opinion that I

should have subtracted depreciation from the full
price I paid, since I had them for five years.

I don't know how familiar you are with
barbells, Mr. Snodgrass, but I can tell you they
look a hell of a lot more impressive in the pages of
Strength and Health Magazine than they do in
one's bedroom. Mine have been lifted maybe half
a dozen times. Once by me, when I lifted them
for the first time and threw my back out for three
weeks; and several times by my mother, when she
had to vacuum under the bed.

I've never seen a depreciation table for
barbells, but even if they were used on a daily
basis, I doubt if they would wear out very fast,
being made of cast iron. In fact, if young Tut-
ankhamen had been a health nut and jerked iron,
I'm sure any barbells found in King Tut's tomb
would be as functional today as they were in old
Tut's time.

Since we'd both feel kind of silly taking this
to the Supreme Court, I suggest we let the
barbell deduction stand.

If you have any further questions about my
deductions as reported on my 1942 income-tax
form, I shall be happy to entertain them.

> Respectfully yours,
> Rolfe Stromburg
> 2nd. Lt., AC

Stromburg dropped the letter in the mailroom slot on
his way to the barbershop. He was now luxuriating in the
old barber chair under the spell of Figaro's strong fingers
massaging the base of his neck, when he heard O'Riley's
voice. He lifted his lids to peer at his copilot, who was
tossing his hat on a peg. "Hey, Pat!"

"How goes it, Swede?"

"Well," said Stromburg, snapping from his reverie,
"our conquering hero has returned from the battle. How'd
it go?"

"Back in one piece. At least physically. Mentally, I

doubt if I'll ever be the same. Those Army grunts are weird. I mean, they're straight off the funny farm."

"So you're not requesting a transfer to the infantry?"

"Geezus! You kidding? I've never been so damned miserable in my life. Think you'd ever see the day when you'd give a month's pay for a pair of dry socks?"

"Can't say as I have."

"Well, I have. And I've eaten so much mud I'll be crappin' adobe bricks for a month."

"So Erich Remarque was right. War in the trenches ain't all that groovy."

"I'll tell you this: I'll take my hat off to those mud-suckin' foot soldiers. Any day of the week. It's not the shooting and the shelling that gets you so much. That's no worse than what they throw at us upstairs. It's just the bone-soakin' *misery!* Those poor bastards are just physically miserable *all* the time. Especially during these rains. Those damn trenches are cesspools. Geezus!"

Stromburg nodded. "It must be hell."

"Hell is where these guys go for R&R. I just took a hot shower at the tent. Felt so good I didn't even notice when the stove blew up. God, it felt good!"

"Well, I'm glad you're back safe and sound, Pat."

"Damned near didn't make it. The last day at the front we were strafed by a couple of fighters. They came over the first time, just shootin' the hell out of everything. As they pulled up, I recognized them. They weren't Germans. They were P-Fifty-ones. *Our own damned planes!* They made several passes, blowin' up the mess tent, strafin' the trenches, even hit the slit trenches—the shit really flew. The infantry guys were shootin' back with everything they had. Talk about a bucket of worms. *Our* Air Corps fighting *our* infantry. No wonder it's takin' so damn long to win this war."

"Looks like we need to improve our ground-support control. The fighters were obviously in the wrong sector."

"You might say that. I'm writing it up in the report I have to file. Be nice if we could join sides and all battle the enemy for a change."

"Well, that's the purpose of the Army Exchange

Program. To get a feel for each other's mission. To learn to coordinate and cooperate." Figaro whisked away the hairs from Stromburg's collar and with a flourish removed the barber cloth. Stromburg rose, surveyed himself in the old cracked mirror tacked to the wall, and grinned at the Italian as he pressed a handful of lire into his palm. "*Grazie*, Figaro. You did your usual fantastic job."

"*Prego, prego, signore. Mille grazie.*"

O'Riley climbed into the barber chair as Stromburg took the vacated milking stool. "You might be interested to know that your infantry exchange officer felt the same about flying with us as you did about fighting with the infantry."

"Oh? What was the ground-pounder like?"

"He was a rough cob. You've probably heard of him. Alex Kebrowski. West Point fullback."

"Kebrowski! You kiddin'?"

"The one and only."

"He's the greatest fullback that ever ate a cleat."

"That's true. But he doesn't think much of airplanes. Or the crews that fly them. In fact, after his first mission he refused to go up again."

"Kebrowski? The greatest fullback to ever come out of West Point . . . refused to fly?"

"Yes. And we had a fairly easy mission at that. Kind of hurts a fellow's feelings when the terror of the gridiron is afraid to fly with you."

"Well, I'll be damned!"

"Said from now on he was even steering clear of tall barstools. He couldn't wait to get back to his trenches."

"And I couldn't wait to get back to this collection of corrosion that we fly."

"Lancaster would have a good quote here. Something about to each his own. A carpenter should stick to his last."

"I guess. If nothing else, this little sojourn made me appreciate my job. In spite of the people I have to work with."

"Glad to hear it." Stromburg studied the ruddy face of his copilot, whose eyelids were closed in ecstasy as the old-fashioned hand clippers were guided up the back of his neck. "I've got some news for you, Pat."

"Oh? Good or bad?"

"Good." Stromburg took a deep breath. "How would you like to be an aircraft commander?"

O'Riley's eyes snapped open. "How would I like to be a *what?*"

"A first pilot. Command your own crew."

O'Riley grimaced. "I thought that's what you said. The answer is no. Negative. Absolutely not. Forget it."

"I'm glad you're wild about the idea. Because some of our senior aircraft commanders are being promoted to group and to wing. There's a shortage of first pilots coming up. Major Diddle had a meeting of aircraft commanders last week, and we came up with a consensus of likely copilots to upgrade to AC. You, old buddy, thanks to my strong recommendation, are number one on the list."

"Why, you bastard! Here you send me off to the holy wars, up to my ass in mud, then you knife me in the back! Of all the crappy—"

Stromburg chuckled. "I knew you'd go for the idea. I'll sure as hell hate to lose you. So will the crew—"

"Then it won't be necessary to go through all that sorrow. You can start upgrading the number two man on the list. As miserable as you are, I'm staying with you."

"You start upgrading tomorrow. And you won't have any trouble, Pat. Hell, you're twice the pilot I am. All you need is to practice some tactical bumps and grinds. Review the emergency procedures. I'll work with you and we'll have you checked out in no time."

"Geezus, Swede! You know what you're saying? I don't want the responsibilities of a damn crew. You know what they'd give me. The newest AC always gets the dregs, the foul-ups, the misfits. Hell, I like our guys. We're a team. Even having to put up with you, and your personality like an open grave, I don't want to change. I'll just finish my missions with our crew—"

"No use running off at the mouth. It's all set. We start tomorrow." Stromburg felt a tug of remorse as he looked at the crestfallen face of his copilot. "Damn it, O'Riley, I'm thinking only of you. I don't want to break in a new copilot. But we have to consider your career progression. Promotions are given to AC's a hell of a lot sooner than they are to copilots. And for your career advancement—"

"Screw my career advancement. I just want to get out of this taffy pull in one piece. With my family jewels intact. I'm not a military man. I'm a dyed-in-the-wool, yellow-bellied PFC—Poor Fucking Civilian. I want to fulfill my lifelong ambition. I want to be a ferry steamer captain on Lake Michigan, cruising between Milwaukee and Luding-ton. I want a wife in Milwaukee. And I want a wife in Ludington. That's what I want. You can take your promo-tion and—"

Stromburg gave the Irishman a benign smile, picked up his hat, went over, and slapped him on the knee. "Tomorrow morning at oh eight hundred it's gear up. You'll like being an aircraft commander."

O'Riley watched his mentor go out the door; then, fuming, he turned to the barber. "Goddamnit, Figaro, why don't you learn English? So you can help me cuss that sonuvabitch out!"

Figaro kissed his fingertips, tossed the kisses at the ceiling. "*Si, si!* Sonuvabitch. *Arrivederci!*"

The jeep labored up the steep grade that was a challenge even for the four-wheeled mountain goat. Strom-burg cursed as he had to slow down to steer around a donkey saddled with milk cans, as its prodding owner deigned to take his half of the road out of the middle. Stromburg shifted into four-wheel drive. "How the hell did you ever find this place, Galvani?"

The tail gunner shifted his sore vitals on the hard seat. "Wasn't easy, skipper. Took some doing."

"I guess. I never did know why these little Italian villages all have to be built on top of a mountain. You'd have to be part eagle to live in some of these rookeries."

"Things haven't changed much. In peace and war, people still want the high ground. Some of these old villages date back to the days before Chirst."

"Well, we're coming to a wall. I hope this is the place."

"This is it. Just go through the gate there, and we're in the fascinating village of Castellucia di Sauri." Galvani winced as a huge cobblestone sent shock waves through the jeep. "I sure appreciate this, skipper. I know you got other things to do on a day off besides tearin' up jeeps."

"Thank our Intelligence officer. This hemorrhoid-hatcher is assigned to him." Stromburg shifted gears. "But after yesterday's mission, we're entitled to a little R&R."

Galvani grimaced at the recollection. "Wasn't that a ball-buster? Three times we went over that damn target before we dropped our bombs. No wonder we got the shit shot out of us."

"Our lead bombardier had his problems. First the weather socked in, screwing up his visual run. Then he had trouble on the second run killing the drift in the jet stream. Eppstein's a stickler for accuracy. He wasn't going to drop until he was sure of pickle-barreling the target."

"While Lieutenant Eppstein was trying to pickle-barrel the target, we lost six airplanes on those two extra bomb runs."

"I'm sure no one feels worse about that than Eppstein. He's a damn good bombardier. He just had a bad day. I thought the crews were going to mob him during debriefing, but we did clobber the target. And that's the name of the game."

"I guess."

Stromburg looked over at the slender young man sitting next to him. "How many times have you met this girl you want me to meet?"

"Maybe half a dozen."

"How the blazes did you ever find her up here?"

"Well, you know, Lieutenant, my folks are from Italy. I was told to look up some of my relatives. So I got chummy with our cook. You know, he married an Italian woman."

"So I understand. With five kids."

"Schultz got him an instant family. Anyway, he did some scouting for me, found there were some Galvanis living right here in this village. So he brought me up in the supply truck a couple of times. That's when I met Marguerita Galvani."

"So she's related."

"She's some kind of far-distant cousin. Her folks have

never met my folks, but there seem to be tribes of Galvanis all over Italy. Anyway, they treat me like a long-lost son."

Stromburg glanced at the canned ham partly concealed by the blanket in the tail gunner's lap. "I can understand why. I'd rather not know where you got the little gratuity there."

"That's good, skipper. 'Cause I'd rather not tell you. But it does pay to stay on good terms with the cook. Turn to the right here."

Heeding the tail gunner's directions, Stromburg circled the fountain in the center of the plaza that was the heart of the little village and started up a narrow lane between two rows of ancient stone houses that held a precarious grip on the steep hillside. The jeep made its way through a small flock of sheep herded desultorily by a toothless antique who saluted them with a gummy grin as they passed; then up the spiraling, rocky path that sorely taxed the jeep's transmission they climbed, until reaching the very top of the hill. Then they pulled up beside a tall, whitewashed wall, parked, and alit from the jeep. As they dismounted, brushing the dust from their uniforms, Stromburg looked around him and whistled. "I'll say this, your Italian relatives really have a view."

"Yes." Galvani pointed down at the valley far below. "If you look closely you can see our airfield. See the runway through the olive grove there?"

"I see it. Our base looks a hell of a lot better from up here."

"That's for damned sure." Galvani led the way through an iron gate in the tall fence. Inside the courtyard they were greeted by a marked contrast to the grubby, peeling exterior of the ancient village. Banks of bougainvillea that somehow defied the chilly January weather burst their blooms on the inner walls of the courtyard. Pots of flowers surrounded a beautifully tiled fountain containing the nude statue of an angelic young boy urinating blissfully into the fountain. Taking in the unexpected beauty of the patio, Stromburg followed his tail gunner as they crossed over to the large, handcarved front door. Galvani pulled the bell cord.

Presently the door was opened by an elderly gentleman. A mane of white hair swept low over the man's craggy face that was preceded by a classic nose borrowed from a Roman statue. Expressive eyes, ignoring the encroachments of crow's-feet at the corners, sparkled out from under shaggy white brows. The man swept Galvani into a big bearhug, kissed him on both cheeks, then held out a large, gnarled hand to Stromburg. "So. You are Lieutenant Stromburg. The pilot of the big bomber Nicholas has told me so much about." Stromburg found his hand being pumped vigorously. "Welcome to the humble house of Vincenzo Galvani."

"I'm glad to meet you, sir."

"The utmost pleasure is mine."

"Nick didn't tell me you spoke English."

Vincenzo Galvani spread his hands expansively. "For many years, Lieutenant Stromburg, I speak the English. I am a maker of the wine. And when one grows the finest grapes in all Italy, one does not sell to the Italians. One sells to the international marketplace. And there one must know the English."

"I see."

"But you did not come to speak the English with me. Let me call my daughters."

"Mr. Galvani," said the tail gunner, holding out the canned ham, "a little something for your table."

"Ah-ha, Nicholas. You should not have done this."

"It's small payment for that case of delicious wine you gave me the last time I was here."

"So you liked the *vino* of Vincenzo Galvani?"

"Best wine I ever drank. I only wished I could get some to my folks in New Jersey."

"Perhaps that can be arranged. I will think on that." He patted the young Galvani on the arm as he ushered the men into the parlor.

It was the first time Stromburg had been in an Italian home, and he looked around with interest. It was not a large place, but evidently the wine business had been good, for the furniture was rich and massive; expensive brocaded drapes softened the windows; the carpets were thick and luxurious. A grand piano commanded a room of its own just off the parlor, and the lamps and decor items exuded a tasteful, Old World grandeur.

"Gentlemen, please take a seat. May I provide you with a little wine?"

"That would be nice," said Stromburg, sinking into a sofa that was deceptively soft.

"The road up to Castellucia can be very dusty. This would call for a glass of tart claret to settle the dust. I will decant a bottle and let it breathe while I find out what has happened to my daughters. You know the ladies. Always they must make the grand entrance."

As the old man left the room, Stromburg turned to his tail gunner. "Daughters? Ladies? He keeps using the plural. I thought there was only Marguerita. One daughter."

"Oh, didn't I mention that Marguerita had a sister?"

"No. You didn't happen to mention that."

"Sorry about that. Marguerita has an older sister. Not bad-looking, either. Once you get used to the harelip. And you don't really notice her club foot unless you're dancing—"

"Galvani! You wily little wop! Have you got something up your sleeve? You wouldn't be trying to fix me up now, would you—"

"Hello, Nicholas."

Both men rose at the sound of the voice and turned their attention to the young lady who had just entered the room. A slender, wasp-waisted figure was carrying a tray containing a wine decanter and glasses. She set the tray on the table, then crossed over to Galvani. He leaned forward and kissed her shyly on the cheek. "Hello, Marguerita."

She turned to Stromburg and held out her hand. "And you are the lieutenant."

"Call me Swede." Stromburg found himself looking down into a lovely face that was surveying him with childlike curiosity through huge, brown eyes one could drown in. Her beaming face was framed by raven-black braided hair that extended down to the middle of her back. Stromburg couldn't help noticing as he took her cool hand

in his that small, firm breasts pushed against the simple
peasant blouse in a way that bespoke a young body still
maturing into womanhood. It was little wonder that
Galvani had been smitten by this fetching, far-distant
cousin. "I'm very happy to meet you, Marguerita."

"Thank you." She moved to the table and started
pouring the wine into glasses. No mean feat, considering
her eyes were glued to the young airman during the whole
procedure. "It was nice of you to come, Lieutenant," she
said, not taking her eyes from Galvani.

"Definitely my pleasure," said Stromburg.

"No," said a low, soft voice. "It is definitely *our*
pleasure to have Nick's lieutenant honor our house."
Stromburg turned to the source of this new voice, which
emanated from the doorway to the music room. He almost
spilled the wine that was being served him as he took a
glass from the tray. "I am Marguerita's older sister.
Esterina."

Framed in the doorway, composing the picture that
had created Stromburg's problem with his wine glass, was
the very beautiful image of a mature Marguerita. The long,
ebony hair was not braided but was coiled in a high bun
over the same lovely face that seemed to be the stamp of
Galvani women. Beautiful brown eyes were spaced wide
over high cheekbones. A full, sensuous mouth was smiling
to show white, even teeth. As this vision entered the room,
borne by a proud, voluptuous body, Stromburg was embarrassed by a little catch in his throat as he found words to say,
"I'm happy to know you, Esterina." He shot a meaningful
look at his tail gunner, who responded with absolute insou-
ciance.

"Nicholas has told us so much about you, I feel we
know you."

Once again Stromburg found a cool, feminine hand in
his. Only this time it was gripped with a firm, almost
mannish handshake. "Yes," he lied. "And our young warrior
had told me much about you folks."

"But I must confess," she said, eyeing him with overt
interest, "you are not what I expected."

"I can imagine what Nick told you. That I have at least

three heads, I'm sure. Tail gunners have never been known to speak kindly of their pilots."

"No. He never said anything derogatory. I guess one just paints images of bomber pilots in the mind's eye. They create such devastating destruction one automatically conjures an image of ruthlessness, fierce hatred—"

"Not this one. I've always been a lover. Not a fighter."

She smiled at him. "I can see that in your eyes, Lieutenant Stromburg."

Embarrassed, he took a long draught from his glass. "Please call me Swede."

"Very well. Swede." She took a glass from the tray.

"If you're through analyzing me, would you mind answering a question?"

"Of course not, Lieutenant . . . Swede."

"How is it that you native Italian Galvanis speak better English than I do?"

Esterina smiled. "I'm sure we do not. But the main reason we speak passable English is because I am a language teacher in our secondary school. I teach English and French."

"So that's it."

"Yes. My father insisted that his children learn at least two languages besides Italian. You see, he had no sons. And in case we wanted to carry on his wine business, he insisted that we be properly educated."

"Your father is a very wise man."

"Yes. Our father is a wonderful man. And, I might add, the best mayor this town ever had."

"Your father is the mayor of Castellucia?"

"He *was* the mayor. For forty years. The job paid nothing, but we did receive the help of the townspeople in building our home up here on the mountaintop."

"It's a beautiful home."

"Thank you. My father had a good business before the war. His wines were very popular."

"Are you going to take over his business?"

She shrugged. "I doubt it. Marguerita is not interested in the wine business. I think she just wants to get married and raise children." She looked over at her sister for a reaction, but Marguerita was in a world of her own, losing herself in the eyes of young Galvani.

"And how about you?" asked Stromburg. "Do you like the wine business?"

"I do. But you see, I am married. And my husband does not like to live in a small village."

"Oh. So you're married."

"Yes. I am married to a teacher."

"Oh."

"He *was* a teacher. But when the war started, he enlisted in the Italian Army. He became an officer and eventually a tank commander."

"Good for him."

"Not entirely. He was captured by the Allies. He is now in a prisoner-of-war camp."

"No! I'm sorry to hear that."

"It is not nearly as bad as it could be. You see, Domenico, my husband, was sent to a POW camp in the United States."

Stromburg chased this revelation with a swig of wine. "Now, wait a minute. You mean to say your husband is in the U.S.A.?"

"Yes."

"Well, I'll be damned."

She smiled at the perplexed look on his face. "It is ironic, is it not? My husband is in your country, you are in his. Neither of you wants to be where you are."

"Where is he in the States?"

"He is in your state of Mississippi. Near the town of . . . Wicksburg?"

"Vicksburg?"

"Vicksburg. Yes, that is it."

"Vicksburg. I didn't even know we had a POW camp there."

"According to his letters, there are three thousand prisoners there. Mostly Germans from General Rommel's Afrika Korps. They are building a model of your Mississippi River."

"They're doing *what?*"

"Your government is taking advantage of cheap labor to

build a very detailed scale model of your Mississippi River Basin. Actually, Domenico is rather enjoying his work. When the project is complete, your engineers will be able to forecast accurately the effects of floods, snowfalls, and other weather phenomena on the river basin, by duplicating them in the model. Then they will know which dams to open, which floodgates to control so they can prevent disastrous floods. I find the information Domenico sends me most interesting."

Stromburg nodded. "So your husband is in Vicksburg, Mississippi. That town played quite a role in our Civil War. I didn't know it was involved in this one, too. That's the damndest thing I ever heard."

"It makes sense to Domenico. As I say, he rather enjoys his work. He is a mathematics teacher."

"No, the Mississippi model makes sense. It's the circumstances that are baffling. General Rommel's crack Afrika Korps is in Mississippi building a model of the Mississippi River instead of trying to level Europe. It's the only part of this war I've seen yet that does make sense."

She smiled as she refilled his glass. "It is interesting, when you stop to think of it. And I am glad for Domenico. Being a prisoner in the United States is so much better than being a prisoner in these European POW camps, I have been told. Domenico has gained ten pounds."

Stromburg grinned. "I wonder how he found the switch from pasta and ravioli to hominy grits and hush puppies?"

"He seems to be surviving nicely. And speaking of eating, I had better go to the kitchen and help Papa. He likes to fix the Sunday dinner."

"Your father? How about your mother?"

"My mother is dead. She passed away when Marguerita was born."

"Oh. I'm sorry."

"Do not be. We get along just fine."

"Yes. I can see that."

"Father does get frustrated these days. He loves to make the good, old-fashioned Italian dinners, and since the war the ingredients just are not available. He is out there now trying to make veal scallopini out of donkey meat. No matter how much you pound donkey meat, it is not going to taste like veal. But he does make excellent pasta, so I do not think you will go away from the table hungry."

"I'm sure of that. I'm very much looking forward to a home-cooked meal. I want to thank you for inviting me along with Nick."

"It is all part of a diabolical plan, I am afraid. How much do you know of Nicholas's intentions?"

"Very little. I have nine men on my crew, and each of them spends most of his time hatching up devious plots that all end up with my giving a command performance before my squadron commander. Sometimes ignorance is bliss."

She laughed. "I fear you will soon be a part of Nicholas's plans. But now, let us all adjourn to the dining room. And eat some of Papa's speciality of the house—*asino cacciatori*."

"Translation?"

"Donkey with tomato sauce."

Stromburg following closely on her heels, Esterina led the way up the curved staircase. "I hope this is not an imposition," he said, "but I have never been in an Italian home before."

"I am happy to show you the house. It will help me to work off the kilo of spaghetti I ate."

"I don't know when I've had a better dinner. Donkey or no donkey. I'll have to think of some way to repay your father."

"Nonsense. Italians love to cook. Father is never happier than when he is up to his elbows in spaghetti sauce." Reaching the head of the stairs, Esterina pointed to the various doors as she spoke. "That is Marguerita's room. This is the bath. And this is the master bedroom." She opened the door to the latter and ushered Stromburg in. "This used to be my parents' room until my mother died. Now father sleeps downstairs in the guest room. The stairs are no longer a match for his arthritis. So while Domenico is away, Papa insists that I use the master bedroom."

"It's magnificent!" Stromburg whistled as he took in the large bedroom. A huge canopied bed piled high with eiderdown bolsters covered the center of the room, flanked by handcarved dressers and wardrobes. A divan was at one side; next to it was an old-fashioned rocking chair. A step up, and the bedroom extended into an anteroom, its raised floor supporting a massive fireplace that glowed with the embers of a log fire.

Esterina crossed over to a small table that supported a tray containing a wine decanter and glasses. She filled two glasses. "A little sherry may help to extinguish the fire of Papa's tomato sauce," she said, handing Stromburg a glass. "I hope you will not think I am being forward, entertaining you in my bedroom." Her eyes met his as she lifted her glass.

He touched her glass. "I'd hardly call this a bedroom. I've seen smaller hotel lobbies."

She smiled as they toasted. "There is something I want to show you." She took his hand and led him past the fireplace to two French doors in the far side of the room. She opened them and led the way out onto a large balcony that extended along the upper story of the house. Crossing to the far edge protected by a wrought-iron railing, she pointed down to the valley below. "If you look closely you can see it."

Stromburg followed her pointing hand and squinted. "Maybe I could see it better if I knew what I was looking at."

"It is your air base. With your blackout curtains, you can barely make it out at night. But there it is."

As he peered, Stromburg found his face very close to her hair. Its clean smell bore just a hint of perfume. "Yes, sir. That's the old outfit, all right."

"I have spent many hours here watching your war. I see your planes take off in the early-morning hours in such strength, the thunder from the engines echoing through the hills. I watch you join up into your formations as you circle overhead, sometimes so many planes they almost blot out the sun. A great air armada off to wreak its terrible vengeance on a hated enemy." She took a sip from her glass. "And then hours later, you return. No longer an invincible armada, but sick and crippled machines, the red flares signaling your aircraft in distress. Many of your bombers are missing. The wail of the ambulances and the fire trucks—"

"Hold on! You paint a very dismal picture of the only war in town."

She turned to him. "You must be a very brave man, Lieutenant Stromburg. To face that day after day."

" 'Bravery' isn't exactly the word. Let's try 'stupidity.' "

"And last week. One of your planes crashed very near our village. Right after it took off."

"I'm sorry. We've lost several planes just after takeoff lately. We're not quite sure why."

"One of its bombs hit our church."

"God! I'm sorry. I hope no one was—"

"No one was hurt. The bomb did not explode."

"Thank God. It shouldn't have. We generally don't arm the bombs until we get near the target."

She touched his arm. "Actually, it was rather humorous. The bomb did not do any damage to the church, but it skidded right through the bathroom. I am afraid it quite upset our village priest."

"I should think it would."

"Yes." She smiled. "Especially since the good father was using it at the time."

Stromburg chuckled. "You're joking."

"Not only that, but it destroyed one of the few flush toilets we have in the village."

"Well, that rips it. When we attack the very seat of the church, that's carrying this war too damn far."

She laughed. "We will survive. But it had done terrible things to Father Zandegrande's morale. Having the only church in the district with—what you call —an outbuilding?"

"Outhouse."

"Outhouse."

"Well, maybe we can do something about that. After all, Italians are no longer our enemy. We should clean up our mess."

"I am glad we are no longer at war." She studied his face. "I do not think I could ever be an enemy of yours, Swede."

He looked down at the smiling face peering up at him in the moonlight. "It would be impossible." He sucked in his breath. "My God, but you are beautiful!"

Her eyes sobered, and she drew near him. "Would you mind very much if I touched you?"

He cleared his throat. "I think that might be arranged."

She took his face in her palms and stroked his cheeks. "It has been over two years since I have been with a man."

"I know how you feel."

"Nicholas tells me you are married."

"Legally I am. Yes."

"I do not quite understand. Your marriage is not good?"

"It's a long story." He put his arms around her. "And it's been a long time since I've touched a woman." He brought his face close to hers. "I have no business doing this."

"No. No business—"

He brought his lips to hers, kissed her deeply on her full mouth. Her hands vacated his face and slipped around his neck, pulling him to her. His arms circled her waist as her body arched into his. He felt the fullness of her breasts crush against his chest as his lips traveled to her throat. She made a little gasping sound, then pushed him from her. "Oh, *Dio mio!*"

"I . . . I'm sorry, Esterina. I didn't mean to—"

She took his hand, turned, and led the way back into the bedroom. "We can blame our feelings on the war, on the misery, on the live-today-and-die-tomorrow philosophy. Or we can be honest. You are a very attractive man, Lieutenant Stromburg. And I have not been held by a man for a very long time. Tonight I would very much like to be held very close by a very attractive man." She started unbuttoning her blouse. "Would you care to remove your clothes?"

Stromburg swallowed hard, coming to grips with this

unexpected situation. "But Esterina, what if your father
. . . or your sister should come up—"

"Marguerita and her Nicholas are far too busy with
their own wooing to be concerned about us. And Papa is
sound asleep." She removed her blouse and started unbuttoning her brassiere. Suddenly she stopped. "I guess I am
being very forward. I took it for granted that you wanted
me as much as I—"

Stromburg started unbuttoning his shirt. "*Want* you?
Good Lord! I was thinking only of you and your reputation."

"Let me worry about that." Wearing only a lacy pair of
step-ins, she went around the room turning down the
lamps, stoking the fire, and refilling their glasses.

The sheets were cool against Stromburg's naked body
as he climbed into the bed, put a bolster under his head,
and watched Esterina finish her chores. Bearing two
glasses, she sat them down on the nightstand, slipped out of
her panties, and stood for a moment at the side of the bed
while she pulled combs from her hair. "Mind if I let my hair
down?"

"Please do." Stromburg licked dry lips as he watched
the firelight flicker across her beautifully proportioned
body, her full, dark-nippled breasts swaying as she removed
the retainers that allowed her hair to cascade down over her
shoulders. And then she was under the sheets and lying on
the pillow next to him.

"We must have no guilt feelings," she said.

"I have no guilt feelings."

"Papa always said people should not sleep together
until they are married. You and I are married. Therefore, it
is perfectly all right."

"I never looked at it quite that way."

"So no guilt feelings."

"No guilt feelings."

And then she was in his arms and their bodies were
one as each reveled in the scents and the tastes and the
touchings of the other.

And suddenly the war was a million miles away.

And far below the lovers, at the air base at the bottom of the hill, the war was about to be a million miles away for Lieutenant Samuel Eppstein, lead bombardier of the 725th Squadron. For at precisely this moment, he shoved the blue-steel muzzle of his .45 service revolver into his right ear, squinted his eyes, and pulled the trigger.

Lieutenant Eppstein left a short note to his parents and a small legacy to the crew members of Stromburg's crew.

Six jars of gefilte fish.

Chapter Eight

Dearest Mom:

Thanks for being so good about writing, Mom. I know it's hard to find time now that you have a job working at Boeing. As best I can divine your job, that "spaghetti" you're soldering will eventually become the electrical nerve center of a B-17. I knew the civilian work force was hard up, but I never thought I'd see the day when my mother would become a factory worker. Just don't let them work you too hard. With you and Sis building airplanes, the Germans will soon have to look to their laurels.

Tell Sis I received her cake. But don't tell her that it was left at the mail center too long and the rats got into it. Before we could stop him, our houseboy, little Luigi, got into what was left and polished it off. He thought the rat leavings were raisins. But they didn't seem to hurt him any; the kid's got a constitution like a goat.

Things are very quiet and routine here. Had some good home cooking the other night at the home of a nice Italian family. And the crew recently inherited some canned fish, so we've been eating royally. I think I'm putting on weight.

Well, I wish there was more to report, but things are dull as dishwater around here. We do manage to keep busy at the USO, however, and my Ping-Pong backhand is really improving.

Since you've been getting letters from Dick Daringer's folks, I'll give you a brief background on another member of our crew. Sergeant Daringer's our flight engineer, and he has one of the most important jobs in the crew. He keeps the airplane's engines running and the equipment maintained. We're lucky to have Dick, as he's very well qualified. He's of medium build, has a hairline moustache, and looks a bit like an emaciated Clark Gable. He sort of rides herd on the other enlisted men and seems to engender their respect and cooperation. He hails from Defiance, Ohio, and has a great sense of humor—a commodity, needless to say, that is very much appreciated during our missions.

Well, according to our Intelligence sources, the Germans are in full retreat from "the Bulge," the Russians have taken Warsaw, and Hungary has declared war on Germany. Surely it's now just a matter of time until the Axis throws in the towel.

Give a big kiss and hug to all the family and save a huge one for yourself. And a special thanks for taking the time to make a bathrobe for little Ann. I know she'll love it. Lordy, how I miss that little rugrat.

All my love,
Swede

In the tiny, cramped office of the squadron commander, Stromburg took the motioned seat in front of the commander's desk and sat down. He tucked his cap under his belt and watched Diddle finish signing papers.

Stromburg didn't care much for his commander. Major Diddle was too flighty; his nervous, neighing laugh was most irritating, and his tic seemed to be getting worse. Diddle didn't fit the mold of a devil-may-care, spit-in-the-wind commander of a flying squadron. Even a bomber squadron.

Diddle signed the last paper, put it in the out-basket on his desk, then picked up an application form and shook it at Stromburg. "This is what I want to talk to you about, Stromburg. This application to marry signed by your tail gunner. No way am I going to approve this."

Stromburg was taken aback. "Sir, I'm not sure I understand."

"You should never have endorsed the application."

"Major, I know how the Army feels about marrying indigenous personnel. But this case is different—"

"They're all different." Diddle leaned back in his chair and locked eyes with Stromburg. "How old is your tail gunner?"

"He's nineteen. Almost twenty."

"He's a bottle-assed kid. Still playing with himself."

"He's old enough to die for his country."

"Oh, don't throw that crap at me, Stromburg. War is a piss-poor primer for marriage. Our young studs come over here at the height of their horniness and try to stick their wick into anything that moves. A stiff dick has no conscience. That's the problem with our goddamn VD rate. But even forgetting the disease, they end up with a pregnant girlfriend and feel they have to take her back to the States. Most of these big-eyed little Eyeties that are puttin' out over here aren't exactly something you'd want to take home to meet Mama."

"You're discounting the effects of this war on the Italians—"

"Like hell I am. I know what the war has done. Prostitution has become the only way some of these little orphans can eat. But let's be practical. Someday this war's going to end. Italy will get back on its feet. In the meantime our young bucks who get involved over here are destined to spend the rest of their lives with some scabby little whore, all because of a restless pecker. I'm not recommending approval of any more marriage requests."

"But sir, how about our cook? You not only approved Sergeant Schultz's marriage, you were best man at the wedding."

"Schultz? He's a horse of a different color. That old fart's no kid. He's pushing fifty. With that puss of his, he's lucky the war came along. He'd still be a bachelor on the Brooklyn docks loading banana boats. You should see the woman he married. Has to weigh at least three hundred pounds. A widow with five kids. War's the best thing that ever happened to them both. She's got a provider for her brood, he's got a warm sack and more woman than he can handle. A marriage made in heaven." Diddle issued a neighing laugh.

With his eyes Stromburg raked the face of the nervous little major. His tic definitely was getting worse. "Very well, sir, I won't push it. The whole thing is academic, anyway. If Galvani wants to marry that pretty little girl, he'll find a way. Army approval or not."

"You're right there, Swede. About all we can really do is try to discourage them. Maybe threaten them a little. Hell, if they've still got hot pants, they can come over after the war and do whatever they want. At least then it won't be our responsibility."

"I understand the Army's position. But this case is different. Galvani's girlfriend is no hooker. She's a beautiful young lady from a fine family. She's a knockout even by stateside standards."

"Wasn't Galvani the tail gunner who tried to peel his joystick like a banana?"

"Yes. It froze to his tail guns."

Once again the high-pitched laugh. "He still got his pole vault in a bandage?"

"As far as I know."

"Well, at least maybe he'll keep it in his pants for a while. Hard to get overamorous when one's jock's in a sling." Diddle sobered, leaned forward in his chair, and studied Stromburg's face. "Enough about your tail gunner. I want to talk to you about some other members of your crew. First, O'Riley. Understand you've signed him off as a first pilot. Can he cut the mustard in combat?"

"Yes. O'Riley's a natural-born pilot. One of the finest—"

"That's not what I asked. Can he command a crew? Inspire them to do their job? Not crack under pressure?"

"Yes. O'Riley might be a little on the lazy side, but the guy's fearless, and the men like him."

"Good. 'Cause he's flying his first mission tomorrow as aircraft commander. He'll be flying number six position in your flight."

"Great."

"And your navigator. Lancaster. Been hearing good things about him. Isn't he sort of a half-assed intellectual?"

"Not sure what a half-assed intellectual is, sir. But Lancaster's one hell of a fine navigator. Once he quits throwing up in the airplane."

"That's a minor problem. Tell him to quit eating breakfast on mission mornings. Should cut things down somewhat."

"He's down to coffee now. Says he has two cups every morning. One going down, one coming up."

"Now about your bombardier. Balzac."

Stromburg winced inwardly. "Yes, sir."

"That little upstart's been a thorn in my side ever since he arrived. He's got more balls than a pool rack."

"I'm afraid so, sir."

"Personally, I hate the little bastard. But as a bombardier, the guy shows promise. At least according to Sam Eppstein."

Stromburg shook his head. "Poor old Sam. What a shocker that was!"

"Yes. But we'll not dwell on that. I've studied the photos on some of your target-of-opportunity missions. I hate to admit it, but Balzac seems to have a pretty good batting average."

"Yes. Balzac's a crackerjack armaments man, and he really knows his Norden bombsight. I'd trust him to lead the squadron . . . even the group. Any day."

"How is he under pressure?"

"He's a volatile little guy. Jumpy as the rest of us during a mission. But on the bomb run it's a different story. He gets so thoroughly engrossed in his bombsight and setting up for his bomb run that he appears completely oblivious to the war around him. Last mission a flak fragment buried itself in his helmet and he didn't even know it until we cleared the target. Then when he saw it, he wet his pants."

"That's good to know. Eppstein's left a hole that has to be filled. Balzac is one of the bombardiers we might groom to fly lead ship."

"He'll deliver for you, Major."

"Let's hope so. Now we come to you, Stromburg. I've had my eye on you for some time. You did fine flying element lead, now you'll be flying deputy squadron lead on occasion. Then, hopefully, squadron lead when you get a little more seasoning."

"Thank you, sir. For the vote of confidence."

"Don't let it go to your head." Diddle released a nervous whinny. "With that bombardier of yours, I thought you might like to have your day brightened a little."

"Thank you, Major. We all have our cross to bear."

"Anything else, Stromburg?"

"Just one thing. The personal effects of Muldoon's crew. They're still in our tent. Serving as our coffee table. I thought maybe the next of kin might like to have—"

"Muldoon?"

"Yes, sir. His crew were the former occupants of our tent. They bought it over Ploesti, I understand—"

Diddle nodded. "Oh, yes. Muldoon. A crazy Irishman. You mean the personal effects are still in your tent?"

"Yes, sir."

"Jesus Christ! I'll have Gonzales take care of it right away."

"Appreciate it, sir."

"Anything else, Stromburg?"

"No, sir."

"Then get your mangy butt outta here."

Stromburg was almost hit in the face with a shovelful of dirt as he approached his tent. Investigating the source of the flying earth, he saw that it was being uprooted by the feverish activities of Balzac and his sidekick, the short, muscular armaments man and chief scrounger, Sergeant Warner. Stromburg watched for a moment, then reached over and tapped Balzac on the shoulder. "May I ask what you're up to now?"

Balzac stopped in midswing long enough to answer, "We're building a trench, Swede. What does it look like we're doing?"

"I can see it's a trench, bombardier. Tell me more."

"It's simple." Balzac continued digging. "With the aid and unstinting assistance of our good friend Sergeant Warner, we're digging a trench in which to lay the electrical cable."

"That's it over there, Lieutenant," said Warner, pausing in the act of wiping his forehead long enough to point to a large coil of electrical wire near the tent.

Stromburg sighed. "Okay, Balzac. What are we up to this time that's going to get me shipped to Siberia?"

"Not a thing, *bwana*. We're merely electrifying our tent. So we won't have to steal any more electricity from the good Major Diddle. And we can throw away the candles. Have honest-to-God electric lights."

"I see. And just how are we going to achieve this miracle? I know. We're going to tap into Colonel Sterling's electricity. Steal it from the group commander. That's a better idea."

"Of course not. We're running this electric cable down to our very own generator."

"Our *what?*"

"We now have our very own generator. From a B-Twenty-four."

"You mean you've scrounged the putt-putt off one of our planes?"

"With the help of our very good friend here, Sergeant Warner. It's off of *Lucky Lady*, the Liberator that crash-landed the other day. *Lucky Lady's* luck ran out. She doesn't need it anymore." Balzac put his hand over his heart and stared skyward. "She's gone to the great airplane graveyard in the sky."

Stromburg made way for little Luigi, who had suddenly materialized at his side. The boy carried a canteen over his shoulder and gave Stromburg a big grin as he wiped a canteen cup with his shirttail and filled it from the canteen. He offered the cup to Stromburg. "Over here, Gunga Din," said Balzac. "Remember, Luigi, you're the water boy for

the hard-toiling troops here. Big-wheel airplane driver can
get his own water. Okay?" Luigi looked up at Stromburg,
shrugged, and took the cup over to Balzac.

"Just where, bombardier, do you propose to put the
generator? Those things are so damn noisy, they'd wake the
dead."

"Right you are, *bwana*. So for that reason we're
putting it down by the latrine. We'll also put a sorely
needed light bulb in the crapper, which should stifle any
malcontents who might otherwise complain about the
noise."

"And the gasoline for the generator?"

"Would you believe it's only going to cost one pack a
week? Again, your friend and mine, Sergeant Warner, has
contacts at the motor pool."

"I'll bet he has. And I have a feeling we've just
allocated the last pack of my cigarette ration."

Balzac wiped his lips and handed the cup back to
Luigi. "See there, Sergeant Warner? What did I tell you?
Do we or do we not have the most compassionate, unselfish
aircraft commander who ever crash-landed an airplane? I
told you our own Lieutenant Stromburg—man among
men, generous to a fault—would be only too glad—nay,
proud—to make personal sacrifices for his men."

Warner took a proffered cup from Luigi, quaffed, then
wiped his mouth with his sleeve. "That's what you said,
Lieutenant."

Stromburg lowered his eyes from their beseeching
look at the heavens and planted them on the sergeant. "If
we may dispense with this unmitigated mule dung a
moment, I'd like to talk to you, Sergeant Warner."

Warner hit a ramrod stance and brought his shovel to
shoulder arms. "Yes, sir, Lieutenant."

"Just continue shoveling and cut out the crap. Balzac
tells me you're something of a jeweler."

Warner grinned. "You mean just because I fixed
Lieutenant Balzac's watch, sir? Nothing really. Clocks are a
hobby of mine. I like to fool around with timepieces—"

"Do you suppose you could do anything with mine?"

Stromburg unfastened the strap and handed his watch to the sergeant. "It's probably just dirty, but it's been stopping occasionally."

"I'll be happy to take a look at it, sir." He fiddled with the stem.

"I'd appreciate it. When you get the time."

Warner pocketed the watch. "I'll check it out tonight."

"Thanks, Sergeant. Oh, and one more thing."

"Yes, sir?"

"As I remember, Balzac told me you were a plumber before the war."

"A plumber's apprentice, sir. Was just about to join the union when the war started."

"I stand corrected. But I take it you can hook up a flush toilet."

"Oh, yes, sir. No problem at all."

"Good. I may have a job for you. But first we need to find a flush toilet. That might provide a challenge even to the squadron's best scrounger."

"Over here, that could present a challenge, yes, sir. But not an insurmountable one. But if you're thinkin' of gettin' one for the officers' crapper here, it ain't quite that easy to install."

"It's not for here. It's for a place already plumbed for a flush john. I want to do a little community relations."

Warner pursed his lips. "Okay. I don't know right offhand where I can find a flusher, but I can start my research." Suddenly a gleam came into his eyes. "I know a great place to start. When you making the next laundry run?"

"My turn comes up next week. Why?"

"Well, if I might tag along, I'll begin my research in Foggia."

"All right, you're on. Just where do you plan to start?"

"Why, Lieutenant, I'm surprised at you. Where else but the seat of all learning? The center of all culture? Madam Grabballi's Palace of Pleasure."

Stromburg was finishing his visual preflight of the bomber. He was peering into the number four engine nacelle when he heard the deep voice say, "See any birds' nests, Lieutenant?"

Stromburg turned to see a sergeant looking over his shoulder into the nacelle. The tall, gaunt NCO had a leathered face in which two soulful, bloodshot eyes overlooked a large nose that sniffed the world cynically. His service cap was supported by a horseshoe of tufted white hair, and his uniform was so large it could also accommodate his twin brother, had he one. "I don't see any, Sarge."

The sergeant brought his hand to his brow in a gesture more migrained than military. "Sergeant Larks, sir. Combat photographer. I'm assigned to your ship for this mission."

Stromburg returned the salute. "Welcome aboard, Larks."

"Thank you, sir. You know my favorite photograph of this whole stinkin' war?"

"Afraid I don't."

"It's a great shot. And I didn't even take it. Shows a robins' nest full of little chicks. Inside the nacelle of a Liberator."

"For some reason birds like to nest in there."

"They say the bomber was taken off the line and not flown till the babies had learned to fly. Then it was put back into service. Ain't that a hell of a message?"

"A hell of a message. Although I'm not sure what it is." Stromburg finished his inspection and turned to appraise the sergeant. There was a B-4 bag loaded with camera equipment and film at his feet. "Need any help loading your gear aboard?"

"No, sir. I'm an old hand at this. Thirty-two missions under my belt."

"Aren't you a little old for being a combat photographer?"

"No, sir. Just look old." He shook a cigarette out of its pack and stuck it into his mouth. "That's what thirty-two missions does. Actually, I'm twenty-nine. Lost most of my hair on a Ploesti raid."

"Looks like you lost a little weight, too. Judging by your uniform."

"Naw. Always been skinny. Have to stand twice to cast

a shadow. I wear my uniform big so I can change the film in my camera." He stuck his hands inside his fatigues and ballooned them out. "That way my pictures never get light-streaked."

"I see. You planning on lighting that cigarette?"

"Naw. Pilots get uptight when I smoke near their airplanes. So I don't smoke cigarettes. I chew 'em." He bit off the end of a Lucky Strike and started chewing. "Result's the same." He spat out a little white ball. "Once you get used to the paper."

"Okay. When you've finished chewing your cigarette, make yourself comfortable in the rear. The lads back there will help you with your flak vest, et cetera."

"I know the ropes, Lieutenant. Just don't leave me up there."

"That I promise."

"And one favor. Please hit the damn target. Embarrassing as hell to develop mission pictures and find our bomb craters from hell to breakfast and the bridge still standin'."

"We'll do our best."

"Three missions to go." Larks took a deep breath and threw his gear into the tail section. "God, I hate airplanes!"

"The last bomb's away!" Balzac's voice was tense over the intercom.

"About time!" roared Ewing, hunching down in the copilot's seat. "Somebody sure as hell kicked over the hornets' nest!" Another flak burst exploded close, making the airplane stagger.

Stromburg racked the bomber over and went into a shallow dive, leading his flight into evasive action off the bomb run. "Those Austrians are pissed."

"We clobbered the bastards!" yelled Balzac. "We made mincemeat out of those marshaling yards. Look! Secondaries! Ammo trains and oil tankers exploding!"

Stromburg craned over to see the havoc below him. A monstrous rolling black cloud was forming over the Linz Marshaling Yards. He had no time to exult in glory as the big hand of a large flak burst suddenly jolted the bomber, hanging Stromburg momentarily by his seat belt. "All right, already! We're through bombing. You guys quit shooting."

"Moderate flak, eh?" shouted Ewing. "I'm gonna kill that frigging Intelligence officer! I haven't seen flak concentrated like this over Vienna! So thick you could roller-skate on it!"

"We sure got pasted!" Stromburg thumbed his intercom button. "Pilot to all stations. I want a battle damage report. Start with you, tail gunner." Stromburg tried to wipe the frost off the windshield created by the steam from his electric gloves as he waited. There was no reply to his request. "Tail gunner from pilot. Do you read, over?" The seconds ticked by with still no response. "Pilot to all stations. Does anyone read the pilot? Over." Stromburg turned to the copilot as nothing but silence greeted his transmission. "Take over, Ewing. I've got to get a damage assessment."

"I got the airplane."

Stromburg relinquished the controls and turned around in his seat. He yelled for the engineer. Daringer appeared, blinking and reeking of gasoline. He was soaking wet. "Yes, sir?"

Stromburg stared at the shivering engineer. "What the hell are you doing?"

"We took a hit that ruptured a fuel line in the bomb bay. I'm trying to fix it."

"Great. Our intercom's out. Can you go to the aft end and get me a battle damage report?"

"Not at the moment, boss. Gas is shooting into the bomb bay like a fire hose. Got to get that line crimped. We're losin' a lot of fuel."

Stromburg nodded. "Carry on. Get Balzac to help." He turned to the copilot. "Can you handle this sieve by yourself, Ewing? I have to go to the rear and check on the crew."

"Go ahead. And check the control cables. We seem to be wallowing like a sperm whale."

Stromburg shot a worried look at his copilot. "I don't like the looks of this." He disengaged himself from the umbilical cords that fastened him to his seat, plugged his oxygen hose into a walk-around bottle, and headed for the rear. At the navigator's station he pulled up short. Lancaster was slumped in his seat, unconscious. Balzac was ministering to him, slapping his cheeks and rubbing his wrists. Stromburg shouted into the bombardier's ear: "Lancaster been hit?"

"His oxygen regulator's knocked out!" shouted Balzac. "He turned blue. Finally got him plugged into this walk-around bottle."

"Good work, Lennie."

"We got to go down, Swede. Now!"

"We can't descend now. Unless you know a tunnel through the Alps. We have to maintain this altitude."

"Lancaster's gonna die! Look at him!"

"He's not going to die. See? He's coming around." Balzac started hitting him on the chest. "That is, if you don't beat him to death."

Lancaster stirred, opened his eyes. "What's going on?"

"A touch of anoxia, Bill," said Stromburg. "You'll be okay. Just suck on that walk-around bottle."

"Feel like I've been on a cheap drunk."

"You'll feel better by the minute. Just keep belting that emergency oxygen."

Lancaster took several breaths, looking around. His eyes returned to Stromburg's face. "Swede, tell me one more time how lucky we are to be in this line of work."

"You never had it so good. Now quit goofing off and figure us a course to Switzerland. We may need it."

"I'll be happy to." Lancaster pulled himself together and addressed his charts. Stromburg turned to the bombardier. "Your patient's going to live. Now, can you give Daringer a hand?"

Balzac nodded and followed Stromburg down to the hatch leading into the bomb bay. As they ventured out onto the catwalk, they were hit by a blizzard of raw gasoline. Two of the bomb-bay doors had been blown off, and Stromburg swallowed hard as he looked down between his shoes to see nothing but five miles of empty space below. He inched along in the gale, holding on to the empty bomb racks. Balzac moved at his heels, shouting above the howling din, "Watch that first step! It's a sonuvabitch!"

Cautiously, inch by inch, they moved across the narrow catwalk, fighting the freezing gasoline that froze their skin and clawed at their eyes. Just as they neared the aft bomb bay where Daringer was working, the gasoline blizzard suddenly shut off. Only fumes remained, swirling around in the slipstream. "You did it!" shouted Stromburg into the engineer's ear.

"Finally got the sucker crimped. But no tellin' how much gas we lost."

"Check the gauges when you get a chance, and give the navigator a report."

"Right, boss."

"And Daringer, what the hell you doing out here without a chute on? One slip on that wet catwalk and—"

"Come on, skipper. There's no room for a chute out here. I had to have freedom of action."

"Okay, okay. But get your ass out of here. Both of you. And be careful!" Clutching each other tighter than they really needed to, Stromburg passed around the engineer and made his way to the hatch at the rear of the bomb bay. And then, his heart in his mouth, he climbed through the rear hatch and into the aft end of the airplane.

As his eyes adjusted to the bright light, they took in a scene of devastation. A large hole filtered in the sunlight just forward of the port gun hatch. Smaller holes in the fuselage admitted light in a random fashion, presenting the somber effect of a planetarium ceiling. Shielding his eyes from the glare, Stromburg saw ammo belts coiled around like giant snakes, the waist guns, unattended, swinging eerily on their mounts. And then, just under the gaping hole, he saw Hannigan and Waverly bending over a figure lying on the floor. Approaching them, Stromburg almost tripped over the big aerial camera lying near the men. His heart hammering, he touched Hannigan on the shoulder. As the waist gunner straightened up, he disclosed a sight that drenched Stromburg with clammy nausea.

The two men were stuffing intestines back into the open stomach of the man lying on the floor. Dazedly, mechanically, almost as if they were stuffing a turkey, the two men, stripped of their gloves, their hands bloody to the wrists, were trying to scoop the long, green, slippery sausages back into their ripped-open cavity.

Dreading to look at the face of the victim, Stromburg finally summoned the courage to slide down the oxygen mask to reveal the features that had turned the color of cigar ash. It was Sergeant Larks, the aerial photographer who had been assigned to his plane. Involuntarily, Stromburg heaved a sigh of relief while trying not to retch. At least it was not one of his crew members. He removed his gloves and put a finger on the man's neck, searching for some sign of life. There was none. "You're wasting your time, men. The man is dead."

Hannigan gave Stromburg a blank stare, then smitten by the realization, he jerked his head and passed his bloody hand across his eyes. "He was standing here taking pictures of the bomb strike," he said. "Next thing I knew he crumpled to the floor like a sack of grain. The poor sucker was disemboweled."

"There's nothing you can do, Hannigan. Get that tarp over there and cover him up. Then get back to your station."

"Yes, sir." Dazedly, Hannigan got to his feet to carry out orders.

Stromburg turned to Waverly. The ball-turret gunner was mumbling to himself as he continued to wrestle with the coiling innards. "You're gonna be okay, cameraman. Soon's I get your slippery guts put back in. You'll be as good as new."

Stromburg took the man's hands. "It's all over, Waverly. The man's gone."

Waverly slapped Stromburg's hands away. "Get away. I gotta help our cameraman. We'll put the innards back, then we'll sprinkle some sulfa on the wound." He made a cackling sound as he fingered a long piece of intestine. "Can't say our cameraman ain't got guts!"

Stromburg drew back and with his open hand slapped the gunner hard on the side of the head. Waverly snapped his head up, looked unbelievingly at Stromburg. "Pull yourself together, man!" Stromburg took Waverly by the shoulder and pulled him erect. "The photographer's gone."

Waverly drew back, staring at Stromburg as he rubbed his cheek. He looked down for a moment as Hannigan covered the corpse, then back into the face of Stromburg. Waverly clenched his jaw and swallowed, shaking his head. "I'm okay, skipper."

"Good." Stromburg patted his arm. "Now get back to your station and get your guns into commission. We're in enemy territory."

"Yes, sir. But first I have to do one thing."

"What's that?"

"Heave up my guts."

"Go ahead."

Stromburg made his way back through the debris to the tail gunner's position, checking the control cables as he went. They seemed to be tight and on their pulleys, but beyond that, Stromburg could not assess their damage. He unholstered his .45 and used its butt to rap on the clam doors that protected the tail gunner's station. Galvani's head poked out. "Hey, Lieutenant. Ain't you at the wrong end of the airplane?"

"Checking to see if you guys came to work this morning. Can't reach you on the intercom."

"It must be shot out. I've been trying to reach you."

"What's the problem?"

"It's the number six airplane in our flight, skipper. It left the formation."

"Number six? Hell, that's O'Riley."

"Yes, sir."

"Oh, shit! Any visible damage?"

"Number four engine trailed smoke. He went down in a wide spiral."

"Christ! O'Riley can't go down on his first mission as AC. No way!"

"He disappeared into the undercast. I didn't see any chutes."

"Okay, Galvani." Stromburg took a deep breath. "Look alive back here. We've taken quite a pasting, but we'll get this bucket of bolts back. Even if we have to land it a piece at a time."

"Skipper, something else happened back here. Did you know we were hit by a fighter?"

"Fighters? No. When?"

"Not fighters. A fighter. Just a few minutes ago."

"I'd better alert the gunners—"

"He's gone now. I didn't even get a shot at him." Galvani turned puzzled eyes on his pilot. "Very weird. Just one plane. Went through the formation like a dose of salts, then climbed up and did a victory roll."

"What kind of plane?"

"I never saw anything like it! It was German, all right, I saw the voided Greek cross. And it went like a bat out of hell. But what's so weird . . . it didn't have a propeller on it. I swear to God, no propeller!"

"No prop? Galvani, you been hitting the deicing fluid again?"

"As God is my witness. No propeller. How could the damn thing fly?"

Stromburg thought for a moment. "Intelligence says the Germans have been researching some kind of jet-propelled airplane. Could it be possible they have them operational?"

'I don't know. But talk about scarin' the hell out of a guy."

"Well, keep your eyes peeled. You can make a full report at debriefing."

"Yes, sir." Galvani glanced over Stromburg's shoulder at the havoc in the waist section. "These waist gunners are sure a crappy bunch of housekeepers. Look at the mess back there."

"Yes. I spoke to them about that." Galvani lived in his own little world, encapsuled like a pupa in his steel-lined cocoon at the very tail of the airplane. Stromburg was glad the photographer's body had been covered by the tarpaulin and was out of view. Then he spotted the hole in the clear plastic that surrounded the tail-gun position. He looked closely at Galvani. "You all right, Nick?"

"I'm okay, skipper. Had a round rattle around in my cage here for a while, but it finally stopped. In my leg." He pulled up the blood-soaked leg of his flying suit to disclose a small gash. "Just a scratch. Already quit bleedin'."

"I'll see that you get some sulfa."

"I'm fine." Galvani grinned. "Now I'll be able to show my grandkids where I got my Purple Heart. Hard to get excited about a peeled pecker."

"Get back to work. All we need now is to get surprised by more enemy fighters."

"Right, skipper." Galvani's head disappeared and the doors clanged shut.

Stromburg headed back toward the cockpit, stopping to check on Waverly, who was crawling back into his ball turret. "Waverly, you all right?"

"Yes, sir."

"You sure? You look pale."

"I'm okay, Lieutenant."

"Okay. Would you mind taking a pack of sulfa out of the medicine kit and taking it to Galvani? He picked up a flesh wound."

"Yes, sir."

As he turned, Stromburg noticed the little spurt of blood that squished out of the top of Waverly's left boot. "Good God, man! You've been hit!"

Waverly looked down at his boot. "I'll be go to hell!"

"You were so occupied trying to save the cameraman, you didn't notice your own wound."

Waverly felt the back of his leg, working up toward his thigh. When he reached his buttock, he let out an oath. "Damn! Feels like I picked up a frag in my butt."

"There's a hole in your suit," said Stromburg, examining.

"Thank God I picked up a hole in my butt."

Stromburg looked at him curiously. "Not sure I follow. Why are you so elated about having a hole in your bottom?"

"Don't you see? If I had to get hit, that's the place to get it. Just think if I'd have lost one of these? One of my milking fingers."

"One of your . . . milking fingers?"

"Yes, sir. I'm gonna get me a herd of cows after the war. Pop's got a ranch, and I'm gonna start a dairy."

"Good for you, Waverly."

"Can you imagine trying to milk a cow without any milking fingers?"

"I expect that would be a problem"

"Yes, sir. I'll take a hit in the ass any old time."

"Okay. But pull down your flying suit. Let Hannigan take a look at you. And stay off your feet."

"But skipper—"

"You heard me. We'll get a pressure pack on to stem the bleeding."

"Not sure I want that waist gunner nosin' around in my behind."

"I think he can be trusted. Under the circumstances."

As Waverly started stripping down his suit, Stromburg explained his plight to Hannigan. The waist gunner started rummaging through the medical kit as Stromburg headed back toward the flight deck.

"It's a slaughterhouse back there," he said to the copilot, buckling himself back into his seat.

"Any dead?" asked Ewing.

"Our cameraman bought it. Almost cut in two."

"God Almighty!"

"Waverly and Galvani picked up a few holes, but they'll make it. We almost took a direct hit in the waist. We're flying a piece of Swiss cheese."

"How about the control cables?"

"They looked okay to me. Still mushy?"

"Could be our low airspeed. You got here just in time to shut down number four engine. We're losing oil pressure fast. And we've lost the turbo supercharger on number one."

"Splendid. We'll have to drop out of formation. We can't hold the others back. Tell Collins to take over the flight lead."

"That would be a lot easier if our radios worked."

"Radios are dead?"

"Along with the intercom."

"Then signal Collins to take over flight lead."

"Roger." As Ewing gesticulated to the pilot of the plane flying formation off their starboard wing, Stromburg started the feathering procedure for the number four engine. As the huge propeller blades slowed to a stop and knifed into the slipstream, Ewing dropped out of the formation in a slow descent.

Stromburg felt a clutch in his heart as he watched the ragtag formation regrouping above him, spearheading white shafts of vapor trails that stood out in the crisp blue sky as the decimated bomber group headed home. His plane was now crippled and alone in enemy territory.

"Your navigator," said Ewing, "has figured out our range with the remaining gas we have. With luck we can just make it to the emergency field at Foggia."

"How about Switzerland?"

"With number four out, I don't think we can maintain altitude to clear the Alps."

"Okay. We'll try to make Foggia. Assessing the situation, we have our intercom and radio shot out, the oxygen system is out at several stations, number four engine is feathered. We are sitting ducks with a crew that's pretty well shot up. Other than that, I don't see any problems, Ewing. Do you?"

"Just one. Here comes an enemy fighter at two o'clock high."

"Splendid." Stromburg started to warn the gunners, then remembered the disabled intercom. Fortunately, Foulette, the nose gunner, was alert, and Dupree had crawled back up into the top turret. As the fighter closed in for the kill, Stromburg was relieved that it did have a propeller, and then the guns started to blink from the wing of the attacking Messerschmitt. He felt his rudder pedals chatter as the fighter's guns stitched holes in the vertical stabilizer. Then the bomber shuddered from the recoil of its own guns as the gunners responded with fire from the nose and top turrets. Red tracers arced into the path of the charging fighter and intercepted. And as the fighter flashed by overhead, it suddenly erupted into an orange and black fireball.

"Hot damn!" roared Stromburg, poking Ewing. "Did you see that? Our gunners actually hit an enemy airplane!"

"That's nice," said Ewing. "About time those freeloaders earned their flight pay."

A cowboy yahoo came from the top turret as Dupree leaned down. "Boss, we got one! Did you see that?"

"I saw it. Now get back to work. Look over there at eleven o'clock."

Above and to the left, barely visible as the sun glinted off their wings, sat a flight of six fighters, their formation so tight their vapor trails merged into one. Instinctively, Stromburg switched his radio to the fighter escort frequency, before remembering the dead radios. Then his heart leaped into his throat as he saw the fighters peel off in precision attack formation and head for his ship. "Well, Ewing, now we know how a sitting duck feels during hunting season. Brace yourself."

"Standing by to hit the bail-out button."

"Here they come!" yelled Dupree. And then, as the German fighters approached, a silver glint shot out of the sun toward the attacking formation . . . and then another . . . and another.

Suddenly Stromburg recognized the silhouette of the fighters that flashed overhead to intercept the attacking Messerschmitts. "God damn!" he roared. "Those are P-Forty-sevens. Our own Thunderbolts!"

"I'll be damned," said Ewing. "Never thought I'd be glad to see a fighter pilot!"

Watching their own private air show from seats on the fifty-yard line, Daringer led the crew in whooping and egging on the Thunderbolts as they broke off the enemy fighter attack and pressed their counterattack. The sky was filled with wheeling, diving, rolling fighting machines bent on annihilation. Long slashes of black smoke began to smudge the clouds as the chattering machine guns took their toll. Three of the Messerschmitts were definitely in trouble, one spiraling down to leave a great black corkscrew in the sky. Then one of the Thunderbolts picked up a round in the engine and began spewing smoke as the pilot bailed out to swing under an oscillating nylon mushroom.

Responding to Daringer's tap on his shoulder, Stromburg looked up at twelve o'clock high to see a formation of three Thunderbolts riding top cover over the stricken bomber, so close they could count the rivets in the huge, cumbersome fighter. "No question about it," mused Stromburg, "we've got to start being nicer to fighter jocks."

"Amen to that," said Ewing. "Might even buy one a drink."

Hours stretched into aeons as the limping bomber made its way over Austria and Corinthia, Lancaster directing the aircraft through the lower valleys of the Alps. The pilots nursed their precious altitude, giving it up foot by foot in deference to the three remaining engines that could not maintain level flight. As they passed into the air space above Yugoslavia, the fighter escort peeled off with a wagging of their wings, their gas tanks sucking fumes, having done their job of fighter protection over enemy territory.

Alone once again and now down to twelve-thousand feet, the bomber was navigated through the mountains of western Yugoslavia, flying at times so low through the valleys the crew members could look up to the snow and pine trees above them. As a threatening ridge loomed ahead in the distance, Stromburg ordered everything on the bomber to be jettisoned that wasn't attached. A string of machine guns, ammo cans, coffee jugs, and flak suits were thrown overboard to violate the pristine, snow-flocked Alpine countryside. Skimming the ridge with scant feet to spare, Stromburg swallowed the heart that had lodged in his throat, then exhaled a giant sigh of relief.

There in front of them were the flat stretches of the Adriatic, which would allow them to continue their descent to lower altitudes and an environment more friendly to sick engines. And now, barring any further mishap to their sorely afflicted aircraft, they just might make it to the emergency airfield at Foggia, just inland of the spur on the boot of Italy.

Chapter Nine

26 January 1945
Sunny Italy

Dear Bob:

Well, how goes it, brother? Thanks for your last letter. I think it's stupid for you to feel guilty just because you're not over here in this mess. You stay home where you belong and take care of that lovely wife of yours and those three house-apes. I don't want to hear any more about it.

Bob, if I don't make too much sense in this letter, it's because I'm kind of drained. I spent the morning writing a letter to Pat O'Riley's dad. My old copilot's been missing in action for a week now. Worst of it is, I feel responsible. It was at my urging that he finally consented to check out as aircraft commander, and now on his very first mission, he gets shot down. Last we saw of his plane it was spiraling down through the undercast with number four engine on fire. Maybe if I hadn't insisted . . .

But hell. I don't mean to dump my troubles on you, Bob. It's just that I've always been able to talk to you, and these letters seem to have a therapeutic value. Sometimes my emotions get so bottled up inside me, I swear to God I'm gonna burst. I have to keep my cool around the crew, and letting it out in my letters to you seems to help. So thanks for being my safety valve, and bear with your younger, screwed-up brother.

I'm not even going to talk about our last mission, but it was a pistol. Suffice it to say, we earned our flight pay.

But enough of this. Yes, I hear from my wife occasionally. Thelma generally sends a cool progress report on how Ann's doing. Yes, I probably should have gotten a divorce before coming overseas, but I just couldn't bring myself to do it because of little Ann. I don't mean to sound like a doomsayer, but I'm beginning to realize there's a good chance I won't be coming back. And if so, there'd have been no reason to put my little girl through the trauma of a divorce. If I do make it back, and believe me I'll bust a gut trying, then we'll be better able to face the problem when I get home. I just wish to hell this thing with Thelma had never happened.

Don't mean for this letter to sound so morbid, but guess I'm just in a crappy mood. I shouldn't be, because the Russians have crossed the old Polish corridor to trap the Germans in East Prussia; and the Reds have reached the Oder River near Breslau. So at least our Allies seem to be making progress.

Am enclosing a little note to Mom. Will you please see that she gets it—without this letter?

All the greatest, old buddy, and a big hug to all your brood.

Love,
Swede

Dearest Mom:

Just have time for a short note. How are you, sweetheart? I enjoyed your last letter, but I'm not too happy about you being put on the swing shift at Boeing. If we're that hard up for airplanes, I'll tell the guys over here to be more careful with the ones we got.

Everything is fine here. Got a nice package of

goodies from Aunt Ruth, and am glad Uncle
Erhard is doing so well. Mail from home sure
takes on a special meaning over here.

To add to your scrapbook, am enclosing a
thumbnail sketch of Sergeant Art Hannigan, our
radio operator and waist gunner. He hails from
Philadelphia, is a bright young buck of medium
build, well-muscled, nice-looking with an infectious grin that he wears most of the time. He's very
cool under pressure, and is somewhat aloof in that
he doesn't get involved in the perennial poker
game and assorted hijinks that're always going on
with the enlisted men. He reads a lot, takes a
correspondence course by mail, and is obviously
going to amount to something when he gets back
home. He handles our radios unless required to
man the waist gun in the rear, and he can send
code at some 27 words a minute. Probably one of
the sharpest RO's in the squadron. We're all very
fond of Art Hannigan.

Tell Sis that I enjoyed getting the pile of
rubber dog doodoo, and we've had a lot of fun
with it. Yesterday morning our bombardier found
it in the bottom of his oatmeal bowl.

I love you bushels, and you needn't apologize
for the peanut butter stains on my letters from
carrying them to the PO in your lunch box on the
way to work. Just keep them coming.

All my love,
Swede

Alone in his tent, Stromburg folded up the two letters,
stuck them into an envelope, addressed it, and picked up
his hat. He was just about to swing through the door when
his bombardier sailed through carrying a fistful of letters.
"Mail call," said Balzac.

"Damn!" said Stromburg. "Looks like I just missed the
mail truck."

"That you did," said Balzac, flipping the letters onto
the bunks of his roommates. "But to atone for your

misfortune, I bring you scads of mail. And a postcard from Florence."

Stromburg picked up the scenic postcard from the stack of mail and looked curiously at the picture of the ancient church on its front. "A card from Florence? Who's it from?"

"I dunno. Didn't have time to read it."

"That's a first." Stromburg turned the card over, read the scrawl in the familiar handwriting, then slowly sank down on his cot. "Why, that no-good sonuvabitch!"

"Yeeeeoowwww!" said Balzac, staring at the calender he had just opened and unrolled. "Would you look at the jugs on that!"

"That miserable bastard. I'm going to kill him!"

"Look at the knockers on that hunka ruffles." Balzac wiped his chin. "Joe's garage in East Chicago puts out the world's greatest calendars. How'd you like to find *that* in your trundle bed?"

Stromburg sat shaking his head, looking off into space. "He sends a goddamn *postcard!*"

Noting the strange look on his pilot's face, Balzac quit kissing the calendar and turned to him. "What the hell are you moaning about?"

Vacuously, Stromburg handed him the postcard. "Here. Read this."

Balzac took the postcard, read it, then his eyes bugged. "Well, I'll bego to hell. So our copilot is alive!"

"The bastard crash-landed in Florence. He's been there a whole week. A whole bloody *week!*"

"I knew you couldn't kill that Irishman. He's too well preserved in the juice of the shamrock."

"A bloody week he's been there! Staying at the American hospital in Florence. Probably diddling every nurse on the staff."

Balzac stared at his pilot. "I don't get it. The bloke's alive. Why are you so upset?"

"Upset? Me upset? I'm going to kill the bastard is what I'm going to do. While he's up there living *la dolce vita*, I've written ten letters to his crew's next of kin. Ten damned letters! And the sleep I've lost agonizing over that Irishman! And the guilt pangs I've suffered for checking him out as AC. Normal procedure when missing in action is to notify one's command by the swiftest possible means. Hell, they have phones in Florence. But does O'Riley call us and tell us he's okay? Hell, no. He sends a goddamn *postcard*! With these Italian mails, it's a wonder it ever got here."

"I think you're being picky, Swede. If I was shot down in one of the most beautiful cities in the world—"

"Up around his shoulder blades. That's where I'm going to kick his ass." Stromburg headed for the door. "Notify the crew. I'll lay on a bird. We'll go pick him up."

"You mean we're going to Florence?"

"That's right."

"Yahoo!" Balzac followed Stromburg out the door. "I suppose this means we have to return O'Riley's personal effects."

"I would say so, yes."

"This presents a small problem. Luigi sold his cowboy boots."

"Then Luigi better buy them back."

Balzac started giggling. "That crazy damn Irishman. Gotta admire a man like that."

Major Diddle did not share Balzac's admiration for O'Riley, nor did he see the humor in the situation. Diddle had also been put to a great deal of trouble in filing the necessary forms that involved missing-in-action reports, and he deeply resented O'Riley's cavalier approach to the conduct of war.

Had O'Riley possessed the foresight to end up in some cruddy POW camp for the duration, all would have been forgiven. But to crash-land in one of the garden spots of Italy and emerge unscathed, then to take a week to notify his command—by postcard—was not to be forgiven. Not to mention the fact that the American 24th General Hospital was located at Florence, a mecca notoriously loaded with American nurses and Red Cross females who not only spoke English but who also were no strangers to deodorant pads. The thought that O'Riley would undoubtedly be capitalizing on this situation prompted a speedy authoriza-

tion of Stromburg's request for an airplane to go to pick up
the errant crew member. The squadron commander sorely
felt the need to repay O'Riley's laissez-faire attitude with
large bites from the hapless pilot's posterior.

The flight to Florence was a little over two hours up
the backbone of Italy, and all the crew save the AC were in
a festive mood. The poker game in the rear of the plane
waged uninterrupted by flak, fighters, and the other usual
nuisances of aerial combat.

When they landed at the Florence airstrip and taxied
over to the operations building, they passed O'Riley's crash-
landed Liberator, which had been towed to a far corner of
the field. There it sat like some huge, molting vulture, its
number four engine a hunk of charcoal hanging from its
mounts, the tread of tires peeling from its wheels like
burned skin. It was obvious O'Riley had made a hot
landing.

In operations, Stromburg was met by a skinny lieutenant wearing the OD armband of the officer of the day, and a
blossoming crop of acne. He introduced himself in a high-
pitched nasal voice as Lieutenant Snively from the 24th
General Hospital and said he had orders to take Stromburg
to Lieutenant O'Riley.

Stromburg gathered his crew around him. He was only
mildly surprised to see that Sergeant Warner, the ubiquitous scrounge artist, was also among his enlisted crew
members. "All right, gents, let me have your attention.
We're going to remain overnight here. Leave at oh eight
hundred in the morning. Some of you might like to go into
town. This is a rare opportunity to sop up a little culture
from this famous city. Or the OD says there's billeting
available at the hospital." He turned to Lancaster. "Our
illustrious navigator and resident intellect will give you a
few words on what you can find in Florence. Bill?"

Lancaster squeezed his brows as he dredged his
memory for some data on Florence. "As I recall, Florence—or Firenze, as the natives call it—played a major
role in the Renaissance. Thanks to such characters as
Leonardo da Vinci, Michelangelo, Dante, Galileo, Machia-

velli, and a great navigator named Amerigo Vespucci, who gave his name to our own country. You can visit the Medici Palace, the Palazzo Vecchio, the Cathedral of Florence, St. Croce Church—"

"That certainly sounds good to us, Lieutenant," said Warner. "Me and the boys would sure like to go into town and sop up a little of that Eyetie culture. Right, fellas?"

There was a chorus of affirmation from the enlisted men.

"I know where you're going to sop up Italian culture," said Stromburg. "Just be damn sure you guys take a pro when you're through." Stromburg turned to his officers. "What are you troops going to do?"

"Balzac and I are going into town," said Lancaster. "I'd like to see where Michelangelo hung his hat."

"Ditto," said Balzac.

"I'll tag along with your bombardier and navigator," said Ewing, who had volunteered for this mission as copilot. "If they don't mind."

"Be our guest," said Lancaster.

"Okay," said Stromburg. "I'll go with the OD and track down O'Riley and his crew. You enlisted troops use the buddy system and remember to make it back for an oh eight hundred wheels-up. Same goes for you alleged officers. You read?"

"Gotcha, *bwana*," said Balzac, saluting with his swagger stick. "I will personally see to it that the men conduct themselves in the usual fashion that has made Crew Three Sixty-nine the envy of the entire Army Air Corps."

"You do that." Stromburg turned to the OD. "Snively, let's go." Snively led the way to his jeep, and the two men swung aboard. "Where are we going?"

Snively started up the jeep and headed out of the parking lot. "We have an officers' club up in the hills. It's a hangout for the medical officers and nurses assigned to the hospital. That's where we'll find O'Riley."

"If there's an officers' club bar, O'Riley will find it."

"This isn't exactly a club, it's the summer home of a land baron that we sort of requisitioned. Not exactly your run-of-the-mill officers' club."

And indeed it was not. The thirty-minute jeep ride terminated in a thickly wooded knoll that suffered a graveled road to corkscrew its way to the top, there to open out on a beautiful villa with magnificent, sweeping grounds.

Stromburg whistled as he took in the marbled columns and the Florentine architecture of the mansion. "So this is your officers' club. You guys got it rough."

"We try to make the best of a miserable situation," said Snively, braking to a halt in the parking lot. "These are indeed the times that try men's souls. The other day the ice machine broke down and we had to drink warm Scotch."

"The things you medics do for your country."

"We all do our bit. But I must confess I feel a bit out of place here at this body-mending station for our Fifth Army casualties."

"Why is that?"

"I'm a gynecologist."

"I see."

"Not too many battle casualties need a gynecologist. I seem to pull OD a lot."

They clambered out of the jeep. "You just hang in there, Snively."

They entered the building, and as Stromburg's pupils grappled with the dimly lit interior, he heard the voice of his copilot. Then he saw the outstretched hands materialize out of the gloom, followed by the handsome Irish face with the half smile tugging at the corners of the mouth. "Hi, Swede. How they hangin', buddy?"

"Don't 'buddy' me, you miserable ingrate," said Stromburg, taking his hand. "I hate your guts."

The half smile broadened into a grin as O'Riley pumped Stromburg's hand. "Swede! Is that any way to talk to an old friend who holds you in nothing but the highest esteem—"

"Save your Irish blarney, O'Riley. You're going to need it when you check in with our squadron commander. Diddle plans to lunch on your butt for about two weeks."

O'Riley sighed. "Fine way to treat a hero who brought back a burning airplane and saved the lives of ten crewmen. I just may not go back."

"You'll go back. With me. At oh eight hundred in the morning. Where's your crew?"

"In town. They'll be back tonight."

"They damn sure better be."

"Now that I've been properly chastised, come on over to my table. You need a beer." O'Riley looked at Snively. "You, too, OD. I'm buying."

Snively shook his head. "Can't do it. I'm on duty. Maybe later."

"You're on. Catch you later."

As Snively headed for the door, O'Riley took Stromburg by the elbow and ushered him through the gloom to a table in the far corner of the room. His eyes adjusting to the dim light, Stromburg took in the opulence of the Italian mansion. "These medics have sure got it made. You sometimes wonder if we really picked the best branch of the service."

"Wait'll you taste this beer." As they sat down, O'Riley filled two glasses from a brimming pitcher. "The Italians may be lousy lovers, but they sure know how to make a good brew."

Stromburg took a deep draft, then licked the foam from his lips. "God, that is good!"

"And wait till you taste the food here. They do things with Spam you wouldn't believe."

"I'm beginning to understand why you were tardy in notifying the squadron."

"I don't understand all the fuss. I notified my squadron."

"Yeah. You notified your squadron. By postcard. They have telephones, you know. Even in Italy. I had to write your Dad a missing-in-action report. Do you know how tough it was to think of something nice to say about you? Took days!"

"I still don't see why everyone's so pushed out of shape. Much ado about nothing."

"What frosted Diddle were all the emergency landing strips you overflew to land here. You know you're supposed to squat on the first emergency runway that'll handle your plane. Not go window-shopping and pick out the emergency field where you have the best chance of getting laid."

"I chose Florence for only one reason: for my stalwart old aircraft commander."

"For me? Hold it. You're losing me in the tight turns."

"For you. Now, pay attention. I knew if I crash-landed in Florence, it would give you an excuse to come pick me up. And it just so happens that an old friend of yours is stationed here. So even your Swedish meatball brain should be able to comprehend that by landing here, you would be able to see your old sweetheart."

Stromburg choked on his beer. "You're saying you landed here so I could see Kathy Wilson?"

O'Riley spread his hands expansively. "Why else?"

"O'Riley, you are so full of it! That idea no more crossed your mind when you were nursing that flaming wreck home—"

O'Riley held up his hand in the Boy Scout oath. "So help me, Swede. Scout's honor. You see the lengths we'll go to for our chieftain?"

"That ain't gonna hack it. No way. You bastard, you owe me."

O'Riley sighed. "Very well. For my little indiscretion, I owe you. And I'm about to pay my debt."

"A pitcher of beer ain't gonna cut it."

"Not beer, m'lad. Something far more exciting."

"You are going to do us all a favor and shoot yourself."

"No. Even better than that." He winked at Stromburg over the top of his beer. "I've arranged a little rendezvous."

"A little rendezvous?" Stromburg looked at his copilot suspiciously. "You've fixed me up before, O'Riley. Thanks but no thanks."

"You're going to like this one." O'Riley looked up as a figure loomed in the doorway. "Ah-ha! Here she comes now." O'Riley rose to greet the newcomer as Stromburg sucked on his beer. Then, as the Irishman brought his guest closer, Stromburg recognized the familiar form. His beer became confused between gullet and windpipe, and as he rose he went into a coughing spasm.

"Hello, Swede."

The hand that extended was warm and soft. Stromburg

took it and wrapped it in both of his. "My God! Kathy Wilson!" He quelled his coughing fit and wiped his nose. "Forgive me. I seem to have inhaled a pitcher of beer."

She smiled. "It's been a long time, Swede."

"A long time." As he seated her, he couldn't help but notice her supple, full figure had not changed, and even the unflattering Red Cross uniform could not hide her nice legs. She took off her cap, shook her head, and flounced her red hair. Stromburg had difficulty swallowing. "You look great, Kathy."

She smiled at him. "Thank you, Swede. War seems to agree with you. Have you lost weight?"

Stromburg nodded. "With a copilot like O'Riley here, I lose my appetite a lot."

She reached over and patted O'Riley's hand. "I like your copilot. He took me to dinner last night."

"I'll bet he did."

"Be kind to him. He went to a lot of trouble tracking me down. So you and I could have this beer together."

"Speaking of which," said O'Riley, "you need a glass, Kathy. I'll get you one." He rose and headed for the bar.

Kathy reached over and took Stromburg's hand. "You're sure a sight for sore eyes, Swede."

"So are you, Kathy. God, you look good!"

"It's just because you're used to dating sheep. Your copilot told me all about it."

"The blabbermouth."

"He's very fond of you."

"The bastard just put me through a wringer. I'm going to castrate him."

"Make it later. Right now I want to talk. And just look at you. I've been homesick lately. Seeing someone from home is doing wonders for my morale."

O'Riley returned with a glass, filled it from the pitcher, and handed it to Kathy. "I hope you two will be able to struggle along without me for a spell. There's a nifty little nurse at the bar that's panting for my muscular body."

"We'll try to muck through," said Stromburg, "in your absence."

Kathy smiled as the lanky pilot headed for the bar. "There's something about Irishmen."

"You're right. That's why I'm going to kill this one. After a very long, slow torture." He looked into her eyes. "I knew you were stationed here. We ran into an old friend of yours in Foggia. Frances Adams. She told us."

"I know. She wrote me all about it. She's a sweetheart."

"Yes. My navigator's been seeing her occasionally."

"So she said."

"You know, I wrote you several times."

She looked surprised. "Oh? I never got your letters."

"I didn't mail them."

"I see. Correspondence was never your long suit."

"Mainly because I didn't know what to say, how to say it, or even if you'd want to hear it if I said it."

"That's dumb, Swede Stromburg. Just because you jilted me and ran off to marry some rodeo queen doesn't mean we can't be good friends."

"I jilted *you!* You were the one who told me to get lost."

"It's because you never wrote to me in college."

"I *did* write to you in college."

"Maybe twice."

"I saw the pictures of you and that college quarterback at Washington State. You weren't exactly pining for my letters."

"Larry was just a good friend."

"So was Thelma."

"But you didn't have to marry her."

"I just wanted to teach you a damn good lesson."

"You did that." She took a long pull from her glass. Then she sat it down, toying with it, making little ringlets on the table. "I'm sorry, Swede. I didn't mean to lip off." She squeezed his hand. "No way to treat an old friend."

"My fault. I seem to have a penchant for flogging dead horses."

She touched her glass to his. "Let's make a toast. No more dead-horse flogging. Let's you and I just roll in nostalgia and speak of the good times."

"Very well. To the good times."

"But first, tell me about your job. O'Riley tells me you're the best pilot in the outfit."

"O'Riley's full of it. I'm a very mediocre pilot who runs around scared shitless most of the time."

"Why, Swede!" She grinned at him. "First time I've ever heard you use that kind of language."

"Sorry, Kathy. Just slipped out. Comes from consorting with too much all-male companionship. And Irishmen."

She laughed. "War does funny things."

"It does at that. I'd have cut my tongue out before using that word around you when we were in school." He smiled at her. "Won't happen again. I'm not used to being in the presence of a lady. I'll watch my tongue."

"Don't worry about it. I've received quite an education here in the hospital. I didn't know there were so many quaint expressions."

"The GI's come up with some winners. What do you do at the hospital?"

"Well, mainly we're in charge of morale. We do what we can for those poor kids—and believe me, most of them are kids—who've been wounded in the front lines. The Fifth Army has taken a lot of casualties."

"I know."

"We administer to their physical and spiritual needs as best we can. We write letters home for those who can't write, see that they get their mail, try to keep them from being either scared or bored to death. Sometimes I think if I ever see another Bingo bean I'll go stark, raving mad."

"It's a thankless job."

"Not really. We have some terrible casualty cases. Soldiers with their arms, legs blown off. If I can help get these kids over a tough hurdle, I feel I've been thanked in a very special way. Last night I spent most of the evening just holding a young man's hand. He'd just had both legs amputated at the hip."

"God! So you do like your job?"

"I didn't say that. I hate my job. Next week I'm being assigned to the burn ward. Swede, you have no idea of the suffering of a horribly burned victim. And just the stench of the ward alone—" She broke off, shuddering.

He squeezed her hand. "I can imagine."

She looked up at him. "I'm sorry. Enough of this kind of talk."

"Yes. Let's talk no more of the war."

"I want to hear all about you. How's your wife?"

"She's fine. Last I heard."

"Good. I understand you have a little girl."

"Yes. Ann. She's the light of my life."

"How old is she?"

"She's going on four."

"I'll bet she's pretty."

"She's turned a few heads in her day."

"May I see her picture?"

"Afraid I don't carry one."

"What? A proud father with no pictures of his daughter?"

"We're discouraged from carrying personal pictures in our wallets. Interrogators in POW camps have been known to capitalize on them."

"Oh. I'd never have thought of that."

"Just another interesting sidebar to our little scrimmage. Now tell me about you, Kathy. Start with the men in your life."

She took a sip of her beer. "There was one white knight in my life. He ran off and married someone else. Since then there haven't been many men."

"Oh, come on! You're an absolute knockout, Kathy Wilson. And you're built like a brick . . . like a tiled latrine. Don't tell me you haven't had your pick of slavering males."

She smiled at him. "You sure you're not suffering from combat fatigue, young man?"

"I'm positive."

"Well then, thank you, sir, for the kind words. Don't get me wrong. I'm not bitter. I've had a couple of infatuations, several crushes—even one lukewarm romance. But no loop-the-loops."

He looked at her intently as he poured a head on their beers. "No loop-the-loops?"

"You know. No cymbal-crashers. No gong-bongers. No loop-the-loops."

"I see. I'm sorry, Kathy. I really am."

"Don't be. I'm quite content. And I believe in the old adage, if you don't play with fire you won't get burned."

"But in your job over here you meet a million guys—"

"I have found out that a hospital in a war zone is the last place in the world to look for a lasting relationship. Everyone wants a one-night stand. That's not for me. I've spent too much time working in the VD ward."

"That would be enough to make one take vows of celibacy."

"And I have one other rule: I don't date married men."

"Does that include an old friend who just happens to be married? Who'd like to take you out on the town tonight?"

"For an old, *old* friend, I might make an exception."

"That's my girl."

"But I can't do it tonight."

He stared at her. "What do you mean, you can't do it tonight? I have to leave in the morning."

"Sorry, Swede. But I have a date."

"A date?"

"Yes, a date. Single women have been known to go out on a date."

"Well, break it, for God's sake."

She lifted her brows. "Break it? You know better than that."

"Look. We haven't seen each other for years. We have just this one night. Who are you dating, the hospital commander?"

"No. I have a date with a very nice corporal. He's a hospital patient."

"A corporal?"

"Yes. I often date enlisted men. I find some officers can be a monumental pain in the butt."

"Couldn't you tell the corporal you'll go dancing with him tomorrow night?"

"We're not going dancing. At least until his stump heals. He has tickets to the opera."

"The opera!"

"Yes. The Italians do not let a little thing like a war preempt *Pagliacci*."

"My God!"

"I'm sorry, Swede. Honestly."

"Hell of a way to treat a war veteran. That's all I've got to say."

She patted his hand. "You'll survive." She looked deep into his eyes. "Swede, will you answer a question honestly?"

"I might."

"If your copilot hadn't arranged this little meeting, would you have looked me up?"

He swirled the beer in his glass, watching it with deep concentration. "Yes." He reached for his wallet, pulled out a piece of paper, and handed it to her. "I had the OD get me the number of your Red Cross office. See?"

She glanced at the paper, then up into his face. "I'm glad."

"For all the good it's going to do. You're busy tonight, and I'm leaving in the morning."

She looked at her watch. "And speaking of which, I must be going. There's a shuttle bus in five minutes."

"To hell with the bus, Kathy. This is ridiculous. Seeing you for just these few minutes is worse than not seeing you at all. If we hadn't met I could go back convincing myself that you'd grown fat, smelled like a hospital, and had turned into a lesbian. But here you are. Looking like a Varga painting. So damned desirable I could eat you alive. And now you're leaving. It's not fair."

She smiled at him. "You're a terrible liar, Lieutenant Stromburg. But you do wonders for a lady's morale." She put on her cap and tucked in her red hair. "Now I really must go."

As she stood, Stromburg rose with her. He reached for her awkwardly. "Suppose just a small kiss between old friends would be permissible?"

"I see nothing wrong with old friends showing a little affection."

He moved to her, took her in his arms, and pressed his lips to hers. What was to have been a peck suddenly turned into a passionate embrace as her arms stole around his neck and pulled him to her. And then with a gasp she pushed him away. "That was hardly an old-friend kiss, Swede Stromburg!"

"Nope," he said, grinning. "But wasn't it great?"

"It was not. Married men should not go around kissing women like that."

"I stand corrected."

"You took advantage. You're a cad."

"I guess I am."

She picked up her bag. "I'm really sorry I have to go. I would love to spend the evening reminiscing."

"Me, too, Kathy."

She looked at him a moment, a mist scudding across her green eyes. "It was good seeing you, Swede."

"It was great seeing you, Kathy." She turned and headed for the door. He yelled after her, "I want to see you again!"

She turned. "I have some leave coming. I'm going to Rome next month. Perhaps—"

"I'm due for R&R. I'll meet you."

"I'll drop you a line." And then she was out of the door.

As the door shut behind her, O'Riley came back to the table, bearing a fresh pitcher of beer. He studied the odd look on Stromburg's face for a beat before saying, "You sure as hell have a way with women. You're alone with Kathy for all of fifteen minutes before you send her flying out the door."

"She had a date, wise-ass." Stromburg snapped out of his reverie and looked over at his copilot pouring a head on their beers. "And, Romeo, you want to tell me about the chick at the bar who was supposedly panting for your body?"

"I made the mistake of getting her under the light." He shuddered. "Can't stand a woman with a handlebar moustache."

"I see."

"But there's no moss on that redhead of yours. Kathy's one gorgeous female."

"She's not my redhead. But you're right. No moss on Kathy Wilson."

O'Riley raised his glass to Stromburg's. "Got a hell of a good idea, Swede."

"Yeah?"

"Let's you and I suck some suds, get banjo-eyed, pissy-assed, stand-up-fall-down, throw-up drunk. And have ourselves one hell of a party."

Stromburg clinked his glass with O'Riley's, knocked back his beer, and shoved the empty glass back at his copilot. "O'Riley, that's the best idea you've ever had."

It was a sad, motley group that gathered in the rear of the airplane the next morning as Stromburg, with no little difficulty, conducted a head count. Although several crewmen were stacked up like cordwood in the aft section, all members of both his and O'Riley's crew seemed to be present and accounted for. Even Sergeant Warner was among those present, if not among the conscious, as he lolled against the bulkhead with a beatific smile on his comatose face, and a porcelain commode nestled tenderly in his arms. Inside the toilet were two bottles of wine embedded in ice, an obvious gift to the aircraft commander who had made the drunken soiree possible. Stromburg was delighted to see that Warner had come through with his request, chilled wine or no. He gave a brief thought as to where and how Warner had come into possession of a nearly new toilet in war-savaged Italy, but his beer-soaked brain was in no condition to wrestle with such weighty matters. So he speedily dismissed it, preferring not to know, anyhow.

One other bit of strange cargo, in addition to the snoring corpses and the porcelain ice bucket, was brought aboard by O'Riley. It was undoubtedly the largest German shepherd puppy in captivity—at least one hundred pounds of paws, tail, tongue, and drool. Although Stromburg was not at all keen about taking the beast aboard, his defenses were quickly knocked down by O'Riley's entreaties that he had won him in a poker game and that the crew desperately needed a mascot. So Stromburg found himself grudgingly acquiescing as the hound slurped his face with a tongue the size of a Ping-Pong paddle.

Stromburg buckled into his seat, losing no time in attaching himself to his oxygen mask and turning on emergency oxygen. He looked over at Ewing. "This is one time we don't have to worry about running out of gas."

"You got that right," said Ewing, energizing the starter on number three engine. "There's enough high-test fumes in the rear end to run these engines for a month."

Chapter Ten

3 February 1945
Chilly Italy

Dearest Mom:

How are you, sweetheart? I received several letters at once from my family yesterday, and it's always so great to hear from you.

I have a little surprise. You remember Kathy Wilson, I'm sure. You always liked her so much. Well, would you believe I saw her for a few minutes last week? She's in the Red Cross, working at an Army hospital in Florence, Italy. She looks absolutely fantastic. In fact, I wouldn't be surprised if some of our soldiers in the Fifth Army didn't become casualties just so they could be taken care of by the beautiful redhead. At any rate, she said to send you and the family her love.

It was my first visit to Florence, and it's a beautiful city. I was surprised to find they still have opera there. The Italians may not have enough to eat, and they do a lot of shivering these cold days, but the Italian opera stars still sing like they're the happiest people in the world. And you know, sometimes I think they are.

Everything is going just fine here. I have Pat O'Riley, my old copilot, back with me. He and our squadron commander had a little misunderstanding, so instead of Pat having his own crew, he will continue flying with me. For some reason I don't understand, this seems to make him very happy. He says he didn't like the responsibilities of a bomber commander.

We have a new addition to the crew, a gargantuan German shepherd puppy that O'Riley brought back from Florence. I have to admit it's an ingratiating beast—if we ever get it toilet-trained—it's all ears, tail, and paws the size of snowshoes. Pat named him DFC (short for Dog Food Converter), and he's having the lads in personal equipment make an oxygen mask for him so he can go along on missions. I wish I could get more excited about this, but Pat had him up in the cockpit on our short flight from Florence, and the dog became so overjoyed, his wagging tail and busy tongue lowered the landing gear, extended full flaps, and feathered one engine. The last straw was when he wet in the navigator's coffee cup. He was finally ousted to the tail section, where he managed to fire off a dozen rounds before the gunners could subdue him.

But the crew has taken a shine to the monster, and if DFC contributes to the morale of the troops, then it looks like I'm stuck. Between the cussed dog and Luigi, our unclaimed orphan, we seem to be taking on a lot of mouths to feed.

Mom, as usual, I'll give you another thumb-nail sketch of one of our crewmen. Herb Dupree is our top-turret gunner, and sort of assistant engineer to Dick Daringer. He hails from Walton, New York, and comes from good farm stock. He's strong as an ox, rather rough-hewn, uses language that would make a marine blush, and is the man in the crew I'd least like to have a fight with. But he's a good man, knows his equipment, and takes his job very seriously. He's also the best aerial gunner we have on the crew. In short, I'm very glad Herb Dupree's on our side.

Well, according to *Stars and Stripes*, President Roosevelt, Churchill, and Stalin met at Yalta

yesterday. I'm sure they met to discuss the final
stages of the war and, I hope, negotiate for a fair
armistice. It looks like the tides of battle are
definitely flowing in our favor at long last, and
before you know it we'll all be coming home.
Needless to say, I'm counting the days.

    Hugs to you, sweetheart, and love to all the
family.

Your Swede

P.S.: I didn't know the movie theaters were selling
war bonds, but I think it's great that you buy one
whenever you go to the movies. Our features over
here are a little sporadic, but if *National Velvet*
with Mickey Rooney and Elizabeth Taylor shows
up, I'll be sure to catch it. Glad you enjoyed it. I
agree, Elizabeth Taylor is a pretty little toad.

Stromburg dropped the letter into the mailroom slot
on his way to see the squadron commander. As he headed
for the ops building, he made a mental search of possible
reasons why Major Diddle had summoned him.

As far as he knew, Balzac had stayed out of trouble for
nearly a week, unless they had found the wine vat Balzac
and O'Riley were brewing raisins in behind the mess hall.
This was doubtful, as Mess Sergeant Schultz's domain was
seldom inspected. It was the IG's theory that the less
people knew about what went into the mess-hall food, the
happier they'd be, so generally the inspectors avoided
Schultz's environs like the plague.

The summons shouldn't be about O'Riley, as Diddle
had already wreaked his vengeance on the hapless copilot,
banishing him forever to the right seat. This was hardly the
chastisement Diddle envisioned, for unbeknownst to him,
O'Riley could not have been more pleased.

Of course, it could be concerning any of his enlisted
crewmen. Daringer, Dupree . . . most likely Galvani, for
the tail gunner had not bowed to Diddle's counseling and
was determined to have the lovely Marguerita Galvani as
his bride. Perhaps the squadron commander had gotten
wind of the impending wedding. . . .

Stromburg's knock on the door was answered by a muffled, "Come in."

Stromburg entered, closed the door behind him, and saluted. "Second Lieutenant Stromburg reporting as ordered, sir."

"At ease, Stromburg."

"Thank you, sir." Stromburg relaxed and looked around. He was surprised to see a civilian sitting in front of Diddle's desk. The man turned to survey him critically.

"Lieutenant Stromburg," said Diddle, "shake hands with Group Captain Witherspoon. From British Intelligence."

Stromburg shook the proffered hand, his mind groping. "Glad to meet you, sir."

"Group Captain Witherspoon has a few questions to ask you, Stromburg." Diddle nodded at the plainclothes officer. "Shoot, Group Captain."

"Very well, Major Diddle." The British officer half turned in his chair to face Stromburg. He was a beefy, slouch-shouldered man who sat on the edge of his chair as though he might be suffering from hemorrhoids. His words were strained through a soggy cigar butt. "I understand you're one of the squadron's up-and-coming aircraft commanders, Lieutenant Stromburg."

"I'm not so sure of that, sir." Stromburg shot an embarrassed look at Diddle, who was eyeing him coldly. "But I am an aircraft commander."

"You have nearly a dozen missions under your belt. During that time you have witnessed several aircraft in your formation blow up shortly after takeoff. Is that not true?"

"Yes, sir."

"Have you any theories as to just why this might have happened?"

Stromburg thought for a moment. "No, sir. Not really. A bomber is a very complex machine. It carries thousands of gallons of highly flammable gasoline. Hydraulic fluid. Bombs. Its electrical system contains hundreds of miles of wires, any of which can create a spark. I don't think our pilots are too surprised when one of our bombers explodes."

"Hmmm." The Intelligence officer leaned back, stroking his upper lip with his index finger. "All of the ingredients for an explosion are there, Lieutenant, to be sure. But we have been doing considerable research on the matter. The Four Fifty-first Bombardment Group has a very high incidence of midair explosions, especially over friendly territory. Much higher, in fact, than any of the other groups in the Fifteenth Air Force."

"Oh? I didn't know that."

"It's true."

Stromburg glanced uncomfortably at his squadron commander. "Are you saying it's pilot error?"

"No. Your flying crews stack up with the best in the Fifteenth."

"Then you must be blaming it on maintenance. Sir, there are no better maintenance men in the whole damned—"

Witherspoon stopped him with a wave of his cigar. "It's not your maintenance, Lieutenant. Don't get your bowels in an uproar."

Stromburg shrugged. "Then, sir, what the hell can it be?"

Witherspoon lowered his head and looked up at Stromburg from under scraggly brows. "We have reason to believe it's sabotage."

Stromburg could only stare at the Intelligence officer, his mouth fumbling for words. "Sabotage? Did you say . . . *sabotage?*"

"Evidence points strongly to that fact. An analysis of the explosions shows that most of them occurred shortly after takeoff, at an altitude of around five thousand feet. The explosions were usually in a lead or deputy-lead ship. Created to cause as much havoc as possible."

Stromburg wagged his head. "But sir—"

"A definite pattern has emerged. It rules out mere coincidence. Now, this is to be regarded as Top Secret. But we have reason to believe there is a saboteur or saboteurs operating on this base."

Stromburg looked numbly at his squadron commander. "So the scuttlebutt is true. I find this hard to believe."

Witherspoon removed the dead butt from his lips and shook it at Stromburg. "You'd better believe it, Lieutenant. Your life is at stake."

"But how could saboteurs blow up a plane in midair?"

"Thermal bombs." Witherspoon replaced his cigar. "An ingenious device that can be set to explode at a given altitude—say, five thousand feet. When the airplane reaches that preselected altitude, a barometric fuse triggers the bomb. Very simple. Very effective."

Stromburg was stunned. "But how do the bombs get on board? Who in hell would do such a thing?"

"It could be anybody. The bombs aren't much larger than a Thermos bottle. There are lots of people milling around a bomber getting it ready for a mission. Maintenance men, fuel attendants, armament personnel—anybody could plant a thermal bomb anywhere on the aircraft when no one was looking. Hell, our saboteur could even be an aircrew member."

Stromburg stared at the portly Britisher. "Now, hold it, Group Captain. No crew member is going to plant a bomb on his own ship."

"Probably not. But how about a crew member from another crew? No one is above suspicion."

"Speaking of crew members," said Diddle, "you have to admit, Stromburg, your crew has more than its share of quirky characters."

Stromburg pulled himself up straight. "Just a minute, sir. You know my crewmen are as efficient and dedicated as anyone on this—"

"Okay, okay, Stromburg." Diddle held up his hands. "Simmer down. No one is pointing fingers at your crew. But you have to admit they're . . . different."

"Different, perhaps. And maybe even a little quirky. But they sure as hell aren't saboteurs."

"I very much doubt if they are," said Witherspoon, removing his cigar long enough to mop his face with a red bandana. "But we're convinced we have a problem. Major

Diddle and I are meeting with you pilots who are flying lead ships. On an individual basis, for security reasons. You will not even tell your crew members. But we want you to keep your eyes and ears open."

"During your visual preflight before takeoff," added Diddle, "take an extra twenty minutes and thoroughly examine your plane. Especially the nosewheel area. It would be easy to toss an explosive device into that section, which is pretty well hidden from view."

"Very well, sir."

"And remember, Lieutenant," said Witherspoon, "this is classified Top Secret. We not only want to apprehend the saboteur, but his connections as well."

"Yes, sir."

"That'll be all, Stromburg," said Diddle.

"Yes, sir." Stromburg saluted, did an about-face, and went out the door, his mind reeling.

Esterina Galvani Tognoli giggled. She and Stromburg were up to their necks in soap bubbles as they languished in the warm bath water. They were facing each other in the tub of the bathroom just off the master suite of the Galvani home. "I thought all airplane pilots had to have superb coordination and the eyes of an eagle," she said, groping for Stromburg's hands.

"True," said Stromburg, continuing his search in the soapy water.

"Then why are you always losing the soap?" She giggled again as his hands brushed her anatomy, which reposed under the billowing suds. "That is definitely *not* the soap."

"Whatever it is, it's great. To hell with the soap."

Laughing, she turned around with her back to him and leaned against his chest. "I have never taken a bath with a man before."

"Not even your husband?"

"No. Domenico would never do such a thing."

"Poor Domenico's loss. Come to think of it, this is my first dunk with a beautiful woman. Or an ugly woman, for that matter."

She scooped up a mound of bubbles and blew them

into the air. "A bubble bath. I never thought I would see another bubble bath. Where did you ever find the crystals, love?"

"I'd rather not know. I just put the request through our local scrounge artist."

"Scrounge artist? I am not familiar with that term."

"Every military unit, no matter how small, always has two things: a resident scrounge artist and a guardhouse lawyer. A guardhouse lawyer knows just enough law to get everyone into a lot of trouble. A scrounge artist is endowed with the ability to find just about anything anyone would want—for a price. Scrounge artists are born, not made."

"That is all very interesting. But if you do not quit searching for the soap, I may be forced to attack you at any moment."

"Seek and ye shall find. I'm still seeking."

"Oh, *Dio mio!*"

"We are blessed with two scrounge artists in our outfit: our bombardier and an armaments NCO. Sergeant Warner is the true professional. He has sort of adopted our crew, and we take him with us on short flights from time to time. Maybe he got the bath salts out of the goodness of his heart."

"Then will you kindly tell him how very much I have enjoyed them? How we used to take such luxuries for granted!"

"I will relay your message."

She clasped his knees and hugged them close to her body. "This is heavenly, *carissimo*. I never want it to end."

"Even if I find the soap?"

"I never want you to find the soap. But please keep searching."

He leaned back, resting his head on the end of the ornate, old-fashioned bathtub with its tiger-clawed feet, and closed his eyes. He idly stroked her smooth, slippery breasts. "I cannot tell you how much you mean to me, Esterina. You have a knack of placing the war a billion light-years away."

She kissed his knees. "And you, my darling, have made the war much more bearable for all of us."

"Your husband is one very lucky man."

"We will not speak of my husband. We will speak only of the two of us. And I think I have found the soap."

Stromburg's eyes snapped open. "I can tell you positively, without a shadow of doubt, that is definitely *not* the soap."

"It sort of feels like the soap."

"It may feel like the soap, but trust me. It is not the soap."

"Very well, it is not the soap."

"On second thought, it could be the soap."

"Yes, it could be the soap." She turned over, and facing him, gave him a long, lingering kiss. "And I just happen to know where there is a soap dish."

The thirteenth mission had turned out to be another glove-steamer.

It was supposed to have been fairly routine—bombing the Korneuburg Oil Refinery in Austria. Intelligence had briefed on only 113 anti-aircraft guns, a fraction of the defense that ringed a fearsome target such as Vienna, and thanks to the round-the-clock bombing of the Allies, the petroleum reserves were virtually dried up, leaving the Luftwaffe all but grounded.

Stromburg had affected an unusually cheerful mien as he conducted his preflight walk-around, trying to look nonchalant as he surreptitiously searched for anything that might resemble a thermal bomb. His crew may have wondered about the unusually diligent inspection, and had they known he was looking for a device that might blow them all to kingdom come, they undoubtedly would have joined in the search. But Stromburg honored the Top Secret classification, and the crew members were not told, so they merely watched in ignorance and became infected with their first pilot's jocular mood. Only Balzac, who was heeding the advice of the squadron's late lead bombardier and who was guessing that the aircraft commander knew more than he was telling, tacitly joined in the preflight search for anything that might look like a detonating device.

In fact, during the first part of the mission it would

have been difficult to convince a casual observer that these
ten cheerful men were winging their way to a rendezvous
where they would be met by a group of very professional
gunners who would be squinting into their highly cali-
brated gunsights for the sole purpose of boring large holes
in their airplane. Evidently the saboteur had taken the day
off, and Stromburg was vastly relieved that no airplanes
exploded in midair as they circled into formation, forming
the foreboding aluminum cloud that would float over the
hinterland to rain its terrible death and destruction.

Over the target, however, things changed dramatically.
The milk run quickly curdled. The guns may have been few
in number, but they were obviously manned by the cream
of Hitler's sharpshooters, for they raised deadly havoc with
the bomb group. Five airplanes were lost on the bomb run;
another two were picked off on the rally after bombs away.
The sky was filled with smoking aluminum and the nylon
blossoms of bailed-out crew members, a stiff price to pay for
the huge black cloud of burning oil that was rising to meet
the straggling formation.

Stromburg had been flying deputy lead for the squadron, and he was just preparing to get back into his slot
following the bombs-away peeloff when the plane shuddered. He felt as well as saw the flak burst they had flown
right into. And then O'Riley stabbed his gloved finger at
the number three engine gauges. "Oh, Geezus!"

Stromburg saw the number three tachometer needle
swing clear around to bounce on its peg, and recognized
the problem immediately. "Runaway prop on number three
engine. Get on the rudder with me, Pat." The two pilots
jammed in the left rudder full travel as the plane veered
sharply to the starboard. "Notify the group we're dropping
out of formation." As O'Riley made the radio call, Stromburg cranked in full left aileron, trying to keep the bomber
from heeling over into a sickening flat spin.

Of all the maladies that can befall an airplane in flight,
few are more dreaded than a runaway propeller. The
constant-speed prop is an engineering marvel when its
governor and component parts are functioning properly. Its
precision gearing, however, is no match for an exploding

155mm shell. Its governor gone, its controls shot out, the propeller was now running wild in flat pitch, creating a drag as effective as if the number three engine mount now bore a barn door. "Won't feather!" yelled O'Riley. "Prop and throttle controls are shot out!"

"Then pull the oil shutoff valve," managed Stromburg, straining with the exertion. "Nothing left to do but freeze it."

"You got it. Oil shutoff valve closed."

"Give me a hand on the aileron. We're losing directional control." O'Riley put his muscle into the controls, backing up the pilot. The ship shuddered, determined to start a slow spiral to the right in spite of the efforts of both men.

"What the hell's going on?" Balzac stuck his head into the cockpit. "You guys got nothing better to do than fly around in circles? We got a problem."

Stromburg glanced at his bombardier. "Heaven forbid we should have a problem."

"We got a bomb bay full of bombs."

"We *what?*"

"I repeat. We got a bomb bay full of bombs. The intervalometer screwed up. I triggered on the lead ship, but our bombs didn't release."

"Oh, great!"

Balzac fanned the steam with his hands. "You guys running a steam bath up here?"

"Balzac, get on the intercom. Tell the crew to prepare to bail out. But don't abandon ship till the alarm bell rings."

"*What?*"

"You heard me. We got a runaway prop. Can't maintain directional control. If that prop doesn't seize damn fast, we'll have to abandon ship. Now, get with it."

"Yes, sir." Balzac's head disappeared from the cockpit, only to reappear seconds later. "Scrub bailout plans, Swede. Lancaster's been hit."

"Oh, Christ!" Stromburg shoved the nose forward as the shuddering aircraft threatened to stall. "How bad?"

"I think it's just a flesh wound. In the upper arm. But he's bleeding like a stuck hog."

"Get a pressure bandage on him. Do what you can."

"We can't bail out and leave Lancaster."

"We're not going to leave Lancaster. Get him into his chute. Prepare everybody for bailout."

"But Swede, ain't no way I'm takin' that nylon escalator—"

"Goddamn it, *move!*"

"Okay, okay!" As Balzac left the cockpit to follow orders, the ship's spiral began to tighten. Stromburg shot a worried look at his copilot. "Why doesn't that bastardly prop seize? With no lubrication it can't overspeed forever!"

"It's taking its time." O'Riley flinched as a flak burst jolted the airplane. "We're a clay pigeon circling here over the target area. I suggest we do something. Even if it's wrong."

"We *have* to do something. This spiral gets any tighter, centrifugal force will pin the crew to their seats. Then they won't be able to bail out."

"Controls are cranked to their limits. She's not holding."

"Okay, Pat. Get ready to evacuate. I'll hold this beast steady while everyone bails out. Go back and help Balzac get a chute on Lancaster. It's time to leave this bucket."

"Balzac can take care of our navigator. I'm staying here with you. It'll take two of us to hold this dude."

"I can handle it, O'Riley. Get your chute on."

"No way."

"Goddamn it, O'Riley! For just once, obey an order! Open the bomb-bay doors and get ready to bail out." Stromburg reached up for the red alarm bell. He lifted its cover and was just about to toggle the switch when O'Riley let out a yelp.

"Hold it, Swede! Look!" Stromburg followed his copilot's pointing finger. "That prop's slowing down!"

As Stromburg watched, the three blades of the propeller suddenly became distinguishable out of the blur that had been the runaway prop. There was a loud, grinding noise; then smoke issued from the propeller dome as the gears and ball bearings, no longer made cool and frictionless by oil's lubrication, seized in a molten red glob of metal. Then the propeller stopped dead in its orbit, liquid metal and smoke streaming from its shaft. "Hot damn!" roared Stromburg. "Now, if the engine doesn't catch fire, we might be able to control this mustang. Pull the fire extinguisher on number three engine."

"Roger. Fire extinguisher activated on number three engine." O'Riley discharged the bottle that flooded the smoldering engine with carbon dioxide. The wallowing aircraft, now not commanded by the gyroscopic stresses and drag of the runaway propeller, slowly heeled back over to a semblance of straight and level flight. The white cloud of fire retardant gushed from the engine, cooling the engine shaft that had threatened combustion. "We lucked out," said O'Riley, monitoring the smoking engine. "The prop didn't disintegrate. Having a prop blade slice through the cockpit can spoil your whole day."

"Yeah," said Stromburg, retrimming the airplane. "But I don't know how much more of this good luck I can stand."

O'Riley released his grip on the controls. "Can you handle it now, Swede?"

"I got it." Stromburg fire-walled the remaining three throttles as another flak burst bounced the airplane. "We've been fish in this rain barrel long enough. Let's haul ass."

"Amen to that."

"Tell the crew to stand down on the bailout alert. Then get a battle damage report."

"Aye, aye, coach."

Stromburg half turned to check on the navigator. Balzac was hovering over him, applying sulfa to the wound. "Balzac."

The little bombardier stuck his head into the cockpit as he unrolled a length of surgical gauze. "Can't you see I'm in surgery? Just fly your damn airplane. Preferably in a straight line."

"How's Lancaster?"

"Bloody but unbowed. I got the bleeding stopped."

"Good man. When you get him patched up, tell him I need a heading for a target of opportunity on the way home. We'll try to get rid of these bombs."

"Roger. He's not in very good shape. His maps and charts are all bloody. But we'll come up with something."

"Okay. We now have directional control and we're almost holding altitude. I've canceled the bailout alert for the time being."

"There goes my chance to join the Caterpillar Club."

"You may get your chance. We're a hell of a long way from home, on three engines. We'll try to get as far as Yugoslavia at least."

"I'm right behind you, *bwana*."

"When you get through with Lancaster, check out your intervalometer. We have to get rid of those damn bombs."

"Yessuh, massah. Now, do you mind if I get back to my operating room?"

"Be my guest."

Minutes rolled into months as the stricken craft plowed through the freezing skies over Austria. Lancaster had proved to be the only casualty, and the plane was now controllable. But even with full power the three laboring engines could not quite hold altitude with the bombs still hanging in their shackles. A few hundred feet per minute had to be sacrificed to keep the struggling bomber several knots above stall speed.

O'Riley's frequent entreaties to drop the bombs over the Austrian landscape just served to make Stromburg more resolute in his convictions. "Damn it, Pat, we didn't get up at the crack of dawn to come all the way over here, risking the lives and limbs of ten good men, to help some Kraut plow up his cabbage patch. We're going to drop those bombs where they'll do some good."

"You buckin' for some kind of medal?"

"You know better than that."

"Well, your motives are laudable, but I'd be more supportive if we weren't losing altitude. I say let's jettison the damn things so we can make it home and live to fight another day."

"The boys have come up with a target of opportunity. It's right on the way home. All we have to do is maintain this heading and we're on the bomb run for marshaling yards in Radkersburg."

"All right, you bullheaded Swede. But we'll be coming in so damn low we'll have to look up to see the target."

"We'll make a good run. Trust me."

"We damn sure better. You know how upset my dog gets if I'm not home to feed him."

Balzac reappeared in the cockpit. "I'm going down to my station, Swede, and fire up the bombsight. The intervalometer's all shot up. We'll have to bypass it. With Daringer's help we'll salvo manually."

"Okay."

"The PPI is out, too. So I'll talk you through the bomb run."

"Roger." Stromburg switched to intercom. "Pilot to crew. We're starting on the bomb run. We don't expect much opposition, but don flak suits and start dispensing chaff." As the crew acknowledged, Stromburg turned to his copilot. "Okay, Patrick. We're about to drop our bombs. I'll fly the airplane, you monitor the engine instruments."

"Righto."

As the bombardier tracked the marshaling yards in his bombsight and set up for the rate and distance, he called the heading corrections off to Stromburg. Closer and closer they came to the bomb-release point as the steam rose in the cockpit. Stromburg steeled himself for the flak bursts that soon would be peppering them. O'Riley placed his flak helmet over his crotch.

"That's it!" yelled Balzac into the intercom. "Salvo the bombs!"

"Bombs away!" echoed Daringer, manually tripping the bomb releases in the bomb bay. The aircraft seemed to grunt with relief, as though a huge enema had just taken effect. Three tons of explosives dribbled toward their mark. Stromburg lowered the bomber's nose and watched with relief as the airspeed began to build up.

"Now, that's more like it," observed O'Riley. "We're actually maintaining altitude."

"I don't get it," said Stromburg, looking around. "No flak. Every marshaling yard in Austria has at least a dozen flak guns."

"We caught 'em with their hands in the sauerkraut jar."

Stromburg shook his head. "I don't understand it."

"All bombs away!" came Balzac's voice over the intercom. "Airplane's yours, Swede. I think we really clobbered that roundhouse."

Stromburg racked over in a tight bank of evasive action. Bombing from a lower altitude than usual, it was easy to see the bomb craters march right up to the railroad tracks and into the marshaling yard buildings as the five-hundred-pound bombs erupted in a fireball of flying bricks and mortar. "By God, bombardier," enthused Stromburg, "you did clobber that target!"

"Of course," said Balzac. "Another pickle barrel for your illustrious bomb-tosser. Damn, I'm good!"

"Just don't break your arm patting yourself on the back."

"No time for that. Have to scrub. Lancaster's bleeding again. I'm due back in surgery." There was a sigh over the intercom. "God, this crew is lucky to have among its members one each Leonard A. Balzac! Truly a man for all seasons."

Stromburg looked over at O'Riley and grunted. "Where in hell did we pick him up?"

"I dunno," replied O'Riley. "But isn't it about time for open season on bombardiers?"

"Should be. While you're checking it out, how about huddling with the engineer and navigator and see if we have enough fuel to make it home?"

"Wilco."

Barring further emergencies, there appeared to be just enough gasoline left to clear the mountains and make it to the airfield at Foggia. But the battle damage report showed that fuel was not the only problem. "Hydraulic system's shot to hell," said Daringer, sticking his head into the cockpit. "We've lost all our hydraulic fluid."

"Any chance of repairing it?" asked Stromburg. "We can get more fluid."

"No. Hydraulic reservoir is full of holes. Won't hold the fluid." Daringer looked at his pilot quizzically. "Anyhow, boss, where the hell could we get more fluid up here?"

"Any kind of fluid will work in a pinch. We'd just have to pass a flak helmet among the crew members. Get a liquid donation from each one."

Daringer made a wry face as he stared at Stromburg. "Yuch!"

"But I guess that's out if the hydraulic reservoir is full of holes."

"Yeah. Thank God. Talk about piss-poor ideas—"

"Okay. So you know what it means not to have hydraulic pressure. We can crank down the landing gear manually if the mechanism isn't shot up. But we won't have any brakes or flaps."

"Nor cowl flaps, nor windshield wipers."

"Roger. With no flaps we'll have to come in hot—which is bad, since we won't have any brakes."

"No brakes."

"So in the event we do reach the emergency field, it's going to be an interesting landing."

"We seem to have our share of interesting landings. Nothing personal, boss."

"Wait a minute." Stromburg squeezed his eyes at the engineer. "I have an idea. Would you get me the slipstick, Dick?"

"The . . . come again?"

"The slipstick. The weight-and-balance slide rule. I have a plan that might be worth trying."

"I'll get it, skipper. But damned if I know how figuring the weight and balance of this *kamikaze* kettle will help a brakeless landing that will be hotter'n a two-dollar shotgun."

"Just get it."

"Yes, sir." Daringer wiped his face with a handkerchief reeking of hydraulic fluid. "There are times when I wonder if I'm really cut out for this line of work."

Stromburg grinned. "You remind me of the circus that couldn't get a replacement for the man they shot out of a cannon."

"I know I'm gonna hate myself. But why couldn't the circus get a replacement for the man they shot out of a cannon?"

"Turned out they weren't making men of his caliber anymore."

"Oh, God!" Daringer looked pained. "I'll ride through a no-brake landing with you, boss. But do I have to put up with this kind of horseshit?"

"Just trying to keep up your morale."

"If it's all the same, I enjoy bad morale. The crappier the better."

"Okay, sorehead. Go get the slipstick."

"All right, Balzac," ordered Stromburg, banking onto the downwind leg over the Foggia air base. "Our radio's out and I can't raise the tower. Fire the red flares."

"Wilco." Balzac stuck the flare gun into its porthole and fired. Two red balls sizzled out of the top of the plane to signify an airplane in distress.

"Gear down."

"Gear coming down," echoed Daringer, turning the crank that would mechanically lower and lock the gear. "By God, it seems to be working!"

"Turning on base leg," said Stromburg into the intercom. "Now everyone remember what you're supposed to do when you hear the alarm bell. Start the second we touch down. Don't acknowledge."

"Geezus!" shouted O'Riley, pointing at the runway. "We're landing smack in the middle of a formation of Lancasters taking off!"

"No choice," said Stromburg. "Not enough fuel to go around. Balzac, keep firing red flares. Turning on final." Stromburg banked over in a shallow turn in deference to the dead engine and lined up with the runway.

"Swede," shouted O'Riley, "we got a red light from the tower! They don't want us to land!"

"Inhospitable bunch of bastards. We'll land right behind that Lancaster starting its takeoff roll. We'll have thirty seconds before the next one starts down the runway."

"Oh, Geezus! We'll never make it!"

"We'll make it. Gear in the green?"

O'Riley checked the landing gear indicator lights. "Negative. Gear's still in the red."

"Daringer," ordered Stromburg, *"crank faster!"*

"I'm crankin', I'm crankin'!"

"Over the threshold," shouted O'Riley. "You're hot-ter'n hell, Swede!"

"I know it! Gotta clear that Lancaster taxiing onto the runway!"

"Gear's still in the red!"

"Screw the gear." With scant inches to spare, Stromburg whistled the distressed bomber over the vertical stabilizers of the British bomber taxiing onto the runway. Then he chopped the throttles, rolled out the trim, and sucked back on the yoke. "Chop the electrical currents!"

O'Riley hit the electrical gang bar. "Ship's dead!"

With a screech of rubber the bomber hit hard, bounced, veered as it encountered the departing Lancaster's slipstream, then settled down with an audible grunt. "Okay, Pat. Hit the alarm bell!"

As the raucous jangle of the alarm bell echoed throughout the plane, there was a flurry of activity as every crew member, including an ashen-faced Lancaster, made a beeline for the aft end of the airplane. "It's not gonna work!" yelled O'Riley. "I told you it wouldn't."

"It'll work!" said Stromburg, fighting the rudder pedals to keep the ship straight as it fishtailed down the runway. "It has to!"

As eight crewmen huddled as near as they could get to Galvani's tail gun, the tail slowly started to settle. And then they heard and felt the rumble as the bomber settled down on its tail. Instantly the forward speed began to decelerate. "Well, I'll be dipped in shit!" shouted O'Riley. "It's working! The damn tail's dragging!"

"I knew it!" Stromburg half rose in his seat to peer over the front of the airplane, which was now rolling down the runway with its nose high in the air and its tail throwing up a rooster tail of sparks as it plowed the runway.

"Don't look now," said O'Riley, craning to look over the top of the nose, "but we're gonna run out of runway before we run out of speed."

Out of habit, Stromburg shoved the brake pedals to the floor. There was no response. In his half-raised position he could see the end of the runway approaching. He thumbed the intercom. "Pilot to crew. Brace yourselves. We're running out of runway!"

And then, fighting the rudder pedals to keep from ground-looping, Stromburg watched the end of the runway slide beneath them, and then they were on the short overrun, and then it, too, disappeared, to be replaced by soft earth. The wheels sank axle-deep into the loam, but the metal behemoth continued its errant course, neatly severing the barbed-wire fence that served as the airdrome boundary, then going on to bisect the perimeter road, barely avoiding a collision with a donkey cart preoccupied with sharing the same slice of real estate. The donkey reared, upsetting the cart, its driver, and several barrels of olive oil as the bomber, its momentum finally sapped, nosed down a gentle incline to come to rest in a drainage ditch. Its idling propellers made several feeble splashes and expired to a silence so still the crew could hear the dust settle.

Stromburg sat rigid in his seat, staring straight ahead, while the deafening drone of the Lancaster taking off scant feet above them ruptured the silence. Then he heard the far-off wail of the meat wagon coming toward them. Stromburg turned to his copilot, who was lighting up a cigarette. "You going to light up that cigarette in here?"

"Yep," said O'Riley, flaming his Zippo.

"Do you know how many regulations you're breaking?"

"I know I don't give a shit."

Stromburg sagged down in his seat. "Neither do I."

O'Riley took a deep drag and blew the smoke toward the ceiling. He picked a piece of tobacco off his lip and turned to Stromburg. "Swede, do you sometimes think the glamor of being an airplane pilot and wearing the wings of silver might be tarnishing just a tad?"

"Maybe just a tad."

Balzac came panting into the cockpit and thrust his head between the two pilots. "Holy donkey hockey!"

"Is everyone okay back there?" asked Stromburg.

"Everyone's okay. Except Lancaster. All the activity got his arm to bleeding again."

"Go back and get him ready. The meat wagon's on the way."

"Wilco, *bwana*." Balzac started to leave, then came back. "You guys got a funny way of landing airplanes."

"Yeah. Tell the crew to get out. I don't think there's enough gas left in this clunker to fill O'Riley's lighter, but with our luck—"

"Roger." The little Pole grinned. "Ya know, if today had been a fish, I'd throw the damn thing back."

Stromburg grinned. "Know what you mean."

As the bombardier disappeared, there was the squeal of brakes outside the aircraft. Stromburg summoned the energy to open the window and look out. A jeep had bounded up, driven by a captain with an AO armband around his arm. The airdrome officer looked up at Stromburg. "What the hell's goin' on?"

Stromburg cupped his ear as another Lancaster thundered overhead. "Say again, Captain?"

"I say, what the hell happened? Ain't you got no brakes?"

"Oh, yes," said Stromburg, settling back down in his seat. "We got brakes. We always land this way."

Chapter Eleven

14 February 1945
Chilly Italy

Dearest family:

Really appreciate your letters, folks. It's great to know what's going on on the home front. The morale officer was right when he said USO shows are fine, but ten of them wouldn't replace one mail call. Thanks to my great family (not to mention the Infernal Revenue Service) I never leave a mail call empty-handed.

I agree with Bob that putting the president of General Motors in charge of the war production effort was the best thing we could do. According to *Stars and Stripes*, Big Bill Knudsen is living up to his boast of "smothering the enemy in an avalanche of production." He turned out (with the help of our mom and sis on the swing shift) sixteen thousand heavy bombers last year alone. Truly, our industrial might will eventually bring the Nazis to their knees. So, Mary, you and Mom keep 'em flying!

The war seems to be going well. The U.S. Third Army crossed the Sauer and Our rivers on a twenty-two-mile front, and Montgomery is launching a British-Canadian offensive. Don't know how much longer Hitler thinks he can hold on, but you have to admire the guy's guts. The paperhanger's going down fighting and scratching all the way.

Mom, everything is just fine here. Most of our flights are pretty dull and boring. And yes, thanks for the castor oil. I'm sure it will come in handy, although constipation doesn't seem to be too much of a problem around here.

Here's another thumbnail sketch for you, Mom. Sergeant Lou Foulette is our nose-turret gunner. He probably looks less like a member of a bomber crew than anyone in the Air Corps. He's a little on the paunchy side, being a complete stranger to exercise in any form; he's a loner, very quiet. You have to pry words out of him with a crowbar. He's quite bookish, always reading, and will probably end up being a teacher. In fact, he has more college education than anyone on the crew, including the officers.

He has a nice, martini-dry sense of humor and a very quick wit once you get him to open up. I seldom see him, even on a mission, for he crawls up into his nose turret before takeoff and stays there until we've landed. About the only time I ever see him is at pay call, and I kid him about being on someone else's crew. But he's good at his job and has never been a bit of trouble.

Foulette does have one idiosyncrasy. He likes to play the violin. Worse, he takes his fiddle along on our missions, which is okay, except he's a very bad violinist. He and our bombardier sometimes entertain us with a duet on the way back from a mission, Foulette on the fiddle and Balzac on the harmonica. It sounds god-awful, but it seems to be keeping the Messerschmitts away. Even a German fighter pilot would think twice before directing machine-gun bullets at a man playing the violin.

Well, I'll have to sign off. Redeye Gonzales, our lovable squadron orderly, has just come by to tell my bombardier and me that our presence is requested at the group commander's office. General Twining, the CG of the Fifteenth Air Force, is visiting our group. During these visits it's customary for the CG to pin on a few medals. Who knows, your far-flung relation just might pick one up. Will let you know.

All my love,
Swede

P.S.: Am enclosing a mail order, Mom. Will you please buy you and Sis something nice for Valentine's Day? Thanks. You're a happy sneeze in the sinus of life, and I love you. I sent little Ann a gold necklace. I hope she gets it.

Redeye Gonzales steered the jeep into the compound of the 451st Bomber Group headquarters, oblivious to the two officers in the rear. Stromburg glanced down at Balzac's shoes. "My God, bombardier, you actually shined your shoes!"

"A few of us military officers take pride in our appearance," said Balzac, buffing his shoes on the back of his pant leg. "Especially when being presented with the Air Medal. Or maybe the Distinguished Flying Cross." He glanced over at his pilot. "And look who's talking. Our splendorous aircraft commander has a polished belt buckle."

"It's a good thing we have Luigi. But I think waxing your swagger stick is carrying things a bit too far."

"Oh, yeah? I don't think the future squadron lead bombardier can look too sharp. When one reaches the lofty pinnacles of command, one must present a model for others to emulate."

"If the brass sees that hat of yours without a grommet, you'll be wearing it where the sun never shines."

"Oh, pshaw. I only wish our navigator were here to bask in this warm glow of recognition."

"He'll be out of the hospital tomorrow. I'm going to Foggia and pick him up. Want to come?"

"Maybe I'd better. I'm not sure he'll get into the same

jeep with you. He says everytime he gets into a conveyance with you, he ends up with large holes in his epidermis."

"Can't say as I blame him. When Lancaster isn't throwing up, he seems to spend a lot of time bleeding."

"We are here, *amigos*," said Gonzales, pulling up in front of the whitewashed building that housed the group commander's office. "Hope you *señors* enjoyed the trip."

"Thanks, Redeye," said Stromburg as the two officers dismounted. "By the way, do you remember the crew of J. D. Muldoon?"

"*Si, señor.* Bought the farm over Ploesti."

"Right. Just thought I'd refresh your memory. The footlocker containing the personal effects of Muldoon's crew is still in our tent. Think you could do something about it?"

"You saying they ain't been shipped to their *familias*?"

"That's what I'm saying."

"Holy *frijóles!* I'll see to it *muy pronto*."

"We'd appreciate that."

Gonzales popped a sloppy salute. "Catch you *señors* later." Then he gunned the jeep. As the vehicle turned around, the officers headed for Colonel Sterling's office.

Stromburg's knock was greeted by a curt, "Enter."

From a ramrod stance, Stromburg swept the room with his eyes. Only two men were present. Colonel Sterling was sitting behind his desk, Major Diddle flanking him on a chair tilted against the wall. "Reporting as ordered, sir," said Stromburg and Balzac in unison, saluting smartly.

Colonel Sterling returned their salute. "Be at ease."

"Thank you, sir," said Balzac as the two men came to a loose parade rest. A sudden stillness brought into sharp focus the noise of Balzac's swagger stick idly slapping the back of his leg.

"I'm sorry you gentlemen missed General Twining," said Sterling, studying the faces of the two men. "He was called back to headquarters. He very much wanted to meet you."

Disappointment showed in Balzac's face. "That's too bad, sir. We very much wanted to meet him. Fine man, the general."

"Yes. However, I will do my best to relay his message." Sterling leaned back in his chair. "I understand, Lieutenant Balzac, you're quite a bombardier."

"Well, sir," Balzac's grin united his ears, "we have been known to paste our target with a respectable bomb plot from time to time. Humility forbids my taking all the credit, however, sir. It's all a matter of crew coordination. I receive a lot of cooperation from our navigator"—he glanced sidelong at Stromburg—"and, of course, our aircraft commander, who provides a solid platform for my bombing calculations."

"Very charitable of you, Balzac, to credit your other crew members. I understand that you had an exceptionally successful bomb run on yesterday's mission. A target of opportunity."

"As a matter of fact, we did, sir. We completely destroyed a marshaling yard. Every one of our bombs did damage. Didn't waste a one. Had to toggle manually, too. A textbook bombing, Colonel Sterling, if I do say so myself."

"Yes. Our target analysis reports indicate you really creamed your target."

Balzac pulled himself up to his full five foot two. "Just doing our job, sir."

"You did a fine job of bombing. Now, will you kindly answer one question?"

"Certainly, sir."

"Why the blundering hell did you have to do your textbook bombing on a marshaling yard in Yugoslavia?"

Stromburg noticed the hard look come into Sterling's eyes. The swagger stick never stopped slapping. "I'm afraid I don't understand, sir."

"Neither did General Twining. That's why he came here personally. You commodeheads blew up one of Tito's shirt factories! For your information, General Tito happens to be on our side!"

Stromburg felt a little trickle of sweat start down his backbone. "Oh, no!"

"You bombed the hell out of Maribor, a small town a few miles inside the Yugoslavian border."

"Sir," managed Balzac through pale lips, "there must

be some mistake. We had positive target identification. Radskerburg is in Austria. It has a little river running through the edge of town. Just like on our target maps—"

"So does Maribor. Only it's thirty miles to the south. And in Yugoslavia. Tito takes a very dim view of having his factory and his railroad cars blown up. What's more important, he expresses his displeasure to President Roosevelt. Then President Roosevelt passes it on down the line to General Twining. And General Twining gets very upset and passes it on down to me. And when General Twining gets upset, I get furious! Just what the hell do you two bimbos think you're doing with my career?"

"So that explains it," said Stromburg, looking vacuously at his bombardier.

"Explains what?" asked Sterling, fighting to control himself.

Stromburg looked at the colonel. "That, sir, explains why there wasn't any flak over the target. I thought it odd at the time."

"Of course there would be no flak over a Yugoslavian town! The Yugoslavs are on our side. At least they used to be. Jesus Christ, Stromburg!"

"I'm sorry about that, sir," said Stromburg. "I really am. I take all the blame."

"You're goddamn right you do. Now you're going to make a complete report. And explain just how you managed to blow up a friendly town's roundhouse and factory."

"Yes, sir. I hope there weren't many casualties."

"Fortunately, very few. It was a holiday. But you raised hell with the shirt factory. Uncle Sam will have to pay for it. I hope to hell it comes out of your salary."

"Seems only fair."

"We no sooner received the report from the Yugoslavs," continued Sterling, boring in, "than we received a protest from the British. It seems you capped this extraordinary feat by landing in the middle of a British bomber formation taking off for a night mission. Christ, Stromburg, you're a busy little beaver. You're a one-man international incident!"

Stromburg shook his head. "I guess it wasn't one of our better days."

"If I had my way, I'd ground your ass. You do more damage that the German V-bombs. But your squadron commander had gone to bat for you. He says you've had a good record up to now. And besides, he's shorthanded. So it looks like you won't be grounded. But we can't let this kind of conduct go unpunished. Do you have anything to say in your behalf before I mete out your thirty lashes?"

Stromburg looked down at the floor. "No, sir."

Suddenly the sound of Balzac's slapping swagger stick increased in tempo. Then the little bombardier spoke up. "Sir, may I say something?"

Colonel Sterling and Major Diddle switched their eyes to Balzac. "Go ahead," said Sterling.

"I think you should know that we got the shit shot out of us over the primary target, and among other things we had a runaway prop. Our navigator was hit. Our bomb intervalometer was shot up and didn't work, so our bombs didn't drop on the primary. The plane was out of control, and we couldn't hold altitude. The order to prepare for bailout was given. But did we bail out? Hell, no! Lieutenant Stromburg, because of his exceptional knowledge of his aircraft, managed to freeze the prop and bring the airplane under control. And did we salvo and waste the bombs? Hell, no. That would have been the easy way out. Stromburg did what he thought was right. He nursed that beat-up airplane to the nearest target of opportunity. Then he dropped his bombs where he thought they'd do some good."

"He picked a hell of a spot, Balzac—"

Balzac held up his swagger stick. "Sir, I'm not finished. We could barely read our navigational maps because they were covered with our navigator's blood. So we charted a course and picked out a target as best we could before our navigator fainted. And once we had identified our target— or thought we had—we nailed it right on the button. If it hadn't been for that little four-minute navigational error, you'd be pinning medals on us instead of trying to swing our asses from the flagpole."

Sterling began to puff up like a pouter pigeon. "Are you quite through?"

Stromburg shot his bombardier a murderous look. "Yes, Colonel Sterling, Balzac is quite through."

"As a matter of fact," said Balzac, squaring his shoulders, "I am not. There's the matter of our landing in Foggia. For your information, our pilot was on three engines, out of gas, no hydraulic pressure, no radio to contact the tower, and with injured aboard. Stromburg brought that sick goose in, drug its tail—which will probably become SOP for a no-brake landing—and set it down in the middle of a formation as slick as you please, without so much as ruffling a tail feather. Now that, gentlemen, is flying. I mean, that's *flying!*"

Stromburg muttered out of the corner of his mouth. "Balzac, will you *shut up!*"

"Yeah, Swede," said Balzac, stopping for breath. "I'm finished."

Sterling exhaled, studying the face of the bombardier. "You are a cheeky little bastard, Balzac."

"Thank you, sir. May I say just one more thing?"

"I don't know why you're asking permission. You don't seem to need it."

"Just one final word, sir."

"By all means. Let's get it all out."

"Does this mean that our request for a three-day pass might not be approved?"

Stromburg was on his second alcohol and grapefuit juice, quietly contemplating the picture on the wall of the officers' club, when Lieutenant Ewing walked in. Ewing hiked his skinny thighs up onto the stool next to Stromburg and started pouring himself a Scotch and grapefruit juice. "Hi, Three Sixty-nine."

"Hi, Ewing."

"Heard you were here. Dropped by to say *adiós*."

"So. It's back to the land of the big PX."

"Yep." Ewing took a long pull from his glass, made a wry face. "Great Godfrey, I'm gonna miss this good booze!"

"Ain't it the truth. My brother's been hoarding a fifth of

Haig and Haig pinchbottle for me. If I drink honest-to-God Scotch, I'll probably throw up."

Ewing took another long drink and wiped his eyes. "God, this stuff would gag a goat."

"How does it feel to complete thirty-five missions?"

"Numb." He turned puddling eyes on Stromburg. "I'm gonna get the hell out of here before they up the number to forty-five. I never thought I'd live to see this day."

"Well, I'm damn glad you did, old buddy. You're a good man."

"Horseshit. I'm just a survivor. The only man out of my crew that hasn't gone home in a wooden planter."

"You're going to forget all that, Ewing. You've been spared. Maybe for a reason. Don't spoil it all by running around hanging crepe."

Ewing reached for a cigarette, lit it with a shaking hand. "You're right. I'm going to turn over a new leaf. Bury the past." He took a long drag. "And maybe someday I'll bury the nightmares." He looked over at Stromburg. "Understand congratulations are in order."

"You mean my promotion?"

"It is now *First* Lieutenant Three Sixty-nine."

"First Lieutenant Stromburg."

"Whatever."

"It was kind of embarrassing for our squadron commander. My promotion came through the same day I received my letter of reprimand for blowing up Tito's shirt factory. Major Diddle was pinning on my silver bars with one hand, handing me a written reprimand with the other."

"The Army, like the good Lord, moves in mysterious ways."

"Well, at least Diddle doesn't hold a grudge. I'm back to flying lead again."

"We give Diddle a hard time, but he's not all that bad underneath. Besides, you should be flying lead. I'm not going to butter up your insufferable ego, but you're the best pilot in the squadron. You'll be operations officer soon."

"That's a lot of bull."

Ewing shrugged. "Have it your way." He splashed half

a glass of alcohol into his glass, added a touch of grapefruit juice, and bolted it. He wiped his mouth, dismounted from the barstool, and batted the tears from his eyes. "God, that's smooth! I'm sure as hell going to miss this place."

Stromburg walked with him to the door. "I want to thank you for being a damn good teacher, Ewing. You taught me what little I know about combat flying."

"If flinching, cringing, and pissing my pants a lot has been helpful, I'm glad to have been of service."

"Don't give me that crap, Ewing. You're going home a hero."

"Oh, hogshit! I'm no goddamn hero. How can I be a hero when I damn near dirty my britches every time we turn on the bomb run? Some fucking hero!"

"Wrong, Ewing. You did that thirty-five times. Like it or not, you're a hero."

"Nope. That's bullshit. Take ninety-nine percent of the guys in our squadron. They're just average, run-of-the-mill, bottle-assed kids. If they weren't battling in the skies over Europe, they'd be home stealing hubcaps, drinking beer, trying to get into the neighbor girl's bloomers. Putting them into a big bomber doesn't make them heroes."

"What is it that motivates our men to go off to battle day after day, knowing the odds they won't come back? What is the ingredient that stiffens their backbones?"

Ewing slitted his eyes at Stromburg. "You really want to know what it is, Three Sixty-nine? What really gives our guys the courage to fly into the jaws of death?"

"I would like to know. Yes."

"Pride. One word. Pride."

"Pride?"

"Pride in one's self. That's what gives you the impetus to go into combat. The same with every man on the crew. Pride in one's own self. An ego trip that rises above every other emotion, including ball-freezing fear. A person does not want to be seen as less than a man in front of his peers. Peer pressure and pride. That's the whole thing in a nutshell. Hell, nobody sets out to be a hero. If there really is such a thing."

"Pride. I'd never have thought of that. Interesting theory."

"As I see it, it's the secret of leadership. You can't instill courage in a man. But you can instill pride. That's why we have all the fuss and feathers of military ceremonies. The pinning on of gongs and medals for achievement, the ceremonial rites of parades and bands and saluting. All to instill pride in one's outfit—in one's self. Forget courage. Give me a crew with pride and I'll give you all the heroes you can use."

"That's fascinating, Ewing. You some kind of closet psychologist?"

"Yep. I'm going home to become a psychiatrist." He grinned for the first time. "A heroic shrink."

"By God, Ewing, you'll make a good one."

"If being a voyeur at the peephole of human emotions can help, I should be well qualified. We certainly run the emotional gamut in our line of work."

"Want an argument, you'll have to pick another subject."

"I want no argument. I just want to get the hell out of here."

"I'm glad you came by."

Ewing held out his hand. "So long, Three Sixty-nine."

Stromburg clasped his hand. "I'd like you to know my name. If you ever get out to the Northwest after the war, I want you to look me up. The name's Stromburg. I'll spell it for you—"

Ewing turned and plodded toward the waiting jeep. "I don't want to know your goddamn name." He swung aboard, popped a waving salute as the jeep started off. "So long, Three Sixty-nine."

"So long, Lieutenant Ewing." Stromburg leaned against the doorway, finished his drink, and watched until the jeep was out of sight.

Stromburg luxuriated in the cool, clean sheets, stretching his muscles. He turned over on his stomach, stuffed the pillow under his chin, and turned to look into the inviting depths of Esterina Tognoli's large, black eyes. "There's a spot right between the shoulder blades."

Esterina smiled, propped herself up on an elbow, and began scratching Stromburg's back with her long nails. "Sometimes, *carissimo*, I think you would rather have your back scratched than make love."

"Just a little higher." He sighed in rapture as he idly watched her naked breasts brush his shoulder with the movement. "There's a time for loving and a time for back-scratching. I say the apogee of ecstasy occurs when they happen simultaneously."

"I will remember that. Am I getting the spot?"

"You are. Indeed, you are. Esterina, I am yours. Body and soul."

"You are very easy to please, my love."

"Who wouldn't be pleased having his back scratched by the most beautiful woman in all Italy. Including Sardinia and Sicily."

"You left out Capri."

"And the Isle of Capri."

She laughed. "It is small reward for the happiness you have helped bring to the Galvani family on this day. The wedding was beautiful."

"It was that. But we could probably have done without Sergeant Foulette's violin and Balzac's harmonica accompaniment. I noticed the dogs were howling for a mile in all directions."

"The dogs just wanted to join in the festivities." She pressed her lips to the nape of his neck. "I will never forget the look on Father Zandegrande's face when he unveiled the gift you gave to his church. Where did you ever get it?"

"A flushing commode is not easy to come by these days. We picked it up in Florence."

"Firenze? You went clear to Firenze?"

"We were there on other business. I just told our squadron scrounge artist that we needed a commode. To replace the one our bomb knocked out. He found one in Florence."

"And what price did you have to pay your scrounge artist to bring such joy to Father Zandegrande?"

"I'm not sure. I haven't gotten the bill yet. Maybe Sergeant Warner just did it out of the goodness of his heart.

Anyway, he's offered to install it in the church. So let's just count our blessings."

"I think Father Zandegrande is still counting them."

"Things have come to a pretty pass when a porcelain commode can bring tears of joy to a priest."

"By American standards I suppose some of our sanitary facilities are quite primitive. Especially in these remote villages. And when one wears as many robes as Father Zandegrande does—"

"I get the picture."

"I would not be surprised"—her kisses traveled down his backbone—"if the good father makes you a saint."

"I'd make one helluva saint." He shuddered. "I don't think you'd better do that."

"And the reception was so lovely. Did not my little sister look radiant?"

"She's a living, breathing doll. I thought Sergeant Schultz was going to have a heart attack when she kissed him."

"He made such a beautiful cake."

"Yes. The old mess sergeant did himself proud."

"And those little finger sandwiches. I wonder what was in them."

"I wouldn't know. And don't ask him. It's common knowledge that the less you know about what goes into Schultz's cooking, the better it tastes."

"It would not have been much of a wedding without you and your friends."

"What really made the wedding was that wine. Best I've ever tasted."

"It was Father's finest. Before the war Daddy stored his best wines in a cave on the outskirts of town. Hiding it from the Germans. It mellows very well there."

"It certainly makes a fellow mellow."

"Speaking of which . . ." She reached over to the nightstand, uncorked the wine decanter, and refilled their glasses. She handed one to Stromburg, who rolled over on his back to take it. She touched his glass with hers.

"To our newlyweds," he said.

"To our newlyweds. I pray they will always be as happy as they were this afternoon."

"They will be. Their marriage is blessed."

She kissed him lightly on the lips. "Their marriage is blessed in heaven. But it is not blessed by your Army, is it, Swede?"

He rolled the glass between his fingers. "No. We did not get Army permission."

"And yet you went ahead with the plans anyway. Will you get into trouble?"

"Probably. But it doesn't matter. I seem to spend more time in hot water than a Maine lobster."

"I am sorry. I just want everything to be perfect for those sweet kids."

"We'll work things out. It's not the Army's intent to discourage marriages like this one. But for every one of these, there are a dozen situations where the Italian girl is just looking for citizenship papers and will marry anyone who can take her out of this battle-scarred country. It's not fair to the soldier, it's not fair to the Italian girl. So the Army officially tries to discourage weddings during wartime."

"I understand."

"I knew you would. We have our Army chaplain who will help them. Father O'Flaherty. We'll get him together with your Father Zandegrande, and the two should be able to move mountains—not to mention a lot of pasta and a case or two of your dad's finest wine."

"Then I will not worry about the Army's permission."

"Please don't." He drained his glass and put it down. "Instead, worry about yourself. For I have this terrible, god-awful yen to kiss your left breast."

"Then I think you should do it."

"I do, too." He did. And then he kissed her right breast. "It's terrible going through life as a boobolic."

She smiled. "A boobolic?"

"I have this thing for boobs. Especially beautiful boobs. Maybe I have the boobonic plague."

She pulled his head to her bosom and held him tight. "Is there a cure for this boobonic plague?"

"Just one." He brought his face up to hers and looked deep into her eyes. "My God, Esterina, you are beautiful."

She kissed his forehead and then the lids of his eyes. "And you are my handsome gladiator."

"Those eyes. I keep fighting the urge to dive into them and never come up."

She laughed softly. "And you are crazy, First Lieutenant Stromburg."

He sobered. "Do you know how very much you mean to me?"

She ran her fingers through his hair. "I know how very much you mean to me."

"I'm a real bastard. But in a way I'm sorry your husband is coming home."

"Yes. In a way, I am, too."

"Maybe I could hold up the prisoner exchange. Bomb a troop ship or something."

She cupped his face in her hands. "That probably would not be a very good idea."

"Probably not."

"There are many chambers in the human heart. One of my chambers is filled with love for my husband. One of the chambers is filled with love for you, my darling."

"I'm not sure I could have mucked through this stupid war this long without you. You've been an island of tranquillity in this sea of horse dung."

"And you have helped fill the agonizing hours of loneliness. And have brought much joy to my family."

"I hope so. I will never forget you, Esterina. Never."

"And you will always have a very special place in my heart." She kissed him softly on the lips. "I know that in the eyes of God what we have done is not evil. Nor sinful."

"Under the circumstances, I doubt if He will get too upset about it." He put his arms around her and pressed her close to him. "We will not see each other again. Will we, Esterina?"

She hugged him tight, and her mouth had trouble with the words. "No, my darling."

He brought his hand to her cheek, felt the dampness there. "I love you, Esterina."

"Oh, and I love you, *carissimo*. With all my heart."

"You will be a part of my dreams as long as I live." He kissed the tears from her cheeks.

"You have given me a happiness I never knew existed."

"Then this is the first time I've been grateful for this war. Were it not for the madmen of this world, you and I never would have met."

"And for that, I could even kiss Mussolini."

He smiled. "Now I must go."

"Yes. You must go. But before you go, one last request."

"Name it."

"I want you to make love to me. I want you to love me like you have never loved me before."

He did.

Chapter Twelve

29 March 1945
Lonesome Italy

My sweet little Ann:

How is my favorite daughter? On this date four years ago, you came into my life. A happy, smiling little bundle of twinkling eyes and leaky plumbing. The very first time I saw you, when you looked up, quit sucking your fist long enough to give me a big, beaming, toothless smile—I was hooked. Even though the nurse said it was gas, from that moment you've been the greatest thing in my life.

Now you are four years old. And not even married. Am I going to have an old maid on my hands?

I'm sure you understand that only this dumbhead war is keeping me from being with you on your birthday. We've put up with this war quite long enough. Now that it's coming between father and daughter on birthdays, it's high time we did something about it. I think we're now doing that, and I should be home before too much longer.

I just want you to know, my sweet, how much I love you. And how very much I miss you. Hopefully, we'll never be apart on another of your birthdays. At least not until that handsome knight comes galloping up on his white charger to sweep you off to his castle.

I'm sure Grandma and Grandpa had a wonderful birthday party. With all the ice cream and cake the rug could handle. Give them a big hug for me.

I hope you received my present. I mailed it over a month ago, but our wartime mails leave something to be desired.

Again, happy birthday, darling. And big juicy smackers and bear hugs.

> XXXXXXXXXXX
> With all my love,
> Pop

"Are you ready for this, *bwana*?" asked Balzac, taking a stance with his left hand behind him, and his .45 automatic poised in his right hand.

"I doubt it, Balzac," said Stromburg, looking nervously at his bombardier as he crawled out of the jeep. "There's something about your projects that I'm never quite ready for." He looked around at the desolate spot, punctuated only by an occasional olive tree. "Why have you summoned me out here to the boonies?"

"Had to be out here in the boonies. Where else could I build a skeet range? I tried to have it down at the motor pool, but some of the guys got nervous just because I shot out the headlights in the colonel's jeep."

"So that's why you've been relegated to the boonies." Stromburg looked over at Luigi. The little tyke was using all his strength to pull back a rubber loop that had been cut from an airplane inner tube. The ends of the rubber loop had been fastened to one end of a long board that was nailed to a tree stump. The loop was being pulled back to the other end of the board, where it was fastened to a trigger affair cut from a large clothespin. After affixing the loop over the trigger, Luigi reached down and picked up a clay pigeon from a nearby pile and placed it in the center of the loop. "That's an ingenious skeet trap. Where in hell did you get the clay pigeons?"

"Sergeant Warner found them in one of the stables. The old admiral who used to own this place must have been

quite a skeet shooter. There are cases of targets. That's why
I thought we should have a skeet range. When we run out
of clay pigeons, we can use Schultz's pancakes." Balzac
cocked his .45 and raised it, then shouted to Luigi, *"Pull!"*

Luigi pulled the jerry-rigged trigger that released the
rubber loop. The rubber snapped back to the end of the
board, carrying with it the clay pigeon. The target flew into
the air in front of Balzac, who took aim with his .45 and
fired. Unscathed, the clay missile flew some fifty yards to
crash into a tree.

"Missed," said Balzac. "Load 'em up again, Luigi."

"Of course you missed, you stupid Polack," said
Stromburg. "You can't shoot skeet with a handgun, let alone
a forty-five. You have to have a shotgun!"

"My good man," said Balzac, "don't you think I know
that?"

"Then why are you—"

"Look around you. How many shotguns do you see?
None, that's how many. So when one doesn't have all one
needs to do one's job, one must improvise."

"But it's a waste of time. You'd have better luck
throwing rocks at it."

"Au contraire, bwana." He shouted at Luigi. "Okay,
pull!"

Again Luigi released the rubber loop that snapped the
target into the air. This time shooting from the hip, Balzac
fired three shots at the disc before it flew into the tree
unblemished. "John Wayne," said Stromburg, "you ain't."

"Those damn pigeons. Just like the Eyeties to come up
with a clay pigeon that doesn't burst when you hit it."

"Right. Well, this is all very interesting, bombardier,
but I have other things to do than stand around and watch
you miss your skeet targets. I'm due at Link Trainer—"

"Don't go yet, Swede. I got you out here because I
want to talk to you. Alone. For some reason our tent is
Grand Central Station."

"All right." Stromburg leaned against the hood of the
jeep and looked closely at his bombardier. "I detect worry
lines. You have a problem, sport?"

"Sort of." Balzac yelled over at his trap-loader, "Take

five, Luigi!" Luigi waved and flopped down on the grass. Balzac picked up a box of shells and joined Stromburg at the jeep. He opened the box of ammunition, removed the clip from the automatic, and idly started inserting bullets into the clip as he talked. "Something's come up, Swede."

Stromburg crossed his arms. "Let's have it."

"Well, you know my stock hasn't been very high lately. Ever since we blew up Tito's shirt factory."

"That's about blown over."

"For you, yes. But now that you're flying lead ship again, I won't be flying with you. No way is Diddle going to let me be the lead bombardier."

"Nonsense. You're a damn good bombardier, Lennie."

"I know I am. But I'm poison now. As long as Diddle is CO, I'll be flying tail-end Charlie."

"Balzac, that's a crock of—"

"No, Swede." Balzac stopped him with a waving palm. "But that's not what I want to talk about. I've been offered a job."

"You what?"

"A job. There's a Major Adams. He's a fighter jock. Flies P-Thirty-eights. He was here on TDY, and I ran into him at the bar. He's experimenting with making a light bomber out of the P-Thirty-eight by placing a bombsight in the nose. He needs a bombardier."

"Put a bombsight in the nose of a P-Thirty-eight? Hell, there's not room enough for a bombardier in the nose of that thing."

"Maybe not for a normal bombardier, true. You may not have noticed, but I'm not exactly built like Joe Louis. I can crawl into the nose of a P-Thirty-eight. That's one reason I was offered the job."

"Well, I'm happy for you. But the military doesn't exactly lend itself to job-shopping. You just don't change jobs whenever the spirit moves you—"

"No problem, Swede. Major Adams will request my transfer through channels. He has a pretty high priority on his project. You know damned well that Major Diddle won't block it. He'll be damned glad to get rid of me. So the transfer is no problem."

"Of all the harebrained—"

"Think of it, Swede. Flying in P-Thirty-eights! The Lockheed Lightning. That fighter is a real hot rod. Top speed over four hundred miles an hour, climbs like a homesick angel. Hotter'n a depot stove. Most fliers would give their eyeteeth to fly—"

"Granted, it's a high-performance airplane. It's also overrated and undergunned. But if that's what you want to do, and you can wrangle a transfer into fighters, what's to talk over?"

Balzac finished loading the clip and rammed it into the gun handle. He looked up at Stromburg. "It will mean leaving the crew. All the guys I came over with. We've become a sort of family."

"I like to think so."

"There's something about flying combat that brings guys closer together."

"Affirmative."

"And I'd miss the hell out of them. I might even miss you."

"Don't get carried away. And don't worry about your old buddies. The guys who have wiped your nose, taken care of your little butt through thick and thin. Just go and sign up with the oversexed zoomies."

"You ain't helping a hell of a lot. Don't you understand, Swede? I'm spinning my wheels here. I'm about as popular with the brass as the old turd in the punch bowl. I'm fighting a losing battle. I'm dead-ended!"

Stromburg looked down into the face of the little Pole, saw the look of frustration there. "I know you have a problem. At least you think you do, which is the same. You also know I'll go to bat for you, you little bastard. But you have to measure the pros and cons. Do what you have to do."

"Yep." The cords stood out in his neck as he clenched his jaw. "I've got to make the decision. Bite the bullet." He motioned to Luigi. "Load 'er up, Luigi." He turned back to Stromburg. "Thanks, Swede. For the talk."

"I'm afraid I wasn't much help."

"You're always a good sounding board."

"Not all that great. What have you decided to do?"

"I'm going to transfer to P-Thirty-eights."

"Sure that's what you want to do?"

"It's what I *have* to do."

"It's what you *think* you have to do."

Balzac shrugged. "Same difference."

"We're going to miss the hell out of you, you little bastard."

"And I'm going to miss the hell out of Crew Three-Sixty-nine." He advanced to the firing line and yelled at Luigi, "*Pull!*"

The target flew into the air. Balzac sighted and squeezed off three rounds. Again the target crashed unmolested into the trees. Balzac blew the smoke from the barrel of the gun. "Just like the damn Eyeties. Making clay pigeons out of cement."

The requisitioned military hospital at Foggia was one of the city's better repair stations, but it was hardly a plush operation. Its stark, antiseptic wards were adequate for the job, however, and it was here that most of the battle casualties among airmen based in southern Italy had their wounds stitched, their holes plugged, and their clap zapped so they could return to the fray.

Stromburg strode down the sterile corridor until he found Ward C, where the corporal at the information desk told him he would find his navigator, and pushed open the swinging doors. He spotted Lancaster in the third bed on the right side of the ward. His cubicle was separated from the other patients in the ward by sheets hanging from tracks in the ceiling. As Stromburg approached, Lancaster put down his book and hailed his pilot. "What do you say, *el jefe?*"

"How goes it, Magellan?"

"Havin' a ball. No place quite like an Italian hospital for a lot of hilarious merriment."

"If you don't like it here, why do you keep coming back?"

"Because I fly with this wild Norski who hates navigators. He likes to see their manly bodies turned into dog food."

"I've decided you're a good man, Lancaster. With your magnetic personality you seem to draw most of the flak. The other crew members appreciate it." Stromburg pulled a chair up to the bed and plunked into it.

"A pox on the other crew members. I've been here so many times I know the whole staff on a first-name basis."

"Well, according to your veterinarian, in a couple of days I can take you away from all of this."

"Back to the old outfit."

Stromburg nodded. "Back to the bosom of your loved ones."

"And back on flying status."

"Soon as your butt heals."

"Wrong." Lancaster patted his book. "Robert Browning nailed it." He turned to a marked passage and read:

> *I give the fight up: let there be an end,*
> *A privacy, an obscure nook for me.*
> *I want to be forgotten even by God.*

Lancaster put down the book and looked up at his pilot. "That's me, Swede. I'm tired of having my carcass ventilated. You know what they pulled out of my butt this time?"

"I shudder to think."

Lancaster reached over to his nightstand and picked up a three-inch shard of clear plastic. "This is what they pulled out of my dimpled derriere. I'm going to have it made into a pair of earrings."

Stromburg took the piece of thick plastic and examined it. "This is part of the navigator's window. Don't you have any respect for government property?"

"I'd appreciate it if the government would keep its property out of my butt."

"The butt is no place for a born hero to get wounded. How the hell did you manage that, anyway?"

"On the bomb run the bombardier asked for the wind drift to crank into his bombsight. I made the mistake of bending over to yell it at him at the same time the flak burst blew out the navigator's window. Christ, does that get your attention!"

"You're lucky it hit you in the butt. Where you're well padded."

"I'll thank you to keep a civil foot in your mouth."

"Well, at least we won't have to worry about our ubiquitous bombardier anymore."

"Oh? What happened to our boy?"

Stromburg told him about Balzac's request for transfer to the P-38 fighter squadron. Then he added, "It was probably the speediest transfer in the annals of military history. Major Diddle never appreciated Balzac's finer points. He personally hand-carried the transfer through."

"So the little character's gone."

"Gone but not forgotten."

"Goddamn!" There was genuine dejection in Lancaster's face. "I'm going to miss that little fart."

"I'll tell you, it's cast a pall of gloom on the crew. It's just not the same. I find that I really miss the little peckerhead. I haven't been called into the CO's office since he left."

"Well, I wish him luck. He got a shafting he didn't deserve."

"Impossible," said a feminine voice. "No flyboy ever got a shafting he didn't deserve."

The men looked up to see Frances Adams standing at the foot of the bed. "Hey," said Lancaster. "Our favorite doughnut-dispenser."

"Hi, Frances," said Stromburg, getting up to give her his chair. "Good to see you."

"Keep your seats, gents. I just came by to make the weekly visit to my favorite hero." She placed a package on his nightstand, went to the side of the bed, and took Lancaster's hand. "This is getting ridiculous, William. Whenever I want to see you, I just call the hospital and ask what ward you're in. You must like the cooking here."

"Love this Army hospital chow. You should have seen dinner tonight. Ever eat roasted roadrunner? Compared to the hash-slingers who poison this hospital, Sergeant Schultz is a graduate of Cordon Bleu."

"Designed," said Stromburg, "to get you goldbricks back to work. This is no time to be lollygagging around in the sack."

"Well," said Lancaster, "they're certainly achieving their goal. A couple of days here and combat looks awfully good. Even flying with you."

"According to the hospital staff," said Frances, "you're the resident boomerang. They no sooner throw you out than you fly right back."

"Talk to my pilot about that," said Lancaster. "He's out to win the prize for the navigator with the most holes."

"So far, I'm way out in front," said Stromburg. "If you count the holes in his head."

"That is no way to talk to my friend," said Frances, giving the patient a kiss on the forehead.

"You're absolutely right," said Lancaster. "I don't mind the enemy shells with my name on it. It's the ones I get addressed to 'Occupant' that I can do without. Want a good deal on a Purple Heart? I got a trunkful."

"Where was the wound this time?" asked Frances.

"I'd rather not say," said Lancaster.

"Oh, come now. You can tell your old Red Cross buddy."

"I'd rather not discuss it."

"He's just bashful," supplied Stromburg. "If he doesn't want you to know, I won't tell." He held up the piece of plastic. "But from now on our friend will be known as Glassass Lancaster."

"Dear God in heaven!" She took the jagged piece and examined it gingerly. "You mean they dug this out of your—"

"I said, I don't want to talk about it."

"You poor baby." She patted his cheek.

"I'm making a pair of earrings out of it. For you."

"For me?" She made a wry face. "How nice."

"They'll make a great conversation piece."

"That they will." She smiled. "Glassass. I like that. It has an euphonic ring. Let me see your wound."

Lancaster looked shocked. "I beg your pardon!"

"Turn over. Pull down your sheet."

"I will not!" Lancaster pulled his sheet up to his chin. "Some things are sacred."

"Ah, come on. I've got six brothers. I've seen bare cruppers before."

"You're not going to see this one."

"Okay, killjoy. Just remember that when you want to see mine."

"Enough of this depraved conversation," said Lancaster. "Here I am on my deathbed, and you two ghouls chatter over my remains like a couple of magpies. I demand a little respect."

"You're right, my love. Enough of this small talk." Frances reached over to the nightstand and picked up the package she had brought. She handed it to Lancaster. "I brought you something."

"Why, Frances!" Lancaster started stripping off the paper. "You shouldn't have."

"No, I shouldn't have. Open with caution."

Lancaster struggled with the wrapping. Then there, nested in the torn paper, was a beautiful, life-sized pheasant, finished in leather. Actual feathers gave a realistic look to the brightly colored work of art. "Why, this is beautiful!" enthused Lancaster. "What is it?"

"It's a decanter." She took it from him to demonstrate. "The head comes off. Just turn it like this." She unscrewed the rooster's head. "Keep it upright when uncorking."

"Well, I'll be damned."

"And be careful. It's full."

"Full?"

She passed it under his nose as he sniffed. His eyes lit up. "To help gag down the hospital food." She looked around to be sure she wasn't being observed. "It's fairly good brandy."

"Frances, you are a sweetheart! I might even start donating to the Red Cross."

"You'd better. That's my liquor ration for a month."

"A holy grail," said Stromburg, "for our holy navigator."

"I'll bring some glasses by later," said Frances. "In the meantime, keep the stopper on that. If these hospital nurses sniff booze in here, they'll raise all kinds of hell. Worse than that, they'll confiscate it and drink it themselves."

"Not likely," said Lancaster. "All these hospital vampires drink is blood. Mostly mine."

"Well," said Stromburg, rising, "I see my navigator is in good hands. I'll get back to the salt mines. Anything you need, Bill?"

"A two-month furlough would be nice."

"Maybe we can swing a two-day pass."

"You're all heart, *el jefe*. Thanks a bunch."

"We need you back," said Stromburg, putting on his hat. "With you and Balzac both gone, the crew's morale is lower than a snake's instep. Get your ass back into the saddle."

Lancaster winced. "Must you use that expression?"

Stromburg shook hands with Frances. "Thanks for coming, honey. You do wonders for the morale of our neurotic navigator."

"My pleasure. Good to see you again, Swede." She looked into his eyes. "I heard from Kathy Wilson last week. She says you two are going to meet in Rome."

"We're sure going to try. How about coming along? We'll cork up Lancaster's holes and have a real soiree."

"How I would love that! But I have to hold down the fort."

"See if you can work something out. We'd love to have you." He turned to Lancaster and gave him a jab on the shoulder. "Pick you up in a couple of days, stud. Hang tough."

"Thanks for coming, Swede. Keep the war going till I get back."

"We'll try." Stromburg turned and strode out of the cubicle.

It was well past midnight. The lights had been turned off in the ward, and most of the ward patients were snoring blissfully. "Greatest idea you ever had," said Lancaster, gazing fuzzily at Frances Adams.

"One thing about being a Red Cross worker," said

Frances, "they don't kick you out after visiting hours. They probably think I'm giving a wounded patient comfort and solace."

He grinned at his visitor, who was leaning back in her chair with her feet on his bed. "That's exactly what you're doing, Angel of Mercy. Comforting and solacing. Let's hear three cheers for the Red Cross. Hip, hip—"

She reached over and put her finger to his lips. "Not so loud, William. You'll wake up the whole ward."

"Why not? They can all join in the party." He brought his glass to his nose and sniffed. "Nothing in the world like the vapors of warm brandy."

"Absolutely nothing," she said, holding her glass in both hands and inhaling deeply.

"But alas, we have a small vexation. Our brandy warmer seems to be bereft of fuel." An inebriated grin lit his face as he looked over at the homemade brandy warmer. A urinal had been placed on two stacks of books, between which Lancaster had placed his flaming Zippo lighter. The contents of the pheasant had been poured into the urinal. He reached over and capped the smoldering Zippo. "Are you, or are you not, beholding the world's greatest brandy warmer?"

"It has to be the greatest. In truth, I have never drunk brandy from a hot bedpan before. We just may have stumbled onto something."

"Have no fear of the bedpan being dirty. I wiped it out very thoroughly with my socks."

"You've always been a bug on sanitation."

"As our little bombardier used to say . . ." Lancaster felt a catch in his throat. "Already I miss the little bastard!"

Frances patted his arm. "Don't dwell on it. What did your bombardier used to say?"

"When one does not have what one needs to do the job, one must improvise. That little fart knew how to improvise." He looked into her eyes. "Did I tell you about the bidet he was building out of an old fuel pump of a crashed German Fokker?"

"No."

He sniffed. "Remind me to do that sometime."

"I'll remind you."

"The war's not going to be the same without that little shit."

"Sacrifice." She reached over and freshened her drink from the urinal. "War seemes to be one monumental sacrifice."

"Ain't it the truth." He held out his glass, and Frances filled it. Then he leaned back on his pillow and studied the ceiling as he recited:

> *The love that asks no questions; the*
> *   love that stands the test,*
> *That lays upon the altar the dearest*
> *   and the best;*
> *The love that never falters, the love*
> *   that pays the price,*
> *The love that makes undaunted the*
> *   final sacrifice.*

"God," she said, "but that's beautiful! Who wrote it?"

"Sir Cecil Arthur Spring-Rice. How's that for a handle? He was the British ambassador in Washington."

"The final sacrifice. Was he talking about losing one's virginity?"

Lancaster shook his head. "I don't think virginity was uppermost in his mind. He was talking about the final sacrifice—dying for one's country." He gave her a lascivious grin. "Do you think losing your virginity is paying the final sacrifice?"

"Nope. I think losing one's virginity should be the down payment on a great sex life."

He moved over to the far side of the bed and patted the pillow. "I agree. Why not bring that ravishing body over here and we'll make a down payment."

She looked at him over the top of her glass and smiled coquettishly. "You mean sacrifice my virginity?"

He patted the pillow. "Why not?"

"I'm afraid it's a little late, my love. My virginity has already been sacrificed."

Lancaster feigned shock. "No!"

"Yes." She giggled. "Sacrificed on the altar of pubescent curiosity."

"Who would be cad enough to seduce you?"

"A nice boy. Cecil Cuthbert, by name."

"Cecil Cuthbert?"

"The same. In the sixth grade. And he didn't seduce me, I think I seduced him. We were supposed to be cleaning the erasers, and he lured me under the teacher's desk."

"Fantastic!"

"More embarrassing than fantastic. He kissed me and we somehow got our braces entangled. We ended up going to the orthodontist in lockstep. Sure took the steam out of my first big seduction."

"That's a beautiful story."

"Had a heck of a time explaining to Mama how Cecil and I happened to get our braces locked. I'll never forget Cecil." She took a long drink and sighed. "Do you remember when you lost your virginity, William?"

"I'll never forget it. My early love life was a disaster. I had acne, wore glasses fashioned from beer-bottle bottoms, and had the coordination of a pixilated pachyderm. So I became a bookworm and got my jollies out of reading. Lived in my own fantasy world. I was a virgin until high school, believe it or not. Then Freda Hamhocker came into my life."

"Freda . . . Hamhocker?"

"Lovely girl." He took a big gulp and wiped his lips. "But I'm afraid her bra size outranked her IQ. We went hiking one day and got lost in the woods. We both ended up sleeping in one sleeping bag. But we kept warm. God, did we keep warm!"

"Good show."

"We might have gone steady, but she found the compass I'd hidden in my Jockey shorts. When she found we had camped in a park two blocks from her father's house, she claimed I had taken advantage of her."

"But of course you hadn't."

"Of course not. She was the one who brought along the sleeping bag." He took another large draught, and set his glass down on the nightstand. "But enough ancient history. As Napoleon said, 'History is a fable agreed upon.' Instead of rehashing old loves, what say we create a new love for tomorrow's hash?"

"You have the nicest way of putting things, William."

"True." He patted the pillow. "If you'd care to join me in my heavenly bower, I'll show you how nice I can really put things."

She shook her head. "I know I'd never say this if it weren't for the brandy, but it sure looks inviting."

"Then divest thyself of thy raiments. And hop into the sack."

"Why, William Lancaster! You're serious."

"Of course I am. We'll cuddle."

"Shame on you! Are you daft?"

"Not daft. Horny. You are a sexy package, Miss Adams. You bring out the beast in me. Let's unite ourselves mentally, spiritually, and most important . . . physically."

"You're absolutely crazy! I should never have brought this brandy."

"Smartest thing you ever did. Start with the shoes."

She kicked her shoes off. "This is against all rules and regulations." She hiked up her skirt and started unrolling her nylons. "I certainly am not going to get into your bed. Just because you took me to dinner at Madam D'Amico's and bought me two fresh eggs—"

"Don't forget the ham and French bread. Now the jacket."

"—gives you no license to lure me into your bed." She drained her glass and started unbuttoning her jacket.

"Just pull the curtain closed there. To be sure we're not disturbed, I'll ring for the nurse. That way we can be assured nobody will show up."

She closed the curtain. "This does not mean I'm getting into bed with you. Certainly not in a hospital ward full of—"

"Now your blouse. That's the good girl. Just fold your clothes and stick them under the bed. Then if someone should drop by, we'll pull the covers over your head and they'll never know you're here."

She folded her clothes neatly and stuck them under the cot. "You can quote Browning and cajole me with your silvery tongue all night, Lieutenant Lancaster, but I am emphatically, definitely not going to—"

"Oooops. A little crowded in these hospital bunks. I'm afraid there's not room enough for your bra. Off with it. There, that's better." He helped her into the bed and covered her with the sheet. "Comfy?"

"Red Cross girls are known for their respectability and high moral conduct. Always rising above such temptations as pleasures of the flesh—"

"Ouch! What the hell—"

"What is it?"

"How did the bedpan get in here? It's hotter'n hell."

"Serves you right for harboring salacious thoughts." She took it from him and placed it on the nightstand. "And thinking for one moment that I'd stoop to—"

"What the hell's that?"

"What's what?"

There was a snapping sound. "That."

"That, you ignoramus, happens to be my garter belt."

"Off with it."

"As I say"—she unsnapped the garter belt—"our reputation will never be compromised while toiling in the line of duty. The Red Cross stands for the highest standards of integrity—"

"True. That's why I never bed anyone but Red Cross girls. Great Godfrey, you snuggle nice."

"—and moral conduct. Reflecting the unassailable values of . . ." She gasped. "Why, William. You haven't a stitch on!"

"Wrong. I have seven stitches on. At least I did. I think one just popped."

"Oh, you poor darling. Let me see."

"No. It's fine."

"Are you sure?"

"Positive."

"You lie very still. As I say, no way am I going to . . . Oh! You shouldn't be doing that, William."

"Sorry. I'll quit."

"Don't. I mean, don't quit. But if you think anything is
going to come of this—"

"If you rather I didn't—"

"My mission is to make you happy. If that gives you
pleasure . . . oh, William!"

"We'll have to take it low and slow. Something
unromantic about the sound of popping stitches."

"This whole thing is positively insane. I am definitely
not going to . . . oh, my God!"

"Promise me you'll be gentle, Frances."

"Oh, sweet William!"

"Gentle, Frances."

"Oh, my dear. I will be gentle."

"Easy, honey. Ouch!"

"Oh, dear Lord. If Cecil Cuthbert had only known
how to do that . . ."

"Frances! I said gently."

"Oh, praise the Lord!"

"Oh, Christ! There goes another stitch!"

"Oh, praise the Lord!" And then her head tilted back
and a rapturous look flooded her face as she lifted her voice
to the heavens in gasping song. "Puhraise the Lord, and
pass the ammunition! Oh, puhraise the Lord, and we'll all
be fuhreeee. . . ."

At the nurses' station outside of Ward C, the night
nurse looked up from her paperwork and cocked her head.
"Lordy! What was that?"

The black corpsman put down the paperback he was
reading and took a swig from his coffee cup. "I didn't hear
anything."

"Sounds like singing. Coming from Ward C."

"I don't hear nothing."

"There it is again. It *is* singing. Sort of singing."

"You're hearing things."

"I am not! Corporal Custer, don't you hear *that*?"

The corporal shook his head and turned back to his
book. "I don't hear nothing."

"Well, I do. That sound would wake the dead. I'm

going to investigate." She picked up her flashlight. "And you should have your ears fixed," she said, rising.

The corporal planted a large hand on her shoulder and shoved her back down. "I just had my ears fixed. Courtesy of that flyboy navigator in bed three." He reached into his pocket and pulled out a twenty-dollar bill. "Half of this Jackson says you didn't hear anything, either."

She studied the black face for a beat, then put down her flashlight and turned back to her paperwork. "As I was saying, Corporal Custer. The wards are unusually quiet tonight."

"You ever had jock itch?"

Stromburg looked across the cockpit at his copilot. "Yeah. I've had jock itch. These damn parachute straps would give anybody jock itch."

"It's funny, but when it clears up, you sort of miss it."

"Not necessarily."

"Well," said O'Riley, "that's the way I feel about Balzac. He was a continual irritation, but now that he's gone, I miss the hell out of him."

"Fletcher is a damn poor replacement for Balzac." Stromburg checked his watch. "Keep your eye on the tower, Pat. Should see a couple of green flares in two minutes."

"Roger, coach. Did you ever see feet like Fletcher's got? He could get a job stamping out forest fires."

"He's a big guy, all right. Or maybe it's just because we're used to a little bombardier."

"He can't help being big. But the guy *can* help smelling like a buffalo skinner. I wonder if Fletcher has taken a shower since he's been here."

"I think he's allergic to soap. Even our tail gunner is complaining, and he's at the other end of the airplane. We're going to have to do something."

"I made a subtle hint. When he came through the flight deck, I sniffed, made a face, and said somebody's deodorant wasn't working."

"Subtlety has always been one of your better traits, O'Riley. What did he say?"

"He said, 'Don't look at me. I'm not wearing any.'"

Stromburg chuckled. "Well, we can always go on oxygen. And we shouldn't show prejudice. Balzac's a tough act to follow."

"I used to think hell was filled with little bombardiers. Now I've decided it's filled with big bombardiers."

"There're the green flares. Mission's on." Stromburg stuck his hand out of the window and waved three fingers. The crew chief pointed his fire extinguisher at the number three engine. "Start engines."

"Starting engines, coach."

Flying lead position, Stromburg was the first to start taxiing. As he lumbered out of the revetment, he was surprised to see a jeep speeding down the taxiway behind them. As it approached, it gave wide berth to the tail section, then swung back alongside behind the wing. Stromburg turned to his engineer. "Monitor the hatch, Daringer. Looks like someone is coming aboard."

"Right, skipper." As Daringer moved to the hatch, Stromburg opened the bomb-bay doors. Without stopping, the jeep's passenger swung from the jeep to the hatch ladder; then the jeep's driver swung away from the taxiing plane and sped on down the taxi strip.

A helmeted head poked into the cockpit. "This the nonstop flight to Hawaii?"

In unison the pilots exclaimed, "Balzac! You little shit!"

Balzac lifted his goggles. "Here I am, you lucky bastards."

"What the hell you doing here?" asked Stromburg.

"Long story. Brief me on the mission."

"What are you talking about? We have a bombardier. All briefed and ready to go."

"You have no bombardier. You have Fletcher. Fletcher could not hit the broad side of a barn if he was standing inside."

"He's one of the best in the squadron. We're flying lead."

"He stinks. Not only does he stink as a bombardier, he stinks period."

"That much is true," said O'Riley.

"I'll get the target info from Lancaster. That gorilla is not flying in my airplane. Get rid of him, *bwana*."

"You know it's not that easy, Balzac. If Diddle knew you were on this plane he's have a coron—"

"Diddle is on leave. Now do you want to bull's-eye the target, or don't you?"

"But what about your jazzy little P-Thirty-eight? That flying hotrod that climbs like a homesick angel? That's hotter'n a depot stove?"

"I don't want to discuss it."

"Talk. Or we'll have Fletcher fan his armpits."

"I'll talk. Suffice it to say that P-Thirty-eights are a tiny damn airplane. You don't climb into it, you put it on like a jockstrap. And when they jerry-rigged the bombardier's station, they left out one very important piece of equipment."

"What's that?"

"A relief tube."

"Aha!" said O'Riley. "So that's it."

"You ever tried holding it for six hours when you're having the pee scared out of ya? You can take the P-Thirty-eight and shove it!"

"Do tell. And that's the only reason our wandering boy has returned?"

"No. Two other reasons. Major Adams and I didn't exactly hit it off. He accused me of being—would you believe this? Cocky."

"Cocky?" Stromburg and O'Riley exchanged glances. "I find that hard to believe," said Stromburg.

"Certainly floored me. The guy's only got one oar in the water."

"And the other reason?" asked O'Riley.

"Well, if you have to know, I missed my old buddies."

"So the truth comes out."

"Right. I never thought I'd miss them so much. The war's just not the same without Luigi and Sergeant Schultz."

"Not to mention DFC."

"That dog I can do without."

Stromburg cuffed him on the side of the head. "We're

glad you're back, you little fart. If you insist on coming, go up and work it out with Fletcher. Just remember that Fletcher's on orders as the bombardier."

"I'll just look over his shoulder. Keep him out of trouble."

"Okay. Now buckle in. We're cleared for takeoff."

"Wilco, *bwana*." The head disappeared.

Stromburg looked at O'Riley, who grinned back. "So the little shit's back home."

"The little shit's back home."

"Is our before-takeoff checklist complete?"

"Checklist complete."

Stromburg gathered up a handful of throttles and shoved them forward. "Then let's see if we can get this groundhog to fly."

Chapter Thirteen

1 April 1945
Scintillating Italy

Dear Bob:

How goes it, brother? This letter will have to be for your eyes only. I've written a separate page you can show Mom.

I'm going to hang, draw, and quarter my bombastic bombardier—if someone doesn't beat me to it. This morning the little bastard started the rumor that all of Madam Grabballi's girls had the clap. This afternoon half the squadron showed up at sick call. When they were all gathered around with their pants at half mast waiting for their penicillin shot, Balzac stuck his head in the door, shouted, "April fool!," and dashed out. Talk about liking to live dangerously. He's locked himself in the latrine for protection, but rumor has it a kettle of tar is boiling over in the enlisted men's area and the chickens are being plucked. It's not that war is so bad. It's bombardiers . . .

I should have heeded your advice when you told me never to volunteer for anything in the Army. I made the mistake of volunteering for a night mission. I can't tell you the target, but it was in Austria. It was supposed to be a milk run, and after twenty missions I figured our crew was entitled to one.

Well, it may have been a milk run, but I don't

think I've been so scared in my ever-lovin' life. I'm sure there wasn't much flak, but at night you swear to God every flak burst is right inside the cockpit. You don't see the explosions so much in the daytime—just a big puff of black smoke to mark the detonation. But at night the red flash of fire lights up the whole sky. Talk about the Fourth of July!

There probably weren't over a dozen ack-ack guns, but as my copilot put it, "I'm sure every damn one of them was pointed at my crotch." Anyway, it did turn out to be a good mission. We clobbered our target and got home with no casualties. I'll certainly doff my chapeau to the English bomber crews; they do this night after night. But I'll never volunteer for another night mission. Your brother has discovered he's a born coward and aims to live to tell about it.

On the plus side, the Allies' strategic bombing is taking effect. By destroying the marshaling yards and the transportation routes, we're depriving the Luftwaffe of fuel for their fighters and bombers, and they seldom attack anymore. As we fly over the German airdromes, we can almost see the poor Kraut fighter pilots sitting in their cockpits down there and shaking their fists at us in frustration.

Now that the tides of war are shifting in our favor, a lot of the rats are deserting the sinking Axis ship. Hungary has now declared war on Germany, and Turkey has joined the side of the Allies. At the Yalta conference, Roosevelt and Churchill have agreed to give eastern Poland to Russia, and Germany is to be disarmed forever. Like chess players, the Big Three are moving countries around like pawns. Yesterday's enemy can be today's friend, and vice versa. We almost need a program to know whom we're fighting. Things keep up like this, I'm going to start thinking global conflicts don't make a hell of a lot of sense.

Anyway, we've crossed the Rhine on a captured bridge at Remagen, and our U.S. tanks are closing a vast trap around the Saar. The Russians are invading Austria, the British have headed into the North German Plain, and their tanks are approaching Münster. We've got the Axis on the ropes and are closing in for the kill. Then we can concentrate on the Japs. But enough of war talk.

Thanks a heap for the pictures of little Ann. Ain't she about the most beautiful young lady ever born? Especially the one where she's wearing Sis's high heels. Sometimes I think the worst part about this cruddy war is taking us away from our loved ones. Especially the kids, when we're missing the precious moments of watching them grow. I just hope they'll remember me when I get home.

Partly for this reason, our little Luigi has become something of a surrogate kid to all of us. Quite frankly, I've become very attached to the little monster, as I'm afraid he has to me. This is going to present a problem when it's time to go home. The Red Cross has come up empty-handed in their search for his family; it seems they've been completely swallowed up by the war.

Between Luigi and that damn beast of O'Riley's, there's certainly no food going to waste around here. If DFC gets any bigger, we're going to enter him in the Kentucky Derby. But at least he's finally tent-trained. Balzac taught him to go over to the squadron commander's tent area to do his business. Needless to say, this necessitated another of my visits to the squadron CO. Sometimes my butt's so sore from being chewed on, I can't sit down. Ain't this war ever gonna end?

Here's one more thumbnail sketch to round out our crew roster, which you can show to Mom. Will Waverly is our ball-turret gunner. Ball-turret gunners are born to the job. They are selected as follows: If someone short-sheets their bed and they don't know it, they're just the right size to be a ball-turret gunner. Anyway, our Waverly is a very good-natured lad who hails from a farming community near Hagerstown, Maryland. He's a stocky individual, and if he gains any more weight we'll have to get him into his ball turret with a shoehorn.

Waverly has one ambition, and that's to own a dairy farm after the war. He has this one fear about combat flying, and that's the possibility that something might happen to his milking fingers. So on our last trip to Foggia, the whole crew went traipsing around to antique shops until they found just what Waverly wanted. He now has a pair of old mail gauntlets—you know, the type knights of old used to wear with their suit of armor—and he wears them on all the missions. His anxieties have ameliorated considerably, which is good, because mine have increased proportionately. When we get all geared up for combat, I sometimes wonder if we're going out after Germans or dragons.

The whole crew goes on R&R next week. The enlisted men have elected to go to the Isle of Capri. The officers are all going to Rome with me. We're very much looking forward to it. Now, don't read anything into this, but Kathy Wilson plans to be there at the same time. We hope to get together.

Well, that's it for now. Tell my movie-buff sister that *The Prisoner of Zenda* with Ronald Colman was on at the mess hall last week. I thought it was a little corny, but maybe it was because the projectionist got the reels mixed up. Anyway, we're looking forward to next week. Sergeant Warner scrounged up a bootleg copy of Hedy Lamarr's *Ecstasy*, and we're all panting for a little culture.

Love,
Swede

P.S.: Tell Mom I think it's a great idea of hers to send all the crew members a card on their birthdays. So I went through all their records and made a list of their birthdays, which is enclosed.

Stromburg sealed the envelope, stamped it, and handed it to Luigi. "Luigi, would you mind dropping this in the mail slot?"

Luigi looked up from the Italian-English dictionary he was making a pretense of studying, planted soulful eyes on Stromburg, and took the letter. "Sure, Swede."

Stromburg looked at him closely. "What's the matter with you? You look like DFC just ate your best friend."

"Ah, I am okay."

"Something's bugging you. Spit it out."

"Naw. Is nothing."

"Spit it out!"

Luigi squirmed uncomfortably. "I been thinking about you going to Roma. You will be gone five or six days. That is roger?"

"That is roger."

"And Luigi will have to stay here. Alone."

"You have to stay here and take care of the tent. And feed DFC. Besides, we can't take you. Against regulations."

"Okay . . . okay." He shuffled toward the door.

"We've made arrangements for Sergeant Schultz to feed you. You'll help out in the mess hall, and you can eat with the kitchen help."

"Sure, Swede." He toyed with the latch on the door. "I will take care of the tent and the dog. And will work in the kitchen."

"We'll bring you back something from Rome. What would you like?"

"Nothing. Is okay."

Stromburg's heart went out to the boy. "That's not really what's bothering you, is it, Luigi?"

Luigi ran his sleeve across his nose. "No. Is okay."

"Come here." Stromburg reached his arms out. "Come tell your old buddy all about it."

Reluctantly the boy turned and walked to within arm's reach of Stromburg. "Okay. Is fine if you to Roma for vacation. I happy to stay here and keep the house. But what will happen to Luigi when war is over? And you leave Italy for good?" Tears started bubbling in the big, black eyes.

"Oh, ho! So that's it!" Stromburg reached out for the boy, put his hands on his skinny shoulders. "So our rough, tough, coyote of the streets knows how to cry."

Luigi pulled out his shirttail, wiped his eyes, and blew his nose. "Luigi not crying."

"No. Of course not." Stromburg pulled him close in a bear hug. "I'm not sure what we're going to do about you when we leave Italy. But we'll work out something. We're not going to leave you here to starve. I promise that."

Luigi sniffed. "I want you to be my papa, Swede."

Stromburg tried to swallow the lump in his throat. "And I would like to have you as my son, Luigi."

The eyes brightened. "Do you mean that? For honest?"

"I really mean that."

"You would not story to Luigi."

"No. I would not lie to Luigi."

Stromburg found his neck in a choking embrace. "Then I will call you Papa. Papa. Instead of Swede."

"Now, hold on. It's not quite that simple—"

"And my name will be Stromburg. Luigi Stromburg."

"Now, wait a minute! There's a lot of red tape and paperwork—"

"My papa is very smart man. He can do anything. I do not worry about little paperwork. Fooey!"

"Luigi! I only said I'd *like* to have you as a son. I didn't say it was even possible—"

"Luigi very lucky to have great flying machine driver as father. I will be good son. You will see." Luigi dashed out the door.

Stromburg watched the door bang on its frame, then his eyes turned slowly to the ceiling as he flopped back on his camp cot. In a voice more beseeching than blasphemous, he muttered, "Jesus Christ."

During its heyday, the Regina Hotel had been one of the finest in all Italy. Its handy location in the center of downtown Rome; its cool, cavernous interior; and its plush decor had beckoned the peregrinating elite of Europe since its opening.

Now its posh tapestries and carpets still lush but a bit frayed, it had been pressed into service as a rest and recuperation mecca for American officers. The grand ballroom was no longer soothed by the melodies of a string quartet but was rocked by an Italian swing band that offered a good wheezing imitation of Glenn Miller; its great dining hall no longer rustled with cashmere and crinoline, but its wing-backed chairs now embraced the pink-twilled flanks of dress uniforms and the slit-skirted thighs of the cream of Rome's prostitutes; and the waiters in their boiled shirts and cuff-frayed black suits served fare more Spamish than splendid. But to the battle-weary refugees from tents and trenches, the tarnish did not show, the patched sheets went unobserved, and the grumbling of indoor plumbing was music to the ears of the servicemen indulging themselves in a week of wine-soaked revelry amid the grandeur that once was Rome.

Stromburg had picked up Kathy Wilson at the Red Cross billets, a requisitioned small hotel not far from the Regina. The short walk from there to his hotel had been awkward, the two trying to make small talk that would mask their nervousness at this strange rendezvous a million miles from home. Kathy was dressed in civvies: a wool skirt, a white blouse over which had been pulled a cardigan sweater. She had captured her red hair in a silk scarf, the ends fluttering behind her in a way that brought a strange dryness to Stromburg's mouth.

Nor had the awkwardness of the meeting been ameliorated by the hostile looks of strolling prostitutes who eyed this attractive redhead as an unknown and unwelcome interloper on their territory. And passing through the revolving doors of the hotel lobby to come face to face with one of Stromburg's squadron pilots had proved most unnerving. The pilot had taken one look at the pretty woman sailing through on the arm of Stromburg, and naturally thinking she was one of the Italian ladies of easy virtue, had released a long, loud wolf whistle and said, "Gawdamighty, Swede, how much did you have to pay for that dish?"

While Stromburg was trying to give him the high sign that his escort articulated in very good English, Kathy answered in a cool voice, "A hell of a lot more money than you have, buster!" A befuddled lieutenant was left spinning in the propwash of the revolving door.

This helped to relieve the tension, and they both burst into laughter upon entering the dining room. "I apologize for my friend," said Stromburg. "Nobody expects to find an American woman in here."

"So I see," she said, looking around at the tables filled with dark-haired women whose natural Italian beauty had been largely hidden under a patina of blue eyeshadow, rouged cheeks, and crimson lips.

"Especially beautiful American women."

She smiled up at him as the maître d' escorted them to a table. "If you think that kind of sweet talk is going to get you anywhere with me, you're absolutely right." Stromburg tipped the majordomo for the good table near the orchestra and seated her.

"There she is! The love of my life." Stromburg looked up to see his copilot pull Kathy up out of her chair and enfold her in a big embrace. "Come into my arms, you gorgeous thing."

"Patrick O'Riley! My favorite Irishman." She planted a big kiss on him as he swung her around.

"It's sure good to see you again."

"And you, Patrick."

"Yes," said Stromburg. "Now I'd invite you to join us, O'Riley, but I'm afraid we only have a table for two—"

"No problem at all," said O'Riley. "As you can see, our industrious navigator is approaching with two more chairs."

"How nice of you to join us," said Stromburg, giving his copilot a look that would frost a flamethrower, "for a moment."

"So this is our Kathy Wilson," said Lancaster, handing O'Riley a chair and seating himself. "Truly she walks in beauty, like the night of cloudless climes and starry skies."

"And all that's best of dark and bright meet in her aspect and her eyes," continued Kathy, and then in unison with Lancaster, "Thus mellow'd to that tender light which Heaven to gaudy day denies."

"Oh, my God!" enthused Lancaster. "Not only is she ravishing, but she knows Byron." He reached for her hand and kissed it gallantly.

Stromburg sighed. "Kathy, meet our navigator. Bill Lancaster. He thinks he's an intellect because he can recite two poems."

"Ignore this barbarian, Miss Kathy. And fly away with me on the wings of love."

O'Riley took her other hand. "Be not smitten by this bookworm, colleen. We Irish must stick together. Let's you and I vacate these commoners and go curl up with a wee dollop of the dew."

"I'm sure glad you leeches showed up," said Stromburg, flagging down the wine steward. "Now all we need is Balzac."

"You called, *bwana?*" Stromburg looked over his shoulder to see Balzac bearing down with three young women in tow. The bombardier looked over at Kathy, and his eyes lit up. "Holy monkey puckey! Look at the knockers on that redhead." And then Balzac winced painfully as Stromburg's shoe connected with his shin.

"Motormouth!" said Stromburg with a hiss. "I'd like you to meet Kathy Wilson. An old friend from the States. Who speaks very good English."

"Oh, shit!" said Balzac, turning crimson. "I mean, dash it all! So you are Kathy Wilson." He liberated one of her hands and took it.

"Kathy," said Stromburg, "you're being pawed by our ubiquitous bombardier, Lennie Balzac. Don't get too close, he drools."

"So you're Swede's bombardier. I've heard much about you."

"And you are *the* Kathy Wilson. Old high-school sweetheart of our lovable *gran patrón*."

"Sometimes it's difficult to understand our diminutive bomb-tosser," said O'Riley. "It's hard to enunciate clearly when one has a mouthful of large foot. A malady our lover boy was born with."

"Oftentimes," retorted Balzac, staring up at O'Riley's Adam's apple, "big copilot get chewed down to size by eager beaver bombardier." He turned to Kathy. "I love you madly and passionately. Let's you and I find a dark corner someplace and plant a crop of war babies."

Kathy smiled up at the three prostitutes hanging on Balzac. "Good idea, but what would we do with your friends here?"

"Ah, yes. My little lovelies. Aren't they sweet? I'm teaching them how to jitterbug."

"Good idea," said Stromburg. "You carry on with your worthwhile pursuits, bombardier, and don't let us detain you."

"That's perfectly all right," said Balzac. "I'll scrounge up four more chairs and join you."

"*Au contraire*. You are going to take your harem back to your own table. And to keep you out of harm's way, our redoubtable navigator and copilot will escort you back."

"Ah, but coach, we want to be with our lovable aircraft com—"

"Out! All of you! Out!"

"Well!" said Lancaster. "That's a fine way to treat an old combat buddy."

"Fine friend," said O'Riley. "I notice he never talks that way when we're at thirty thousand feet, flat on our backs, fighters zooming in from every direction—"

"Right," said Balzac. "He always did say we were like the Four Musketeers. One for all, and all for one. And then Lady Jane pops into the picture—"

"Will you kindly," said Stromburg, "hike your scurvy butts the hell outta here?"

"Well, that does it!" said O'Riley, rising. "Come, men. Let's kiss Miss Kathy good-bye." O'Riley pulled her up, bent her over, and planted a long kiss on her. Lancaster and

Balzac followed suit as Stromburg sat at the table, drumming his fingers.

"Remember," said Balzac, reluctantly separating from her, "if this pervert so much as lays a hand on you, just scream. We'll all come running to your rescue."

"I'll remember that."

Balzac turned to Stromburg. "Good-bye, former friend." He haughtily gathered up his three women and departed, followed by his copilot and navigator.

"Whew!" exhaled Stromburg. "Did you ever see such a group of lechers? I thought they were going to pitch a tent."

"I think they're marvelous," said Kathy. "And your bombardier is the cutest thing I ever saw."

"*Cute!* That little piranha has aged me ten years. They're all rotten. Rotten to the core."

"Hear, hear." Kathy smiled at him as the waiter arrived with their wine.

Stromburg sampled the wine that was splashed into his glass, nodded appreciatively at the steward, and when the glasses were filled, he touched Kathy's with his. "I'm not all that crazy about the bubbly, but it seems only fitting that this special occasion be toasted with champagne. To two old friends, Kathy."

"May we always be good friends, Swede." They drank.

"I can't tell you how much I've been looking forward to this moment."

"Me, too. I want to catch up on all the juicy gossip from home."

"We'll have five full days to do that. I've arranged some tours. We'll have to see the Colosseum, of course, the Roman fountains, the catacombs—"

She squeezed his hand and looked at him with sad eyes. "I'm afraid I can't, Swede."

"What do you mean, you can't? You got something against Roman culture?"

"I love Roman culture. It's the Roman calendar I hate. I have to go back tomorrow morning."

He looked at her in disbelief. "Oh, *no!*"

"Oh, yes. Two of the girls had to go home on emergency leave. I shouldn't have come at all."

"You certainly should have! You're as entitled to R&R as anyone I know!"

"Not really. But I did want to see you. Even if it meant only for an evening."

"Of all the crappy—"

"Now, Swede, don't spoil what little time we have together. Or I'll really be upset."

He simmered down. "Damn it to hell. You've just knocked all my plans into a cocked hat."

"I am sorry." She clenched his hand tightly. "I really am. Now let's be grateful that we have this much time together."

"Okay. I'll be grateful. You know anybody who'd like half a dozen tour tickets?"

"You'll use your tickets." She looked around the room. "A tall, handsome aviator could have his pick of any of these beautiful Italian women."

"As long as the tall, handsome aviator's flight pay holds out."

"You'll soon be rid of this old, square American, and then you can really have some fun on your leave."

"I happen to have a thing for old, square Americans." He touched her glass with his. "But you're right. We'll not brood about our misfortunes. We'll enjoy each other's company while we can."

"That's my Swede."

"To you, Kathy. I never thought we'd be having a glass of champagne in Rome together."

"No. In my dreams it was always Paris. To you, Swede." They drank, then she tore her eyes from his. "That's delicious wine."

"Personally, I prefer Italian wine to the French."

"And I think I'm going to prefer Rome to Paris." The orchestra started up with a slow rendition of "I'll Be Seeing You." "That's a pretty good orchestra."

"Not bad. Care to dance?"

"If I can stand up without my Army boots. First time I've worn pumps in ages."

"Just hang on to me."

The two of them were feeling no pain. Stromburg clutched the champagne bottle to his chest as he looked down at Kathy Wilson, smiling insouciantly. "What do you mean I can't come in, Kathy?"

She leaned against the door. "Swede, there are two reasons you can't come into my hotel room. One, these Red Cross rooms are off limits to members of the opposite sex. You, my friend, are definitely a member of the opposite sex." She hiccuped. "And two," she held up three fingers, "I have a roommate. A roommate who is not a member of the opposite sex." She hiccuped again. "More's the pity."

"Wait a minute. You know we can't go to my hotel. I'm sharing it with those three yo-yo's you met. The place is a zoo. Now you tell me we can't go into your hotel room?"

"That's right." She smiled up at him sweetly.

"Then come on." He grabbed her hand. "We'll go find a hotel room we can go into."

"No, love." She held steadfast, snapping him back. "We're going to do nothing of the kind."

Stromburg tapped his watch. "Kathy, look! It's only two o'clock. We have the night ahead of us—"

"I am not going to spend the night tramping around Rome looking for a black-market hotel room. Just so you can try to take advantage of me. Besides"—she hiccuped again—"I got the hiccups."

"Kathy, the last thing in the world I want to do is try to take advantage of you."

She grinned at him impishly. "Well, then I might try to take advantage of you." She giggled. "And I don't think your mother would like that."

"Look. We have a full bottle of champagne. We can't let it go to waste."

She looked up at him, saw the disappointment in eyes that were focusing with some difficulty. "No. Of course we can't waste a bottle of champagne." She took him by the elbow and guided him over to the stairs. She sat down on the top step, patting the carpet beside her. "Park yer carcass right here beside me, Swede Stromburg."

He sat down, giving her a sidelong look. "This is ridiculous. Our only night in Rome, and we're spending it on the stairs of a fourth-rate hotel. I'm gonna go find a hotel room—"

She pulled him back. "Open the champagne. We'll have a farewell drink"—she looked up at him through eyelids that were threatening to descend—"then I'm going to bed. I'm being picked up at oh six hundred in the morning."

"That leaves us four full hours—"

"Pour the champagne," she said, hiccuping.

Grumbling, he reached into his pockets, pulled out two wine glasses, and popped the champagne cork. He caught the fizz in one of the glasses, topped it, and handed it to Kathy. "This is ridiculous. When we could be in a nice, quiet hotel room."

She reached over, put her finger on his lips. "Swede, you know I do not sleep with married men."

"I wasn't planning on doing a hell of a lot of sleeping."

"I know." She patted his arm. "We're not having a one-night stand. Even in romantic Rome."

"Look, Kathy. Forget I'm married. I'm not really, you know."

"I understand you're very much married."

"I am still married in the eyes of the law. I am married in no one else's eyes."

She looked at him over the rim of her glass. "Do you want to tell me about it?"

"No. I don't like to talk about it."

"Maybe it will help. Take a big drink and tell me all about it."

"You really want to know?"

"I really want to know."

"All right." He skoaled his drink and poured himself another one. "In school. When you told me to get lost. I guess I got tangled up with Thelma on the rebound. I—"

"I never told you to get lost."

"Do you want to hear this story or not?"

"I want to hear the story."

"All right. Thelma was a pretty little thing when I first met her. She could ride a horse like the wind—"

"She looked very hard to me. She bought her makeup by the pound."

"One more interruption and I'm gonna go find a hotel room."

"Sorry, Swede. No more interruptions. I promise." She tried to stifle a hiccup.

"Now pay attention. I soon found out Thelma had a drinking problem. Not just social drinking . . . she started at breakfast. Instead of cornflakes, she'd have a beer. Or sometimes she'd have beer on her cornflakes."

"Yuch!"

"As you know, they have treatment centers for alcoholics. I tried to get her into one. But the problem was, she'd never admit to being an alcoholic. Therefore, she refused treatment. She would sometimes polish off a case of beer a day. She got all bloated, bleary-eyed, started looking like the *Graf Zeppelin.*"

"Oh, Swede, I'm sorry."

"That's not the worst part. What really ripped it was her morals. Or lack thereof. She'd get into her cups and start making passes at anything that wore pants. And her taste was atrocious. Some of the things she brought home defied description. One time I came home to find her in bed with a Norwegian bullfighter. Ever hear of a Norwegian bullfighter?"

"No."

"I never did, either. Till I came home and found one in my bed."

Kathy shook her head. "This is unbelievable."

"I gave her her walking papers. Sent her home to her mother."

"Did that do any good?"

"She dried out for a couple of months, became halfway decent again. So, because of Ann, I took her back. Then I came home one night to find her in bed with the bartender from a local pub. This time we split up for good."

"Why didn't you get a divorce?"

"About this time my orders came for overseas. I figured that if I didn't make it back from the war, Ann wouldn't have to know about our problems. And if I did come back, I'd work out something after the war. So I sent

Ann to her mother's folks, who happen to be good, solid citizens, and came overseas."

She took his hand. "My poor baby. I'm terribly sorry."

"Not too sorry. I'm sure I'm as much to blame as she is. I must be an ogre to live with. Why else would she have to slop Budweiser over her shredded wheat to face me in the morning?"

"I have never lived with you, but I know you well enough to know that you could never be an ogre."

"I'm not so sure. Anyway, that's the story. I don't mean for it to sound maudlin. You're the first I've ever told it to, and I haven't got the hang of telling it."

"I'm glad you confided in your old friend." She dabbed at her eyes, sniffing. "And now, here you are. On my doorstep."

"Here I am. So if you want to get technical, I guess you could say you were out with a married man."

"Thanks for telling me, Swede. I know it hurt."

"It did." He started to rise. "Now can we go find a hotel room?"

"No."

He scowled at her. "What do you mean, no?"

"I said I do not sleep with married men." She snuggled against his shoulder. "I also do not sleep with unmarried men."

"I should hope not."

"Good. Then you understand."

"No. I think this case is a little different. After all, how long were we sweethearts before you told me to get lost?"

"I never told you to get lost. And that has nothing to do with it."

"It has *everything* to do with it." He polished off his drink and refilled their glasses. "You probably think I'm some kind of sex fiend, hopping from bed to bed. Truth is, a Tibetan monk gets more rolls in the hay than I do."

"My poor *bambino*." She turned his head to look into his eyes. "Don't tell me you have led a chaste life while you've been fighting the big war."

"It's true. A chaste, virtuous life."

"Come on, now, buddy. It's your old friend you're

talking to. The one that had to sit on your hands in the backseat of your brother's Pontiac when we used to neck in the graveyard."

"Well, there was one small detour from the path of righteousness."

"Oh?" She straightened up. "I want to hear all about it."

"No."

"Come on. Tell your old friend all about your debauchery."

"I don't know why I even mentioned this. It certainly was not debauchery. Nor was it cheap or sordid."

"It sounds fascinating. Tell me more."

He cleared his throat. "I had a very nice relationship with a beautiful Italian woman."

She nodded. "I can understand that. Some of these Italian prostitutes are beautiful."

"She was not an Italian prostitute. She was a schoolteacher."

"Oh?" The edge of eagerness dulled. "A schoolteacher? How did you meet her?"

"She's the sister of a young lady my tail gunner married. Comes from a fine Italian family."

"I see."

"It was a very short affair. But it was unforgettable."

"If it was so unforgettable, why was it so short?"

"Her husband came home."

"My God! She was married?"

"Yes."

"Swede Stromburg!" She pulled away from him. "Shame on you."

"I didn't want to talk about it. You insisted."

"I'm sorry I did. You consorting with a married woman!"

"You make it sound sordid. It was not. I think our relationship actually preserved my sanity during this cockamamie war. What little I have left. And I know I was good for her." He took a large quaff from his glass. "Actually, it was very beautiful."

"I'm sure her husband will agree."

"He will never know."

She shook her head. "Swede Stromburg!"

"Will you kindly quit saying that?"

"This has certainly been an evening of soul-baring."

"Thanks to this third bottle of champagne. I was rather hoping we'd get around to baring something besides souls."

"You've shocked me."

"Well, at least I cured your hiccups."

She looked up at him, sniffing. "I'd rather have my hiccups back."

"Listen, Miss Holier-than-thou. Don't tell me your bloomers haven't slipped occasionally since last we met. A gorgeous gal who's roamed the world—"

"My bloomers, as you so elegantly put it, have stayed exactly where they belong. They will be lowered only for my husband on our wedding night."

"Oh, my God! You sound like something from the Stone Age."

She held her empty glass up to him. "And no matter how many glasses of champagne you pump into me, young man, that fact will not alter. You may refill my glass."

He filled her glass. "That's final?"

"That's final."

"Then there wouldn't be much point in getting a hotel room."

"You're beginning to get the picture."

"In spite of the fact that I'll be back at war next week, facing the grim reaper, flying my crew into combat against overwhelming odds—"

"You can also stow that. I've had that sprung on me by real pros."

"I'm sure you have. But wouldn't it be horrible, Kathy, if I were killed in the war and our love were never consummated?"

"That would be sad. Only thing sadder would be to consummate our love and then you not get killed in combat."

"Kathy Wilson! That was a crappy thing to say!"

She looked up at him, her lids drooping in spite of her best efforts. "I say death before dishonor."

"Okay. I give up."

"You do? You are waving the white flag of truce in the battle for my chastity?"

"I surrender. I'm no match for you and your virginity. You win. You can go through life forever kicking yourself for letting this chance go by. I hope to hell you lose the key to your chastity belt."

"Now who's saying crappy things?"

"Finish your drink. I'll deposit you at your door."

She put her head on his shoulder, closed her eyes. "You are mad at me."

"I am not mad at you."

"Then kiss me."

"I don't want to kiss you."

"Then would you like to unbutton my blouse?"

"No. I don't want to unbutton your blouse."

"You can, you know."

"I do not unbutton blouses on hotel stairways."

"Okay. Then you may escort me to the door."

"Very well." With some effort he got her to her feet, but she collapsed after several steps. He picked her up in his arms.

"I think I may have had one bubble of champagne too much."

"Quite possible," he said with a grunt.

With great concentration she opened both eyes wide. "You hate me, don't you, Swede?"

"No. I could never hate you."

"It would be very easy to go to bed with you. You are a very desirable man."

"I can see you're having a terrible time controlling your lust." He carried her over to the door and stood her on her feet. She looked up into his face, her eyes suddenly serious.

"Seeing you again has stirred old feelings. I just don't want to relight an old torch."

"Would that be so bad?"

"You hurt me deeply when you got married, Swede. I don't want to reopen old wounds."

"Reopen old wounds? Hell, mine never closed. Do

you know how much I love you, Kathy? And have always loved you since the first day I saw you fall into that mud puddle?"

She smiled wanly. "Love me, Swede? That's funny talk from a man who's married to someone else, and who sleeps with married women when their husbands are away." She touched his cheek. "No, Swede. I'm not going to be hurt like that again."

"Goddamn! I've explained all that. Don't shut me out, honey!"

"I'm not going to shut you out. I'm just not going to let you in. Not now, anyway. Maybe when the war is over we can see how we feel about each other. Providing we're both single and sleeping alone. Then, if there is still an attraction, we'll face it on our own terms. Not as victims of romantic Rome, cheap champagne, or a stupid war."

"You're gambling that we'll still be around after the war."

"We'll be around." She fumbled in her purse for her key, found it, and turned it in the lock. "Thank you for an interesting evening."

"You're welcome." He looked down at her face for a long time. Then he kissed her softly on the lips. His mouth traveled to the tip of her nose, then to her eyelids, and finally to her hair. He held her very tight.

Then she turned the knob, slipped inside the door, and closed it quietly.

Chapter Fourteen

10 April 1945
Springtime Italy

Dearest Mom et al.:

How's my favorite girl? Don't let them work you too hard, honey. And stay off the swing shift. Can't have you losing your beauty sleep.

Hope you got the postcards from Rome. Now that I'm back in my nice, snug tent, it's hard to realize that I spent nearly a week in the Eternal City that all roads lead to.

We had a great time. Saw all the sights that Rome is famous for and got lots of rest. They have a nice USO in Rome, and the boys and I had a lot of fun playing Ping-Pong and brushing up on our reading.

I did get to see Kathy Wilson for one evening. We had dinner together and went dancing. She's still pretty as a peony. She's going to make some lucky guy a great wife.

Well, this profile on Nick Galvani, our tail gunner, will complete the sketches of the guys on Crew 369, probably the greatest gang of cowhands who ever saddled up a B-24. I hope you've saved these letters, just in case I ever get around to doing a book on this looney war. I seriously have my doubts I ever will . . . it's just too unbelievable. Any self-respecting editor would pass it up, as lacking credibility.

Anyway, Galvani hails from New Jersey, and

is a thin, wiry Italian with a mop of black, curly hair that comes down low over a swarthy face. His big, soulful eyes draw attention from a rather large Roman nose, and with his firm jaw and jutting chin he presents a quite handsome countenance to the world. He's a compulsive worrier, is more nervous than a pregnant fox in a forest fire. But given that, he's a very likable guy. He's generous to a fault, mixes well with the officers and enlisted men, and is a crackerjack of a tail gunner. I'm sure you recall my letters describing his recent wedding to a very pretty Italian girl from a small village nearby. We are now working on getting the marriage legalized by the Army so Nick can take his bride with him when we return to the States.

You know, Mom, in a way it'll be kind of sad when the war is over. We won't miss the war, of course, but I will miss my crew. There's something about flying combat that seems to forge a real friendship in the crucible of fire. Something very special.

Since brother Bob is following the progress of the war on his wall map at home, I'll give you the latest from our Intelligence briefings so he can plot it. We've sprung the trap on eighty thousand Germans in Holland. The Russians have driven into Vienna. Fires are raging in Bremen from the British bombardment, and our Ninth Army troops have entered Hanover. And to help finance our flight pay, General Patton has seized a huge gold hoard.

So everybody's busier than a long-tailed pussycat in a room full of rocking chairs, trying to button this thing up over here. It can't last much longer.

Give everyone a big kiss for me, and keep a bushel of boodles for yourself.

> Your number two son,
> XXXXXXXXXXXX
> Swede

Stromburg addressed the V-Mail, and stuck it into his flying helmet so he wouldn't forget to drop it into the mail slot on the way back to his tent. He finished off a crumbly doughnut, chased it with a swig of cold coffee, and listened with detachment as Major Diddle wound up the debriefing.

"So you gents made a damn good showing today. Using heavy bombers to strike enemy troops in close ground support takes precision bombing. We have a communiqué from the Canadians fighting in Bologna saying that we made mincemeat out of their opposition, and the war should soon be over in Italy.

"Don't let it go to your head, but you guys can take pride in a job well done. Since Stromburg here led the mission, we're going to celebrate and let him buy the drinks."

There was a chorus of hear, hears as the tired crew members, still wearing their heavy combat gear, clumped toward the door of the briefing room. Stromburg gathered up his personal equipment to follow, when he felt Major Diddle's hand on his shoulder. "Stromburg, got a minute?"

"Yes, sir." Stromburg turned to face his squadron commander.

"You know that Captain Benson bought the farm trying to wipe out the Bressanone Railroad bridge while you were on leave."

"Yes, sir. Goddamn shame. Benson was a fine troop."

"Yes." Diddle reached for his pack, shook out a cigarette. "Benson was a good head." He skated a kitchen match across his bottom, watched it flare. "His death has created a vacancy in the outfit. One that has to be filled." He lit his cigarette and squinted at Stromburg through the smoke. "How'd you like to be the new operations officer?"

Stromburg was genuinely astonished. "Me? The number one squadron screw-up?"

"We've all done our share of screwing up. And you have a crew that's made great contributions to your problems."

"Wait a minute, Major. My bombardier and navigator led the group today. You can't say they didn't perform."

266 *William C. Anderson*

"They performed. Always liked your navigator, that's why Lancaster's flying lead. But that bombardier of yours. If you didn't squeal like a castrated cat every time I threatened to replace him—"

"Balzac may be a character. But he's one of the best bombardiers in the group, sir. And you know it."

"Providing we can get him to bomb the right target. Granted, in the air he's good. That's why he's flying lead. But on the ground . . . I'm going to kill the little bastard. Do you know what he's trained that damn dog of yours to do? I'm up to my ass in dog shit!"

"Know what you mean. There are times when I fight homicidal tendencies myself. But to know him is to love him."

"I don't intend ever to find out, because I don't want to know him that well." Diddle blew a cloud of smoke at the ceiling. "Orders making you the new ops officer will be cut this afternoon."

"Does this mean I won't be able to fly with my crew?"

"You're the ops officer. One of your duties is crew scheduling. Work it out."

"Yes, sir."

"With the job, providing the war lasts long enough, comes a pair of tracks."

"I don't care about the promotion. I just want to finish up my missions with my crew and go home."

"Wouldn't we all."

"Thank you, sir, for the vote of confidence. I'll do the best job I can."

"I know you will. That's why you're getting the job."

"Now if that's it, sir, I think I could use a shot of mission whiskey."

"Carry on, ops officer." As Stromburg headed out, Diddle called after him. "Oh, there's one more thing that happened while you were on R&R. A bit of bad news."

Bill Lancaster cursed the darkness as he tripped over the threshold of the door that provided access to the officers' latrine tent. As he unbuckled his pants to confront the rude six-holer, he noticed the figure sitting in the far corner. "Swede, is that you?"

Stromburg sniffed and wiped his eyes. "It's me, Bill."

Lancaster winced as he introduced his bare cheeks to the cold boards. "I'm sure going to miss this crapper." He looked over at Stromburg, his eyes adjusting to the gloom. "I say, Swede, if one is to heed Nature's call, wouldn't one be well advised to lower one's britches?"

"Just came in here to be alone for a minute."

"Sorry I invaded your sanctum sanctorum."

"No sweat."

"But to quote Socrates, when you gotta go, you gotta go."

"Socrates knew whereof he spoke." Stromburg blew his nose.

Lancaster looked over at him curiously. "Swede, you all right?"

"Just a touch of hay fever."

"Right. Hay fever."

"Backs my sinus up."

"Yeah." Lancaster toyed with the roll of stateside toilet paper in his hand. "Lots of hay in an olive grove. Do you want to tell your old spongy-shouldered navigator about it?"

Stromburg wiped his nose, stuffed his handkerchief back into his pants. "Major Diddle laid one on me. Kinda got me in the crotch."

"I'm listening."

Stromburg looked at his navigator. "You remember Lieutenant Ewing?"

"Ewing? Hell, yes. No-name Ewing. Weird character. Didn't want to know anyone's name."

"That's Ewing. A damn fine pilot."

"I thought he rotated back to the States."

"He left just before we went on R&R."

"So what about him?"

"The guy's dead."

Lancaster's jaw dropped. "How could Ewing be dead? Hell, he finished his missions. Thirty-five of them."

"Affirmative. He bought the farm in a damn jeep! On

the way to the Bari airport to catch his flight home. The poor bastard bought it in a *jeep!*"

"Good Christ!"

"Thirty-five times that poor sucker faced death. Thirty-five times he sweat his life's blood out through his pores. Every one of his crew was killed except him, and he gets to go home. On his way he buys it in a *goddamn jeep!*"

"What the hell happened?"

"Got sideswiped by an Army truck and ran off the road. One of *our* trucks! Rolled down an embankment. Killed him and the driver. They found Ewing's body in the jeep. It took half an hour to find his head."

Lancaster shuddered. "Christ Almighty!"

Stromburg sniffed, reached for his handkerchief. "I don't know why that got to me in the solar plexus. We've seen a lot of death, but this thing with Ewing really hit below the belt. The Big Man upstairs must really be pissed. This just ain't fair."

"Hard to understand the Grand Scheme, Swede."

Stromburg wiped his nose. "Sorry about this. I'm making an ass of myself."

"You're entitled."

Stromburg stood up and headed for the door. "You know, navigator, I'm getting so I don't care much for this game anymore."

"Know what you mean. I wouldn't get too upset if they canceled it for lack of interest." He studied Stromburg's profile in the dim light. "You sure you're okay, Swede?"

"I'm fine." He stopped at the door, looking out at the setting sun. "We've got ten more missions to go. We gonna make it?"

Lancaster looked down at his half roll of stateside toilet paper, measured its thickness. "Yep. We're just gonna make it."

Group Captain Cecil Witherspoon's florid face looked even redder in contrast to the white barber's cloth that was pinned around his neck. As Stromburg entered the barbershop, Figaro greeted him with a sweeping gesture of the brush he was using to soap the back of Witherspoon's neck.

The British Intelligence agent forced the words around the cigar butt that was clamped in the corner of his mouth. "Greetings, Stromburg."

"Hello, Group Captain Witherspoon." Stromburg took a seat on one of the stools. "Major Diddle said you wanted to see me."

"Thanks for coming by. Would have dropped into your office, but if we can talk while I'm getting my ears lowered, it'll save some time."

"No problem. I need a haircut, anyway."

"Understand you're the new ops officer."

"Rumor has it."

"Congratulations, old chap."

"Thank you, sir."

"It is in your new capacity that Major Diddle wanted me to check with you. Seems we must lay on a flight."

"Oh?"

"We have a very important dignitary visiting the squadron this afternoon. He'll be arriving by staff car with General Twining on an inspection tour. The VIP wants to fly back to London this evening. Can you handle that?"

"Of course."

"Naturally we will want your best crew to man the mission. Major Diddle suggested you take the flight yourself."

"I'm not the best pilot, but I have the best crew. I'll be happy to fly the mission."

"Excellent."

"May I inquire as to the identity of this VIP?"

"I'm afraid we'll have to keep that under wraps for security reasons. Suffice it to say, he's a very, very important person who is vital to the conduct of the war. I will say this much: You'll recognize him when he comes aboard."

"Very well, sir. I'll go back now and have maintenance set up our best bird. And alert the crew. Anything else?"

"That's about it. Suggest you start standing by for an immediate takeoff around nineteen hundred."

"Yes, sir."

"And better throw on an extra thermos of coffee. And a bottle of good brandy, if you can scare one up."

"Wilco."

"That's all I can think of at the moment."

"Then I'll excuse myself and attend to my chores."

"Do that. And again, congratulations on the promotion, old chap."

"Thank you, sir."

"Okay, coach," said O'Riley, "checklist complete up to starting engines. We're ready to crank number three."

"Roger," said Stromburg. "Stand by." He turned to face Lancaster and Balzac, who were looking over his shoulder. "Navigator, you think you can find London?"

"Of course. Have you never read George Robert Sims?"

"Afraid not."

"He wrote 'The Lights of London Town.' 'O gleaming lamps of London, that gem the city's crown, What fortunes lie within you, O lights of London Town?' We'll just home in on the lights. Like a blind dog in a butcher shop."

"Sorry I asked. I don't think your Sims ever heard of blackout curtains." Stromburg turned to Balzac. "Unless you have plans for bombing London, I presume we are carrying no bombs."

"That is affirmative, *bwana*. No bombs. The Limeys have been behaving themselves."

"Since you will be dropping no bombs, that leaves you with lots of free time on your hands. You will spend that time wet-nursing our VIP."

"My pleasure, sir. I have it from a reliable source that our VIP is Miss Betty Grable. She is winding up a USO tour, and it is our lot to transport her to London Town."

"In that case, I trust you have coffee and sandwiches aboard?"

"Aye aye, *bwana*. I handled that myself."

"And the brandy?"

"Thanks to Sergeant Warner. There's a small matter of six packs of cigarettes you owe to—"

"I don't want to hear about it." Stromburg turned to his copilot; "I checked the front end, Pat. Did you give the rear a damn good inspection?"

"Just like you said. It's clean as a whistle." He looked closely at his pilot. "Relax, Swede. You're as jumpy as spit on a hot stove."

"I just want everything to go smoothly for our VIP. This might be a golden opportunity to sabotage an airplane, if the VIP is as important as we've been led to believe."

"That's a happy thought. You mean even the ops officer has no idea of our VIP's identity?"

"Not the slightest."

"Well, all I can say is he's one lucky cuss." O'Riley reached over and punched Stromburg on the shoulder. "To be riding with our brand new ops officer. You little dickens, you. Making ops officer."

"As they say, it's a dirty job, but someone has to do it."

"Don't knock it. It's getting us a trip to England. Always wanted to see London. Maybe I'll run into my dad."

"We'll RON at an Eighth Air Force base. We'll see how the Hollywood Air Force *really* lives."

"To hell with the Hollywood Air Force," said Balzac. "It's those pretty English women I lust for. Did you know they all take horny pills?"

"I did not know that," said Lancaster.

"True. Tigers in heat. Every bloody one of them."

"Could be," said Stromburg. "But you'll only have twenty-four hours to find out."

"We may not be able to get to *all* the English women in twenty-four hours," said Lancaster.

"I'm sure," said Balzac, "we can count on the rest of the crew to lend a hand. Or whatever."

"Top of the evening, sirs." Balzac and Lancaster made way as Sergeant Warner stuck his head into the cockpit.

"Ah," said O'Riley. "How goes it with our resident scrounge artist?"

"Miserable. I did not receive my invitation to accompany my favorite flying crew on this special mission."

"Sorry, Warner," said Stromburg. "No hitchhikers this time."

"Bad news. At your destination, Madam Grabballi has a very exciting branch office—"

"You know our destination?"

"No. But I'm sure Madam Grabballi has a branch office there."

Stromburg grinned. "We'll take you with us next time, Warner. We're taking the laundry run next week."

"Okay, Lieutenant. I'll hold you to that. In the meantime, I got something for you." He disappeared, to emerge seconds later with a large angel-food cake. In it were stuck several birthday candles.

"Where in hell did you get that?" asked O'Riley.

"I have my ways and means. It's a birthday cake for that character in the rear of the plane. We were gonna celebrate in the enlisted men's tent, but since you got this special mission, the guys can enjoy it with their poker game."

"That's real thoughty, Warner," said Stromburg. "We'll send it back when we get airborne."

"Do that. And don't forget to light the candles."

"We'll light the candles."

"Roger, sir. Have a good trip. You *sure* you don't need a good armaments man on this mission?"

"Quite sure."

"Well, you won't have any fun. But make the best of it, sir."

"We'll try. Thanks, Warner."

As Warner disappeared, O'Riley pointed out at the ramp. "Here they come, Swede."

Stromburg looked out to see a staff car gliding into the revetment. It was preceded and followed by Military Police jeeps. As the lead jeep pulled to a stop under the wing, Major Diddle jumped out to trot over to the staff car and open its door. A stooped figure alighted, to be silhouetted in the moonlight. The breath caught in Stromburg's throat as he took in the bowler hat, the cigar clamped in the jutting jaw.

"Holy hades!" uttered O'Riley. "Is that who I think it is?"

"It can't be!"

"It sure as hell is! Winston Churchill! In the flesh. Our passenger's Winston Churchill!"

"Well, I'm a monkey's uncle!"

Dumbfounded, the pilots watched as Diddle helped the portly gentleman dismount. The staff car driver took a small valise from the trunk of the car and followed the two men to the ladder that led up the hatch in the rear of the airplane. Stromburg thumbed the intercom button. "Pilot to waist. Look alive back there. Our passenger is coming aboard."

"Yes, sir," responded Hannigan. "He's coming up the ladder now." There was a brief pause, then, "Oh, my God!"

Stromburg turned to Balzac. "Lennie, you better go back to the waist and see that our VIP is comfortable. I'm afraid our crew members back there are in a state of shock."

"Right, *bwana*." Balzac headed for the aft section.

With the passenger aboard and the hatch closed, Major Diddle came around to the front of the airplane and made a circling motion with his forefinger. "Start number three," commanded Stromburg.

"Firing number three," said O'Riley, energizing the engine and toggling raw gasoline into its cylinders.

With a wheeze the engine caught, backfired its protest, then smoothed out its reciprocation as the huge propeller flayed the dust in the revetment. Engines four, two, and one followed suit. Stromburg gave the motion to clear the bomb-bay door area and ordered the doors closed. He gave the signal to pull the chocks; then, receiving the thumbs-up signal from Major Diddle, he started taxiing to takeoff position. "Pilot to waist. Everyone buckled in back there?"

"The crew's buckled in," replied Galvani. "Lieutenant Balzac is strapping in our passenger. Geez, skipper, you never told us it was Winnie Churchill. Wait'll I tell my grandkids about this!"

"Keep an eye on him. Make sure he's comfortable."

"Yes, sir."

"And if you're smart, you won't let him into your poker game. From what I hear, you'll end up in London with empty pockets."

"I'll tell the boys."

"When our passenger is strapped in, tell Balzac to come forward for takeoff."

"Yes, sir."

"Ain't this a kick in the head," said O'Riley. "Ole Crew Three Sixty-nine ferrying the one and only Winston Churchill." He looked around the dark field. "It's odd we don't have a fighter escort."

"I suppose that's the reason for all the security," said Stromburg. "A fighter escort would draw attention to a lone bomber."

"Well, I hope they know what they're doing."

"I do, too." Reaching the warm-up area adjacent to the active runway, Stromburg weather-vaned the bomber into the wind to complete his run-up. "Number one engine's still a little cold, Pat. We'll let 'er warm up for a minute before we check the mags."

"Roger."

Balzac stuck his head between the two pilots. "Everything's secure in the rear, *bwana*. Ready for takeoff."

"Is our passenger comfortable?" asked Stromburg.

"Seems to be. He's sucking on a coffee cup and smoking a cigar."

Stromburg snapped around. "You mean he's back there *smoking?*"

"You got it."

"Christ, that's against regulations!"

"*You* go back and tell the Prime Minister of England to put out his cigar."

"Smell any gas fumes? Be embarrassing as hell if this crate blew up."

"It wouldn't dare."

"You got a point." Stromburg checked the engine instruments. "Okay, Pat. Cylinder-head temperatures are in the green. Let's check the mags and complete the run-up."

"Roger."

For a few moments the pilots busied themselves with a careful check of the engines, then ticked off the last items on the before-takeoff checklist. "Okay, Pat. Ask the tower if we can sever these surly bonds of earth, as our navigator puts it." As O'Riley contacted the tower, Stromburg switched to intercom. "Pilot to all stations. Prepare for immediate takeoff."

"Roger, sir," responded the tail gunner.

"We're cleared into takeoff position, Swede," said O'Riley.

"Roger. Takeoff checklist complete?"

"We're ready to go."

"Then let's go."

Stromburg taxied the huge airplane onto the runway and lined up. "Dingbat from Hiccup Tower," came over the radio, "you're cleared for takeoff."

"Roger," replied O'Riley. "Dingbat rolling."

Stromburg brought the power up slowly, pushing all four throttles to their stops. Then he released the brakes and took a good grip on the controls as the lightly loaded airplane sprang forward in rapid acceleration.

The four propellers whining at high RPM, O'Riley monitored the engine instruments. "Everything's in the green, coach. Airspeed climbing . . . forty . . . fifty . . ." Stromburg sighted down the dimly lit runway, kicking rudder to keep the bomber on a straight course. " . . . seventy . . . eighty . . ."

"Holy shit!" Suddenly Stromburg's hand yanked back on the throttles, his feet jamming on the brakes.

"What the bloody hell you doin'?" roared O'Riley. "Everything's in the green—"

"Abort! Abort!" yelled Stromburg, fighting the rudders as the brakes took hold.

"Swede, what the screechin' blazes—"

"Give me full flaps. Open the cowl flaps. Throw out an anchor!"

O'Riley obeyed the orders, the smell of burning rubber permeating the cockpit as the squealing tires grappled with the pierced steel planking of the runway. Stromburg alternately applied and released the brakes, striving to cool the tires before they exploded from the heat. Slowly the charging behemoth was brought to rein, decelerating with a force that caused the crew to strain against their safety belts.

"Pat, notify the tower we're aborting and returning to our hardstand."

"Roger."

O'Riley carried out instructions as he nervously watched the end of the runway fast approaching. When it was obvious the bomber was going into the muddy overrun, Stromburg roared, "Hang on!" and thrust the left brake and rudder to the floor. Although the craft had nearly arrested its forward momentum, the plane ground-looped with enough speed almost to tip over on one wing.

"Holy donkey hockey!" yelled Balzac, sticking his head into the cockpit. The plane shuddered to a halt, its propellers stirring up a miniature cyclone of dust. "That was one helluva fast trip!"

Stromburg wiped his forehead with a gloved hand and took a deep breath. "I never thought this thing could ground-loop. It can!"

"That is *not* recommended procedure," said O'Riley. "Would you kindly enlighten your copilot as to just what the bloody hell is going on?"

Stromburg shoved the throttles forward and began taxiing back up the runway. "I will enlighten you. After we have the after-landing checklist."

"Make that the after-ground-loop checklist. And I don't think we got one."

"Tell the tower to have Sergeant Warner meet the aircraft."

"Warner?" O'Riley cocked an eyebrow at his pilot. "Did you say Sergeant Warner?"

"Affirmative." Stromburg turned to the bombardier. "Lennie, go back and inform our pasenger that we're returning to our revetment. When we've parked, I'll explain."

"Roger," said Balzac. "I'd like to sit it on that myself. This trip was so fast our navigator didn't even have time to throw up."

Stromburg taxied back to the revetment, and with the guiding flashlight of the waiting crew chief, turned in and spun the plane around. He opened the bomb-bay doors, and they had no sooner rolled up their tracks than the crew chief clambered up to stick his head into the cockpit. "What's the problem, Lieutenant?"

"The bird's okay. I'm not even cutting the engines. Tell Sergeant Warner to come up here. On the double."

"Yes, sir." At this moment the armament jeep rolled up. Sergeant Warner dismounted and was approached by the crew chief. In front of the hooded lights of the jeep the two men were profiled in a quick conference; then Warner nodded and headed for the bomb bay. In another moment he appeared on the flight deck. "Yes, sir. You came back for your armaments chief. I knew you would."

"Not exactly," said Stromburg, shouting to be heard above the idling engines. "You know, Sarge, funny things come into the mind of a pilot on a takeoff roll. Did you know that?"

Warner gave him a blank look. "Can't say as I do, Lieutenant. No, sir."

"Really funny things. Weird things. Like birthdays."

"Birthdays, sir?"

"Birthdays. For instance, I made up a list of my crew members' birthdays last week. To send to my mother, so she could remember the guys with a birthday card. The list struck me as quite odd, for none of the crew was born during the first six months of the year. Don't you think that's odd?"

"I'm not sure what you're getting at, Lieutenant."

"I think it's odd. And it stuck in my mind. Do you know what month this is, Sergeant?"

"It's April, of course."

"April. Right. Ergo, none of my crew has a birthday this month."

Warner licked his lips. "That is odd. I must have gotten my dates mixed up. I could have sworn that Waverly had a birthday—"

"No. No birthday." Stromburg turned to Lancaster. "Bill, that birthday cake you're holding. See if Sergeant Warner would like a piece."

Lancaster held out the cake. Warner recoiled. "No thanks, sir. I'm not big on sweets."

Stromburg took the cake from Lancaster and thrust it at the sergeant. "I said take a slice, Sergeant!"

In the dim light of the cockpit, Warner's eyes flicked

from face to face, finally coming to rest on Stromburg's. "I said I don't care for cake, Lieutenant."

"Maybe this is why you don't care for cake!" Stromburg's hand shot forward, diving deep into the angel food. He groped around wrist-deep in the frosting. Then a triumphant look came into his face as his probing fingers closed around something. Very carefully he extracted a tubular, metallic object, dripping with cake icing and crumbs. Gingerly he scraped the frosting from it and held it up for all to see. "That, gentlemen, is what a thermal bomb looks like. Happy birthday."

Fascinated by the deadly looking explosive being held by Stromburg, none of the crew members noticed Warner's hand steal into the jacket of his fatigues. The next thing they saw was the blue nose of the .45 being whipped out in the sergeant's hand.

Stromburg stared at the gun, then his eyes traveled to the wild look on the sergeant's face. "Put down the gun, Warner. Before someone gets hurt."

"Someone is going to get hurt." He flicked beads of sweat from his forehead with the palm of his hand. "Tripped up by a goddamn birthday list! I gotta hand it to you, Stromburg."

"Hand it to my mama. It was her idea."

"All right, I'll hand it to your mama. Now you hand me the bomb."

"I'd rather not. These things can be danger—"

Stromburg felt the cold muzzle of the automatic in his ear. "The bomb, Stromburg."

Stromburg handed over the explosive. "You want the bomb, Sergeant, it's yours."

Warner removed the gun from Stromburg's ear, warily turned it on the crew in the cockpit as he wiped the bomb off on his pants. "This bomb is set to go off at four thousand feet."

"In other words," said Stromburg, "as soon as we reached four thousand feet we'd be another grim statistic."

"A statistic, yes. Grim? Depends on whose side you're on."

"So you're the saboteur who's been planting the bombs in our planes. How many have you sabotaged, Warner? Five . . . ten . . . more?"

"This will make an even dozen."

"You've been responsible for killing over one hundred and twenty Americans. Not to mention the dozen bombers you took out of commission. Why, Warner?"

"Why?" Warner wiped the sweat from his face with his arm. "Because I have my orders. Like you, Stromburg, I am a good soldier. I just happen to be working for the other side."

"Wow!" said Balzac, his eyes bulging. "Are you a Kraut?"

"I am a German. Oberleutnant Hermann Rhineman at your service."

"You sure as hell had us fooled," said Balzac. "I always liked you."

"I am a very likable person, Balzac. I wish I could say the same about you."

"Why you sonuvabitch!"

Warner grunted. "There's no more time for chitchat. As I said, this thermal bomb has been set to detonate at four thousand feet. In the hands of a skilled armaments expert, it can be reset as a time bomb." He took a small hex key from his pocket and turned the bomb over in his hand. "And I am a very skilled armaments expert."

"As well as skilled in clock mechanisms," said Stromburg, remembering his watch that Warner had repaired. "Just what do you intend to do? I don't like people messing around with live bombs in my cockpit."

"You won't have to worry much longer. A simple adjustment—" he located a small opening in the nose of the device and started to insert the hex key—"and we'll have an explosive with a very short fuse. Just long enough to let me clear the airplane before it meets with a tragic accident. An accident, happily, that will wipe out all the evidence that Sergeant Warner, the camp scrounger, ever had anything to do with sabotage."

"I guess you know," said Balzac, "that if you detonate that bomb it means no more trips to Madam Grabballi's."

"Such are the tragedies of war." Warner inserted the key into the bomb and prepared to turn it, when a crescent wrench came whistling down from behind to catch him squarely on the shoulder. Howling with pain, he dropped his gun and jerked around to face the source of surprise. Balzac fruitlessly scrambled for the gun, which skittered across the flight deck and fell through the bomb bay to the Tarmac below.

Warner writhed in agony as he faced the assailant who had sneaked up behind him. "Who the hell are you?"

"Group Captain Witherspoon." Without his turned-up coat collar, his bowler hat, and his cigar clamped in his mouth, Witherspoon's resemblance to the Prime Minister was not nearly so pronounced. "I am with British Intelligence."

"So!" Warner's face reflected the pain as he rubbed his shoulder. "This whole thing was a trap!"

"A trap, I might add, that sprang rather nicely. Thanks in large measure to the cooperation of Lieutenant Stromburg. Now if you'd care to hand over that device, we can conclude this messy business."

"The bomb." Warner's eyes traveled down to the device he still clutched in his left hand. As he stared at it, this had a mesmerizing effect on the men on the flight deck as they watched him slowly extend it toward Witherspoon. Then, caught completely flat-footed, the Intelligence officer nearly doubled over as a sharp elbow was rammed into his ample midriff. Before anyone could move, Warner leaped from the flight deck onto the catwalk of the bomb bay, then onto the Tarmac below. Like a cat he scooped up the .45 lying on the ground and ducked under the belly of the plane to circle around in front of the spinning propellers.

There, framed in the hooded lamps of his jeep he stood poised, the bomb in his left hand, the automatic and the hex key in his right. Grimacing with the pain of his shoulder, with great effort he fumbled the key into the bomb without dropping the gun. He yelled up at Stromburg, who was staring down at him through the open pilot's window. "As I said, Stromburg, your plane will be number twelve. A twist of this key—" a stab of pain smacked him, and he lowered his arm to flex his fingers—"and all your worries will be over."

Stromburg snapped around, his eyes frantically searching the flight deck. "For God's sake, somebody do something! Before that bastard lobs that bomb into the airplane."

"I'll go after him," said Balzac, heading for the bomb bay. "That sonuvabitch owes me!"

"It's my job." Massaging his stomach, Witherspoon shouldered Balzac out of the way and jumped down onto the bomb-bay catwalk. As he did so there was a loud report and the sound of a bullet ricocheting through the bomb bay. "Ah, the bloody bastard!" Witherspoon pulled himself back up into the flight deck, dragging a leg that was spurting blood.

"You will not make that mistake again!" shouted Warner, waving the smoking .45. "You will all stay in the airplane!"

"Okay, okay," said Stromburg, raising his hands. "We'll all stay here quietly while you fix your bomb."

"That would be advisable." Again Warner fumbled with the key, experiencing difficulty juggling the key, the gun, and the bomb.

Stromburg turned to face the men looking over his shoulder. "Anyone got a gun?"

The men shrugged. "This was supposed to be a ferry mission, Swede," said Balzac. "No armament."

"Good God!" Stromburg looked down at Witherspoon, who was sitting on the floor being tourniqueted by Lancaster. "Don't you have a gun, Group Captain?"

Witherspoon shrugged. "We never carry the bloody things. Damn dangerous." He looked down at his leg. "Look what one just did to me."

"Well, there's only one thing left to do."

Stromburg looked out of the window at Warner, who had finally fumbled the hex key into its hole. "Now," said Warner triumphantly, "just a twist of the wrist and *voilà*—"

"Hang on!" commanded Stromburg. He thrust his legs forward and with his toes released the brakes, at the same time nudging the throttles forward. Preoccupied with arming the bomb, Warner never looked up as the plane lurched forward, the lethal propellers biting the humid air. And then there was a strange sound above the noise of the engines, not unlike that of a machete cleaving a ripe melon.

The red arc of the number two propeller flung a ringlet of red goo through the open cockpit window. As the two pilots looked in amazement at the carnage raining onto the flight deck, O'Riley's amazement turned to horror as a recognizable piece of anatomy landed in his lap. With the utmost disgust, he reached down with thumb and forefinger and picked it up to throw it out of the cockpit.

It was the nose of Herr Oberleutnant Hermann Rhineman.

Chapter Fifteen

15 April 1945
Italy

Mr. Elwood Snodgrass
Internal Revenue Service
District Office
Boise, Idaho

Dear Mr. Snodgrass:

Thanks for you prompt reply to my recent letter.

It warms my cockles to discover that our Internal Revenue Service does have a heart of gold. I appreciate your approving my deduction for the barbells I gave to the Salvation Army.

About the entertainment deduction you question. I don't feel nearly as strongly about that as I did about the barbells. If you want to knock out my $18.50 bill for peanuts to entertain the squirrels when I was manning a lookout station for the U.S. Forest Service, I won't fight it.

I don't know if you ever manned a lookout station on top of the tallest mountain in the Kaniksu National Forest, but if you ever did, you know how lonely it gets. If it weren't for the blue jays and the squirrels, there would be no one to talk to for weeks on end. I actually looked forward to an occasional forest fire to liven things up. So I entertained the squirrels and the birds with an occasional peanut binge, and they entertained

me. If that isn't an entertainment expense, I don't
know what is. However, as I say, I don't feel as
strongly about this as I do about the barbells, so if
you want to disallow my deduction and refigure
my tax, be my guest.

Nice hearing from you, and it's mighty comforting to know we have men of your caliber
manning the Treasury during these perilous
times.

> Sincerely,
> Rolfe Stromburg
> 1st Lt., AC

Stromburg scrounged around in his writing pad for a
stamp, licked it, and stuck it on the V-mail. Then he put his
writing aside and leaned back on his camp cot. He had
brought it outside of the tent to absorb the warm sunlight of
the spring day. He closed his eyes and was just about to
drop off when he sensed a shadow falling across his face.
Shielding his eyes, he looked up to see the stooped figure of
Group Captain Witherspoon blocking out the sun. He sat
up, started to rise.

"Mornin', Stromburg," said the Englishman, using his
crutch to push down on Stromburg's shoulder. "Don't get
up."

"Good morning, Group Captain."

"I'm on my way back to London. Just thought I'd drop
by to say cheerio."

"Glad you did, sir." Stromburg made room on his cot.
"Have a seat."

"For a moment." Witherspoon folded his portly body
and perched on the end of the cot, favoring his leg.

"Can I fix you a cup of tea? Or something?"

"Hate tea. All Englishmen, according to Agatha Christie, are supposed to love tea. I detest the stuff."

Stromburg grinned. "We have some stronger stuff over
at our club. It's embalming fluid, but no one seems to
mind."

"The way I feel this morning, embalming fluid might
be just the ticket. But we'll make it another time."

"Very well, sir. How's the leg?"

"Not bad. Considering it has a bit of a hole in it. I am definitely getting too old to be filling this flaccid torso with unwanted metal."

"Should you be walking?"

"No. Definitely not. My superiors, however, have never been known for their compassion. I have a lorry waiting to take me to Foggia."

"I wish you a speedy recovery, sir."

"Thanks, old chap." Witherspoon pulled out a cigar, started to peel off its wrapper. "I was quite impressed with the way you handled our little affair last night. Jolly good show."

"All I did was respond to a knee-jerk reaction. I can't take credit for that."

Witherspoon grunted as he rolled the end of the cigar in his mouth. "You took care of our saboteur quite nicely. We picked up his accomplice this morning." He studied Stromburg as he flared a silver lighter and stuck it to his cigar. "You interested in who it was?"

"I think I know."

"Do you now?"

"Yes. I have a feeling we'll be looking for a new barber."

Witherspoon peered at him through the smoke. "You're in the wrong branch of the service, old man. You should be in Intelligence."

"It doesn't take Agatha Christie to figure that out. When you picked the barbershop to tell me about an upcoming classified mission, I knew you secretive cloak-and-dagger boys would never do that unless you wanted the saboteurs to get the message."

"Even though your barber speaks not a word of English?"

"I have a hunch Figaro speaks better English than I do."

"As a matter of fact, he does. You colonists butcher our language something fierce."

Stromburg grinned, then sobered. "There's something about a barbershop that brings out the loquacity in a man.

Especially when we thought the barber didn't speak English. I'm sure we all talked too damn much."

"Yes. A tonsorial parlor is a great listening post. Salvadore Giuseppi, your barber's real name, kept your Sergeant Warner well informed."

"Christ, what a shocker that was! To find our armaments man was a German agent."

"Not too uncommon, old chap. The Germans have a very sophisticated Intelligence network—in many ways far superior to ours, I'm afraid. Your Sergeant Warner, alias Hermann Rhineman, immigrated with his family to the United States when Hermann was a lad. Hermann was raised, schooled, and naturalized in your country. Even joined the American Army. But his father never severed his ties with mother Germany. When the Nazis came into power, it was easy to conscript the services of young men like Hermann."

"My God! Our military must be swarming with Nazi agents."

"Hardly. Ninety-nine percent of the Germans who immigrated to your country are good Americans. Most of them hate the Nazis as much as we do. It's just the oddballs we have to be alert to."

"And how about the Italian barber?"

"Strictly amateur. The Italians make lousy undercover agents. Mainly because none of them can keep a secret. Salvadore Giuseppi worked for the Germans on a free-lance basis. He was paid so much for each Intelligence tidbit. Strictly small-time."

"Then it wasn't exactly a big sabotage ring."

"Hardly. Pretty much a two-man operation. Under the supervision of German Intelligence. But they can be most annoying. And do a lot of damage."

"We would have been the twelfth bomber liquidated. That's a lot of men." Stromburg mulled this. "I do think it was a little tacky not letting me know that you were using my airplane to set a trap. I don't know who was more surprised, me or the saboteur."

"There was a good reason for not letting you in on it."

"What was that?"

"Because, my dear fellow, you were not above suspicion."

"*What?*"

"Neither you nor your crew."

Stromburg's eyes hardened. "Wait a minute. You actually suspected *me?* And members of my *crew?*"

"I said you were not above suspicion. You were hardly a prime suspect, but we don't rule anyone out in a situation like this. Did you ever suspect your armaments chief, Sergeant Warner?"

"No."

"So there you are. Nothing personal, old cock."

Stromburg looked into the bulldog face of the group captain. "With all due respect, sir, you are one devious sonuvabitch."

A slow grin lit the Englishman's face. "I plead guilty to that. All Englishmen are devious. How else do you think we got you Yanks to come over here and fight our war?"

Stromburg chuckled. "You blokes are still smarting from the pasting we gave you in the Revolutionary War."

"Quite possibly. I'm not at all sure you colonists should have cut the umbilical cord."

Stromburg's smile faded as he watched the smoke curl up from Witherspoon's cigar. "Funny thing, Group Captain."

"What's that, old chap?"

"Last night. When I released the brakes on the airplane. I knew I was about to make hamburger out of a fellow human being." He looked into the Englishman's eyes. "And I never hesitated for a second."

"If you had, he'd have lobbed that bomb into the cockpit. Then *we'd* have been hamburger. It's kill or be killed. Personally, I think you made the right decision."

"I guess."

"You're learning the insidious craft of war, old man."

"But I never felt a thing. All I saw was the face of Captain Sheridan. A pilot who was blown up with his crew on one of our missions. Victims of this little man who was standing in front of the propellers."

"You did the only thing."

"I guess." His eyes locked with Witherspoon's. "I did it. And I'd do it again. But the fact remains that I made sausage out of a living, breathing human. And I felt *nothing!* I still feel nothing. Is this what war does to a person?"

Witherspoon took a long drag on his cigar, exhaled, then painfully lumbered to his feet. "Hope to run into you again, Stromburg."

Stromburg rose with him. "You didn't answer my question."

"Beastly nuisance this." Witherspoon tucked his crutch under his arm. "Today they are burying your president in Hyde Park."

"Yes."

"I think President Roosevelt was a good leader."

"Roosevelt's the only president I can remember. He'd have had my vote for his third term if I'd been old enough to vote."

"If you'd been old enough to vote. Godfrey, the Yanks did send a bunch of bloody kids over here to save our derrieres."

"You still haven't answered my question."

"Did you feel anything when your president died?"

"Hell, yes. He's always been a sort of father figure. I'm sure I'm not the only one who shed a few tears."

"I'm sure. He was a victim of this war, also." Witherspoon stuck out his hand. "Good-bye, Stromburg. And thanks for saving my life."

"Don't mention it." Stromburg shook his hand. "You're not going to answer my question."

Witherspoon removed the cigar from his mouth, spat into the dust. "I thought I just did." He replaced the soggy stogie, clamped down on it, turned, and limped toward the road.

3 May 1945
Italy's scuffed boot

Dear Brother Bob:
     This is the last letter I'll write from Italy.
Our bomb group flew its final mission from

here on 26 April. Pretty much a milk run, we bombed the Sachensburg marshaling yards in Austria. Our war in Europe is just about kaput.

Benito Mussolini and his mistress, Clara Petacci, died a grisly death at the hands of Italian Partisans. Adolf Hitler is dead, along with his mistress. Maybe these guys should have stayed home and tended to business instead of screwing around with loose women. According to Hamburg radio, Admiral Karl Doenitz announces himself new head of Germany and says the war will go on.

He's whistling "Dixie," of course, because German troops in Italy and southern Austria have surrendered, Berlin has fallen to the Russians, Field Marshal Von Rundstedt has been captured by U.S. troops, and our Allied planes are ripping up the Nazis attempting to escape from Germany into Denmark by sea. It is now just a matter of days.

Damned shame Roosevelt couldn't have lived just a few more weeks to witness the Armistice. Seems like most of the lead actors in our little drama won't be around for the final curtain.

I have so very much to be thankful for. To date I still have all my crew members in one piece. Granted, a couple are being held together by bandages, but unbelievably, Crew 369 has beaten the odds, and we'll be going home with thirty missions under our belts. It all seems too good to be true.

For some reason best known to the high brass, we're getting ready for a mass flyover of one thousand planes as a sort of victory salute to our European Allies. One thousand planes! An aluminum overcast. Can you imagine getting that many planes together and all flying in the same direction? It's gonna be a lotta grins.

Well, Bob, I'll soon be seeing you, and Mom, and Sis, and Ann . . . and all my crazy relatives,

before you know it. So give them all a big hug,
and start bottling that home brew!

Love and hugs to everyone,

Swede

A few days later, on May 7, 1945, all German troops
unconditionally surrendered.

For several days all of Europe was caught up in a wild,
free-swinging orgy of unbridled revelry. Blackout curtains
were ripped down; lights were turned on in the cities;
hoods were removed from automobile headlights. Food
being hoarded for the duration was trotted out, to be
chased down by all types of alcoholic beverages, ranging
the spectrum from sparkling champagne to strained Sterno.
There were parades, and wild, tumultuous gatherings, and
dancing in the streets. It was Mardi Gras and bacchanalia
and New Year's Eve and the World Series all wrapped up in
one great explosive release from the stiflings and horrors of
world war.

Nor were the Americans ignored in this frenzy of
jubilation. Treated like liberators, they were festooned with
flowers, smothered with kisses, welcomed to bedchambers.
And certainly no exceptions were the men of the 451st
Bomb Group. For seventy-two hours military regulations
were ignored, rank had no privilege, the high brass were
Bacchus and Dionysus.

The men of the 725th Squadron were particularly
jubilant in their celebration of war's end by virtue of
Nicholas Galvani, tail gunner extraordinaire. The young
bridegroom had not only plucked the fairest flower of
Vincenzo Galvani's garden but also had found himself the
beneficiary of the winemaker's finest stock as well, to
commemorate this momentous occasion suitably. The men
of the lucky squadron were not only high on the hog in the
libation department when a jeepload of Galvani's finest
wine arrived, but they also had designs to be high on the
hog in the culinary department when Sergeant Schultz
decided to have a luau.

Schultz's plans to roast a pig had to be modified

somewhat, due to a paucity of pigs and a plethora of sheep in the area. Probably one of the first luaus in history to feature baked sheep, the party had germinated so nicely that not a soul complained of eating meat wrapped in wool. Augmented with baked ham and fried Spam, the banquet Schultz prepared not only cleaned out the mess-hall larder preparatory to moving but also served as a repast fit for a king.

Redeye Gonzales was detailed to take a truck into town and return with the pick of Madam Grabballi's litter, and the communal mess hall was turned into a dance hall for officers and NCO's alike. The radio from Crew 369's tent furnished the music, amplified by two excellent speakers found among Sergeant Warner's personal effects.

Lancaster commandeered a jeep and drove into Foggia to pick up Frances Adams, and she, in turn, brought along several Red Cross workers to join in the celebration. Even the dedicated Red Cross ladies were swept up in the magic of the moment, and for once eschewed doughnuts and coffee for luaued lamb and medicinal alcohol, the latter the fruit of a raid on the squadron dispensary.

O'Riley and Balzac quickly cut the two best-looking ladies out of Lancaster's small herd, leaving a rather horse-faced woman named Gertrude, with clicking teeth and a mammoth bosom, to become completely enamored of Stromburg.

Even copious amounts of Galvani's best wine could not quite prepare Stromburg for the doting woman, whose teeth turned out to be false, along with her bosom. Stromburg actually toyed with the possibility of ditching the female Ichabod Crane, and taking a jeep ride up the torturous trail of the mountain village to see the voluptuous Esterina Galvani just one more time, but even his anesthetized brain could visualize the folly and embarrassment of meeting up with her husband, who was now home.

And for a while he considered stealing an airplane and going to Florence to spend this uninhibited celebration with his one true love, Kathy Wilson. But this idea, too, crashed upon the rocks of fuzzy reality, for his condition was such that he could barely find the latrine, let alone the city of Florence in an airplane.

And so it came to pass that for two days and nights the members of the 725th Squadron reveled in an orgiastic foofoorah of drunken debauchery, wild womanizing, and overindulgence in alcoholic spirits of such magnitude that Bacchus surely must have twirled in his grave.

That is, all except the operations officer of the squadron; for First Lieutenant Stromburg spent the time playing horseshoes with a horse-faced woman named Gertrude, who hailed from Bozeman, Montana. Score: Stromburg, 7 games; Gertrude, 49.

Balzac climbed down the rear-hatch ladder, turned to look around at the empty revetments on both sides of the runway. He crossed over to Stromburg, who was checking the fuel cocks under the bomber's wing. "Swede, it's gettin' damn eerie around here." He looked over at the tent area, where a group of Italians was gathering. "I'm for gettin' the hell out of here. Look out there. The natives are going into a war dance."

"I've about finished the preflight," said Stromburg, tasting the wing petcock drippings for signs of water. He made a wry face and spat. "You'll be happy to know we have no condensation in the fuel."

"I'm happy to know that something on this bird is okay. Look at this rust bucket! You and your frigging promotion to ops officer. Not only are we the last ones to leave this frigging place, but we also end up with the worst frigging airplane in the frigging squadron."

"Inexperienced crews can't handle in-flight emergencies like veteran crews. So naturally the oldest crews get the oldest airplanes to take home. Would you have it any other way?"

"Hell, yes! If I were ops officer, I'd give the best airplanes to the oldest crews. They've earned them."

"Wish I'd thought of that."

"You didn't notice Major Diddle hanging around till the last dog was hung to vacate this place. He went home in a brand-new B-24J. Why did you have to volunteer for roll-up?"

"I didn't volunteer for roll-up. Major Diddle had to be the first out to make arrangements along the ATC route for the rest of the squadron that's following him. It's the ops officer's job to be the last one to leave. Besides, I gave all you crew members the opportunity to leave on any aircraft you wanted. You all volunteered to stay and go home with me. So quit your bellyachin'."

"That's because you caught us when we had the granddaddy of all hangovers. Thank God the Germans don't surrender every day. My follicles are still afire."

"I cannot be responsible when one disdains temperance in one's drinking habits. I asked you to play horseshoes, but I couldn't get you out of the hayloft. So don't come bleeding to me."

"It was that little brunette Red Cross worker from Oshkosh. She had this thing about hay. You ever spend two days in a hayloft?"

"Not that I recall."

"Wow!"

"Anyway, look at the record. Every one of our planes got off successfully. Even *Boxcar Beulah* got off the ground and is headin' back to the beautiful U.S. of A."

"And we get stuck with the biggest ramp queen of them all!" Balzac walked forward and stared up at the faded picture of the coffee can that had been painted on the nose. "Who in hell would name a plane *Maxwell House*?"

"Some old crew long ago. Remember the radio commercial? Maxwell House is good to the last drop. Rather droll, what?"

"Droll ain't the word. Let's just hope to hell this next trip ain't the last drop."

"You're a worrywart, Balzac. There'll be no flak, no fighters. I've forgotten how to fly an airplane that isn't full of holes."

"Are you grousing at our aircraft commander, bombardier?" asked O'Riley, loping up to the plane. He was being half dragged by the leash attached to DFC. "You are a long way from home to be lipping off to the pilot of your airplane." He addressed the dog. "Set 'er right there, boy." DFC dropped the huge B-4 bag he had been carrying in his mouth, and O'Riley threw the bag on board. Then he tugged the tether, pulling the huge hound over to the front of the plane. "Now, pee on the nosewheel, DFC. That's a good doggy. You know how nasty the boys in the rear get when you pee on their coffee jug."

"Goddamn it, O'Riley!" Balzac watched in horror as the dog lifted its leg to vent a fire-hose stream on the nosewheel tire. "I've told you a dozen times! Not on the nosewheel! You know damn well where the nosewheel goes when the gear is retracted."

"Refresh my memory."

"Into the bombardier's compartment! That's where! And you damn well know it! How'd you like to swim around in dog pee?"

"Heavens to Betsy, bombardier, you are right." O'Riley bent down to the dog. "DFC, don't you ever do that again. Naughty dog."

DFC repented by lapping his master's face with his Ping-Pong-paddle tongue while Balzac beat the side of the aircraft and said with a moan, "God deliver me from such cretins. And make me never have to go to war in the company of copilots again!"

"Are you sure you want to take that beast back to the United States, O'Riley?" asked Stromburg. "Dogs are supposed to go through some kind of immunization program."

"I thought we made a deal. You wouldn't squawk about DFC, and we'd all help you smuggle Luigi in."

"Luigi's different, for God's sake. He's a human being. Sort of. It would be sheer savagery to leave an orphan here at the hands of these people. They don't have food enough for themselves, let alone a poor orphan bastard."

"True. But if you're worrying about immunization for dogs, wait'll you lock horns with Immigration. They're rougher than cobs."

"We'll smuggle him in some way. Then we'll sort out the paperwork later. I'm not leaving him here to scrounge like an alley cat."

"You may end up adopting him."

"Then so be it. Okay, a deal's a deal. But keep the dog

out of the cockpit. I'll not have him up there feathering engines and eating crew members."

"God, what a grouch. I've made arrangements for him in the rear. Our tail gunner's going to take care of him."

"Okay." Stromburg looked at his watch. "All the enlisted men aboard, Balzac?"

"Yes, sir. All present and accounted for. Poker game's already in progress. So far Luigi's won three pots."

"Then if our navigator should make an appearance, we can mount the blue."

"Speak of the devil. Here comes our illustrious Magellan now." Balzac's eyes narrowed. "Holy monkey puckey! Who's that with him?"

Lancaster came double-timing into the revetment, carrying something in his arms. He was being closely followed by what appeared to be a small parade. As he came puffing up to the plane, he handed his burden to Stromburg while he bent over to catch his breath. Stromburg folded back the blanket in his arms and looked down into the cherubic face of an Italian baby. "Good Christ!"

As Lancaster caught his breath, Sergeant Schultz came staggering up, half carrying his three-hundred-pound Italian wife. She in turn was carrying another child. Four more stair-stepped children came panting up at their heels. It was the entire family of the recently married mess sergeant.

"Leapin' lasagna!" said Balzac. "What have we here?"

"Swede," said Lancaster, panting, "it's gettin' mean out there. The Italians have just stormed the mess hall."

"Why not?" asked Stromburg. "It's theirs. The whole base has reverted back to the Italians."

"It's not the fact that they're claiming it. It's the *way* they're claiming it. It's an angry mob. Spoiling for trouble."

"Then best we get under way."

"We're going to have to take Schultz and his family with us."

"*What?*"

"Besides us, Schultz is the last American on the base. He was going to evacuate himself and his family on the last truck after giving the remaining mess hall food to the

Italians. But they've rioted and commandeered his truck. We have to take them along."

"But Bill, we have no accommodations for passengers! This is not exactly Pan Am flight three oh seven! We have no seats, very crude sanitary facilities, no extra food—"

"And no choice," added Lancaster. "We can't leave them here."

"We got food," said Sergeant Schultz. He thrust his hand into the huge bosom of his wife and came up with a wheel of cheese and a round loaf of bread. "And we got wine. Turn around, Luisa." Schultz started to reach up her dress.

"Okay, okay," said Stromburg, stopping him. "I'd rather not know where Luisa is smuggling wine. But it's a long flight. Have you milk for the baby?"

Schultz reached over and planted a large paw on his wife's breast. "Lotsa milk. Luisa's part Guernsey. Wanna see?"

"No, I don't want to see."Stromburg handed the baby to its mother, and forced a smile on the bewildered woman to put her at ease. "Okay, Luisa. Load your family into the rear of the plane. We'll try to make you all as comfortable as possible."

"Thanks, Lieutenant," said Schultz. "I ain't gonna forget this." With Balzac's help they started loading the brood aboard.

"It's a good thing I went by the mess hall to pick up the coffee jugs," said Lancaster. "They were about to lynch poor old Schultz."

"What the hell has gotten into these people? They're supposed to be our Allies. Yesterday they were throwing flowers."

"Human nature," said Lancaster. "Ever since we occupied Italy, we've called the shots. We're the subjugators. Now that our forces are decimated, they're seeking retribution. And fighting over the spoils. You know, when Mussolini was toppled from power, it was his own Italian Partisans who filled him full of lead."

Stromburg shook his head. "It doesn't make a hell of a lot of sense."

"I've yet to see any part of this stupid imbroglio that does make any sense."

Stromburg nodded. "Sometimes you get the feeling war was designed by the Marx Brothers." He watched the last of Luisa's brood being helped up the ladder into the rear of the plane. "But I do know one thing: I'm beginning to understand how Noah felt when it came time to load the Ark."

"'Philologists, who chase a panting syllable through time and space, Start it at home, and hunt it in the dark. To Gaul, to Greece, and into Noah's Ark.' William Cowper said that."

"I don't particularly give a shit. Get your butt aboard." As Lancaster climbed in, Stromburg looked out across the revetment. A dozen or so Italians with pitchforks were heading for the plane. "O'Riley, get up there and start engines. Toss me a fire extinguisher. I'll stand fireguard." O'Riley passed Stromburg one of the plane's extinguishers and climbed into the right seat. Stromburg scurried around to confront the number three engine. "Crank 'er up, Pat!" he yelled at O'Riley through the open copilot's window.

O'Riley began energizing the switches that would start number three to rotating. The engine fully primed, the propeller started to turn as the whining starter engaged. There was one desultory cough producing a huge backfiring smoke ring, but the engine refused to start. O'Riley energized the starter for nearly a full minute, the huge propeller gyrating slowly.

"Come on, baby. *Start!*" muttered Stromburg. "We have to get the hell outta here!" And then he noticed the raw gas dripping from the bottom of the engine. "She's flooded, Pat. Let 'er cool a minute. Then crank 'er with the mixtures lean."

"Roger," replied O'Riley. "Hope to hell our battery hangs in there. It's about shot."

Stromburg moved to where he could check on the advancing Italians. They were coming closer to the revetment. He shouted up at O'Riley. "Tell the tail gunner to crank his guns around and point them at the Italians."

"Why, Swede? We have no ammo aboard."

"The Italians don't know that. Tell Galvani to yell at them to keep their distance, while he trains his guns on 'em."

"This is crazy!"

"So is being shish-kebabbed on a pitchfork. Toss me the flare gun and a package of flares. In case that doesn't work."

"You got it." O'Riley carried out orders. Stromburg rammed a flare into the flare gun as he watched the advancing peasants. He heard Galvani's voice ring out in strident Italian as the tail-turret guns swiveled menacingly to point directly at the group. The men stopped in their tracks, assessing this new situation.

"Try 'er again!" yelled Stromburg, grabbing the fire extinguisher. "She's gotta start this time." Again the starter whined, was engaged, and the blades started turning. This time there was a cough, a backfire, another cough. Then nothing. "Sonuvabitch!"

"We're losing our battery!" called out O'Riley.

"That happens, we're gonna lose the ball game. We have no putt-putt. Cool 'er for a few seconds, then try again. Got the booster pump on?"

"Of course I got the booster pump on!" O'Riley shot his pilot a look of disdain at the stupidity of the question, checked the booster-pump toggle switch, and sheepishly flicked it on.

"Okay, Pat!" yelled Stromburg. "Give 'er another go!"

Once again the tribladed propeller was slowly energized. It barely turned over as the nearly drained battery gave a last boost. And then the engine coughed. It coughed again, as several of the cylinders started firing. And then it kicked over, and with a roar that sounded to Stromburg like "The War of 1812 Overture," it rattled and banged into a rough reciprocation. Under O'Riley's practiced fingers, it smoothed out into a steady roar that was music to their ears. With the number three engine running and activating its generator, there was now power to start the three other engines.

In quick succession Stromburg stood fireguard as numbers four, two, and one engines kicked into life. The

Italians milled around in confusion, intimidated by the tailguns staring down at them, and the smoke and propeller blast washing over them. As Stromburg tucked the fire extinguisher under his arm and headed for the flight deck, several of the braver peasants separated from the group and started talking animatedly.

Stromburg was about to throw his fire extinguisher on board and follow it, when Lancaster suddenly loomed in front of him, stabbing his finger at something behind him. He shouted. "Swede! Coming up behind you!"

Stromburg whirled around just as a jeep came bouncing up behind the wing. An American MP was at the wheel, and there was one passenger in the front seat. As the vehicle skidded to a halt, the passenger dismounted, and the MP reached behind him to throw out a duffel bag. Stromburg stared in mute astonishment as the passenger approached. "Got room for a hitchhiker, Swede?"

"Kathy!" Stromburg stared into the green eyes of Kathy Wilson.

"I just got my orders to return to the States. I knew your squadron was rotating. I was hoping you might have room."

"Kathy! Don't you know we can't carry civilian passengers in a combat airplane?"

"No." Her face fell. "I didn't know. I thought that under the circumstances—"

"So far I've broken roughly eight thousand regulations on this mission. And we're not even off the ground yet. So hop aboard."

"Oh, Swede. Bless you." She started to kiss him but was interrupted by the jeep driver.

"I'll throw the lady's duffel bag aboard, sir," said the MP. "Then I'm gettin' the hell outta here. I suggest you do the same."

"We're going to do that, Sergeant," said Stromburg, watching the MP speedily transfer words into action. Kathy's baggage aboard, the MP jumped back into his jeep, made a squealing turn, popped Stromburg a salute, and hightailed it back down the taxi strip.

"That's a very nice man," said Kathy, waving good-bye at the speeding jeep.

"A nice man," said Stromburg, taking her arm, "would have stayed here and fought off the Eyeties while we got airborne. Now hustle your bustle." He steered her to the bomb bay and helped her up onto the flight deck.

He was about to·follow her, when he sensed the commotion behind him. Two of the Italians had crawled up onto the bomb-bay catwalk, the one in the lead carrying his pitchfork at the ready. Stromburg shoved Kathy up onto the flight deck, turned to face the oncoming peasants. He folded out the horn of the fire extinguisher, pointed it at the nearest man, and squeezed the trigger. An instant, hissing cloud of freezing carbon dioxide issued from the extinguisher, enveloping the bomb bay. Half blinded and clawing at the choking fog, the two men leaped down from the catwalk and staggered away from the plane, gasping and fighting the slipstream.

Stromburg clicked off the extinguisher, leaped up to the flight deck. "Close the bomb-bay doors, Pat. Now!" He tossed his flare gun to Lancaster. "Use this if they try to damage the plane." He jumped into the left seat, buckling his safety belt as he pushed the throttles forward. "Let's get the hell out of here!"

The plane bounced over its chocks, spun out of the revetment, and started bouncing down the taxiway to the runway. Stromburg turned his head to issure orders over his shoulder. "Navigator, make Kathy comfortable back there. Hold her on your lap for takeoff."

"If you insist," said Lancaster, complying with orders. He addressed the passenger. "Now, you just hug me real tight, Kathy. Atta girl."

"Pat," ordered Stromburg, "check with the rear. Tell 'em to buckle in for takeoff."

"Roger, coach."

"How we doing on the checklist?"

"Down to engine run-up."

"Skip it. We're not even checking the mags. We have no choice but to try to get this bucket airborne. If the mags are acting up, I don't want to know about it."

"That being the case, coach, firewall the throttles and blast off. Look over there—this is one time you won't have to get the tower's permission."

Stromburg glanced over at the control tower. Italians were swarming over it like ants, breaking the glass, dismantling the lights. "This is eerie, isn't it?"

"Unbelievable."

They swung onto the runway in a sweeping turn, Stromburg firewalled the throttles, and the old airplane started porpoising down the runway. He reached over to the peter heater hanging from the cockpit ceiling and gave it a tug. "Here goes nothin'. Come on, old girl. Lift your skirts."

The spring rains had turned the Italian terrain into an undulating green blanket that passed below the belly of the old bomber as it lumbered into the clear skies. It banked over after takeoff, circling one last time to allow its crew members to take a final look at the verdant aerie that had been their nest for the past six months. Even the poker game was interrupted as each man, locked in his own thoughts, stared mutely out of the plane as it buzzed over the old homestead that now was bristling with rampaging Italians.

The half year had been only a few grains of sand in the hourglass of time, but for the men of Bomber Crew 369 it would provide a hundred Mays of memories: some humorous, some terrorizing, some warm and cherished, some so unspeakable they would blot themselves from the memory banks forever. In its short span, it had bonded friendships in the hot forge of combat that would stand the test of a lifetime; it had accelerated the aging process that changed immaturity to responsibility, acne to ulcers. Undeniably, the ten men of Bomber Crew 369 would never be the same men, for they had witnessed at first hand the horrors of mortal combat as a closely knit team; they had been stripped of their outer shells to lay bare their innermost fears, hates, and loves for all the world to see.

All told, Stromburg was proud of his crew. None of them had come up seriously wanting. He was even fairly pleased with himself. He was sure as hell no hero, but he had comported himself with a certain consistency, if not with style, and he could live with the face that glared back at him from the shaving mirror in the morning. But most important of all, he was bringing his crew back in one piece. They had made a dent in the dispensary, and they had reaped a harvest of Purple Hearts, but unless the last bouts with Madam Grabballi's girls dictated otherwise, they would bear few permanent scars. And for this, Stromburg was proud.

Gathering altitude, the bomber passed low over the little village of Castellucia and its residents who had offered life-saving surcease from the rigors of war. Stromburg banked over the hilltop house of Vincenzo Galvani and waved a final, silent farewell to the Galvanis, especially the beautiful woman below who was having a late luncheon on the balcony with her husband.

Esterina Galvani Tognoli stood and waved her napkin, as she knew the last airplane from Cerignola contained two people she would always love and probably would never see again: her little sister, who had stowed away on the big bomber to be with her husband; and the aircraft commander, who had stolen a piece of her heart to take with him to America.

"That is the last of the Americans," said her husband, Domenico. "And I cannot say I am sorry they are gone."

"They are our Allies," said Esterina, bringing her napkin to her cheek. "We must not forget that."

"No. I have no hatred for the Americans. They are a crazy bunch. But they mean no harm."

"No harm." Esterina wiped her eyes. "I am going to miss the Americans. They have their faults. But the world would be a very dull place without them." And under her breath she whispered, "Good-bye, Lieutenant Swede Stromburg. Good-bye, *carissimo*."

The plane passed low over the Catholic church with the elegant spire that stabbed the afternoon sky and that housed another Italian who was not eager to see the Americans leave—for precisely at this instant, Father Zandegrande was responding to a summons from Nature and was settling his ample flanks atop the new fixture that had been installed in his tiled retreat. As he gathered his voluminous robes around him in sanitary comfort, he crossed himself and offered a hosanna to the young pilot in the airplane roaring overhead who had so effectively redressed a most indelicate grievance. "God be with you, young American aviator," he offered up in Italian.

The old bomber quit the Italian mainland coast and chugged out across the Tyrrhenian Sea toward Palermo, one of the checkpoints en route to Marrakech in Morocco, where its crew would land to complete the first leg of the journey home. From there the Air Transport Command would route the bomber on to the Azores, thence to Gander Field in Newfoundland, then on to Bradley Field in Connecticut, its final destination.

Maxwell House was perking along in commendable fashion, a hiccuping number four engine the only clue that the old dowager had long been queen of the ramp. In deference to aging arteries and the possibility of cardiac arrest, Stromburg had throttled back the old matron to long-range cruise, sacrificing alacrity for longevity.

Stromburg felt a tap on his shoulder. He turned to look into the green eyes of Kathy Wilson. "I never realized," she said, "that this was such a huge airplane."

Stromburg turned the controls over to O'Riley, then stretched back to address the navigator. "Bill, I'll trade you places. Can you navigate from up here for a spell?"

"Aye, aye, *el jefe*. I'm doing strictly pilotage at the moment. What better place to do it than in the pilot's seat?"

They switched places, Lancaster crawling into the left seat. Stromburg poured two cups of coffee from the flight-deck jug, then sat down next to Kathy on a footlocker that had been stowed in the navigator's station. "Yes," he said, handing her a cup, "it's amazing how an airplane can be so damned big on the outside and yet be so cramped on the inside. How's everything in the rear end?"

"As you say, cramped. But everyone's morale is so high at going home, I don't think anyone minds."

"Luigi still winning the poker game?"

She laughed. "He is something else! Those eyes. Is he going to be a charmer!"

"He already is. He charmed me into taking him back to the States. I've stuck my neck out from here to Ellis Island."

"And the rest of your passengers are interesting. Especially that beautiful Italian girl."

"I would hardly call Luisa beautiful. Prolific, perhaps, but beautiful—"

"I don't mean the mess sergeant's wife. I mean Marguerita. What a knockout she is."

"Marguerita? The tail gunner's wife?"

"I believe so. She has to be the prettiest—"

"Marguerita *aboard?* In my airplane?"

"Of course. I thought you knew."

"I had no idea. That little bastard smuggled her aboard. I must have half of Italy back there. What's the penalty for smuggling aliens? Or police dogs? God only knows what other contraband the enlisted men have hidden in the rear. It's a wonder this menace to public safety got off the ground."

"Not to mention old beat-up Red Cross gals."

"Not to mention beautiful Red Cross gals. I will end up in the pokey and they'll throw away the key. No way to treat a conquering hero."

"I will come visit you every day. And will bake you a cake with a file in it."

He reached for her hand. "You would do that for me?"

She looked into his eyes and smiled. "I think I just might."

"Does this mean there's a chance we might get together?"

She took a sip of her coffee. "I don't know. There are a lot of hurdles to leap."

"Yes. In just a couple of dozen years I've managed to get my life more confused than an Ethiopian fire drill. A lousy marriage, a wonderful daughter, an illegal alien, a true love who won't have anything to do with me—"

"And just who is this true love?"

"You know damn well who it is."

"Well, if it's me, we'll just have to wait and see. There's the small matter of you being a married man—a condition that's hardly going to endear you to my folks if you should come a-courtin'."

"I'll take care of that. I plan to get a divorce, anyway."

"Sometimes that's easier said than done. And there's your daughter. You're sure to have a custody battle."

"I know. I'm not looking forward to that."

"And there's the war in the Pacific to button up. We'll probably both have to go. And there's the problem of—"

He put his hand over her mouth. "Enough. Since we'll have to face these gargantuan problems, I say we should definitely enjoy while we can. Would you care to join me in the ball turret? Maybe fool around a little?"

She laughed, reached over, and gave him a kiss on the nose. "I'll say one thing for you, Stromburg. You never give up. If perseverance is what it takes, you'll go far."

He squeezed her hand. "I love you, Kathy. Even if you don't want to join me in the ball turret. God, how I love you!"

"And I love you, too, you crazy moron. Sometimes I wish I didn't love you so much." She put her arms around him and gave him a kiss so steaming that he spilled his hot coffee all over himself and didn't even know it.

And some of the coffee spilled down on the footlocker they were sitting on, almost blurring the stenciled lettering that read:

"The personal effects of J. D. Muldoon's Crew 234."

Author's Afterword

As stated in the Foreword, there was indeed a Bomber Crew 369 assigned to the 725th Squadron of the 451st Bomb Group of the Fifteenth Air Force stationed in Italy. Only the names have been changed to protect the privacy of these individuals.

It has now been over forty years since these young warriors became men in the firestorm that raged over Europe during the global conflict of World War II. It might be of interest to know what happened to the members of Bomber Crew 369 during the ensuing years.

Dick Daringer, engineer, returned to Defiance, Ohio, after the war, where he pursued the trades of plastering and factory work. He joined the Ohio National Guard and rose to the rank of captain before retiring. He is still married to his high-school sweetheart and has three children and ten grandchildren.

Art Hannigan, radio operator, became a conductor with SEPTA—the rapid-transport company in Philadelphia—where he has worked for thirty-seven years. He has been married even longer to the same wife and has five children and two grandsons. He plans on retiring soon.

Herb Dupree, top-turret gunner, got into heavy construction following the war and helped build the St. Lawrence Seaway and the Glen Canyon Dam before joining a forklift truck company in Greene, New York. He has had three wives and four children, and he survived a near-fatal heart attack in 1983. He now resides in St. Augustine, Florida.

Lou Foulette, nose gunner, attended the University of Michigan and Wayne State University. He has been married twice and has two daughters. He now resides in Taylor, Michigan, and is an instructor of political science at a local community college. He has given up the violin.

Will Waverly, ball-turret gunner, was reemployed by Fairchild Aircraft until 1963, when he went to work for the State of Maryland Motor Vehicle Administration as an investigator. He has one wife and one daughter. He never got the chance to use his milking fingers.

Nick Galvani, tail gunner, had his marriage sanctified with three children and four grandchildren. He became a production manager in a company that produced precision jet-engine parts. After two triple-bypass open-heart operations, he now lives quietly with his wife in Kensington, Connecticut.

Of the officers, Bill Lancaster, navigator, became a successful design engineer for Ford Motor Company in Dearborn, Michigan. He married a childhood sweetheart, sired three children, and became a trustee on the Dearborn Board of Education.

Lennie Balzac, bombardier, incongruously became principal of a series of grammar schools in Southern California. He married a college sweetheart and fathered a son and a daughter. Prudent real-estate ventures paid off, and he now resides in a beach home at the exclusive community of Corona Del Mar, California.

Swede Stromburg, pilot, remained in the service until 1964, when he retired as a lieutenant colonel to pursue a writing career. He eventually married his redhead and issued fifteen books, one son, and another daughter.

Pat O'Riley, copilot, is the only member of Bomber Crew 369 unaccounted for. It is rumored that he achieved his dream of being a deck officer on a Lake Erie steamer, and was lost at sea during a storm in 1968. This rumor has never been substantiated.

Randomly selected from all walks of life, there was nothing particularly distinguished about the officers and men who comprised Bomber Crew 369. They had no unusual aptitudes nor appetites for war. They had no special combat training before reporting for duty. They were something of a ragtag bunch, having virtually nothing in common but a strong and sometimes misguided feeling of patriotism.

These ten men were no braver nor more daring than any other bomber crew of the Second World War. Like their compatriots, they reaped their share of medals: Distinguished Flying Crosses, Air Medals, Battle Stars, Presidential Citations, and Purple Hearts. Bomber Crew 369 was unique only in that it did beat the odds and did not suffer the normal attrition rate of flying crews; to a man, the same crew that went overseas in 1944 returned as a unit in 1945.

There was magic in the cold-crisp skies over Europe in the 1940s, when men fought a pitched battle in their flying machines; no ambiguities of motives or purpose, the battle lines clearly drawn. No war will ever again be as simple, as uncomplicated, as clearly defined as the Allies versus the Axis of World War II.

In 1982 at Colorado Springs, Colorado, the 451st Bomb Group held its first reunion. Most of Bomber Crew 369 attended. Crew cuts and flat guts had long since surrendered to hair too thin and bellies too fat; bifocals covered eyes more prone to water than sparkle; and war stories had gotten better with each retelling.

Yet, underneath the hubbub of reunion, underneath the clamor and din of hotel banquets and dinner dances, there was a certain something that set these men apart from the usual conventioneers. Maybe it was the recapping of the sharing together of young people coping in a young world. Maybe it was the rugged castings of friendships forged in fire. Maybe it was the special camaraderie of men frozen together in time and space.

Whatever it was, the aerial war was a mystical, magical, terrorizing, yet wonderful moment in their lives. It was a brief page in the history of this republic that will forever capture the imagination and the fantasy of the free spirit—these men who fought in the crystal stillness five miles above the earth.

Winston Churchill spoke eloquently of the airmen of

his Fighter Command in the House of Commons when he said, "Never in the field of human conflict was so much owed by so many to so few."

As for Bomber Crew 369, no one could have envisioned a more fitting requiem for these airborne gladiators than poet Sam Foss when he penned:

> *And in the average man is curled*
> *The hero stuff that rules the world.*

WILLIAM C. ANDERSON

California, 1986

ABOUT THE AUTHOR

WILLIAM C. ANDERSON is a retired Air Force Colonel whose experience as a bomber commander in Germany during World War II formed the basis for this book. As an author he has a distinguished list of book and film credits. *The Hurricane Hunter, Penelope, Adam, M-1,* and *Bat-21* are only a few of his better known works.